Swee

They're out for ... and the reward
couldn't be sweeter…or sexier…

3 passionate novels!

In March 2006 Mills & Boon bring
back two of their classic collections,
each featuring three favourite
romances by our bestselling authors…

SWEET REVENGE

Rome's Revenge by Sara Craven
The Sweetest Revenge by Emma Darcy
A Seductive Revenge by Kim Lawrence

ROYAL PROPOSALS

The Prince's Pleasure by Robyn Donald
A Royal Proposition by Marion Lennox
The Sheikh's Proposal
by Barbara McMahon

Sweet Revenge

ROME'S REVENGE
by
Sara Craven

THE SWEETEST REVENGE
by
Emma Darcy

A SEDUCTIVE REVENGE
by
Kim Lawrence

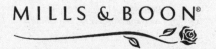

MILLS & BOON®

*MILLS & BOON and MILLS & BOON with the Rose Device
are registered trademarks of the publisher.*
Harlequin Mills & Boon Limited,
Eton House, 18-24 Paradise Road, Richmond, Surrey, TW9 1SR

SWEET REVENGE © by Harlequin Enterprises II B.V., 2006

Rome's Revenge, The Sweetest Revenge and A Seductive Revenge
were first published in Great Britain by Harlequin Mills & Boon
Limited in separate, single volumes.

Rome's Revenge © Sara Craven 2001
The Sweetest Revenge © Emma Darcy 2001
A Seductive Revenge © Kim Lawrence 2000

ISBN 0 263 84662 8

05-0306

*Printed and bound in Spain
by Litografia Rosés S.A., Barcelona*

ROME'S REVENGE

by

Sara Craven

Sara Craven was born in South Devon, and grew up surrounded by books in a house by the sea. After leaving grammar school she worked as a local journalist, covering everything from flower shows to murders. She started writing for Mills & Boon® in 1975. Apart from writing, her passions include films, music, cooking and eating in good restaurants. She now lives in Somerset.

Sara Craven has appeared as a contestant on the Channel Four game show *Fifteen to One* and is also the last ever winner of the 1997 *Mastermind of Great Britain* championship.

Don't miss Sara Craven's exciting new novel
Wife Against Her Will
out in May 2006 from Mills & Boon
Modern Romance™

CHAPTER ONE

THE charity ball was already in full swing when he arrived.

Rome d'Angelo traversed the splendid marble foyer of the large Park Lane hotel and walked purposefully through the massive archway which led to the ballroom. A security man considered asking for his ticket, took a look at the dark, uncompromising face and decided against it.

Inside the ballroom, Rome halted, frowning a little at the noise of the music and the babble of laughter and chat which almost drowned it. In his mind's eye he was seeing a hillside crowded with serried rows of vines, and a hawk hovering silently against a cloudless sky, all enshrouded in a silence that was almost tangible.

Coming here tonight was a mistake, and he knew it, but what choice did he have? he asked himself bitterly. He was gambling with his future, something he'd thought was behind him for ever. But of course he'd reckoned without his grandfather.

He accepted a glass of champagne from a passing waiter, and moved without haste to the edge of the balcony, which overlooked the ballroom floor. If he was aware of the curious glances which pursued him, he ignored them. By this time he was used to attracting attention, not all of it welcome. He'd soon learned in adolescence the effect that his six-foot-three, lean, muscular body could generate.

At first he'd been embarrassed when women had eyed him quite openly, using his broad-shouldered, narrow-hipped frame to fuel their private fantasies. Now he was simply amused, or, more often, bored.

But his attention tonight was focused on the several hundred people gyrating more or less in time with the music below him, his frowning gaze scanning them closely.

He saw the girl almost at once. She was standing at the edge of the dance floor, dressed in a silver sheath which lent no grace to a body that was on the thin side of slender and made her pale skin look tired and washed out. Like a shinny ghost, he thought critically. Yet she'd probably dieted herself into that condition, boasting about the single lettuce leaf she allowed herself for lunch.

Why the hell couldn't she be a woman who at least looked like a woman? he wondered with distaste. And how was it, with all her money, no one had ever shown her how to dress?

For the rest, her shoulder-length light brown hair was cut in a feathered bob, and, apart from a wristwatch, she seemed to be wearing no jewellery, so she didn't flaunt her family's money.

She was very still, and quietly, almost fiercely alone, as if a chalk circle had been drawn round her which no one was permitted to cross. Yet he could not believe she was here unescorted.

The Ice Maiden indeed, he thought, his lips twisting with wry contempt, and definitely not his type.

He'd met them before, these girls who, cushioned by their family's riches, could afford to stand aloof and treat the rest of the world with disdain.

And one of them he'd known well.

His frown returned.

It was a long time since he'd thought about Graziella. She belonged strictly to his past, yet she was suddenly back in my mind now.

Because, like the girl below him, she was someone who'd had it made from the day she was born. Who didn't have to be beautiful or beguiling, which she was, or even civil, which she'd never been, because her place in life was preordained, and she didn't have to try.

And that was why Cory Grant, in turn, could stand there, in her expensive, unbecoming gown, daring the world to keep its distance.

Dangerous things—dares, he thought, his firm mouth twisting.

Because the challenge implicit in every line of her rigid figure was making him wonder just what it would take to melt that frozen calm.

Then a slight movement focused his gaze more closely, and he realised that her hands were clenching and unclenching in the folds of the silver dress.

He thought, Ah—so there's a chink in the lady's armour, after all. Interesting.

And right on cue, as if she was suddenly conscious that she was being watched, she looked up at the balcony and her eyes met his.

Rome deliberately let his gaze hold hers for a long count of three, then he smiled, raised his champagne glass in a silent toast and drank to her.

Even across the space that separated them he could see the sudden burn of colour in her face, then she turned and walked away, heading for the archway which led to the cocktail bar.

If I was still gambling, he thought, what odds would I give that she'll look round before she gets to the bar?

It seemed at first he'd have lost his money, but then, as she reached the entrance, he saw her hesitate and throw a swift glance over her shoulder, aimed at where he was standing.

The next second she was gone, swallowed up by the crowd inside the bar.

Rome grinned to himself, then drank the rest of his champagne, setting the empty glass down on the balustrade.

He took his mobile phone from the pocket of his tuxedo and dialled a number.

When his call was answered, he said, his voice cool and abrupt, 'I've seen her. I'll do it.'

He rang off, and went back the way he'd come, his long, lithe stride carrying him across the foyer and out into the chill darkness of the night.

Cory hadn't wanted to come to the ball. And particularly she hadn't wanted to come with Philip, who, she guessed, had been set up by her grandfather to bring her.

She thought, I really wish he wouldn't do that, but her inner smile was tender. She knew that Arnold Grant only wanted the best for her. The problem was they'd never agree on what that 'best' was.

In Arnold's view it was a husband, wealthy, steady and suitable, who would provide her with a splendid home and, in due course, babies.

For Cory it was a career, not even remotely connected with Grant Industries, and total independence.

Currently, she drew an over-generous salary as Arnold's personal assistant, which meant that she organised his diary, made sure his domestic life ran smoothly, and acted as his hostess and companion at social events.

She felt a total fraud, knowing full well that all those activities could have fitted easily into her spare time, enabling her to do a job where she earned the money she was paid.

But Arnold insisted that he could not do without her, and had no hesitation in playing the old and frail card if he sensed she was near to rebellion.

Being allowed to move out of the big family house in

Chelsea and rent a modest flat of her own had been a major concession it had taken her nearly a year of argument and cajolery to win.

'How can you think of leaving?' he'd protested pitifully. 'You're all I've got. I thought you'd be here with me for the few years I have left.'

'Gramps, you're a monster.' Cory had hugged him. 'You're going to live for ever, and you know it.'

But although she no longer lived under his roof, he still felt he had *carte blanche* to meddle in her affairs.

And this evening was a case in point. He was a major contributor to the charity in question, and she was there to represent him, accompanied by a man who'd probably been blackmailed into bringing her.

Not, she decided, a pretty thought.

And so far it was all pretty much the disaster she'd expected. She and her escort had barely exchanged half a dozen words, and she'd seen the fleeting expression on his face when she'd emerged from the cloakroom.

You think this dress is bad? She'd wanted to say. You should have seen the ones I turned down. And I only bought it because I was running out of time and desperate, although I recognise a giant sack which also covered my face would have been a better choice.

But of course she'd said nothing of the kind. Just steadied her sinking heart and allowed him to take her into the ballroom.

And when Philip had dutifully asked her to dance with him she'd rewarded him by stepping on his foot. A painful process when your shoes were size sevens.

After which he'd hastily offered to get her a drink, and disappeared into the bar. That had been almost fifteen minutes ago, and it was more than time she went to look for him.

For all he knew, she thought, she could be lying on the floor, her face blackened and her tongue swollen with thirst.

She sighed under her breath. She always felt such a fool at these events. Such a fish out of water. For one thing, at five foot nine she was taller than most of the women. She was almost taller than Philip, which was another nail in the evening's coffin. Thank God she'd worn low heels.

She was a lousy dancer, too, she acknowledged with detachment. She had no natural rhythm—or even basic coordination, if it came to that. If she could find no one else's feet, she would fall over her own instead.

And she could usually manage a maximum of two minutes' bright social chatter, before her brain went numb and her pinned-on smile began to hurt.

At this moment she could only think how much she'd rather be at home, curled up with a book and a glass of good wine.

But now she really ought to move, before people thought she'd been actually glued to the spot, and make an attempt to find her unfortunate escort.

Maybe she could plead a sudden migraine and let him off the hook altogether, she thought.

She wasn't sure when she first became aware that someone was watching her.

Probably wondering if it was just the dress, or whether she'd genuinely been turned into a pillar of salt, she thought, glancing indifferently upwards.

And paused, conscious that her heart had given a sudden, unexpected lurch.

Because this was not the sort of man to give her even a passing look under normal circumstances.

And as their eyes met, some warning antenna began to send out frantic messages, screaming *Danger*.

He was immaculately dressed in conventional evening

clothes, but a bandanna around his unruly mane of curling
dark hair and a black patch over one eye would have suited
him better.

Although that was utter nonsense, she castigated herself.
He was probably a perfectly respectable lawyer or accoun-
tant. Certainly no buccaneer could afford the arm and leg
tonight's tickets had cost.

And it was time she stopped goggling like an idiot and
beat a dignified retreat.

But, before she could move, he smiled and lifted the
glass he was holding in a silent toast.

Cory could feel one of the agonising blushes that were
the bane of her life travelling up from her toes.

All she had to do was turn her head and she would find
the real recipient of all this attention standing behind her,
she thought. Someone blonde and gorgeous, who knew how
to wear clothes and probably how to take them off as well.
Someone who could make a remark about the weather
sound like an explicit sexual invitation.

I'm just in the way, she told herself.

But there was no one standing behind her. There was
herself. And he was looking at her, and only her, smiling,
as if he was watching. Waiting for her to do something.

Cory felt a sudden drop of sweat slide between her
breasts like ice on her heated skin. Was aware of a swift
flurry in her breathing.

Because she wanted to go to him. She wanted almost
desperately to walk across the ballroom and up those wide
marble stairs to where he was standing.

But, even more potently, she wanted him to come to her
instead, and the swift, unexpected violence of that need
jolted her out of her unwelcome trance and back to reality.

She thought, My God—this is crazy. And, more determinedly, I've got to get out of here—now…

She wheeled, and walked swiftly towards the cocktail bar and the errant Philip.

She risked a quick look over her shoulder and realised with mingled alarm and excitement that he was still there, still watching her, and still smiling.

My God, she thought again shakily. Philip might not be very exciting, or even marginally attentive, but at least he doesn't look like a pirate on his night off.

She looked round the crowded bar and eventually spotted him, sitting at a corner table with a bunch of his cronies, and roaring with laughter.

It was paranoid to think she might be the subject of the joke. Indeed, all the evidence suggested that he'd completely forgotten about her.

So—I'm paranoid, she thought with a small mental shrug. But once bitten...

At the bar, she asked for a white wine spritzer, and was just about to take her first sip when someone touched her shoulder.

She started violently, sending half the contents of her glass sloshing over the hated silver dress, and turned, half in hope, half in dread.

'Cory?' It was Shelley Bennet, an old schoolfriend, who now worked full time for the charity. 'I've been looking all over the place for you. I'd begun to think you'd chickened out.'

Cory sighed, mopping at herself with a minute lace hanky. 'No such luck. Gramps was adamant.'

'But surely you haven't come on your own?' Shelley's frown was concerned.

'My partner's over there, taking a well-deserved break,' Cory said drily. 'I may have broken his toe.' She hesitated. 'Shelley, when you were in the ballroom just now, did you notice a man?'

'Dozens,' Shelley said promptly. 'They tended to be dancing with women in long frocks. Strange behaviour at a ball, don't you think?'

'Well, this one seemed to be on his own. And he didn't look as if dancing was a major priority.'

Ravishment, maybe, she thought, and looting, with a spot of pillage thrown in.

Shelley's eyes glinted. 'You interest me strangely. Where did you see him?'

'He was up on the balcony.' Cory gave a slight frown. 'Usually you know exactly who's going to be at this kind of occasion, yet he was a total stranger. I've never seen him before.'

'Well, he seems to have made quite an impression,' Shelley said with affectionate amusement. 'You look marginally human for a change, my lamb, rather than as if you'd been carved out of stone.'

'Don't be silly,' Cory said with dignity.

Shelley's eyes danced. 'How much to look down the guest list and supply you with a name, if not a phone number?'

'It's not like that,' Cory protested. 'It's just such a novelty to see a new face at these things.'

'I can't argue with that.' Shelley gave her a shrewd look. 'Was it a nice new face?'

'No, I can't say that. Not *nice*, precisely.' Cory shook her head. *Not 'nice' at all.* 'But—interesting.'

'In that case I shall definitely be reviewing the guest list.' Shelley slipped an arm through her friend's. 'Come on, love. Point him out to me.'

But the tall stranger had vanished. And, but for the empty champagne glass on the balustrade in front of where he'd been standing, Cory would have decided he was simply a figment of her imagination.

'Snapped up by some predatory woman, I expect,' Shelley said with a sigh. 'Unless he took a good look at the evening's entertainment potential and decided that charity begins at home.'

Actually, he was taking a good look at me, Cory thought, rather forlornly. And probably writing me off as some sad, needy reject.

Aloud, she said briskly, 'Not a bad idea, either.'

She hailed a lurking waiter, and wrote a brief note of excuse to Philip on his order pad. 'Would you see that Mr Hamilton gets this, please? He's at the corner table in the cocktail bar.'

Shelley regarded her darkly. 'Are you running out on me, too—friend?'

''Fraid so,' Cory told her cheerfully. 'I've put in an appearance, so my duty's done and Gramps will be mollified.'

'Until the next time,' Shelley added drily. She paused. 'And what about your escort?'

'He's done his duty, too.' Cory smiled reassuringly. 'And I'd hate to have to fight off a token pass on the way home.'

'Maybe it wouldn't be token,' said Shelley. She was silent for a moment. 'Love, you aren't still tied up over that prat Rob, are you? You haven't let him ruin things for anyone else you might meet?'

'I never give him a thought,' Cory said, resisting an impulse to cross her fingers. 'And even if I believed in Mr Right, I can tell you now that Philip doesn't measure up.'

Shelley's eyes gleamed. 'Then why not opt for some good, unclean fun with Mr Wrong?'

For a brief moment Cory remembered a raised glass, and a slanting smile, and felt her heart thump all over again.

She said lightly, 'Not really my scene. The single life is safer.'

Shelley sighed. 'If not positively dull. Well, go home, if

you must. I'll ring you tomorrow and we'll fix up supper and a movie. The new Nicolas Cage looks good.'

'I had no real objection to the old Nicholas Cage,' said Cory. She gave Shelley a brief kiss on the cheek, and went.

The cab driver was the uncommunicative sort, which suited Cory perfectly.

She sat in the corner of the seat, feeling the tensions of the evening slowly seeping away.

She needed to be much firmer with Gramps, she told herself. Stop him arranging these dates from hell for her. Because she'd laughed off Philip's bad manners, and ducked the situation, that didn't mean she hadn't found the whole thing hurtful.

He'd left her standing around looking stupid, and vulnerable to patronage by some stranger who thought he was Mr Charm.

A hanging offence in more enlightened times, she told herself, as she paid off the cab and went into her building.

One disadvantage of living alone was having no one to discuss the evening with, she thought wryly, as she hung her coat in the wardrobe.

She could always telephone her mother, currently pursuing merry widowhood in Miami, but she'd probably find Sonia absorbed in her daily bridge game. And Gramps would only want to hear that she'd had a good time, so she'd have to fabricate something before she saw him next.

Maybe I'll get a cat, she thought. The final affirmation of spinsterhood. Which at twenty-three was ridiculous.

Perhaps I should change my name to Tina, she thought. There Is No Alternative.

She carefully removed the silver dress, and placed it over a chair. She'd have it cleaned, she decided, and send it to tonight's charity's second-hand shop. It would do more good there than it had while she'd been wearing it. Or had it really been wearing her?

Moot point, she thought, reaching for her moss-green velvet robe. And paused...

She rarely looked at herself in the mirror, except when she washed her face or brushed her hair, but now she found she was subjecting herself to a prolonged and critical scrutiny.

The silver-grey silk and lace undies she wore concealed very little from her searching gaze, so no false comfort there.

Her breasts were high and firm, but too small, she thought disparagingly. Everywhere else she was as flat as a board. At least her legs were long, but there were deep hollows at the base of her neck, and her shoulderblades could slice bread.

No wonder her blonde, glamorous mother, whose finely honed figure was unashamedly female, had tended to view her as if she'd given birth to a giraffe.

I'm just like Dad and Gramps, she acknowledged with a sigh. And if I'd only been a boy I'd have been glad of it.

She put on her robe and zipped it up, welcoming its warm embrace.

She dabbed cleanser on to her face, and tissued away the small amount of make-up which was all she ever wore. A touch of shadow on to her lids, a glow of pink or coral on her soft mouth, and a coat of brown mascara to emphasise the curling length of the lashes that shaded her hazel eyes. Her cheekbones required no accenting.

From the neck up she wasn't too bad, she thought judiciously. It was a shame she couldn't float round as a disembodied head.

But she couldn't understand why she was going in for this kind of personal assessment anyway. Unless it was

Shelley's reference to Rob, and all the unhappy memories his name still had the power to evoke.

Which is really stupid, she thought quickly. I should put it behind me. Move on. Isn't that what we're always being told?

But some things weren't so easy to leave behind.

She went across her living room into her small galley-kitchen and poured milk into a pan, setting it on the hob to heat. Hot chocolate was what she needed. Comfort in a mug. Not a stony trip down memory lane.

When her drink was ready, she lit the gas fire and curled up in her big armchair, her hands cupped round the beaker, her gaze fixed on the small blue flames leaping above the mock coals.

One day, she thought, she'd have a huge log fire in a hearth big enough to roast an ox.

In fact, if she wanted, she could have one next week. One word to Gramps, and mansions with suitable fireplaces would be laid open for her inspection.

Only, she didn't want.

She'd found out quite early in life that as the sole heiress to the Grant building empire the word was hers for the asking. That her grandfather was ready to gratify any whim she expressed. Which was why she'd learned to guard every word, and ask for as little as possible.

And this flat, with its one bedroom and tiny bathroom, was quite adequate for her present needs, she thought, looking round her with quiet satisfaction.

The property company who owned it had raised no objection to her getting rid of the elderly fitted carpets and having the floorboards sanded and polished to a gleaming honey shine.

She'd painted the walls a deep rich cream, and bought a

big, comfortable sofa and matching chair covered in a corded olive-green fabric.

She'd made a dining area, with a round, glass-topped table supported by a cream pedestal and a pair of slender high-backed chairs, and created an office space with a neat corner desk which she'd assembled herself from a pack during one long, fraught evening, and which held her laptop, her phone and a fax machine.

Not that she worked at home a great deal. She'd been determined from the first that the flat would be her sanctuary, and that she would leave Grant Industries behind each time she closed her door.

Although she could never really be free of it for long, she acknowledged with a smothered sigh.

But she used her home computer mainly to follow share dealings on the Internet—an interest she'd acquired during her time with Rob, and the only one to survive their traumatic break-up. A hobby, she thought, that she could pursue alone.

It had never been her parents' intention for her to be an only child. Cory had been born two years after their marriage, and it had been expected that other babies would follow in due course.

But there had seemed no real hurry. Ian and Sonia Grant had liked to live in the fast lane, and their partying had been legendary. Sonia had been a professional tennis player in her single days, and Ian's passion, apart from his wife and baby, had been rally driving.

Sonia had been playing in an invitation tournament in California when a burst tyre had caused Ian's car to spin off a forest road and crash, killing him instantly.

Sonia had tried to assuage her grief by re-embarking on the tennis circuit, and for a few years Cory had travelled with her mother in a regime of constantly changing nannies and hotel suites.

Arnold Grant had finally intervened, insisting that the little girl come back to Britain to be educated and live a more settled life, and Cory's childhood had then been divided between her grandparents' large house in Chelsea and their Suffolk home, which she'd much preferred.

Sonia had eventually remarried, her second husband being American industrialist Morton Traske, and after his death from a heart attack she'd taken up permanent residence in Florida.

Cory had an open invitation to join her, but her mother's country-club lifestyle had never held any appeal for her. And she suspected that Sonia, who was determinedly keeping the years at bay, found her a secret embarrassment anyway.

Their relationship was affectionate, but detached, and Cory found herself regarding Sonia very much as a wayward older sister. Most of the mothering in her life had been supplied by her grandmother.

Beth Grant had been a serenely beautiful woman, confident in the love of her husband and family. The loss of her son had clouded her hazel eyes and added lines of sadness to the corners of her mouth, but she had given herself whole-heartedly to the rearing of his small daughter, and Cory had worshipped her.

However, it hadn't taken long for Cory to realise there was another shadow over her grandmother's happiness, or to understand its nature.

The feud, she thought wearily. The damn feud. Still alive even after all these years.

It had been the only time she'd known her grandparents to quarrel. Seen tears of anger in Beth Grant's eyes and heard her voice raised in protest.

'This can't go on,' she'd railed. 'It's monstrous—farci-cal. You're like children, scoring off each other. Except it's more dangerous than that. For God's sake, stop it—stop it now…'

Her grandfather's answering rumble had been fierce. 'He started it, Bethy, and you know it. So tell him to give it up. Tell him to stop trying to destroy me. To undermine my business—overthrow my companies.'

Arnold Grant had smiled grimly. 'Because it hasn't worked, and it never will. Because I won't allow it. Anything he does to me will be done back to him. And he'll be the one to call a truce in the end—not me.'

'The end?' his wife had echoed bitterly. 'What kind of truce can there be when you're trying to annihilate each other?'

She'd suddenly seen Cory, standing in the doorway, and had hustled her away, chiding gently.

'Gran,' Cory had asked that night, when Beth had come to tuck her into bed, 'who's Matt Sansom?'

'Someone who doesn't matter,' Beth had said firmly. 'Not to me, and, I hope, never to you. Now, go to sleep, and forget all about it.'

Wise counsel, Cory thought, grimacing, but sadly im-possible to follow. And, since her grandmother's death six years before, the enmity between the two men seemed even more entrenched and relentless.

Only last week her grandfather had been gloating be-cause he'd been able to filch a prime piece of real estate which Sansom Industries had been negotiating for from un-der their very noses.

'But you don't even want that site,' Cory had protested. 'What will you do with it?'

'Sell it back to the bastards,' Arnold had returned with a grim smile. 'Through some intermediary. And at a fat profit. And there isn't a damned thing that old devil can do about it. Because he needs it. He's already deeply committed to the project.'

'So he'll be looking for revenge?' Cory had asked drily.

Arnold had sat back in his chair. 'He can try,' he'd said with satisfaction. 'But I'll be waiting for him.'

And so it went on, Cory thought wearily. Move and counter-move. One dirty trick answered by another. And who could say what damage was being done to their respective multi-million empires while these two ruthless old men pursued their endless, pointless vendetta? It was a chilling thought, but maybe they wouldn't be content until one of them had been the death of the other.

And then there wouldn't be anyone to carry on this senseless feuding.

Cory herself had always steadfastly refused to get involved, and Matt Sansom's only heir was the unmarried daughter who kept house for him. There'd been a younger daughter, too, but she'd walked out over thirty years ago and completely disappeared. Rumour said that Matt Sansom had never allowed her name to be mentioned again, and in this case, Cory thought wryly, rumour was probably right.

Her grandfather's enemy was a powerful hater.

She shivered suddenly, and got up from her chair.

In her bedroom, she tossed her robe on to a chair and unhooked her bra. And paused as she glimpsed herself in the mirror, half naked in the shadows of the lamplit room.

She thought with amazement, But that's what he was doing—the man on the balcony—undressing me with his eyes. Looking at me as if I was bare...

And felt, with shock, her nipples harden, and her body clench in a swift excitement that she could neither control nor pardon...

For a moment she stood motionless, then with a little cry she snatched up her white cotton nightdress and dragged it over her head.

She said aloud, her voice firm and cool, 'He's a stranger, Cory. You'll never see him again. And, anyway, didn't you learn your lesson with Rob—you pathetic, gullible idiot? Now, go to bed and sleep.'

But that was easier said than done. Because when she closed her eyes, the dark stranger was there waiting for her, pursuing her through one brief disturbing dream to the next.

And when she woke in the early dawn there were tears on her face.

CHAPTER TWO

ROME walked into his suite and slammed the door behind him.

For a moment he leaned back against its solid panels, eyes closed, while he silently called himself every bad name he knew in English, before switching to Italian and starting again.

But the word that cropped up most often was 'fool'.

The whisky he'd ordered earlier had been sent up, he noted with grim pleasure. He crossed to the side table, pouring a generous measure into a cut-glass tumbler and adding a splash of spring water.

He opened the big sliding doors and moved out on to the narrow terrace, staring with unseeing eyes over the city as he swallowed some of the excellent single malt in his glass. He put up a hand to his throat, impatiently tugging his black tie loose, ignoring the dank autumnal chill in the air.

He said quietly, almost conversationally, 'I should never have come here.'

But then what choice did he have, when the Italian banks, once so helpful, had shrugged regretful shoulders and declined to loan him the money he needed to revitalise his vines and restore the crumbling house that overlooked them?

And for that, he thought bitterly, he had Graziella to thank. She'd sworn she'd make him sorry, and she'd succeeded beyond her wildest dreams.

He'd intended his trip to London to be a flying visit, and

totally private. He'd planned to stay just long enough to negotiate the loan he needed, then leave immediately, without advertising his presence.

But he'd underestimated his grandfather, and the effectiveness of his information network, he realised, his mouth twisting wryly.

He'd barely checked in to his hotel before the summons had come. And couched in terms he hadn't been able to refuse.

But he couldn't say he hadn't been warned. His mother had been quite explicit.

'Sooner or later he'll want to meet you, and you should go to him because you're his only grandchild. But don't accept any favours from him, *caro*, because there's always a payback. Always.'

Yet he still hadn't seen the trap that had been baited for him.

He'd been caught off guard, of course. Because Matthew Sansom had come to him first. Had simply appeared one day at Montedoro right out of the blue.

Rome had been shaken to find himself staring at an older version of himself. The mane of hair was white, and the blue eyes were faded, but the likeness was undeniable, and not lost on Matt Sansom either.

The shaggy brows had drawn together in a swift glare of disbelief, then he'd recovered. 'So—you're Sarah's bastard.'

Rome inclined his head. 'And you're the man who tried to stop me being born,' he countered.

There was a smouldering silence, then a short bark of laughter. 'Yes,' said Matt Sansom. 'But perhaps that was a mistake.'

He swung round and looked down over the terraces of vines. 'So this is where my daughter spent her last years.'

He sounded angry, almost contemptuous, but there was a note of something like regret there, too.

He stayed two nights at Montedoro, touring the *vigneto* and asking shrewd questions about its operation, and paying a visit to the local churchyard where Sarah was buried beside her husband, Steve d'Angelo.

'You have his name,' Matt said abruptly as they drove back to the villa. 'Was he your father?'

'No, he adopted me.'

The pale eyes glittered at Rome. 'Card-sharp, wasn't he?'

'He was a professional gambler.' Rome was becoming accustomed to his grandfather's abrasive style of questioning. 'He was also a brilliant, instinctive card player, who competed for high stakes and usually won.'

'And you followed in his footsteps for a while?'

Rome shrugged. 'I'd watched him since I was a boy. He taught me a lot. But my heart was never in it, as his was.'

'But you won?'

'Yes.'

Matt peered through the window of the limousine with a critical air. 'Your stepfather didn't invest much of his own winnings in the family estate.'

'It came to Steve on the death of his cousin. He'd never expected to inherit, and it was already run down.'

'And now you've taken it on.' That bark of laughter again. 'Maybe you're more of a gambler than you think, boy.' He paused. 'Did your mother ever speak about your real father?'

'No,' Rome said levelly. 'Never. I got the impression it wasn't important to her.'

'Not important?' The growl was like distant thunder. 'She brings disgrace on herself and her family, and it doesn't matter?'

Just for a moment Rome caught a glimpse of the harsh, unforgiving tyrant his mother had run away from.

'She was young,' he said, his own voice steely. 'She made a mistake. She didn't have to do penance for the rest of her life.'

Matt grunted, and relapsed into a brooding silence.

That was the only real conversation they'd had on personal subjects, Rome recalled. They'd seemed to tacitly agree there were too many no-go areas.

His grandfather had sampled the wine from Rome's first few vintages with the appreciation of a connoisseur, drawing him out on the subject, getting him to talk about his plans for the *vigneto*, his need to buy new vats for the *cantina* and replace the elderly oaken casks with stainless steel.

Looking back, Rome could see how much he'd given away, in his own enthusiasm. Understood how Matt Sansom had deliberately relaxed the tension between them, revealing an interested, even sympathetic side to his nature.

The offer of a low-cost loan to finance these improvements had been made almost casually. And the fact that it wasn't a gift—that it was a serious deal, one businessman to another, with a realistic repayment programme—had lured Rome into the trap.

It had only been later, after the deal had been agreed and his grandfather had departed, that he'd begun to have doubts.

But it was finance he needed, and repayments he could afford, he'd thought. And it would be a definite one-off. Once the last instalment had been paid, he would look for future loans from more conventional sources.

He remembered a night in Paris when both Steve and himself had emerged heavy winners from a private poker game which had been scheduled to last a week. The other players had been quietly spoken and beautifully dressed, and the air of power round the table had been almost tangible, and definitely menacing.

'Are we going back?' he'd asked eagerly, but Steve had shaken his head.

'Never return to a pool where tigers come to drink,' he'd told him, and they'd caught the next plane back to Italy.

It was a piece of advice that had lingered. But Rome had told himself that his grandfather's loan was a justifiable risk. The first and last visit to the tigers' pool.

Over the past two years communication between them had been brief, and usually by letter.

Rome had assumed that it would remain that way.

So the curt demand for his presence had been an unwelcome surprise.

Matt Sansom lived just outside London, in a house hidden behind a high stone wall and masked by clustering trees.

'Disney meets Frankenstein' had been Sarah d'Angelo's description of her childhood home, and, recovering from his first glimpse of the greystone, creeper-hung mansion, its bulk increased by the crenellated turrets at each end, Rome had found the description apt.

A quiet grey-haired woman in an anonymous navy dress had answered the door to him.

'Rome,' she said, a warm, sweet smile lighting her tired eyes. 'Sarah's son. How wonderful. I didn't believe we'd ever meet.' She reached up and kissed his cheek. 'I'm your aunt Kit.'

Rome returned her embrace, guiltily aware he'd assume she was the housekeeper.

He said, 'I didn't believe I'd ever be invited here either. I thought my existence was too much of a blot on the family honour.'

He was waiting for her to tell him that his grandfather's bark was worse than his bite, but the expected reassurance didn't come.

Instead, she said, 'He's waiting for you. I'll take you up to him.

'He's resting,' she added over her shoulder, as she led the way up the wide Turkey-carpeted staircase and turned left on to a galleried landing. 'He's been unwell. I was afraid it was his heart, but the doctor's diagnosed stress.'

If the house looked like a film set, then Matt Sansom's bedroom emphasised the impression. It was stiflingly hot and airless. The carpet was crimson, and so were the drapes, while the vast bed was built on a raised dais. And in the centre of it, propped up by pillows, was Matt himself.

Like some damned levee at eighteenth-century Versailles, Rome thought, amused, then met the full force of his grandfather's glare and realised this was no laughing matter.

He said, 'Good evening, Grandfather. I hope you're feeling better.'

Matt grunted and looked past him. 'Go downstairs, Kit,' he directed abruptly. 'You're not needed here.'

Rome swung around. 'Aunt Kit,' he said pleasantly, 'I hope you can make time for a talk before I leave.'

She nodded, darting an apprehensive glance at her father, then slipped from the room.

'You can bring us some coffee in half an hour,' Matt called after her as she closed the door.

Rome's brows lifted. 'Is that my aunt's job?'

'It is tonight. I've given the staff the evening off.' Matt gave him a measuring look. 'And you're very quick to claim family relationships.'

'Are you saying we're not related?' Rome asked levelly.

'No. I've decided to acknowledge your existence. But in my own time, and in my own way.'

'Am I supposed to be grateful?'

'No,' said Matt. 'You're expected to do as you're told.' He gestured at the carafe and glass on his night table. 'Pour me some water, boy.'

'As we're dispensing with common courtesy, may I tell you to go to hell, before I walk out?' Rome, tight-lipped, filled the glass and handed it to the old man.

'No,' Matt said. 'Because you can't afford to.' He allowed Rome to assimilate that, then nodded. 'Now, pull up that chair and listen to what I have to say.' He drank some water, pulling a peevish face. 'What do you know of Arnold Grant?'

Rome paused. 'I know that you've been lifelong business rivals and personal enemies,' he said quietly. 'My mother said that the feuding between you had poisoned life in this house for years. That's one of the reasons she—left.'

'Then she was a fool. She should have stayed—helped me fight him instead of disgracing herself.' He reached under his pillows and pulled out a folder. He extracted a magazine clipping and thrust it at Rome. 'Here he is.'

Rome gave the photograph an expressionless look. He saw a tall thin man with iron-grey hair, flanked by two prominent politicians.

He said, 'What of it?'

'I'll tell you precisely what.' Matt thumped the bed with his fist. 'He came at me again recently. I was negotiating for some land for a shopping development. I'd had plans drawn up, paid for test drilling and consultancy fees—and he did a secret deal—stole it from under my nose. Cost me hundreds of thousands of pounds, and not for the first time either. But, by God, it will be the last. Because I'm going for him, and this time it's personal.'

Rome was alarmed at the passion vibrating in the older man's voice. At the veins standing out on his forehead.

He said quietly, 'Someone once said the best revenge was to live well. Have you thought of that?'

'I intend to live well.' Matt's eyes glittered. 'After I've dealt Arnold Grant a blow he'll never recover from. And this is where you come in.' He paused. 'He has two weak spots—and one of them's in that photo. See the girl standing on the end?'

Rome gave the cutting a frowning glance. 'Yes.'

'That's his only granddaughter. She's not much in the way of looks but he thinks the sun shines out of her, and it's through her that I'm going to bring him down.' He paused. 'With your help.'

Rome put the cutting down, and rose. He said, grimly, 'Let's hold it right there. I don't know what you're contemplating, and I don't want to.'

'Always supposing you have a choice.' Matt leaned back against his pillows. 'Now, stay where you are and listen. You're going to meet this girl, and you're going to persuade her to marry you. I don't care how.'

For a moment Rome stared at him, then he said quietly and coldly, 'I'm not sure if this is a serious proposition, or a sick joke. If it's the first, the answer's no, and if the second, I'm not even marginally amused.'

'Oh, I mean it,' Matt said. 'And you'll do it. If you know what's good for you. Now sit down.'

The threat was unequivocal, and Rome felt tension grating across every nerve.

He thought, This is crazy. I have to reason with him...

Resuming his seat, he looked back steadily at his grandfather. 'I make wine. I don't take part in feuds. And I'm not interested in involvement with some unknown girl. There are plenty of tame studs for hire out there who'll fulfil your requirements. They might even enjoy it. I wouldn't.'

'You make wine,' Matt Sansom said softly, 'only while you still have a vineyard. If I called in my loan, you'd have to sell up. And believe that I'll do exactly what I need to.'

'But you can't.' Rome stared at him, horrified. 'I've made every payment...'

'But I'm having a cash-flow problem—I've just lost out on a big deal and have to recoup my losses.' Matt allowed himself a thin smile of satisfaction. 'And think of the consequences,' he added. 'Your workers will be out of jobs, your house will crumble into ruins, and you'll be picking a living from the casinos again. Is that what you want?'

Rome said, between his teeth, 'No.'

'Then be sensible. You'll have no problem with the Grant girl. There's no regular man in her life. She'll fall into your hand like a ripe apple from a tree.' He laughed hoarsely. 'She was engaged at one point, but threw her unfortunate fiancé, over a fortnight before the wedding. Nearly broke him up, I gather. You'll understand that, I dare say,' he added, darting Rome a lightning glance.

Rome was suddenly rigid. He said icily, 'You have done your homework.'

'Knowledge is power. And Arnie Grant doesn't know I have a grandson—which is his second weakness.'

Rome shook his head in disbelief. He said, 'You actually expect me to marry this girl—whatever her name is?'

'She's called Cory,' Matt said. Something flickered in his eyes, then vanished. 'It's a family name. But she's known as the Ice Maiden, because she freezes men off. And you won't marry her,' he added with a wheezing laugh. 'Because when Arnie Grant discovers your real identity— that you're my grandson and illegitimate at that—he'll move heaven and earth to stop it. To get rid of you from her life.

'That's why a hired stud won't do. It has to be you. Because Arnie Grant will want you to go away—to disappear before the truth comes out and turns him into a laughing stock, together with his precious child. And he'll pay you to do just that.

'But he'll know that I know,' he added gloatingly. 'That I set him up—and he'll have to live with that humiliation for the rest of his life. It will finish him.'

He nodded. 'You'll be able to name your own price, and whatever he offers you, I'll match. And you can consider the loan paid off, too.'

'I could do that anyway,' Rome flashed. 'I came over here looking for finance. I can repay you from my new borrowing. I don't need your dirty bargain.'

'Ah,' Matt said softly. 'But you may find that money's not as readily available to you as you thought. That you're not considered a good risk. In fact, I'd offer generous odds that your luck—and your credit—have run out.'

Rome rose and walked out to the window. Afternoon was fading into evening, and a breeze was stirring the rain-soaked shrubs in the garden below.

He thought of the thick autumn sunlight falling on Montedoro, the rich gleam of the earth and the pungent scents of the *cantina*, and felt a bleakness invade his very soul.

The vineyard had become his life. Its workers were his people. He was not prepared to let them go to the wall.

He said without looking around, 'So, you've poisoned the wells for me. Did you do the same in Italy?'

'I didn't have to. A man called Paolo Cresti did it for me. He thinks you're having an affair with his wife.'

Rome swung back to face him. 'That's a lie,' he said coldly. 'I haven't set eyes on her since her marriage.'

Matt's smile was thin. 'That's not what she's let her husband believe. You should have remembered the old saying—hell have no fury like a woman scorned.'

Rome stared at him bitterly. 'I should have remembered much more than that,' he said. He walked back to the bed and picked up the cutting. 'Has it occurred to you that this girl may not find me attractive?'

'Plenty of women have, by all accounts. Why should she be an exception?'

'And I may not fancy her,' Rome reminded him levelly.

'But you'll fancy the money you'll get from old Grant.' Matt leered at him. 'Just keep thinking of that. And keep your eyes shut, if you have to.'

Rome's mouth twisted in disgust. He looked down at the photograph. 'This tells me nothing. I need to see her properly before I decide.'

'I can't argue with that.' Matt handed him an elaborately embossed card from the folder. 'A ticket in your name for a charity ball at the Park Royal Hotel tomorrow night. She'll be there. He won't. You can look her over at your leisure.'

There was a tap at the bedroom door, and Kit Sansom appeared with a tray of coffee.

'We shan't need that,' her father said. 'Because Rome is leaving. He's got some serious thinking to do.' His smile was almost malicious. 'Haven't you—boy?'

Rome hadn't spent all the intervening time thinking, however. He'd attempted to make contact with some of the financial contacts on his list, but without success, no one wanted to know him, he realised bitterly. Matt Sansom had done his work well.

And now, for Montedoro's sake, he was committed to

the next phase of this war of attrition between two megalomaniac old men.

He groaned, and tossed down the rest of his whisky. If ever he'd needed to get roaring, blazing drunk, it was tonight.

As he walked back inside to refill his glass, someone knocked at the door of his suite. A porter faced him.

'Package for you, sir. Brought round by special messenger.' He accepted Rome's tip, and vanished.

Frowning, Rome slit open the bulky envelope. He realised immediately that he was looking at a complete dossier on Cory Grant—where she lived, how she spent her spare time, where she shopped, her favourite restaurants. Even the scent she used.

No detail too trivial to be excluded, he acknowledged sardonically.

But it was chillingly thorough. Matt must have been planning this for a long time, he thought. And the screwed-up land deal was just an excuse.

He poured himself another whisky, stretched out on the bed and began to read.

'You made me look a complete idiot,' said Philip. 'Walking out like that.'

Indignation added a squeak to his voice, Cory thought dispassionately. And who needed a man who squeaked?

She kept her tone matter-of-fact. 'I didn't think you'd notice I was gone.'

'Oh, come off it, Cory. I told you—I ran into some old friends—lost track of time rather. And I'm sorry if you felt neglected.' He paused. 'But I'll make it up to you.' His voice became chummy, almost intimate. 'Why don't we have dinner? I promise I'll give you my undivided attention.'

Cory gave her cordless phone receiver a look of blank disbelief.

She said politely, 'I don't think so, thanks. We don't have enough in common.' Except, she thought, that your father is one of Gramps's main sub-contractors, and you realise you may have rocked the boat.

'Look, Cory.' He sounded hectoring again. 'I've apologised. I don't know what else you want me to say.'

'Goodbye would do quite well.'

'Oh, very amusing. Know something, Cory? It's time you got off that high horse of yours and came down to earth, or you're going to end up a sad old maid. Because I don't know what you want from a man. And I suspect you don't know either.'

She said, 'It's quite simple, Philip. I want kindness. And you just don't qualify.'

She replaced her receiver, cutting off his spluttering reply.

She should have let her answering machine take the call, she thought. She simply wasn't up to dealing with Philip's efforts at self-justification after her disturbed night.

And she wasn't up to dealing with the reasons for the disturbed night either.

With a sigh, she went into her tiny kitchen, poured orange juice, set coffee to percolate and slotted bread into the toaster.

Gramps would be next, she thought, eager to know how the evening had gone, and she'd make up a kindly fib to satisfy him.

Only it wasn't her grandfather who rang almost at once, but Shelley.

'Cory—are you there? Pick the phone up. I have news.'

Cory hesitated, frowning slightly.

Her 'hello' was guarded, but Shelley didn't notice.

'I've found your mysterious stranger,' she reported happily. 'I did a quick check, and he bought one of the last tickets. His name's Rome d'Angelo. So, the ball's in your court now.'

'I don't see how.'

Shelley made an impatient noise. 'Come on, babe. You won't find many men with that name to the square acre. I'd start with directory enquiries.'

'Perhaps—if I wanted to find him,' Cory agreed, her lips twitching in spite of herself.

'I thought he'd made a big impression.'

'But not one I necessarily wish to repeat.' God, Cory thought, I sound positively Victorian. She hurried into speech again. 'Thanks for trying, Shelley, but I've made a major decision. If I get involved again, I want someone kind and caring, not sex on legs.'

'You could have both. Isn't this guy worth a second look?'

'I doubt if he was worth the first one,' Cory said drily. 'I'm sorry, love. I'm a hopeless case.'

'No,' Shelley said. 'You just think you are. So, if you're not going man-hunting, what do you plan for your day?'

'I'm doing the domestic thing.' Cory narrowed her eyes to stare at a ray of watery sun filtering through the window. 'And I may go over to the health club for a swim later.'

'Well, take care,' Shelley advised caustically. 'Too much excitement can be bad for you. I'll call you next week.' And she rang off.

As Cory replaced her own handset, it occurred to her that the unknown Rome d'Angelo was almost certainly that kind of excitement. Bad for you.

And best forgotten, she told herself dismissively.

*   *   *

The health club was rarely very busy on Saturday mornings, and today was no exception. Cory found she had the pool virtually to herself. She had always loved swimming, finding her own grace and co-ordination when she was in the water, and she could feel the tensions floating out of her as she cut through the water.

Afterwards she relaxed on one of the comfortable padded benches set back around the pool, and read some of the book she'd brought with her, but to her annoyance she found her concentration fragmenting.

In spite of herself, she kept thinking of the previous evening, and that brief, disturbing glimpse she'd had of Rome d'Angelo.

She found herself trying the name over in her mind, silently cursing Shelley as she did so.

I really didn't need to know his identity, she thought. He was easier to keep at bay when he was an anonymous stranger.

Although she'd been aware of a connection between them, as powerful as an electric current.

Suddenly, shockingly, she felt her body stir with excitement, as if she'd been touched. As if her mouth had been kissed, and her breast stroked gently to pleasure. Beneath the cling of her Lycra swimsuit her nipples were hardening to a piercing intensity, her body moistening in longing.

Cory sat up, pushing her hair back from her face.

It's time I took a shower, she thought, her mouth twisting. And maybe I should make it a cold one.

The changing rooms on the floor above were reached by lift. The women's section was beautifully equipped, with mounds of fluffy towels, gels and body lotions and other toiletries, hairdriers, and a selection of all the popular fragrances in tester bottles for the clients to try.

Cory didn't linger today as she usually did. She show-ered swiftly, then dressed in her usual weekend uniform of jeans and a plain white tee shirt.

She'd have some lunch at the salad bar on the ground floor before it got busy, she decided, as she shrugged on her leather jacket and picked up her tote bag. She was on her way out when she swung round, went back to the vanity unit, and sprayed her throat and wrists with some of her favourite 'Dune'.

And why not? she demanded silently as she made for the wide central stairway.

She was two thirds of the way down, head bent, moving fast, when she suddenly felt her warning antennae switch to full alert, and glanced up, startled.

She saw him at once, standing at the bottom of the stairs, looking up at her.

Recognition was instant, sending her pulses into overdrive.

She felt her lips frame his name, then stiffened in sudden, almost violent negation. Because he couldn't be here—he *couldn't be...*

Her foot caught the moulded edge of the step, and she stumbled. As she fell, she grabbed at the rail and managed to check her headlong descent, but she couldn't prevent herself sliding down the last half-dozen steps on her hip, and landing in an untidy huddle at his feet.

She lay for a moment, winded, hearing a buzz of comment, aware of shocked faces looking down at her. Of one face in particular, dark and coolly attractive, with vivid blue eyes fringed by long lashes, a high-bridged nose, and a mouth redeemed from harshness by the sensuous curve of its lower lip.

She realized too that he was kneeling beside her, and she was lying across his knees, his arm supporting her.

His voice was low and resonant with a faint accent she could not place.

'Don't try to move. Are you hurt?'

'No.' The denial was swift, almost fierce, and she pushed herself up into a sitting position. 'I'm fine—really. It was just a stupid accident.'

She was going to have the mother of all bruises on her hip, but she'd deal with that tomorrow. At the moment, her main concern was getting out of the club with what little remained of her dignity.

But his hand was on her shoulder, forcing her to stay where she was.

'Maybe I should take you to the nearest casualty room—get you checked over.'

'There's no need for that. No damage has been done.' She hunched away from him. She felt dazed, her body tingling, but instinct told her that had more to do with his hand on her shoulder than the tumble she'd just taken.

'Then perhaps you'd take me instead.' His face was dead-pan, but there was a glint in those amazing eyes. 'I'm not used to having girls fall at my feet, and shock can be dangerous.'

'Oh, really?' Cory glared at him as she hauled herself painfully upright. 'Now, I'd say you'd spent your adult life stepping over recumbent women.'

Oh, God, she thought, appalled. What am I doing? I can't believe I just said that.

His brows lifted. 'Appearances,' he said softly, 'can be deceptive. Something I also need to remember,' he added quietly as he, too, got to his feet.

Cory was almost glad to see one of the physiotherapists hurrying towards them. She answered his concerned questions, declined having her ankle examined, and agreed to fill out an accident report.

'But later.' Rome d'Angelo took her arm, and apparent control of the situation. 'Now the lady needs something to drink.'

Cory hung back, trying not to wince. She was altogether more shaken than she'd realised, but the fall was only partly responsible.

Now she needed to get away before she made an even bigger fool of herself.

She said, controlling the quiver in her voice, 'I'm really all right. There's no need for you to concern yourself any more.'

'But I am concerned,' he said softly, as the crowd began to melt away. 'You threw yourself, and I caught you. And I'm not prepared to put you down yet. So, are you going to walk to the coffee shop with me—or do I have to carry you?'

Cory heard herself say, 'I'll walk.' And hardly recognised her own voice.

CHAPTER THREE

THIS is lunacy, thought Cory, and I should run out of here and have myself committed immediately.

But she couldn't. For one thing, she was too sore to run anywhere. For another, her wallet and keys were in her tote bag, which Rome d'Angelo must have rescued after her fall and which was now hanging from one muscular shoulder as he waited at the counter in the coffee shop.

So, she said, perforce, to stay where she was, perched in rigid discomfort on one of the pretty wrought-iron chairs at the corner table he'd taken her to.

Round one to him, it seemed.

And all she had to do now was ensure there wasn't a round two.

Because every instinct she possessed was warning her yet again that this was a man to avoid. That he was danger in its rawest sense.

Anyone with a year-round tan and eyes like the Mediterranean was out of her league anyway, she reminded herself drily. But the peril that Rome d'Angelo represented went far deeper than mere physical attraction.

It's as if I know him, she thought restlessly. As if I've always known him...

She felt it in her blood. Sensed it buried deep in her bones. And it scared her.

I'll drink my coffee, thank him politely, and get the hell out of here, she thought. That's the best—the safest way to handle this.

She was by no means the only one aware of his presence,

41

she realised. From all over the room glances were being
directed at him, and questions whispered. And all from
women. She could almost feel the *frisson*.

But then, she certainly couldn't deny his eye-catching
potential, she acknowledged unwillingly.

He was even taller than she'd originally thought, topping
her by at least five inches. Lean hips and long legs were
emphasised by close-fitting faded denims, and he wore a
collarless white shirt, open at the throat. A charcoal jacket
that looked like cashmere was slung over one shoulder,
along with her tote bag.

He looked relaxed, casual—and powerfully in control.

And she, on the other hand, must be the only woman in
the room with damp hair and not a trace of make-up.
Which, as she hastily reminded herself, really couldn't matter less…

Pull yourself together, she castigated herself silently.

She saw him returning and moved uneasily, and un-
wisely, suppressing a yelp as she did so.

'Arnica,' he said, as he put the cups down on the table.

'Really?' Her brow lifted. 'I thought it was *café latte*.'

'It comes in tablet or cream form,' he went on, as if she
hadn't spoken. 'It will bring out the bruising.'

'I think that's already escaped,' Cory admitted, wincing.
She eyed him as he took his seat. 'You know a lot about
herbal medicine?'

'No.' He smiled at her, his gaze drifting with deliberate
sensuousness from her eyes, to her mouth, and down to her
small breasts, untrammelled under the cling of the ancient
tee shirt, and then back to meet her startled glance. 'My
expertise lies in other areas.'

Cory, heart thumping erratically, hastily picked up her
cup and sipped.

'Yuck.' She wrinkled her nose. 'This has sugar in it.'

'The recognised treatment for shock.' Rome nodded. 'A hot, sweet drink.'

'I fell down a couple of steps,' she said. 'I'm sore, but hardly shocked.'

'Ah,' he said softly. 'But you didn't see your face just before you fell.' He paused, allowing her a moment to digest that. 'How did you enjoy the ball?'

Pointless to pretend she hadn't noticed him, or didn't recognise him, Cory realised, smouldering.

She managed a casual shrug. 'Not very much. I didn't stay long.'

'What a coincidence,' he said softly. 'Clearly, we feel the same about such events.'

'Then why buy a ticket?'

'Because it was in such a good cause. I found it impossible to resist.' He drank some of his own coffee. 'Don't you like dancing?'

'I don't think it likes me,' she said ruefully. 'I have this tendency to stand on peoples' feet, and no natural rhythm.'

'I doubt that.' Rome leaned back in his chair, the blue eyes faintly mocking. 'I think you just haven't found the right partner.'

There was a brief, seething silence, and Cory's skin prickled as if someone's fingertips had brushed softly across her pulse-points.

She hurried into speech. 'Talking of coincidences, what are you doing here?'

'I came to look over the facilities.'

'You live in the area?' The question escaped before she could prevent it.

'I plan to.' He smiled at her. 'I hope that won't be a problem for you.'

Cory stiffened. 'Why should it?'

'My appearance seems to have a dire effect on you.'

'Nothing of the kind,' she returned with studied coolness. 'Don't read too much into a moment's clumsiness. I'm famous for it. And London's a big place,' she added. 'We're unlikely to meet again.'

'On the contrary,' he said softly. 'We're bound to have at least one more encounter. Don't you know that everything happens in threes?'

Cory said shortly, 'Well, I'm not superstitious.' And crossed her fingers under cover of the table. She hesitated. 'Are you planning to take out a membership here?'

'I haven't decided yet.' His blue gaze flickered over her again. 'Although, admittedly, it seems to have everything I want.'

'And separate days for men and women,' Cory commented pointedly, aware that her mouth had gone suddenly dry.

'Except for weekends, when families are encouraged to use the place.' His tone was silky.

Cory played with the spoon in her saucer. 'And is that what you plan to do? Bring your family?'

His brows lifted. 'One day, perhaps,' he drawled. 'When I have a family.' He paused again. 'I'm Rome d'Angelo, but perhaps you know that already,' he added casually.

Cory choked over a mouthful of coffee, and put her cup down with something of a slam.

'Isn't that rather an arrogant assumption?' she demanded with hauteur.

He grinned at her, unabashed. 'And isn't that a defence rather than a reply?'

'I don't know what you're talking about,' Cory said, feeling one of those hated blushes beginning to warm her face. Oh, no, she appealed silently. Please, no.

He said, 'Now it's your turn.'

'To do what?' *Fall over again, send the table crashing, spill my coffee everywhere?*

'To tell me your name.'

She said with sudden crispness, 'I'm grateful for your help, Mr d'Angelo, but that doesn't make us friends.'

'I'd settle for acquaintances?' he suggested.

'Not even that.' Cory shook her head with determination. 'Ships that pass in the night.'

'But we didn't pass. We collided.' He leaned forward suddenly, and, in spite of herself, Cory flinched. 'Tell me something,' he invited huskily. 'If I'd come down to the ballroom last night, and asked you to dance—what would you have said?'

She didn't look at him, but stared down at the table as, for a few seconds, her mind ran wild with speculation, dangerous fantasies jostling her like last night's dreams.

Then she forced a shrug, only to wish she hadn't as her bruises kicked back. 'How about, ''Thank you—but I'm here with someone.''?'

Rome's mouth twisted. 'He seemed to be doing a great job.'

'That's none of your business,' Cory fought back. 'Will you please accept, Mr d'Angelo, that I don't need a saviour, or a Prince Charming either.'

'And your circle of friends is complete, too.' He was smiling faintly, but those incredible eyes glinted with challenge. 'So what is left, I wonder? Which of your needs is not being catered for?'

Cory's face was burning again, but with anger rather than embarrassment. She said, 'My life is perfectly satisfactory, thank you.'

He was unperturbed by the snap in her voice. 'No room for improvement anywhere?'

'I have simple tastes.'

'Yet you wear Christian Dior,' he said. 'You're more complicated than you think.'

Suddenly breathless, Cory reached down for her tote bag, jerking it towards her. Then rose. 'Thanks for the coffee,' she said. 'And for the character analysis. I hope you don't do it for a living. Goodbye, Mr d'Angelo.'

He got to his feet, too. His smile held real charm. 'Until next time—Miss Grant.'

She'd almost reached the door when she realised what he'd said, and swung round, lips parting in a gasp of angry disbelief.

But Rome d'Angelo wasn't there. He must have used the exit that led straight to the street, she realised in frustration.

Her mouth tightened. So, he liked to play games. Well, she had no intention of joining in—or of rising to any more of his bait.

But at the same time she found herself wondering how he'd found out her name. And what else he might know about her.

And realised that the swift shiver curling down her spine was only half fear. And that the other half was excitement.

'You've met her? You've talked to her?' Matt Sansom's laugh rasped down the telephone line. 'You don't waste much time, boy.'

'I don't have a lot of time to waste,' Rome reminded him levelly. 'I have a life to get back to, and work to do.' He paused. 'But believe this. She isn't going to be any kind of push-over.'

'That's your problem,' his grandfather snapped. 'Failure doesn't enter the equation. What woman can resist being swept off her feet?'

In spite of himself, Rome felt his mouth curve into a reluctant grin as he remembered angry hazel eyes sparking defiance at him from the floor. Remembered, too, how slight she'd felt as he'd lifted her. Felt a small sensuous twist of need uncoil inside him as he recalled her pale skin, so clear and translucent that he'd imagined he could see the throb of the pulse in her throat as he'd held her. As he'd breathed the cool sophisticated fragrance that the heat of her body had released.

'This one could be the exception,' he drawled. 'But I've always preferred a challenge.'

'So when will you see her again?' Matt demanded eagerly.

Rome smiled thinly. 'I'll give her a couple of days. I need the time to find an apartment—establish a base.'

'I've told Capital Estates to prepare a list of suitable properties,' Matt barked. 'They're waiting for your call. And don't stint yourself. You need a background that says money.'

And he rang off.

Rome switched off his mobile and tossed it on to the bed, frowning slightly.

Well, he was committed now, and there was no turning back, he thought without pleasure. But Montedoro was all that mattered. All that could be allowed to matter.

And he had somehow to overcome his personal distaste for the means he was being forced to employ to save his vineyard.

Although, to his own surprise, not every aspect of the deal was proving as unpalatable as he'd expected.

Cory Grant was the last girl he would normally have pursued, but he could not deny she intrigued him. Or perhaps he just wasn't used to having his advances treated with such uncompromising hostility, he thought, his mouth twisting in self-derision.

Whatever, he'd enjoyed crossing swords with her in this preliminary skirmish.

The invisible circle still surrounded her, but within it she wasn't as prim and conventional as he'd thought. Under that ancient tee shirt she'd been bra-less, and at one moment he'd found himself, incredibly, fantasising about peeling the ugly thing off her, and discovering with his hands and mouth if her rounded breasts were as warm, and soft, and rose-tipped and scented as his imagination suggested.

But that wasn't in the equation either, he reminded himself grimly. Because he intended to keep all physical contact between them to an absolute minimum. He'd have quite enough to reproach himself for without adding a full-scale seduction to the total.

So, he was planning an old-fashioned wooing, with flowers, romantic dates, candlelit dinners, and a few—a very few—kisses.

Not as instantly effective as tricking her into bed, he thought cynically, but infinitely safer.

Because sex was the great deceiver. And great sex could enslave you—render you blind, deaf and ultimately stupid. Make you believe all kinds of impossible things.

Just as it had with Graziella.

He sighed harshly. Why hadn't he seen, before he'd got involved with her, that behind the beautiful face and sexy body she was pure bitch?

Because a man in lust thought with his groin, not his brain, was the obvious answer.

And at least he wasn't still fooling himself that he'd been in love with her.

In bed, she'd been amazing—inventive and insatiable—and he'd been her match, satisfying the demands she'd made with her teeth, her nails, and little purring, feral cries.

But when he'd asked her to marry him—laid his future and Montedoro at her feet—she'd burst out laughing.

'*Caro*—are you mad? You have no money, and the d'Angelo vineyard was finished years ago. Besides, I'm going to marry Paolo Cresti. I thought everyone knew that.'

'A man over twice your age?' He looked down at the lush nakedness she'd just yielded to him, inch by tantalising inch. 'You can't do it.'

'Now you're talking like a fool. Paolo is a successful banker, and wealthy in his own right.' She paused, avid hands seeking him, stroking him back to arousal. 'And my marriage to him makes no difference to us. I shall need you all the more, *caro*, to stop me from dying of boredom.'

For a long moment he looked at her—at the glittering eyes, and the hot, greedy mouth.

He said gently, 'I'm no one's piece on the side, Graziella.' And got up from the bed.

Even while he was dressing—when he was actually walking to the door—she still didn't believe that he was really leaving her. Couldn't comprehend his revulsion at the role she'd created for him.

'You cannot do this,' she screamed hysterically. 'I want you. I will not let you go.'

Up to her marriage, and for weeks afterwards, she'd bombarded him with phone calls and notes, demanding his return.

Then had come the threats. The final hissed vow that she would make him sorry.

Something she'd achieved beyond her wildest dreams, he acknowledged bitterly.

At first, he'd thrown himself into life at Montedoro with a kind of grim determination, driven by bitterness and anger.

But gradually, working amongst the vines had brought a
kind of peace, and a sense of total involvement.

And that was something he wasn't prepared to lose
through the machinations of a lying wife and a jealous husband.

Since Graziella he'd made sure that any sexual encoun-
ters he enjoyed were civilised, and strictly transient, conducted without recrimination on either side.

But Cory Grant did not come into that category at all,
so it was far better not to speculate whether her skin would
feel like cool silk against his, or what it would take to make
her face warm with sensual pleasure rather than embarrassment or anger. In fact, he should banish all such
thoughts from his mind immediately.

Even though, as he was disturbingly aware, he might not
want to.

For a moment he seemed to breathe her—the appealing
aroma of clean hair and her own personal woman's scent
that the perfume she'd been wearing had merely enhanced.

He felt his whole body stir gently but potently at the
memory.

Ice Maiden? he thought. No, I don't think so. And
laughed softly.

'You're very quiet today.' Arnold Grant sent Cory a narrow-eyed look. 'In fact, you've been quiet the whole weekend. Not in love, are we?'

Cory's smile was composed. 'I can't speak for you,
Gramps, but I'm certainly not.'

Arnold sighed. 'I thought it was too good to be true. I
wish you'd hurry up, child. Help me fulfil my two remaining ambitions.'

Cory's brows lifted. 'And which two are those today?'

'Firstly, I want to give you away in church to a man who'll look after you when I'm no longer here.'

'Planning another world cruise?' Cory asked with interest.

Arnold frowned repressively. 'You know exactly what I mean.'

Cory sighed. 'All right—what's your second ambition?'

Arnold looked saintly. 'To see Sonia's face when she learns she's going to be a grandmother.'

Cory tutted reprovingly at him. 'How unkind. But she'll rise above it. She'll simply tell everyone she was a child bride.'

'Probably,' her grandfather agreed drily. He paused. 'So is there really no one on the horizon, my dear? I had great hopes you'd hit it off with Philip, you know.' He gave her a hopeful look. 'Are you seeing him again?'

Cory picked up the cheques she'd been writing for the monthly household bills and brought them over to him for signature. 'No, darling.'

'Ah, well,' he said, 'it wasn't obligatory.' A pause. 'What was wrong with him?'

This time she sighed inwardly. 'There was—no chemistry.'

'I see.' He was silent while he signed the cheques. As he handed them back, he said, 'Are you sure you know what you want—in a man?'

'I thought so, once.' She began to tuck the cheques into envelopes. 'These days, I'm more focused on what I *don't* want.'

'Which is?'

Eyes like a Mediterranean pirate, she thought, and a mouth that looks as if it knows far too much about women and the way they taste.

She shrugged. 'Oh, I've a list a mile long. And I need

to catch the post with these—and call at the supermarket before I go home. I haven't a scrap of food at home.'

'Then stay the night again.'

'Gramps—I've been here since Saturday.'

'Yes,' Arnold said. 'And I'm wondering why.'

'Does there have to be a reason?' Cory got up from the desk, the graceful flare of her simple navy wool dress swinging around her.

'Usually when you descend like this you have something you want to tell me.' His eyes were shrewd. 'Something on your mind that you need to discuss.' He paused. 'Or you're hiding.'

'Well, this time it was just for fun.' Cory dropped a kiss on his head on her way to the door. 'So, thank you for having me, and I'll see you tomorrow.'

She couldn't fool Gramps, she thought ruefully, as she posted her envelopes and hailed a taxi.

She'd gone straight home from the health club on Saturday, changed, thrown some things in a bag, and turned up on his doorstep like some medieval fugitive looking for sanctuary.

And all because Rome d'Angelo had known her name.

How paranoid can you get? She asked in self-denigration. It didn't follow that he also knew her address—or that he'd seek her out.

Although he'd said they would meet again, she reminded herself with disquiet. But perhaps he'd simply been winding her up because she'd made it so very clear she didn't want his company.

Undoubtedly he enjoyed being deliberately provocative, she thought, remembering the considering intensity of his gaze as it swept over her, making her feel naked—as if all her secrets were known to him.

'A tried and tested technique if ever I saw one,' she

muttered to herself, and saw the cab driver give her a wary glance in his mirror.

For once, the supermarket wasn't too busy, and she had leisure to collect her thoughts, dismiss Rome d'Angelo from her mind, and concentrate on what she needed to buy.

She picked up some bread, milk, eggs and orange juice, then headed for the meat section. She'd buy some chops for dinner, or maybe a steak, she thought, sighing a little as she remembered the clear soup, sole Veronique, and French apple tart that Mrs Ferguson would be serving to her grandfather.

She swung round the corner into the aisle rather too abruptly, and ran her trolley into another one coming in the opposite direction.

She said, 'Oh, I'm so sorry,' then yelped as her startled gaze absorbed exactly who was standing in front of her.

'You,' she said unsteadily. 'What the hell are you doing here?'

'Buying food,' Rome said. 'But perhaps it's a trick question.'

'In this particular supermarket?' Her voice cracked in the middle. 'As in—yet another amazing coincidence?'

'I told you that things ran in threes.' He looked understated but stunning, in casual dark trousers and a black sweater, and his smiling gaze grazed her nerve-endings.

'So you did.' She took a breath. 'You're following me, aren't you? Well, I don't know what happens where you come from, but here we have laws about stalking—'

'Hey, calm down,' Rome interrupted. 'If I'm following you, how is it my trolley's nearly full, while yours is still almost empty? The evidence suggests I got here first.'

'Well, I'm damned sure you've never been in this shop before,' she said angrily.

'Because you'd remember?' He grinned at her. 'I'm flattered.'

'Not,' she said, 'my intention.'

'I believe you. And, actually, I'm here, like you, because it's convenient. I live just round the corner in Farrar Street.'

'Since when?'

He glanced at his watch. 'Since three hours ago.'

'You're telling me you've found a place and moved in— all since Saturday morning?' Cory shook her head. 'I don't believe it. It can't all happen as quickly as that.'

'Ah,' he said gently. 'That depends on how determined you are.' His gaze flickered over her, absorbing the well-cut lines of her plain navy coat, the matching low-heeled shoes, and her hair, caught up into a loose coil on top of her head and secured by a silver clasp. 'Another change of image,' he remarked. 'I've seen you dressed up at the ball, and dressed down at the club. Now you seem to be wearing camouflage.'

'Working gear,' she said curtly. 'Now, if you'll excuse me, I have my own trolley to fill.'

But he didn't move. 'You must take your job very seriously.'

'I do,' she said. 'I also enjoy it.'

'All appearances to the contrary,' he murmured. 'I thought British companies were adopting a more casual approach.'

'My boss is the old-fashioned type,' she said. 'And I must be going.'

Rome leaned on his trolley, his eyes intent as they examined her. 'I hoped it might be third time lucky,' he said softly.

'Tell me something,' she said. 'Does the word "harassment" mean anything to you?'

He looked amused. 'Not particularly. Now, you tell me

something. In these politically correct times, how does a man indicate to a woman that he finds her—desirable?'

'Perhaps,' Cory said, trying to control the sudden flurry of her breathing, 'perhaps he should wait for her to make the first move.'

Rome's grin was mocking. 'That's not an option I find very appealing. Life's too short—and I'm an impatient man.'

'In that case,' Cory said, having yet another go at tugging her trolley free, 'I won't keep you from your shopping any longer.'

Rome propped himself against the end of the shelving, and watched her unavailing struggles with detached interest.

'Maybe they're trying to tell us something,' he remarked after a while.

'Oh, this is ridiculous.' Cory sent him a fulminating glance, then shook the entangled trolleys almost wildly. 'Why don't you *do* something?'

His brows lifted. 'What would you like me to do?' he asked lazily. 'Throw a bucket of cold water over the pair of them?'

Cory's lips were parting to make some freezing remark that would crush him for ever when she found, to her astonishment, an uncontrollable giggle welling up inside her instead.

As she fought for control, Rome stepped forward and lifted his own trolley slightly, pulling the pair of them apart.

'There,' he said softly. 'You're free.' And he walked away.

Cory stood, watching him go.

So, that was that, she thought. At last he'd got the message. She knew she should feel relieved, but in fact her reaction was ambivalent.

She moved to the display cabinet, took down a pack containing a single fillet steak, and stared at it for a long moment.

Then, on a sudden impulse, she followed him to the end of the aisle. 'Mr d'Angelo?'

He turned, his brows lifting in cool surprise. 'Miss Grant?' The faint mockery in his tone acknowledged her formality.

She drew a breath. 'How do you know my name?'

'Someone told me,' he said. 'Just as someone told you mine—didn't they?'

Cory bit her lip. 'Yes,' she admitted unwillingly.

'So, now we both know.' He paused. 'Was there something else?'

'You were very kind to me when I fell the other day,' she said, stiffly. 'And I realise that my response may have seemed—ungracious.'

She paused, studying his expressionless face.

'I hope you're not waiting for a polite denial,' Rome drawled at last.

'Would there be any point?' Cory returned with a faint snap.

'None.' He sounded amused. 'Is that it—or are you prepared to make amends?'

'What do you mean?' Cory asked suspiciously.

Rome took the pack of solitary fillet steak out of her hand, and replaced it on a shelf.

He said quietly, 'Have dinner with me tonight.'

'I—couldn't.' Her heart was thudding.

'Why not?'

'Because I don't know you.' There was something like panic in her voice.

He shrugged. 'Everyone starts out as strangers. I'm

Rome, you're Cory. And that's where it begins. But the choice is yours, of course.'

She thought, And the risk…

In a voice she hardly recognised as hers, she said, 'Where?'

'Do you like Italian food?' And, when she nodded, 'Then, Alessandro's in Willard Street, at eight.'

Cory saw the smile that warmed his mouth, and her own lips curved in shy response.

She said huskily, 'All right.'

'Good,' he said. 'I'll look forward to it.' He turned to go, then swung back. 'And you won't need this.'

His hand touched her hair, unfastening the silver clasp, releasing the silky strands so that they fell round her face.

He said softly, 'That's better,' and went, leaving her staring after him in stunned disbelief.

CHAPTER FOUR

'YOU don't have to do this,' Cory told her reflection. 'You don't have to go.'

It was seven-fifteen, and she was sitting in her robe at her dressing table, putting on her make-up. And starting to panic.

She couldn't believe that she'd capitulated so easily— that she'd actually agreed to meet him, against all her instincts—and counter to her own strict code, too. Rule One stated that she never went out with anyone whose background and family were unknown to her.

And Rome d'Angelo could be anyone.

Except that he was quite definitely someone. Every hard, arrogant line of his lean body proclaimed it.

He walked away, she thought. And I should have let him go. It should have ended right there. And it certainly need not go any further.

She put down her mascara wand, and thought.

Rome d'Angelo might know her name, but that was all, she told herself with a touch of desperation. Her telephone number was ex-directory, and he couldn't know where she lived—could he?

On the other hand, these were obstacles that could easily be overcome by someone with enough determination.

So—she needed a contingency plan, she thought, frowning, as she fixed her favourite gold and amber hoops in her ears.

Well, she could always sub-let the flat and find somewhere else to live in a totally different part of London.

Somewhere she could lie low and wait for Rome d'Angelo to go back to wherever he'd come from.

As she realised what she was thinking, Cory sat back, gasping. Was she quite mad? she asked herself incredulously. Was she seriously contemplating uprooting herself—going into hiding to avoid nothing more than a casual encounter?

Because Rome d'Angelo wasn't here to stay. He was just passing through. She knew that as well as she knew the pale, strained face staring back at her from the mirror.

And he was clearly looking for amusement along the way.

But, on the scale of things, she would never be the number one choice for a man in search of that kind of diversion, she acknowledged with stony realism. So, why had he asked her?

Of course he was new in town, and probably didn't know many people as yet, but that would only be a temporary thing. A single man of his age with such spectacular looks would soon be snowed under with invitations. He wouldn't have enough evenings—or nights—to accommodate the offers that would come his way. Maybe she was just a stopgap.

Cory grimaced as she fastened the pendant which matched the earrings round her throat.

For a moment she wished she was Shelley, who wouldn't hesitate to date Rome d'Angelo, whatever the terms, and who would frankly revel in the situation. And then wave him a blithe goodbye when it was over.

'You only live once,' Cory could hear her saying. 'So, go for it.'

And she wouldn't be able to credit the kind of heart-searching that Cory was putting herself through.

But then Shelley had never had someone like Rob in her

life, Cory reminded herself defensively. Had never known what it was like to suffer that level of betrayal. Never needed to armour herself against the chance of it happening again.

And yet, as Shelley had warned, Rob was in the past, and she couldn't use him as an excuse to shelter behind for ever.

She had her own private fantasy that some day in the future she'd meet someone kind, decent and reliable, who would love her with quiet devotion, and that she'd make a happy life with him. It was up there with the house in the country and the log fires, she thought with self-derision.

But, in the meantime, until that day arrived, maybe she needed to be more relaxed about men in general, so that she'd be ready for the man of her dreams when he showed up.

And Rome d'Angelo would be excellent material for her to practise on. To remind her, just for a short time, what it was like to talk, laugh and even flirt a little.

Because that was precisely as far as it was going. Flirting was fun—and it was relatively safe, too, because it was conducted at a distance.

She gave herself a long look in the mirror, noticing that there was a faint flush of colour in her cheeks now, and that her mouth glowed with the lustre she'd applied.

She'd brushed her hair until it shone, and it hung now in a soft cloud on her shoulders. As he'd stipulated, she thought, her mouth curling in self-mockery.

For a moment she recalled the swift brush of his hand as he removed the clip, and felt herself shiver with a kind of guilty pleasure.

As a gesture, it was pure cliché, of course, but still devastatingly effective. It had been several minutes before she'd been able to stop shaking, gather her scattered thoughts, and finish her shopping in something like normality.

So, that was something she definitely could not afford, she thought, biting her lip. To let him touch her again.

She got up and slipped off her robe. The simple flared woolen skirt she put on was the colour of ivory, and she topped it with a matching long-sleeved sweater in ribbed silk.

She checked the contents of her bag, flung a fringed chestnut-coloured wrap round her shoulders, and left.

It was only a five-minute walk to Alessandro's, and she found her steps slowing as she approached, taking time out to look in the windows of the boutiques and antiques shops which lined the quiet street.

The last thing she wanted was to get there first, and let him find her waiting. She might as well have 'needy' tattooed across her forehead.

Of course, he might not be there at all, she realised, halting a few yards from the restaurant's entrance. Perhaps he'd instantly regretted his impulsive proposition and decided to stand her up instead.

Which would be neither kind nor considerate, but would certainly solve a lot of problems.

She peered cautiously through the window, into the black glass and marble of the foyer bar. It was already crowded, yet she saw him at once.

He was leaning against the bar, and he wasn't alone. He was smiling down into the upraised face of a dynamically pretty redhead in a minimalistic black dress and the kind of giddy high heels that Cory had never contemplated wearing in her life.

She was standing about as close to him as it was possible to get without being welded there, and one predatory scarlet-tipped hand was resting on his arm.

As Cory watched, her whole body rigid, the other girl reached into her bag and produced a card which she tucked into the top pocket of Rome's shirt.

Cory felt as if she'd been punched in the stomach. She wasn't prepared for the pain that slashed at her. Pain that came from anger, and something less easy to define or understand.

Her lips parted in a soundless gasp, and for a moment she was tempted to slip away into the night. Then some new arrivals came up behind her, and one of the men was holding the door for her, and smiling, and she was being swept along with the crowd into the restaurant.

Rome was looking towards the door, scanning the new arrivals, and when he saw Cory he straightened and, with a swift word to his companion, began to make his way over to her.

He was wearing light grey trousers which moulded his lean hips and emphasised his long legs, a charcoal shirt, open at the throat with the sleeves turned back over tanned forearms, and an elegant tweed jacket slung over one shoulder.

He moved with a kind of controlled power, and as the crowd parted to allow him through, heads turned to look at him.

Cory stood helplessly, staring at him, as the force of his attraction tightened her throat.

He said, '*Mia cara*, I thought you would never come.'

And before Cory could move or speak, she found herself pulled into his arms, and his mouth was possessing hers in a long, hard kiss.

She was too stunned to struggle, or protest. And if she had it would have made little difference. The arms holding her were too strong. The lips on hers too insistent. All she could do was stand there—and endure…

When he let her go at last, there were two angry spots of colour burning in her face. She was aware of amused stares, and murmured remarks around them.

She said in a fierce strangled whisper, 'How dare you?'

He looked amused. 'It took great courage, I admit, but, as you saw, it was an emergency.'

She said coldly, 'I imagine you can take care of yourself. You didn't need to drag me into it.'

'Perhaps,' he said. 'But the temptation was irresistible.'

'Then I hope you find having dinner alone equally appealing.' Her voice bit, and she half turned.

'No,' he said. 'I should not.' He made a brief, imperative gesture with one hand, and Cory suddenly found herself surrounded. A hostess appeared beside her to take her wrap, a waiter was asking deferentially what the *signorina* would like to drink, and Alessandro himself, wreathed in smiles, was waiting to conduct them to their table.

Somehow, walking out had become impossible. Unless she made the kind of scene which made her blood run cold.

Tight-lipped, she took her seat, and accepted the menu she was handed.

He said, 'Thank you for staying.'

Her voice was taut. 'You speak as if I had some choice in the matter.'

'Is that going to rankle all evening?' His brows lifted, and he spoke seriously. 'I've made you very angry, and I'm sorry, but it was a situation calling for drastic action. The lady was becoming persistent.'

'And you couldn't cope?' Cory lifted her eyebrows in exaggerated scepticism. 'You amaze me. And most men would be flattered,' she added.

'I'm not most men.'

'I've noticed,' Cory said with faint asperity. 'Yet you took her card.'

She stopped dead, aghast at another piece of blatant self-betrayal.

I should have been cool, she berated herself. Shrugged the whole thing off, instead of letting him know I'd noticed every detail. My stupid, stupid tongue...

'I was brought up to be polite,' Rome returned across her stricken silence. He removed the little pasteboard oblong from his pocket and tore it into small pieces, depositing the fragments in a convenient ashtray. 'But I prefer to do my own hunting,' he added softly, the blue eyes seeking hers across the table.

'I've noticed that, too,' Cory said. 'And you're also very persistent.'

He sent her a questioning glance. 'You have a problem with that?'

She shrugged. 'How you conduct your private life is no business of mine. You're an available man. You can please yourself whom you see.'

'Not always,' he said. 'Not when the lady remains evasive. Or even hostile.'

He was silent for a moment, then he said evenly, 'We haven't got off to a very good start, Cory. So, if I've ruined everything, and you really want to go, I won't stop you.'

She believed him. But the waiter was bringing their drinks, and a dish of mixed olives, and suddenly it all seemed too complicated. Besides, the performance so far had attracted quite enough attention, she reminded herself wryly.

He added, 'But I hope you won't.'

'Why should it matter?'

'As I've already indicated, I hate eating alone.'

Her voice was flat. 'Oh.'

'Among other reasons,' he went on casually. He paused.

'But perhaps I should keep those to myself, in case I put you to flight after all.'

His gaze captured hers, mesmerising her, then moved with cool deliberation to her mouth. She felt her skin warm under his scrutiny—her pulses leap, swiftly, disturbingly.

She managed to keep her voice under control. 'I suspect I'm actually too hungry to leave.'

His mouth curved into a faint grin. 'So it's worth enduring a couple of hours of my company for the sake of Alessandro's food?'

'I don't know,' Cory said composedly. 'They might have changed the chef.' And she picked up the menu and began to read it.

A small victory, she thought, as his brows lifted in amused acknowledgment, proving that she might be reeling, but she wasn't out.

When they'd given their order, Rome said, 'So—what are the rules of engagement?'

She looked at him questioningly. 'What do you mean?'

'Kisses are clearly forbidden.' He gave a slight shrug. 'I was wondering whether there are any more taboos you're meaning to impose.'

'I already broke my major rule simply by turning up tonight,' she said. 'I think that's enough for one evening.'

'Ah,' he said softly. 'But this particular night is still very young.'

Cory took a sip of her Campari and soda. 'Perhaps we could dispense with comments like that.'

He shrugged a shoulder. 'Very well. Shall I say instead how mild it is for the time of year? Or calculate how many shopping days are left until Christmas?'

Cory bit her lip. 'Now you're being absurd.'

'And you, Miss Grant, are being altogether too serious.'

He studied her for a moment. 'Do you behave like this with all your dates?'

'I usually know them rather better than I know you.'

Remembering the squeaking Philip and other disasters, Cory surreptitiously crossed her fingers under cover of the tablecloth.

'Never a move without the safety net in place,' Rome mocked.

She lifted her chin. 'Perhaps. What's wrong with that?'

'Don't you ever get sick of security? Tired of measuring every step?' The blue eyes danced, challenging her. 'Aren't you ever tempted to live dangerously, Cory *mia*?'

She met his glance squarely. 'I thought that was what I was doing.' She leaned forward suddenly, clenched fists on the table. 'Why am I here tonight—having dinner with—a mysterious stranger?'

'Is that how you see me?' he was openly amused.

'Of course. You appear out of nowhere, and then you're suddenly all round me—in my face at every turn. I don't understand what's going on.'

'I saw you,' he said quietly. 'I wanted to know you better. Is that so surprising?'

Yes, she thought. *Yes.*

She lifted her chin. 'Why—because you felt sorry for me—leading contender in the Worst Dressed Woman contest?'

He said slowly, 'I promise you—pity never entered my mind.' There was an odd silence, then he went on, 'So—what can I do to become less of a mystery?'

'You could answer a few questions.'

He poured some mineral water for them both. 'Ask what you want.'

Cory hesitated, wondering where to begin. 'Why are you called Rome?'

'Because I was born there.' He shrugged. 'I guess my mother was short on inspiration at the time.'

'What about your father?'

Rome's mouth twisted. 'He wasn't around to ask. I never even knew his name.'

'Oh.' Cory digested that. 'I'm sorry.'

'There's no need,' he told her levelly. 'My mother made a mistake, but she had enough wisdom to know that it didn't have to become a life sentence. That she could survive on her own.'

'But it can't have been easy for her.'

'Life,' he said, 'is not a cushion.' He paused. 'Or not for most of us, anyway.'

Sudden indignation stiffened her. 'Is that aimed at me?'

'Are you saying you've grown up in hardship?' There was a strange harshness in his tone.

'Materially, no,' Cory said curtly. 'But that's not everything. And you're not exactly on the breadline yourself if you can afford a place in Farrar Street, over-priced tickets to charity bashes, and the joining fee at the health club.'

He shrugged. 'I make a living.'

'And how do you do that?' she said. 'Or is that part of your mystery?'

'Not at all.' Rome smiled at her, unfazed by the snip in her voice. 'I sell wine.'

'You're a wine merchant?' Cory was disconcerted. There was something about him, she thought, something rough-edged and vigorous that spoke of the open air, not vaults full of dusty bottles.

'Not exactly,' he said. 'Because the only wine on offer is my own.'

She stared at him. 'You own a vineyard?'

'Own it, work in it—and love it.'

His voice was soft, suddenly, almost caressing. This was

a man with a passion, Cory realised. And the first chink he'd shown in his armour.

Would his voice gentle in the same way when he told a woman he loved her? she wondered. And had he ever said those words and meant them?

Instantly she stamped the questions back into her subconscious. These were not avenues she should be exploring.

She hurried back into speech. 'And is that why you're in London? To sell your wine?'

A selling trip was unlikely to last long, she thought, and soon he would be gone and her life could return to its cherished quiet again, without troubling thoughts or wild dreams.

'Partly,' he said. 'I'm always looking for new markets for my wine, of course, but this time I have other business to transact as well. So my stay will be indefinite,' he added silkily. 'If that's what you were wondering.'

Wine-grower and part-time mind-reader, Cory thought, biting her lip.

It was a relief when the waiter arrived to take their order, and there were decisions to be made about starting with pasta or a risotto, and whether she should have calves liver or chicken in wine to follow.

When everything, including the choice of wine, had been settled, and they were alone again, he said, 'Now may I ask you some personal questions?'

'I don't know.' She could feel herself blushing faintly as she avoided his gaze. 'Maybe we should keep the conversation general.'

'Difficult,' he said. 'Unless we sit at separate tables with our backs to each other. You see, *mia bella*, you're something of a mystery yourself.'

She shook her head, attempting a casual laugh. 'My life's an open book.'

'If so, I find the opening chapters immensely intriguing,' Rome drawled. 'I keep asking myself who is the real Cory Grant?'

Her flush deepened. 'I—I don't understand.'

'Each time we meet I see a different woman,' he said softly. 'A new and contrasting image. The silver dress was too harsh for you, but tonight you're like some slender ivory flower brushed with rose. The effect is—breathtaking.'

Cory discovered she was suddenly breathless herself. She tried to laugh again. To sound insouciant. Not easy when she was shaking inside.

'Very flattering—but a total exaggeration, I'm afraid.'

'But then, you don't see with my eyes, *mia cara*.' He paused, allowing her to assimilate his words. 'So, I ask again, which is the real woman?'

Cory looked down at her glass. She said huskily, 'I can't answer that. Maybe you should just choose the image you like best.'

'Ah.' Rome's voice sank to a whisper. 'But so far that image is just my own private fantasy. Although I hope that one night it will become reality.'

His eyes met hers in a direct erotic challenge, leaving her in no doubt over his meaning. He wanted to see her naked.

She felt her pulses thud as she remembered her certainty that he'd been mentally undressing her at the ball, and her colour deepened hectically.

She said unsteadily, 'Please—don't say things like that.' And don't look at me like that, she added silently, as if you were already sliding my clothes off.

His brows lifted. 'You don't wish to be thought attractive—desirable?'

'Yes, one day—by the man I love.'

Oh, God, she thought. How smug that sounded. How insufferably prim. As if she'd turned into the heroine of some Victorian novel. And waited for him to laugh.

Instead he sat quietly, watching her, his expression unreadable.

At last, he spoke. 'Tell me, *cara*, why are you so afraid to be a woman?'

'I'm not,' she denied. 'That's—nonsense. And I really don't like this conversation.'

Rome's brows lifted sardonically. 'Have I broken another rule?'

'I'd say a whole book of them.' She wanted to drink from her glass, but knew that he'd see her hand trembling as she picked it up and draw the kind of conclusions that she could not risk.

'No kisses and no questions either.' Rome shook his head. 'You don't make it easy.'

She forced a taut smile. 'But life isn't a cushion. I'm sure someone said that once. And here comes our first course,' she added brightly.

She hadn't expected to be able to swallow a mouthful, but the creamy risotto flavoured with fresh herbs proved irresistible, and the crisp white wine that Rome had ordered complemented it perfectly.

She said, striving for normality, 'We should be drinking your own wine.'

'Perhaps next time. Alessandro and I are about to strike a deal. I came here early so I could talk to him.'

'Until you got sidetracked, of course.'

'Ah, yes,' Rome said meditatively. 'I wonder if she has a rule book.'

'If so, it'll be the slimmest volume in the western hemisphere,' Cory said acidly, and stopped, appalled. 'Oh, God, I sound like a complete bitch.'

'No.' Rome was grinning. 'Merely human at last, *mia cara.*' And he raised his glass in a teasing toast.

As the meal proceeded, Cory found to her surprise that she was beginning to relax, and even enjoy herself.

The conversation was mainly about food. It was a nice, safe topic, but even so Cory found herself silently speculating about the man opposite her, talking so entertainingly about Cajun cooking.

Rome's life might now be centred on an Italian vineyard, but it was obvious that he was a cosmopolitan who'd travelled extensively. There was still so much she couldn't fathom about him, she thought restlessly.

She wondered about his parentage, too. His mother presumably had been Italian, so he must have derived those astonishing blue eyes from his unknown father. An English tourist, she thought, with an inner grimace, enjoying a holiday fling with a local girl, then going on his way without knowing a child would result. However strong Rome's mother had been, she would have had to struggle in those early years.

And how had an illegitimate city boy ended up growing wine in the Tuscan countryside?

No, she thought. There were still too many unanswered questions for her to feel comfortable in his company. So it was as well she had no intention of seeing him again—wasn't it?

The tiny chicken simmered in wine and surrounded by baby vegetables was so tender it was almost falling off the bone, and Cory sighed with appreciation as she savoured the first bite.

'You are a pleasure to feed.' Rome passed her a sliver of calves liver to taste. 'You enjoy eating.'

'You sound surprised.'

'You're so slim, I'd half expected you to be on a permanent diet like so many women,' he acknowledged drily.

Cory shook her head. 'I'm not slim, I'm thin,' she said. 'But no matter how much I eat, I never seem to put on weight.'

He said softly, 'Perhaps, *mia cara*, all you need is to be happy.'

The words seemed to hang in the air between them.

She wanted to protest—to bang the table with her hand and tell him that she was happy already. That her life was full and complete.

But the words wouldn't come. Instead, she found herself remembering the scent of his skin, the hard muscularity of his chest as he'd held her. The warm seductive pressure of his mouth in that endless kiss…

And she felt the loneliness and fear that sometimes woke her in the night charge at her like an enemy, tightening her throat, filling her mouth with the taste of tears.

She bent her head, afraid that he would look into her eyes and see too much.

She said in a small, composed voice, 'Please save your concern. I'm fine. And this is the best chicken I've ever had.'

She resisted a temptation to refuse dessert and coffee and plead a migraine as an excuse to cut the evening short. Because something told her that Rome would recognise the lie, and realise he'd struck a nerve. And she didn't want that. Because already he saw too much.

Instead she embarked on a lively account of her one and only visit to Italy on a school cultural exchange visit.

'The school we stayed at in Florence was run by nuns,' she recalled. 'And every night we could hear them turning these massive keys in these huge locks, making sure we couldn't escape.' She lowered her voice sepulchrally, and Rome laughed.

'Would you have done so?' He poured some more wine into her glass.

'I got to a point where I felt if I saw one more statue or painting I'd burst,' Cory confessed. 'I never knew there could be so many churches, or museums and galleries. We never seemed to have a breathing space. And, really, I'd rather have spent every day at the Uffizi alone.'

'But you weren't allowed to?'

She shook her head. 'The teachers hustled us round the city at light speed. They seemed to think that if we stood still for a moment we might be abducted—or worse.'

'Perhaps they were right,' Rome murmured. He paused. 'Will you ever go back there?'

'Perhaps one day. To wander round the Uffizi at my own pace.'

He was silent for a moment. Then, 'Florence is a great city, but it isn't the whole of Tuscany,' he said quietly. 'There is so much else to see—to take to your heart.' He drank some wine. 'It would make a wonderful place for a honeymoon.'

Cory took a deep breath. 'I'm sure it would,' she said coolly. 'And if I should happen to marry, I'll keep it in mind.'

'You have no immediate wedding plans?' He was playing almost absently with the stem of his glass.

She said crisply, 'None—and no wish for any.'

'How sure you sound.' He was amused. 'Yet tomorrow you might meet the man of your dreams, and all your certainties could change.'

The last time I dreamed of a man, Cory thought with a pang, it was you...

Aloud, she said, 'I really don't think so.' She picked up

the dessert menu and gave it intense attention. 'I'll have the peach ice cream, please—and an espresso.'

'Would you like some *strega* with your coffee, or a *grappa*, perhaps?'

'Thank you,' she said. 'But no.' Because it's nearly the end of the evening, and I need to keep my wits about me, she added silently.

She ate her ice cream when it came, and sampled some of Rome's amaretto soufflé, too.

Alessandro himself brought the small cups of black coffee. He said something in Italian to Rome, who responded laughingly.

Cory was convinced they were talking about her. She was already planning in her mind how to couch her refusal when Rome asked to see her again, which she was sure he would.

Alessandro turned to her. 'You enjoyed your dinner, *signorina*?'

'It was wonderful,' she said. 'Absolutely delicious. Far better than the steak and salad I was planning.'

'So lovely a lady should never eat alone,' Alessandro told her with mock severity, and went off smiling.

To Rome, she said politely. 'Thank you. It was a very pleasant evening.'

'Pleasant?' His mouth was serious, but his eyes were dancing. 'Now, I'd have said—interesting.'

'Whatever.' Slightly disconcerted, Cory reached for her bag. 'And now I must be going. It's getting late.'

Rome glanced at his watch. 'Some people would say the evening was just beginning.'

'Well, I'm not one of them,' Cory said shortly. 'I have work tomorrow.'

He grinned at her. 'And anyway, you cannot wait to run away, can you, *mia cara*?'

He came round the table and picked up her wrap before she could reach it herself. As he put it round her, she felt his hands linger on her shoulders, and the faint pressure sent a shiver ghosting down her spine, which she told herself firmly was nerves, not pleasure.

She took a step away from him. Her voice sounded over-bright, and her smile rather too determined as she turned to face him. 'Well—goodnight—and thanks again.'

His brows lifted mockingly. 'Isn't that a little premature?' he drawled. 'After all, I have still to see you home.'

'Oh, but there's no need for that,' she said quickly. 'It's only a short distance—'

'I know exactly where it is,' Rome interrupted. 'And I still have no intention of allowing you to return there unescorted, so let us have no more tiresome argument.'

She stared at him. Her voice shook a little. 'Is there anything—anything you don't know about me?'

He laughed softly, '*Mia bella*—I have only just begun, believe me. Now—shall we go?'

And she found herself walking beside him, out into the damp chill—and the total uncertainty—of the night.

CHAPTER FIVE

THEY walked in silence, not touching, but Cory was heart-stoppingly aware of the tall figure moving with lithe grace at her side. She had half expected him to take her arm or her hand, and was grateful for the respite. Which was all it was.

Because she had no idea what would happen when they reached their destination.

She couldn't feel shock or even mild surprise that, as she'd feared, he'd discovered where she lived. Not any more. Every defence she had seemed to be crumbling in turn.

Which one would be next? she wondered, with a slight shiver.

Rome noticed instantly, but misinterpreted her reaction.

'You're cold.' He slipped off his jacket and draped it over her shoulders.

'Thank you.' Her fingers curled into the warm, soft cloth, gathering it round her like a barricade. Which was a mistake, because inextricably mingled with the smell of expensive wool was the now familiar scent of Rome himself, clean, totally male and almost unbearably potent. Reminding her of those few pulsating moments in his arms when her shocked senses had not just breathed him—but tasted him...

She hurried into speech. 'But you'll be frozen.'

'I don't think so.' There was a smile in his voice. 'I spend too much out of doors in all kinds of weather.'

'Oh,' she said. 'Yes—of course.'

She could hear the click of her heels on the pavement, hurrying slightly to keep up with his long stride. The air was cool, and there was a sharp dankness in the air which made her nose tingle.

She told herself, with an inward sigh, 'It's going to rain.'

'Is that a problem for you?' His answer, laced with faint amusement, alerted her to the fact she'd spoken aloud.

'Not really.' A faint flush warmed her face. She didn't want him to think she was making conversation for the sake of it. 'If you live in England, you can't let rain bother you too much. And when we lived in the country everything—the grass, the leaves—was so washed and—fragrant afterwards, I even began to like it. But here in the city the rain just smells dirty.'

'You liked the country best?' His tone was reflective. 'Then what made you leave?'

'The house wasn't the same after my grandmother died,' Cory said, after a pause. 'Too many memories. So my grandfather decided to sell it and base himself entirely in London. I don't blame him at all for that, but I miss the old place just the same.'

'Where was the house?'

'In Suffolk.' Her voice was soft with sudden longing. 'There was an orchard, and a stream running through the garden, and when I was a child I thought it was Eden.'

'It was the other way round for me,' Rome said, after a pause. 'I was brought up in cities, and I have had to wait a long time to find my own particular paradise.'

'But you have it now?'

'Yes,' he said, with an odd harshness. 'I have it, and I mean to keep it.'

Cory turned her head to look at him in faint bewilderment, and stumbled on an uneven paving flag.

Instantly Rome's hand shot out and grasped her arm, steadying her.

She felt the clasp of his fingers echo through every bone, sinew and nerve-ending. Was aware of her body clenching involuntarily in the swift, painful excitement of response. Bit back the small gasp that tightened her throat.

Turned it into a breathless laugh instead. 'Oh, God—I'm so clumsy. I'm sorry. Perhaps it was the wine. I'm not accustomed to it…'

'You don't usually drink wine?' He looked down at her, brows lifting.

'Rarely more than one glass.' Her smile was rueful. 'So I'll never make your fortune for you. Isn't that a shocking admission?'

'It confirms what I suspected,' Rome said, after a pause. 'That you work hard, and take your pleasures in strict moderation.'

She wrinkled her nose. 'That makes me sound very dull.'

He smiled back at her. 'Not dull, *mia cara*.' His voice was suddenly gentle. 'Merely—unawakened.'

She stared at him, her lips parting in surprise and uncertainty. When he halted, it took her a moment to realise that they'd actually reached the front door of her flat.

And some kind of moment of truth, she thought, her heart lurching half in panic, half in unwilling excitement.

As she fumbled in her bag for her key, she heard herself say in a voice she barely recognised, 'Would you like to come in—for some more coffee?'

His hesitation was infinitesimal but fatal, cutting her to the core.

'I cannot *mia bella*.' He sounded genuinely regretful, but it was rejection just the same. 'I have to go back to the restaurant and close the deal with Alessandro.'

She said, 'Oh.' Then, 'Yes—I see.'

She rallied, fighting down the disappointment that was threatening to choke her. Fighting to conceal from him that he had the power to hurt her.

She said brightly, 'Well—thank you for a lovely meal.'

'The gratitude is all mine, Cory *mia*.' He took the hand she did not offer and raised it to his lips, turning it at the last moment so that his mouth brushed her inner wrist, where the telltale pulse leapt and fluttered uncontrollably at the brief contact.

'And perhaps I had better have my jacket,' he went on conversationally as he released her. 'Unless, of course, you wish to keep it.'

'No—no—here.' Almost frantically she rid herself of its sheltering folds and pushed it at him. 'Goodbye.' She turned away, stabbing her key into the lock.

He said softly, 'I prefer—goodnight.'

As the door opened at last, she allowed herself a quick glance over her shoulder, but he was already yards away, his long stride carrying him back to his own life—his own preoccupations.

Cory thought, So that's that, and went in, closing the door behind her.

Rome cursed savagely under his breath as he walked away. What in hell was the matter with him? he demanded silently. His grandfather had been right. She was ready to fall into his outstretched hands.

All he'd had to do was walk through that door with her and she'd have been his. Total victory with minimum difficulty, he thought cynically.

A victory that he'd wanted, starkly and unequivocally, as the unquenched heat in his body was reminding him. The whole evening had been building to that moment.

And yet—unbelievably—inconceivably—he'd held

back. Made a paltry excuse about an appointment that was actually scheduled for the next day.

And she'd known. The street lighting had taken all the colour from her face and turned her eyes into stricken pools.

And suddenly he'd found himself wanting to pick her up in his arms. To hold her close and bury his face in the fragrance of her hair, and keep her safe for ever.

Perhaps the wine had affected him, too, he derided himself.

Because he'd planned a verbal seduction only, he reminded himself tautly. He'd intended to entice her with spoken caresses and half-promises, and a hint of passion rigorously dammed back. Yet scrupulously ruling full physical possession out of the equation.

Probably because he'd never visualised it as a genuine temptation, he acknowledged ruefully.

So what had changed—and when?

At what moment had she ceased to be a target—and become a woman?

It was when I called her 'unawakened'—and realised it was true, he thought.

She'd been engaged to be married. It was unrealistic to suppose she hadn't been involved in a sexual relationship with her fiancé. Yet his experience told him that, sensually and emotionally, she was still a virgin.

That maybe the Ice Maiden image was born from disappointment rather than indifference. That all the potential for response was there, waiting, just below the surface.

He'd felt it all evening in the swift judder of her pulses when he'd touched her, in the tiny indrawn breaths she hadn't been able to conceal. And in the sudden trembling capitulation of her mouth as he'd kissed her.

Shock tactics, he'd told himself at the time, when he'd

seen her standing there, the wide eyes filling with accusation. An expedient designed merely to prevent her from sweeping out and reducing his chances of saving Montedoro to nil.

He hadn't expected to enjoy it so much. Or to want so much more so soon either. That was an added complication he could well do without.

That, indeed, he *would* do without. Because he wasn't some adolescent at the mercy of his hormones, he reminded himself bluntly. He had control, and he would use it from now on.

But he hadn't anticipated Cory Grant's own hunger, he thought, his mouth tightening.

He realised now what it must have cost her to issue that faltering invitation. Had seen the shock in her eyes when he'd stepped back.

But perhaps in the greater scheme of things that was no bad thing, he told himself tersely. He would stay away for a few days, he decided. Keep her guessing. Allow her to miss him a little, or even a lot, before he made another approach. And then, just when she thought it was safe to go back in the water...

Because he couldn't afford any softening, whatever the inducement. He had to stay focused—cold-blooded in his approach. He had too much at stake to allow any ill-advised chivalrous impulses to intervene.

And if he'd created an appetite in Cory Grant, he could use it. Feed it tiny morsels rather than a full banquet. Until she could think—could dream—nothing but him, and the denial he was inflicting on her senses.

And that voluptuous ache in his own groin would simply have to be endured for now, he thought grimly.

When all this business was behind him, and Montedoro was safe, he would indulge himself. Take a break in Bali or the Caribbean. Find some warm and willing girl looking for holiday pleasure, and tip them both over the edge during long hot moonlit nights.

Someone who did not have bones like a bird and skin like cool, clean silk. Or a wistful huskiness in her voice when she spoke of her childhood.

He sighed restlessly and angrily, and lengthened his stride.

The Ice Maiden, he decided broodingly, would have been altogether easier to cheat.

Cory leaned back against the door of her flat, staring sightlessly in front of her, trying to steady the jagged breathing tearing at her chest.

'I don't believe I did that.' Her voice was a hoarse, angry whisper. 'I can't believe I said that.'

I'm not drunk, she thought. Therefore I must be mad. Totally out of my tree.

And now, somehow, I have to become sane again. Before I end up in real trouble.

She shuddered, crossing her arms defensively across her breasts.

She'd just issued the most dangerous invitation in her life—and somehow she'd been let off the hook. Rome had turned her down, for reasons she couldn't even begin to fathom but for which she had to be grateful, she told herself resolutely.

Only, she didn't feel grateful. She felt bewildered, bruised and reeling. Lost, even. And humiliated in a way she'd sworn would never happen again.

She eased herself slowly away from the door and fastened the bolt and the security chain before heading for her bedroom. She didn't put on any of the lights. She just went in and fell across the bed, without removing her clothes or her make-up. Curling up in the dark like a small animal going to earth to escape a predator.

And a lucky escape it had been. For all the anguish of emotion assailing her, she could not deny that.

Because Rome and she inhabited two different worlds. And the fact that those worlds had briefly collided meant nothing. Because soon he would be gone. Back to his vineyard and his real life. A life that did not include her but which would encompass other women.

And she would remain here, and go on working for her grandfather, as if nothing had happened. So it was important—essential—that nothing did happen. Or nothing serious, anyway.

She couldn't afford any regrets when Rome had gone.

Although it might already be too late for that, she thought, turning on to her stomach and pressing her heated face into the pillow.

Since that night at the ball, she'd scarcely had a quiet moment. He'd invaded her space, filled her thoughts, and ruined her dreams.

In the aftermath of Rob, she hadn't allowed herself to think about men at all. It had been safer that way. But just lately she'd had a few enjoyable fantasies about meeting someone whom she could love, and make a life with, and who would love her in return.

But even this cosy daydream had been snatched away. And in its place was a much darker image. One that churned her stomach in scared excitement, and made her body tremble.

It wasn't love, she told herself. It was lust, and she was ashamed of it. She'd believed she wanted Rob, but that had been a pallid emotion compared with this raw, arching need that Rome had inspired.

He seemed etched on her mind—on her senses. He was

in this room with her now. In this darkness. On this bed. His hands and mouth were exploring her with hot, sensuous delight, and she stifled the tiny, avid moan that rose in her throat.

I don't want this, Cory thought desperately. I want to be the girl I was before. I might not have been very happy, but at least my mind and body belonged to myself alone.

She also had to live with the shame of knowing that this need was purely one-sided. Because Rome had been able to walk away without a backward glance.

Yet her main concern was her own behaviour.

She'd never made the running with men—not even with Rob. She'd allowed him to set the pace throughout their relationship.

She was too shy—too inhibited—to set up an agenda that included sex on demand, even with the man she planned to marry.

Until now, tonight, when she had suddenly stepped out of character.

And much good it did me, she thought bitterly.

Although going to bed with Rome would have been an even greater disaster, for all kinds of reasons.

When she saw him again—if she saw him again—she would be safely back in her own skin, she told herself, and playing by her own rules. She would take no more risks. Especially with someone like Rome d'Angelo.

She would be back in control.

And the loneliness of the thought brought tears, sharp and acrid, crowding into her throat.

'Old Sansom's playing a cool game over this land deal,' Arnold Grant remarked. 'I was sure there'd be an approach from some go-between by now. So what's the old devil up to? What's he got up his sleeve now?'

He waited for some response from his granddaughter, and when none was forthcoming swung his chair round to look at her, only to find her sitting staring out of the window, not for the first time that day.

'What's the matter with you, girl?' he demanded. 'Are you in a trance, or what?'

Cory started guiltily. 'I'm sorry, darling. I guess I'm a bit tired.' She forced a smile. 'I was out on the town last night.'

'Quite right, too.' Arnold surveyed her, narrow-eyed. 'Although one night shouldn't put those shadows under your eyes. You look as if you haven't slept for a week. No stamina, you young ones.' He paused. 'So—who were you out with? Do I know him?'

Cory sighed. 'Yes, Gramps, you do indeed know *her*.' She stressed the pronoun. 'Shelley and I went to the cinema, then had a meal in a Chinese restaurant. I really enjoyed it.'

Which was pitching it a bit high, she silently admitted. The film had been good, the food delicious and Shelley great company, but Cory had been on tenterhooks in case her friend brought Rome d'Angelo into the conversation again, which had rather taken the edge off the evening.

I'm being thoroughly paranoid, she thought.

Arnold snorted. 'Well, you don't look or sound as if you had a wonderful time. You've been quiet all week, girl. Not your usual self at all.'

'In other words, I'm boring, and you're going to replace me with a glamorous blonde,' Cory teased.

'God forbid,' Arnold said devoutly. 'And you're not boring, child. Just—different.' He gave her a sharp look. 'Is it man trouble?'

'No,' Cory said, her throat tightening. 'No, of course not.'

It wasn't really a lie, she defended silently. Because there was no man to cause trouble—not any more.

She hadn't heard from Rome, or set eyes on him, all through this endless week.

She'd filled her days with activity—work, food-shopping, cooking, cleaning the flat to a pristine shine.

But the nights had been a different matter. Sleep had proved elusive, and she'd spent hours staring into an all-pervading blackness, longing for oblivion.

She'd used her answering machine to screen her calls, but she could have saved herself the effort because none of them had been from him.

On the street, her senses felt stretched to snapping point as she scanned the passers-by, looking for him. As she glanced over her shoulder, expecting to find him there.

Only, he never had been.

So that particular episode was clearly over and done with almost before it had begun, she told herself determinedly. Rome had found someone else to pursue—metal more attractive. And, in the long term, that was the best—the safest thing.

It was the short term she was having trouble handling.

'Money, then?' Arnold persisted. 'Are those sharks of landlords giving you trouble? Do you want my lawyers to deal with them?'

'Absolutely not,' Cory protested. 'They're a very reputable property company.'

'Hmm.' Arnold was silent for a moment. Then, 'If you've got yourself into debt, child, you can tell me. I could always raise your salary.'

'Heavens, no.' Cory was aghast. 'I don't earn half what you pay me as it is.'

'I'll be the judge of that,' her grandfather said gruffly. 'So what's the problem?'

Cory shrugged. 'It's nothing serious,' she prevaricated. 'It's probably all the wet weather we've had. I may be one of these people who needs the sun. I'm just feeling in a bit of a rut—not too sure where my life is going. That's all.'

It was his turn to sigh, his face set in serious lines. 'Ah, child. You need to go to parties. Meet more people. If my Beth hadn't been taken, she'd have seen to it. Arranged a social life for you. Made sure you enjoyed yourself.' He shook his head. 'But I'm no good at that sort of thing. I've let you down.'

'Oh, Gramps.' Cory's tone was remorseful. 'That's not true. And I hate parties.'

'Nevertheless, you need a change of air—a change of scenery,' Arnold said with decision. 'I'm going down to Dorset this evening, to spend the weekend with the Harwoods. Why don't you come with me? They're always asking about you. And that nephew of theirs will be there, too, on leave from the Army,' he added blandly. 'You remember him, don't you?'

Yes, Cory remembered Peter Harwood. Good-looking in a florid way, and very knowledgeable about tank manoeuvres. Keen to share his expertise, too, for hours on end. Not an experience she was anxious to repeat.

She said gently, 'It's a kind thought, Gramps, but I don't think so. I—I have plans of my own.'

And now he would ask what they were, and she would be floundering, she thought, bracing herself mentally.

But, blessedly, the phone rang, diverting his attention, and the awkward moment passed.

As she was preparing to leave that evening, Arnold halted her with a hand on her arm. 'Sure you won't come to Dorset?'

'Absolutely,' she said firmly.

He nodded glumly. 'Any message for young Peter?'

Her swift smile was impish. 'Give my regards to his tank.'

But she would do something positive this weekend, she determined. She wasn't going to waste any more time phone-watching.

Rome had appeared in her life, and now he had gone again, and she should be feeling thankful, instead of this odd hollowness, as if the core of her being had been scooped out with a blunt knife.

But I'll get over it, she told herself resolutely. I did before. I can again.

And as a first step, she didn't go to the health club in the morning. Just in case Rome had decided to use it after all and she ran into him there—literally as well as figuratively, she thought, remembering their previous encounter with a grimace.

Instead she'd go to Knightsbridge and indulge in some serious window shopping. Maybe have lunch at Harvey Nicks, and spend the afternoon at the cinema, or a theatre matinée.

Or she might go to a travel agency and book herself some winter sunshine.

Except that she already knew what she was going to do. What she always did when she was at a loose end, or troubled. Although she had no real reason to feel like that, she reminded herself. Not any more. Because, with luck, that particular trouble was past and gone.

Nevertheless, she would go to the National Gallery and look at the Renaissance paintings. It might be a very public place, but it was her private sanctuary, too. Her comfort zone.

And that was what her life needed at this particular moment, she thought. Not shopping, or long-haul holidays, but tranquillity and beauty.

She would let those exquisite forms and colours work their magic on her, and then, when she was calm and in control, with her life drawn securely round her once more, she would plan the rest of her day.

She dressed swiftly in a simple grey skirt with a matching round-necked sweater in thin wool, tied a scarf patterned in grey, ivory and coral at her throat, and thrust her feet into loafers. Then she grabbed her raincoat and an umbrella and set off for Trafalgar Square.

The Gallery was having a busy morning. Cory threaded her way between the school parties and guided groups of tourists until she reached the section she wanted. Thankfully, it was quieter here, as most of the crowds seemed to have been siphoned off to some special exhibition, and she wandered slowly from room to room until she found the *Mystic Nativity* by Botticelli and a seat on a bench facing it.

It had always been her favourite, she thought, as she drank in the clear vibrant colours. She loved the contrast between the earthiness of the kings and shepherds, come to do honour to the kneeling Virgin and her Child, and the ethereal, almost terrifying beauty of the watching angels.

Usually just a few minutes in front of it melted away any stress she might be experiencing. But today it wasn't having the desired effect, and after a while she got up restlessly and walked on.

She paused to look at another Botticelli—the great canvas of *Venus and Mars*—staring for a long disturbing moment at the languid beauty in her white and gold dress, with a world of secret knowledge in her face, and the conquered, sated man next to her.

What would it be like, she wondered, to have that kind

of sexual power? To bewitch a man, and leave him drained, and at your mercy?

Love winning the ultimate victory over war, she thought as she turned away.

She would go and get some coffee, she decided, and then probably revert to Plan A and the shopping expedition to Knightsbridge.

She was on her way out when she saw the portrait. She'd noticed it before on previous visits—a young man in his shirtsleeves, his curling hair covered by a cap, turning his head to bestow a cool and level glance on his observers.

But this time she went over to take a much closer look. She stood motionless, her hands clenched in her pockets, staring at the tough, dynamic face, with the strong nose, the firm, deeply cleft chin and the high cheekbones, as if she was seeing it for the first time.

Aware of the slow, shocked beat of her heart. Because, she realised, if Rome d'Angelo had been alive in the sixteenth century, he could have modelled for this portrait by Andrea del Sarto.

Since their first meeting she'd had the nagging feeling that she'd seen him somewhere before, and had been trying to trace the elusive resemblance. And now, at last, she'd succeeded. He'd been here all the time. In her sanctuary. Waiting for her.

She shook her head, her lips twisting in a little smile.

She said softly, 'Your eyes are the wrong colour, that's all. They should be blue. Otherwise you could be him— five hundred years ago.'

And heard, from behind her, as she stood, rooted to the spot in horrified disbelief, Rome's voice saying with cool dryness, 'You really think so? You flatter me, *cara*.'

CHAPTER SIX

CORY looked down at the polished floorboards at her feet, praying they would open and swallow her.

The last time she'd felt such a complete idiot had been standing on her own doorstep as Rome walked away, she thought detachedly, feeling the first scalding wave of embarrassment wash over her. And, before that, when she'd taken that spectacular dive at his feet.

Now she'd let him catch her standing there talking to herself, for God's sake. Speaking her thoughts aloud, as she often did. And this was once too often.

She turned slowly, her face still flushed.

He was standing about a yard away, unsmiling, the brilliant eyes slightly narrowed, his damp hair curling on to his forehead. He was wearing narrow black trousers, with a matching rollneck sweater, and carrying a russet waterproof jacket over one arm.

Cory lifted her chin in challenge. 'There's a saying about eavesdroppers.'

Rome nodded. 'I know it. But your comments were hardly derogatory. And you would never have made them to my face.'

'What are you doing here?'

'Just like you—looking at Renaissance paintings.'

'So, you just happened to—turn up?' Her tone was incredulous.

Rome shrugged a shoulder. 'I can hardly visit the Uffizi,' he returned coolly. 'But it's true that I hoped I'd find you here,' he added.

She wished she could stop shaking inside. She said haughtily, 'I can't imagine why.'

Rome's brows lifted. 'No, *mia bella*? I think you do your imagination less than justice. Except where this portrait is concerned.' He looked past her, studying it reflectively. 'Is this really how you see me?'

Cory's flush deepened. 'You can't deny there is a resemblance,' she said defensively. 'And he's not named in the portrait. He could be one of your ancestors.'

Rome's mouth twisted. 'I doubt it, but it's a romantic thought.'

'From now on I'll try and keep them under control,' Cory told him with bite. 'Do enjoy your art appreciation.'

As she made to walk past him, he detained her with a hand on her arm.

'You're not leaving?'

It was her turn to shrug. 'I've seen what I came to see.'

'And so have I,' he said softly. 'Another intriguing co-incidence. So—now we have the rest of the day ahead of us.'

She said thickly, 'You take a hell of a lot for granted, Mr d'Angelo. And I have other plans.'

'Do they involve anyone else?'

'That's none of your business.'

'A simple no would be enough.' The blue eyes were dancing suddenly, and her mouth felt dry. His voice was suddenly coaxing. 'Take pity on me, Cory *mia*. Cancel your arrangements and spend the day with me instead.' His smile coaxed, too. Disturbingly. 'Help me play tourist.'

She bit her lip. 'I don't think that's a very good idea.'

'You haven't given it a chance,' he said. 'It might improve on acquaintance and—who knows?—so might I.'

In response, her own mouth curved reluctantly. 'Don't you ever take no for an answer?'

'That, *mia bella*, would depend on the question.' His voice was silky. 'But I promise you one thing, Cory Grant. When you say no to me and mean it, I'll listen.'

There was a brief heart-stopping pause, then he said abruptly, 'Now, will you come with me? Share today?'

He held out his hand steadily, imperatively, and almost before she knew what she was doing she allowed him to take her fingers—clasp them.

He nodded, acknowledging the silent bargain, then moved off, making for the main exit, sweeping her along with him so fast that Cory practically had to jog to keep up.

She said breathlessly, 'Just a minute—you haven't told me yet where we're going.'

'First—to the car park.'

'You've—bought a car?'

'No, I've leased one.'

'And then?'

He gave her a swift sideways glance. He was smiling, but there was an unmistakable challenge in the blue eyes.

He said softly, 'Why, to Suffolk, of course, *mia cara. Avanti.*'

She said, 'It is a joke, isn't it? You're not really serious?'

They were out of London now, and travelling towards Chelmsford, as Cory registered tautly.

'Am I going in the wrong direction?' Rome asked. 'I was aiming for Sudbury.'

'No,' she said. 'No—that's fine. But I still don't know why you're doing this.'

The car was dark, streamlined and expensive, and he handled it well on the unfamiliar roads—as she was grudgingly forced to admit.

'I'm tired of concrete,' he said. 'I thought you would be, too.'

'Yes—but you don't just—take off for Suffolk on the spur of the moment,' Cory said warmly. 'It's a long way.'

'And we have the rest of the day.' He flicked a glance at her, a half-smile playing round his mouth. 'Would you prefer to turn back? Visit another art gallery—or perhaps a museum?'

'No,' she said slowly. 'No—I don't want to do that.'

She wasn't sure it was possible to turn back either. Not now. Not ever. She felt as if she'd taken some wild, momentous leap in the dark.

She said, almost beseechingly, 'But it's all happened so fast...'

'I think it was the way you talked about it,' Rome said, after a pause. 'I could tell how much it had meant to you. And I was curious to see something that could put that note of yearning into your voice. It made the distance seem immaterial.'

'Oh.' Her throat tightened.

'And I would do the same for you,' he added casually. 'If you come to Italy, I'd show you all the places that were important to me.'

'Even your vineyard?'

He laughed. 'Maybe even that.'

'Well, I hope you won't be disappointed in Suffolk. It's quite a gentle landscape. There aren't any towering cliffs or sweeping hills. And the beaches are all dunes and shingle.'

Rome shrugged a shoulder. 'I'll chance it.'

Cory watched curiously as he negotiated a busy junction with effortless ease.

She said stiltedly, 'You're a very good driver.'

'I've been driving for a long time.' He slanted a glance at her. 'You don't have a car?'

She shook her head. 'It's never seemed worth it. Not in the city. For work and shopping I tend to use the Underground, or taxis.'

'Unfortunately we don't have those conveniences at Montedoro, so one's own transport is a necessity.'

She nodded. 'Have you visited East Anglia before?'

'No,' he said. 'I've only been in London. Why?'

'Because you seem to know the way so well. And without any prompting from me.'

There was another slight pause, then he shrugged again. 'We have road maps even in Tuscany. And I'm capable of working out a route for a journey.'

'Which means you must have planned this in advance,' Cory said slowly. She turned her head, staring at him. 'Yet you had no means of knowing that we'd meet today. Or ever again, for that matter.'

'You're wrong about that.' His voice was quiet. 'Because I knew I would see you again, Cory *mia*. And so did you. If not today, then at some other time. And I could wait.'

Yes, she thought, with a sudden pang. He would be good at that. Was that why he'd kept away all week? Making her wait—making her wonder?

She said bitterly, 'I don't think I know anything any more.'

'Do you wish you hadn't come? Perhaps you'd rather be back at your National Gallery, fantasising about an image on canvas.' His tone was sardonic. 'Do you prefer oil paint to flesh and blood, *mia*?'

She flushed. 'That's a hateful thing to say. And not true.'

'I'm relieved to hear it.'

Cory bit her lip. Glancing up at the sky, she said, with

asperity, 'It seems to have stopped raining. I suppose you arranged that, too.'

Rome laughed. 'Of course. I want this to be a perfect day for you, *cara*.'

Cory relapsed into a brooding silence. But it didn't last long—how could it, when she began to recognise familiar landmarks and favourite bits of countryside?

In spite of herself, she felt anticipation—even happiness—beginning to uncurl inside her.

'We'll be in Sudbury soon,' Rome remarked at last. 'Do you want to stop and look round?'

'Gainsborough was born there,' she said. 'They've turned the house into a gallery for some of his work. But maybe we've looked at enough paintings for one day.'

'Where do you suggest we go instead?'

'Lavenham's quite near,' she said. 'And it's really beautiful—full of old, timbered houses.'

'Is that where you used to live?'

She shook her head. 'No, our house was nearer the coast—in a village called Blundham.'

'I'd very much like to see it,' Rome said, after a pause. 'Would you mind?'

'No,' she said. 'Why should I? But, at the same time, why should you want to?'

'To fill in another piece of the puzzle.' He was smiling again, but his voice was serious. 'To know you better, *mia bella*.'

Cory straightened in her seat. She said crisply, 'Isn't that rather a waste of time—when you'll be gone so soon?'

He said softly, 'At the moment, my plans are fluid.' And paused. 'Tell me, is there somewhere in Lavenham that we can have lunch?'

She said huskily, 'Several places.' And stared determinedly out of the window as she allowed herself to wonder what he might mean.

The bar at the Swan Hotel opened into a maze of small rooms. They found a secluded alcove furnished with a large comfortable sofa and a small table, and a cheerful waitress brought them home-made vegetable soup followed by generous open sandwiches, with smoked salmon for Cory and rare roast beef for Rome. She chose a glass of white wine, dry with an underlying flowery taste, while Rome drank a sharp, icy Continental beer.

On their way to the hotel they'd visited the market place and seen the old Corpus Christi guildhall, now a community centre, and the ancient market cross.

The rain had well and truly stopped now, and a watery sun was making occasional appearances between the clouds, accompanied by a crisp breeze.

Cory was telling him over the sandwiches that a number of the shops they'd passed dated from the Tudor period, when she stopped with a rueful laugh.

'What am I doing?' She shook her head almost despairingly. 'I'm trying to teach history to someone who was born in Rome.'

He grinned. 'Different history, Cory *mia*. And don't stop, please. I'm enjoying my lesson. Why was Lavenham important?'

'Because of the wool trade. It was a major centre. Then came the Industrial Revolution, and the power looms, but there was no coal locally to run them, so the woollen industry moved north.' She smiled rather sadly. 'We may have missed out on the dark, satanic mills, but now we have nuclear power plants instead.'

'So, tell me about Blundham.'

'I'm afraid you'll be disappointed.' Cory finished her

wine. 'It's just an ordinary little village. We don't get too many tourists, apart from birdwatchers and walkers.'

'I hope our arrival won't prove too much of a shock,' Rome said drily, as he paid the bill.

But, in the end, the shock was Cory's.

They arrived at Blundham after a leisurely drive through narrow lanes. On the face of it the village, with its winding main street lined with pink-washed cottages, looked much the same. She recognised most of the names above the shops, and the pub, which had been rather run down, had received a much needed facelift, with window boxes, smart paintwork, and a new sign. It all had the same rather sleepy, prosperous air that she remembered.

'Why are there so many pink houses?' Rome queried, as he slowed for the corner.

Cory shook her head. 'It's just a traditional thing. You'll see it everywhere in Suffolk.' She pulled a face. 'My grandfather told me that originally they mixed the plaster with pigs' blood to get that particular colour, but I don't know if it's true or if he was just winding me up.' She leaned forward eagerly. 'If you take the left-hand fork down here, it will bring us to the house.'

'Who does it belong to now?'

'A London couple. He was something in the City, and she wanted to play the country lady.' Cory frowned slightly. 'I didn't like them much, and nor did my grandfather. He said they'd find it too big, and too isolated. In fact, he told them so, and the agents were furious. But they came up with the asking price, so they got it.'

Rome said slowly, 'Only it seems they didn't keep it.'

He brought the car to a halt beside a big estate agency sign attached to the front wall with 'Sold' blazoned across it.

And, in smaller letters, 'Acquired for the Countrywide Hotel Group.'

'A hotel. Oh, no, I don't believe it.' Cory sat for a moment, rigid with dismay, then scrambled out of the car. She peered through the tall wrought-iron gates. 'They haven't just sold it, they've actually moved out and left it empty. Look—the garden's like a jungle.'

She pushed at one of the gates, and it opened with a squeal of disuse.

'Countryside Hotels came sniffing around when we put the house on the market, but Gramps turned them down flat. He wanted it to remain a private home. That's why he sold to the Jessons.' She shook her head. 'I can't tell him. He'll be so upset.'

'Perhaps not,' Rome said quietly as he followed her up the overgrown drive. 'After all, he said it himself. Too big and too isolated. Maybe the Jessons gave it their best shot.' He put a hand on her shoulder. 'Cory, are you sure you wish to do this? Shall we go back to the car and drive up the coast?'

Her voice was subdued. 'We've come all this way. So I may as well say goodbye. And it could be worse,' she added, with a forced smile. 'It could have been bought by Sansom Industries and pulled down.'

She was half expecting a question or a comment, but Rome said nothing. Just gently removed his hand as they walked on towards the house.

It was redbrick, built on three storeys, with tall chimneys and mullioned windows.

'It's a good house,' Rome said, as they walked round to the rear. 'Simple and graceful. It doesn't deserve to be empty.'

'My room was up there. The window on the end.' Cory pointed. 'I chose it because at night I could hear the sound of the sea. Usually it was gentle and soothing, but when there were storms it would roar, and Gramps said it was a monster, eating back the land.'

'Didn't that give you nightmares?' Rome asked drily.

'No.' She shook her head decisively. 'Because I knew I was safe and loved. And the monster would never reach me.'

Or not then, she thought, with a pang. Her nightmare had begun with Rob...

'What's wrong?'

She started almost guiltily. Rome was watching her, frowning a little.

'Nothing—why?' She forced a smile.

'Your face changed,' he said. 'One moment you were remembering. The next you looked sad—almost scared.'

Cory paused. Shrugged. She said quietly, 'Maybe Memory Lane is a dangerous place.'

His mouth twisted. 'You think the future holds more security?' There was an odd note in his voice—almost like anger.

No, she thought with sudden desolation. Not if it holds you...

She said quietly, 'I try to live one day at a time—and not look too far ahead.'

She moved off determinedly along the stone terrace. 'Now I'll show you my grandmother's sunken garden. She used to grow roses there, and the most marvellous herbs.'

She reached the top of the stone steps and stopped dead, drawing a swift painful breath. Because the garden, with its tranquil paths and stone benches, had gone. In its place was a swimming pool, surrounded by an expanse of coloured tiles. Even the old summer house had been supplanted by a smart changing pavilion.

Cory's throat tightened. She turned and looked up into Rome's cool, grave face.

She said, like a polite child, 'Thank you for bringing me here, but I've seen enough and I'd like to go home, please.'

Then her face crumpled and she began to weep, softly and uncontrollably, the tears raining down her pale face.

Rome said something quiet under his breath. Then his arms went round her, pulling her close. His hand cradled her head, pressing her wet face into the muscular comfort of his chest.

She leaned against him, racked by sobs. He smelt of fresh air and clean wool, and his own distinctive maleness, a scent that seemed at the same time alien and yet totally familiar. She breathed him, filled herself with him, as her hands clung to his shoulders, her fingers twisting feverishly in the fine yarn of his sweater.

As she cried, he murmured to her, sometimes in English but mostly in Italian. While she didn't understand everything he said, instinct told her they were words of endearment, words of comfort.

And she felt his lips brush her hair.

She lifted her head and looked up at him, a sob still catching her throat, her eyes bewildered—wondering.

The long fingers touched her drenched lashes, then gently stroked her cheek, pushing back the strands of dishevelled hair. And all the time she watched him silently.

She felt him straighten, as if he was going to put her away from him, and whispered, 'Please…'

For a moment he was still. Taut. The dark face was stark, the blue eyes narrowed, suddenly, and burning.

And when he moved it was to draw her close again. But not, this time, for consolation.

He kissed her forehead, then, very softly, her eyes, as if he was blotting her tears with his lips.

She sighed, her body bending like a willow in his arms in a kind of mute offering. And then, and only then, he found her mouth with his.

She was more than ready. She was thirsting, starving for him. Her lips parted, welcoming the heated thrust of his tongue. Their mouths tore at each other in a kind of frenzy. She forgot to think, to reason, or to be afraid. There was nothing—*nothing*—but this endless kiss. This was what she'd been born for, and what she would die for if need be, she told herself, her brain reeling.

When he lifted his head at last, she was shaking so violently she would have collapsed but for his arm, like an iron bar, under her back.

He said her name swiftly, harshly, then bent his head again. He was more deliberate this time, more in control, his lips exploring her wet cheeks, the hollow of her ear and the leaping pulse in her throat, lingering there as if he was tasting the texture of her skin.

Then he kissed her lips again, fitting his mouth to hers with sensuous precision, letting his tongue play with hers, teasing her lightly, wickedly, into uninhibited response.

His free hand slid inside her sweater and moved upwards, pushing the encumbering folds away and seeking the soft mound of her breast. Stroking her gently, feeling the aroused nipple hardening against his palm under the thin camisole she wore, as she arched against him.

He lifted his head and stared down at her for a long moment, his eyes slumberous, urgent, as he studied the effect of his caress.

For a moment she returned his gaze, then her lashes swept down, veiling her eyes, as she waited for him to touch her again.

This time she experienced the shuddering thrill of his mouth against her, suckling her scented, excited flesh through the silk covering. Circling the rosebud peak with his tongue, coaxing it to stand proud against the damp and darkened fabric.

Cory could feel the heat of him—the male hardness—against her thighs in implicit, primitive demand, and heard herself moan swiftly and uncontrollably in need and surrender.

It was a small sound, but it broke the spell. Snapped the web of sensuality which held them.

Between one instant and the next Cory found herself released—free. And Rome standing three feet away from her, trying to control his ragged breathing.

He said quietly, as if speaking to himself, 'I did not—intend that.'

Hands shaking, Cory dragged her sweater back into a semblance of decency.

She said, in a voice she barely recognised, 'It was really my fault. You got—caught up in an overspill of emotion, that's all.'

'No,' he said harshly. 'It was entirely mutual. Have the honesty to admit it.'

There was a tense silence. Cory looked down at the flagstones. 'Are you—sorry it happened?'

'No—but I should not have allowed it, just the same.' He sounded weary, and a little angry. 'We had better go.'

She was still trembling as they walked back to the car. Her lips felt tender—swollen—and she touched them with a tentative finger.

'Did I hurt you?' He noticed, of course.

'No,' she said.

But it was a lie.

Because in those brief rapturous moments in Rome's

arms she had given him the power to hurt her for all eternity.

And eternity, she realised painfully, might already have begun.

CHAPTER SEVEN

THE clouds had returned with a vengeance, and the North Sea was a sullen grey as they drove up the coast road.

There was silence inside the car, but not the companionable sort, born of long familiarity. The enclosed atmosphere simmered with tension, and some other element less easy to define.

Cory sat huddled into the passenger seat, staring rigidly at the white-flecked waves emptying themselves on to the banks of shingle.

She did not dare look at Rome, who was concentrating almost savagely on his driving.

The advance and retreat of the sea was like a symbol of her own life, she thought, pain twisting inside her. One moment she was being carried along on an inexorable tide of passion. The next she was abandoned, stranded. Left clinging to some inner emotional wreckage. And she wasn't sure how much more she could take.

Any student of body language, she thought, would take one look at her and say 'defensive'. But they didn't know the half of it. The faint lingering dampness of her camisole against her skin was an unwanted but potent reminder of the subtle plunder his lips had inflicted.

Her entire being was one aching throb of unsatisfied longing.

While being shut with him in this confined space was nothing less than torture.

She sat up with sudden determination.

'Could you stop the car, please?—I'd like to go for a

walk—clear my head.' She shot a swift, sideways glance at his set, remote profile. 'If that's all right,' she added.

'Of course,' he said coolly. 'It's a good idea.' He paused. 'Something we both need, perhaps.'

The wind was freshening, blowing in unpleasant gusts from the sea, and Cory took off the scarf knotted at her neck and struggled to tie it over her hair instead.

'May I help?' Rome came round the car to her side.

'No.' Her mouth was suddenly dry, her heart pounding as she thought of his fingers touching her hair, brushing against her throat. 'No, I can manage. Thank you.'

He shrugged on the russet jacket, his eyes hard. 'As you wish.'

He set off and she followed, picking her way across the sliding shingle, filling her lungs with the cold salt-laden air as she battled with the wind.

Apart from clusters of sea birds hunched at the edge of the sea, and a couple exercising a small dog in the distance, they had the long stretch of beach to themselves.

Rome strode ahead, apparently impervious to the chill of the wind, or the increasing dampness in the air, and Cory found she was struggling to keep up with him.

Hey, she wanted to shout. This is my environment, not yours. How dare you be so at home here, when I feel alienated of—a stranger…?

At the top of the shingle bank, the elderly hulk of a fishing boat had been left to end its days, and Rome paused in the shelter of its remaining timbers, shading his eyes as he stared out to sea, watching the progress of a solitary oil tanker on the horizon.

As she joined him breathlessly, he gave her an unsmiling glance. 'How are the cobwebs?'

'They didn't survive the first minute.' She leaned against

the bow of the boat, steadying her flurried breathing and attempting to rearrange her scarf.

Rome resumed his scrutiny of the tanker, his expression unreadable. Silence hung between them.

Eventually, Cory cleared her throat. She said, 'I think I owe you an apology.'

'For what happened between us earlier?' Rome shook his head. 'We must share any blame for that.'

'I didn't mean—the kiss.' And what a polite euphemism that was, she thought wryly, for all that had really gone on.

'What, then?' His mouth was hard and set.

She said steadily, 'For bursting into tears all over you. I'm not usually such a wimp—I hope. It was just such a shock. The village looked just the same, so I'd convinced myself that Blundham House would, too. That it would still be there waiting for me, caught in some time warp, and that all I had to do was show up.' She shook her head. 'Stupid, or what?'

'Unrealistic, perhaps. But I encouraged that by bringing you here. I should not have done so. I just—needed to get out of London, and I thought you did, too.' He was still staring at the horizon, and his voice was bitter with self-accusation. 'This whole day was a bad mistake.'

Hurt twisted inside her. She said quietly, 'Rome—we both lost our heads for a while. But it's no big deal, and it certainly isn't irretrievable.'

His laugh was brief and humourless. 'You don't think so?' He turned to look at her. 'Cory, you can't be that naïve. You must see it has changed everything.'

She tried to look into his eyes, but they were hooded, unfathomable.

She forced a smile. 'Perhaps I'm due for a change.'

'That,' he said, 'would be unwise.'

'Then maybe I'm just tired of being sensible,' she threw back. 'But if you're not—I can learn to live with it.'

His mouth tightened. '*Dio*, I wish it were that simple.'

Cory leaned her shoulder against the boat, needing its support suddenly.

She said huskily, 'Rome—is there some—some reason why we shouldn't be—together?'

She'd meant to say 'someone else', but found she couldn't speak the words aloud.

He said bleakly, 'Any number of reasons, *mia cara*. Do you wish me to list them for you?'

No, she thought with swift anguish. Because one of them could be another woman's name. And more than she could bear.

That damned scarf was slipping again. She untied it, thrusting it into the pocket of her raincoat, glad to conceal the fact that her hands were shaking.

She said in a low voice, 'And what if I said I didn't care? That I want to forget the past and live just for the present?' She bit her lip. 'And let the future take care of itself.'

There was a tingling silence. Cory could almost feel the tension emanating from him.

He said, 'You don't know what you're saying, Cory. And you deserve better than that. You deserve a future.' He flung back his head in sudden anger. 'Dear God—what an unholy mess.'

She could taste blood from her ravaged lip. 'Then—again—I'm sorry. And I'll have to stop saying that.'

She looked past him at the sea, iron-dark now, like the sky above it. Saw a cloud advancing across the water, whipping up the surface like cream.

She said, 'We should get back to the car. There's a squall coming.' She added carefully, 'And, however it's turned out, it was good of you to give me this day. I'll remember it always. But I don't think there should be any more of them. When we get back to London, we should say good-bye.'

He said harshly, 'You think that's possible?'

'No,' she said. 'Essential.'

And gasped as the sheet of rain she'd seen approaching arrived in an icy torrent which drenched them relentlessly within seconds.

Rome swore, and grabbed her hand. 'Run,' he ordered.

The rain swirled at them, driven viciously by the wind, as they stumbled back across the treacherous shingle, struggling to keep their footing. They were breathless and half blinded when they reached the car.

Rome thrust Cory into the passenger seat, then dived in beside her. They sat for a moment, listening to the roar of the wind and the fierce drumming of the rain on the car roof.

Rome reached into the glove compartment and produced a packet of tissues.

He said wryly, 'For the moment, this is the best I can offer.'

Cory used a handful of them to blot the worst of the moisture from her face and hands. But she could do little about her hair, which was sticking to her scalp, and even less about her soaked clothing, now adhering clammily to her skin.

Even her eyelashes were dripping, she thought ruefully.

And Rome was in no better state.

She said doubtfully, 'It might be quicker to go back by the motorway…'

'Perhaps,' he said, starting the car. 'But I have a better idea.'

They drove back the way they had come. After a mile or so, Rome turned down a narrow lane.

'Where are we going?' Cory was shivering.

'I saw a hotel signposted on the way here. I'd planned to take you there for tea. We'll use their facilities to get dry instead.'

'But we can't do that. They won't allow it.'

'We have no choice,' Rome told her coolly. 'And nor do they. If we drive back to London in this state, we're risking pneumonia.'

He drove in between two tall brick pillars and up a winding, tree-shaded drive.

Through the rivulets of water still running down the windscreen, Cory got an impression of a large creeper-clad building with lights blazing cheerfully from its mullioned windows.

Rome brought the car to a halt in front of the main entrance.

He said, 'Wait here, while I see what can be done.'

Her lips were still framing another protest when he disappeared, leaving her with the beat of the rain for company.

Peering out through the streaked and misty windows, she could see a number of other cars parked nearby, and this heartened her.

If the hotel was busy, it wouldn't want extra waifs and strays dropping in because they'd been caught in a storm, she thought, easing her wet skirt away from her legs with distaste.

But even if the hotel rolled out the red carpet for them, she still couldn't go in there. Not with Rome.

The journey back to London was going to be difficult enough, and she didn't want to prolong the remainder of her time in his company.

And spending even a few hours with him in a remote

country hotel was bound to force on them the kind of intimacy she could never risk again.

Pneumonia, she thought, would almost be preferable.

She was so deep in her own unhappy thoughts that she was unaware of Rome's return until her door was opened abruptly.

'They can take us.' He handed her a big coloured umbrella. 'The porter will show you where to go, while I park the car. And I'll even be the soul of chivalry and let you have the first hot bath.'

Cory stared at him. She said huskily, 'You mean you've reserved a room?'

'Naturally. We'll need some privacy while our clothes are being dried.'

She said fiercely, 'Our day out is over, Rome. I thought I'd made that clear. And I'm not signing off by joining you in some seedy hotel room that you rent by the hour.'

'By the night, actually. Although it's our own business how long we stay. And I've brought you here because we're both very cold and very wet. This is dire necessity, Cory, not some elaborate seduction ploy.'

Her face warmed. 'We can't stay here. I won't. It—it's out of the question.'

'Then you're asking the wrong questions. Cory—don't be difficult. It's still pouring with rain, and I'm getting soaked again.'

She said stubbornly, 'I want to go back to London.'

'You shall.' His tone was gritty. 'But first I intend to have a bath, some food, and my clothes dried and pressed by the hotel valet service. I don't think that's unreasonable.' He paused. 'However, if you prefer to stay here, alone and dripping, and making yourself ill in the process, that is entirely your own decision. But in that case be good enough not to give me your cold.'

He paused again. 'Don't argue any more, *carissima*. I would carry you in, but the staff might get the wrong impression and give us the bridal suite.'

Cory gave him a fulminating look, and left the car with as much dignity as she could assemble at short notice.

The porter, small, balding and jolly, awaited her. 'Good afternoon, madam, and welcome to Hailesand Hotel. What a shame about the weather.' He relieved her of the wet umbrella. 'We've put you in the Garden Suite, and it's just down here.'

Cory found herself squelching down a thickly carpeted corridor. The porter threw open the door at the end with a flourish.

'This is the sitting room, madam.' He bustled around lighting lamps. 'The main bedroom's through that door on the right, and the bathroom's opposite, with the other bedroom next to it. Not that you'll need it, of course, but it's nice for families.'

'Yes,' was all Cory could manage.

'I'll put a match to the fire, shall I? Make things cosier for you,' he added with satisfaction as flames began immediately to curl round the kindling in the dog grate. 'And if you leave your wet clothes in the bedroom the housekeeper will collect them for you. You'll find complimentary robes in the wardrobe, and plenty of nice toiletries in the bathroom, so just relax and make yourself at home.

'Your husband said you'd be wanting tea,' he threw back over his shoulder on the way to the door. 'Just ring down to the desk when you're ready and I'll bring it—and some more logs for the fire.'

'Thank you,' Cory said, feeling as if she'd been bowled over by a giant teddy bear.

'You're welcome, madam.' He twinkled at her, and went out, leaving Cory to the confusion of her own thoughts.

Her initial reaction was thankfulness that they were in a suite, and not a double room. So at least she'd be able to maintain some kind of distance from him during their brief stay, she told herself painfully.

Her second thought was that if they had to stay somewhere while their clothes dried, this would seem the perfect choice.

Even without the fire the room would have been cosy, she thought, viewing the thickly cushioned twin sofas with their chintz covers which flanked the fireplace.

There was a small round dining table in one corner, and a bookcase crammed with a tempting selection of paperbacks.

The walls were hung with watercolours of local scenes, and there were bowls of fresh flowers everywhere. Old fashioned French windows offered access to the gardens beyond. Or would when it wasn't lashing with rain, Cory amended, with another shiver. Which reminded her what she was there for.

She eased her feet out of her shoes and peeled off her sodden tights, then padded across to the bathroom.

As she ran hot water into the tub, adding a sachet of freesia bath oil for good measure, she realised the friendly porter hadn't exaggerated. The pretty basket of toiletries even had toothbrushes and paste.

The main bedroom was attractively decorated in blue, the faint severity of the tailored bedspread and plain drapes offset by a cream carpet lavishly patterned in forget-me-nots.

Was that a subtle hint? Corey wondered, as she stripped off her wet clothes and put on the smaller of the two cream towelling robes from the wardrobe. If so, it was unnecessary.

Eventually, she hoped—she prayed—she would be able

to put the events of these few enigmatic days behind her. But not yet.

She put her discarded garments in the linen laundry bag she found in a drawer, but decided she would rinse out her own undies and dry them quickly on a radiator.

The robe was a perfectly discreet cover-up, but she'd feel awkward and self-conscious being so nearly naked in front of Rome.

For her own peace of mind, she needed more than one layer, she thought, her mouth twisting.

She took the other robe into the sitting room and draped it over the arm of the sofa, where he would see it, and placed the laundry bag beside it.

Then she went to have her bath, carefully turning the little brass bolt on the door first.

She lay half submerged in the scented bubbles like a mermaid on a rock. Except she felt that she was the one being lured to her doom, she thought, letting the water lap softly over her breasts and gasping a little at the sensation.

She had never been so aware of her own body before, nor of its unexpected capacity for pleasure.

But then, she had never before felt such overwhelming physical desire for a man as she did for Rome.

Not even Rob, whom she'd believed she loved, had been able to arouse such a fierce, unbridled need in her.

Perhaps if he had things would have been different between them, she thought, biting her lip.

But all that dizzying, aching passion for Rome had to be counterbalanced by the questions about him that remained unanswered.

It troubled her that she still knew so little about him. It genuinely shocked her that she'd been on the point of giving herself to a man who was still virtually a stranger to her. And who—one day, one night—would walk away, back to his own life. Leaving her bereft.

So the wise thing was to step back herself before she was tempted again. Before any real harm was done.

One of the nuns at her convent school had lectured the girls regularly on avoiding 'occasions of sin'. And Sister Benedict would have placed Rome in that category without a second thought.

He was the occasion, the sin itself, and the ultimate need for repentance all united in one lethal package.

She knew the right thing was never to see him again, even if the anguish of it made her want to moan out loud.

But she wouldn't sit at home brooding about what might have been. She would stop being so selective—so reclusive. She would do as her grandfather wanted. She'd go out and meet people, and somehow, sooner or later, she would find someone who would make this deep, aching hollow inside her disappear.

It was just a matter of time.

She shampooed her hair, rinsed out her camisole, briefs and tights, and folded them in a towel over her arm.

She combed her wet hair back from her face, and took a long objective look at herself. The sleeked back hair left her no defences at all, and she was all eyes and cheekbones, and soft vulnerable mouth.

But she couldn't stay in here, as if she was clinging to sanctuary. Somehow she had to endure the next few hours—survive them. And to do that she had to confront the man in the next room, whether angel or demon. And she had to do it now.

She took a deep breath, then opened the bathroom door and went into the sitting room.

Rome was standing by the French windows, staring into the gathering darkness. He was bare-legged, and the sleeves of the robe were folded back, exposing muscular forearms. His skin looked very dark against the pale fabric.

He turned slowly and looked at her, his expression watchful, almost wary. She had the sense of strong emotion rigorously controlled. Of a battle that had been fought and won during her absence.

She had to resist an impulse to tighten the sash of her robe—to draw its lapels closer together.

Behave calmly, she adjured herself silently. Treat the situation as if it was normal. As if it's not a problem.

She said, 'I'm sorry I took so long.' Then, shyly, 'This—this is a lovely place. Log fires and tea on demand.'

He smiled faintly. 'Give me ten minutes, then order some.' He paused. 'Our clothes will be a couple of hours, so I had them bring us a dinner menu. We can eat here.'

'Oh.' She couldn't keep the note of dismay out of her voice, and his brows lifted mockingly.

'The restaurant demands smart casual dress, *cara*,' he drawled. 'I doubt we would qualify. Also, we might be a little conspicuous.'

She said, 'I was hoping we'd be on our way back to London before dinner.'

'How eager you are to be off,' Rome commented caustically. 'You have a date tonight, perhaps?'

Cory did not meet his gaze. 'No—just a life to get back to.'

He said softly, 'Ah, yes, of course.'

He walked across the room, heading for the bathroom. As he passed Cory he bent, so that his mouth was almost brushing the delicate curve where her neck joined her shoulder, and inhaled with frank appreciation.

He said, 'You smell—exquisite, *mia bella*. Like some rare flower.'

Her body stiffened with almost unbearable tension. She kept her voice level with an effort. 'Thank you.'

She remained where she was until she heard the click of the bathroom door signal that she was alone.

Then she moved, like an automaton, to one of the sofas, and sank onto the edge of it, staring at the flames that were leaping round the logs. Consuming them. Burning them out.

Knowing that this could happen to her, too.

She thought, Oh, God, I have to be careful—so careful.

And found herself wondering if it was not already too late...

CHAPTER EIGHT

ROME tossed the disposable razor into the waste basket and rinsed his face. As he reached for a towel he paused, staring at himself in the mirror above the basin, his eyes bleak with self-condemnation.

Yet he couldn't blame himself totally for the present situation, he argued. He wasn't responsible for the weather which had stranded them here.

And although he'd been desperate to get away from London and out of his grandfather's aegis, he hadn't planned to take Cory with him. Not at first.

'What's happening with the girl?' Matt had demanded on the telephone, not for the first time. 'Why aren't you seeing her?'

Rome's brows drew together. 'Are you having me watched?' he asked coldly.

'That's my business. I've made an investment in you, boy,' Matt barked. 'And I protect my investments.' He paused. 'You took her to dinner, I understand, and that's good. But why haven't you followed it up?'

'Because I want her to ask herself that,' Rome said levelly. 'I want her to miss me.'

'Or forget all about you,' Matt said contemptuously. 'You could lose all the ground you've won.'

'You should have used the hired stud.' Rome's tone was short. 'You'd have found him more amenable to orders. I do this my own way. That was the agreement.'

'Then do it faster,' his grandfather snapped. 'This delay

is costing me money. You'd better make some progress this weekend, or you'll be hearing from me again.'

Rome replaced his receiver with a thud, his mouth grim. The temptation to tell Matt Sansom to go to hell was almost overwhelming.

But he couldn't afford that—yet.

He had no plans to contact Cory until the middle of next week. He wanted her intrigued—seriously bewildered—and with her guard down.

He retrieved the hated dossier and glanced through it, wondering where she was and what she was doing. An item about the National Gallery caught his eye. It seemed to be one of her favourite weekend haunts, and instinct suggested that it might be the kind of place she'd choose if she was troubled about something. If…

When he actually found her there he expected to feel mildly elated that he'd been able to predict her movements—and her mood—with such accuracy. Instead, he felt winded—as if someone had punched him savagely in the gut. He found himself leaning against a doorframe, almost gasping for breath.

Even then he didn't intend to approach her. He was, he told himself, just checking. And she had no idea he was there, watching her. So it would be easy to slip away.

Only to find himself walking across to her, as if impelled by some unseen force.

He didn't mean to mention the Suffolk trip either. After all, it was just an idea, still in the planning stage. He was saving it for later, like the cherry on the cake. Proof of how caring he was, he derided himself.

So why had he suddenly found himself blurting it out? Almost hustling her out of the Gallery and to his car as if she might suddenly drift through his fingers and vanish?

He shook his head in exasperation.

He'd given way to a series of crazy impulses—and this was the result.

And then he'd compounded all previous errors by kissing her. And not the studied kiss he'd taken in the restaurant, which had been solely intended to rattle her. To teach her in one swift lesson how fragile that cool reserve of hers really was.

No, the truth was that he'd wanted to feel that soft mouth of hers trembling under his again. Had needed it with sudden desperation.

But he hadn't anticipated her body's shaken response—or that she'd—offer herself with such candour.

He still wasn't sure where he'd found the strength to pull back. Perhaps some lurking shred of decency had reminded him that sex was not on offer. His decision. And that he'd be taking her under false pretences. Which she didn't deserve.

He sighed impatiently—angrily.

Because, at the same time, a small hard voice in his head was telling him that he was a fool. That this was the perfect opportunity to fulfil his deal with Matt.

By dawn tomorrow, he thought cynically, he could persuade Cory to be his wife—or anything else he might ask of her.

And then he'd be done with his grandfather's machinations and free to get on with his own life. Off the hook.

Which was what he wanted.

All that he wanted.

He tossed the towel aside and reached for his robe, tying the belt firmly round his lean waist.

And all he had to do, he told himself, was walk back into the next room and take it.

Because nothing could be too high a price to pay for Montedoro—could it?

He looked back in the mirror, but this time all he could see in his eyes was confusion.

Cursing under his breath, he switched off the light and went into the sitting room.

Cory was curled up in a corner of one of the sofas, a magazine open on her lap which she was reading with elaborate concentration.

On the table in front of her was a tray of tea, newly arrived.

Rome halted, his mouth twisting involuntarily. He said softly, 'How very domestic.'

She looked up at him. Apart from a faint flush in her cheeks, she appeared totally composed.

She said sedately, 'Except that I don't know if you take milk and sugar.'

He stretched out on the opposite sofa, smiling at her. 'Just milk, please. But I like my coffee black.' He paused. 'Do you think you'll remember?'

Cory busied herself with the teapot. 'I can just about manage that—for one evening.'

She put the cup where he could reach it. Poured her own tea. Made a studied return to her magazine.

The room was silent but for the splash of rain on the windows and the crackling of the logs in the fireplace. The warmth had dried her hair, turning it into a silken cloud round her face.

One strand drifted across her cheek and she pushed it back, knowing, in spite of herself, that the small gesture had not been lost on him. That he was reading her with the same close attention that she was paying her magazine. And probably learning far more.

He said, 'I didn't know you played golf.'

'I don't.'

'Then why read a golfing magazine?'

'I—I'm thinking of taking it up,' she said defensively, and was immediately furious with herself for perpetrating such an obvious and ridiculous lie.

'You've come to the right place,' Rome said lazily. 'When I was registering, the place started heaving with frustrated and very damp golfers, all forced off the links by the weather.'

She'd hoped to use the magazine as a barricade, but clearly that wasn't going to work, so she tossed it aside.

She said, 'When do you think our clothes will be returned?'

He shrugged. 'What's the hurry?' He smiled again, his gaze tracing the open neckline of her robe. 'I like you better the way you are.'

Cory bit her lip. 'I don't,' she said shortly, resisting an impulse to draw the lapels closer and tighten her sash. 'I'd prefer to be dressed and out of here.'

'Don't hold your breath,' Rome advised with a shrug. 'I gather this is a hotel that prides itself on service. Our clothes will be brought back when they're ready, and not a moment earlier.'

Cory studied him for a moment, frowning. 'It's odd,' she said, 'but sometimes you don't sound Italian at all.'

'There's nothing strange about it,' he said. 'I was accidentally born there. But I doubt that I have any genuine Italian blood.'

She said, 'But surely your mother…'

'My mother was English,' he said. 'She quarrelled with her family and ran off to Europe, and she happened to be in Rome when I was born. That's all.'

She said, 'Oh.'

He grinned sardonically. 'Disappointed, *cara*?' he challenged. 'Now that you know I can't be descended from del Sarto's model?'

She flushed. 'Don't be absurd. And please stop calling me *cara*,' she added with asperity.

'Then what shall I call you?' Arms folded behind his head, fingers laced, he regarded her. 'Darling—my love—my sweet?'

She did not look at him. 'No, thank you.'

'You make things very difficult.' He spoke softly, faint laughter in his voice. 'Italian is such a beautiful language for making love.'

'It's also just a pretence,' she said quietly. 'When you're not Italian.'

There was a silence, then, *'Touché,'* he murmured. 'Which I believe is French.' He paused. 'Does it matter so much—my not being Italian?'

'It doesn't matter at all. Except…'

'Tell me.'

She smoothed the towelling robe over her thigh. 'Except that I never seem to get to know you—know who you really are. Or what you want.'

Her voice lifted in a kind of appeal. She felt him hesitate, and waited.

But Rome's eyes were hooded. He said lightly, 'At the moment, my priority is dinner. Have you looked at the menu yet?'

'Yes.' Cory fought down her disappointment. Whenever she thought she was getting close to him, he retreated to a distance again. But why?

She cleared her throat. 'I thought—the pâté, followed by the beef in red wine.'

'That's what I'm having.' His voice was cool. 'And as we're clearly soulmates, you can stop wondering about me, *mia bella*—and worrying.'

But Cory, watching him rise lithely to his feet and cross

the room to telephone their order, knew it could never be that simple.

Because instinct was telling her that knowledge could be dangerous. And that sometimes it was better—and safer to go on wondering...

He said, 'Tell me about your grandmother.'

Dinner was over, and they were lingering over coffee. The food had been delicious, and, to Cory's surprise, Rome had ordered a bottle of dark, velvety wine to accompany their meal.

As he'd filled their glasses, she'd said doubtfully, 'Do you think that's wise?'

'You'd have preferred a Bordeaux?'

She'd said, 'I was thinking about later...' and had flushed when he'd raised his eyebrows and begun to laugh.

She'd said hurriedly, 'I meant you shouldn't drink and drive.'

'I'm disappointed.' He had still been grinning. 'But I promise to stay well within the limit,' he'd added softly. 'On all counts.'

Which, Cory thought, smouldering, had been enough to kill anyone's appetite stone dead.

Yet, strangely, she'd eaten every crumb of pâté, and done full justice to the rich and fragrant casserole. The wine, too, lingered on the palate.

Now, the table had been cleared by an efficient young waitress, and the tray of coffee she'd brought had been placed on the table by the fire.

Cory would have preferred to stay at the dining table, which had conferred a kind of much-needed formality to the proceedings.

She was listening all the time for the knock on the door which would announce the return of their clothing.

Her camisole and briefs had quickly dried on the bedroom radiator, and she was now wearing them again under her robe. They were only a fragile form of protection at best, but she felt better—safer with them on.

But she wouldn't really relax until she had the rest of her things back.

All through dinner she'd been taking surreptitious glances at her watch as she marked the way time was passing all too quickly.

If they didn't leave here soon, she thought, it might be too late...

Then mentally berated herself for being over-fanciful.

She had no real reason to feel threatened. Rome had been the perfect dinner companion, chatting with her on all kinds of topics, sounding out her opinions, even arguing lightly at times.

So far the conversation had been general. But now Rome's question about Beth had moved it back to the personal again.

She moved restively. 'My grandmother? Why do you want to know?'

'Because the two of you were clearly close, and I'm interested.' He paused. 'Does it hurt you to talk about her?'

Cory's smile was suddenly tender. 'No, not really. She was just a lovely person—very gentle, and calm, and she and my grandfather adored each other. She told me once it was love at first sight—although when they met she was actually engaged to someone else.'

'Who also, presumably, found her gentle and lovely.' Rome grimaced. 'It must have been a bitter pill for him to swallow.'

'Yes,' Cory admitted. 'But Gran had already realised they weren't right for each other. She was going to break off the engagement anyway. Meeting Gramps was just the final impetus she needed.'

'And what about you?' Rome said. 'Do you believe in love at first sight?'

She drank some coffee. She said, 'I suppose there has to be a real initial attraction in any relationship. But on the whole I think love should build up from trust—friendship—respect.'

'How very virtuous,' he said softly. 'And what about passion—desire—the touch of someone's hand that tells you the world has changed for ever? Does that mean nothing?' He paused. 'Or is that what scares you?'

This, she thought, was what she'd been dreading from the first.

He didn't have to put a hand on her. This line of questioning could strip her naked emotionally.

The atmosphere in the room seemed to have thickened suddenly—become electrically charged. The heat from the burning logs had become too intense. The brush of the towelling robe against her bare skin was almost more than she could endure.

She said, too vehemently, 'I'm not scared.' And wondered precisely whom she was trying to convince.

'Then why won't you look at me?'

Somehow, she made herself lift her head. Meet his gaze.

His mouth was smiling faintly, making her remember how it had felt on hers. His eyes were caressing her—pulling away the thick enveloping folds of the robe. Uncovering her, she thought dizzily, for his private delight.

He hadn't laid a finger on her, but the mere possibility had the power to make her body moisten and melt. And he had to be aware of it. Had to know what he was doing to her...

And she had no defences. Technically, she wasn't a virgin. Her brief time with Rob had dealt with that on a physical level. But sensually, and emotionally, she was untouched. And she knew it. As he must, too.

She said swiftly, huskily, *'Don't...'*

'Why not?'

She could think of a host of reasons, including all the high-flown phrases about respect and trust that she'd already trotted out.

But they all seemed unimportant against the burning reality of need. It was crude and it was violent, and it was tearing her apart. So that all she could do was stare at him wordlessly—and wait.

He said again, quietly, 'Why not?'

And this time it was an affirmation of a decision already made. A pact that had been agreed.

The tap at the door was a jolt to her senses as sudden and shocking as a blow, so that she almost cried out.

Rome got to his feet and went to the door. She heard a murmur of voices, and then the porter was there with their clothes, beautifully pressed under plastic covers, draping them carefully over the arm of a sofa.

She thought, My reprieve. And part of her wanted to laugh hysterically, while the other half wanted to cry...

She heard a stranger using her voice, thanking him, and asking him politely to take the coffee tray away.

'Certainly, madam. Is there anything else I can get you this evening—or your husband?'

And heard Rome say, 'No, that's fine. We have everything we need, thanks. Goodnight.'

She found she was repeating the words 'everything we need' over and over in her head.

When Rome came back to the sofa, she began to babble. 'They think we're married. Even though I'm not wearing a ring.' She spread out bare hands. 'See. Isn't that absurd?'

'Ludicrous,' he said, and his voice was very quiet.

'And you were right,' she hurried on. 'They've made a really good job of the valeting. Everything looks as good as new. And I reckon if we hurry we can still be back in London before midnight...'

Her voice tailed off with a gasp as Rome knelt in front of her, taking her shaking hands in his and holding them.

He said gently, 'Cory, we're not going anywhere tonight. You know it, and so do I, so let's stop pretending.'

She heard herself say in a voice she hardly recognised, 'Yes.'

He got to his feet, drawing her up with him, then lifted her into his arms as if she were some tiny featherweight and carried her into the bedroom.

The big shaded lamps were burning on each side of the bed, and the cover had been turned back. Rome put her down gently against the pillows and came to lie beside her. She was trembling, but she made no protest as he undid the sash of her robe and parted its folds.

He looked at her for a long moment, the dark face arrested, intent. Then he said huskily, *'Mia bella.'* He raised her slightly, freeing her arms from the encumbering sleeves, then dropped the robe on to the floor beside the bed.

The long fingers trailed slowly across the swell of her breasts above the lace edging of her camisole, then cupped her chin, lifting her face for his kiss.

Her lips parted on a small sigh, welcoming him. The pressure of his mouth was slow and sweet as it explored hers, while his hands began their own journey of conquest, stroking the length of her slender body in one considered act of possession.

The silk she was wearing shivered against her skin at his touch. She felt him ease the camisole upwards, and closed her eyes as he drew it gently from her body and discarded it.

The room was warm, but she was suddenly cold, turning on to her side away from him, wrapping her arms round her body.

He put his arm round her, pulling her back against him, and she realised he was naked. And not merely naked, but deeply and powerfully aroused.

Rome put his lips against her throat, just below her ear, making the tell-tale pulse leap to the brush of his mouth. His fingers shaped the curve of her shoulder, and she trembled like a frightened bird under his hand.

He kissed her throat again, and the sensitive nape of her neck, moving the silky tendrils of hair aside with his lips.

He whispered coaxingly, 'Take your hands away, *mia cara*. Don't hide from me. I want to know everything about you.'

'There isn't a great deal to learn.' She tried to make a joke of it, but her voice was too small and too breathless.

'Oh, you're so wrong,' he told her softly. 'I have to find out what you like.' He let his lips travel down her throat to the delicate hollow at its base. 'And what you may not like.' He ran a tantalising finger down the centre of the back she kept turned to him, making her flinch and gasp. His hand moved round, closing on her hip for a moment, then drifting down to her slender thigh, where it lingered, warm, sensuous and quite deliberate.

'And what you might enjoy if you tried,' he whispered.

Her whole body seemed to shudder. Then she twisted away from him, swiftly, almost violently.

She said in a suffocated voice. 'I—I can't do this. I thought—but I can't.'

Rome stayed still for a long moment, his eyes fixed thoughtfully on the long, vulnerable line of her back. Then he moved, too, taking the pillows and piling them up behind him. He reached for her, ignoring the small stifled sound she made, and drew her back beside him, holding her in the crook of his arm with her face against his shoulder.

He pulled the sheet over them, covering himself to the waist and tucking the embroidered hem across her breasts.

He said, 'Is that less threatening?'

She said on a sigh, 'I suppose.' She hesitated. 'You must think I'm a terrible fool.'

He dropped a kiss on her hair. 'Don't try to read my thoughts,' he told her gently. 'Because you're way off target.'

'Don't you—mind?'

'I'm disappointed, of course,' he said. 'But, ultimately, the decision was always yours to make.' He paused, allowing her to digest that. 'However, I'd be interested to know why you changed your mind. If you can tell me.'

There was a charged silence, then she sighed again, a small desolate sound.

She said, 'You've seen how clumsy I am. I can hardly walk across a room without falling over my feet, or someone else's.'

'I saw you fall once because you were startled,' he said. 'That's all, and scarcely a federal case.'

'It's not all,' she threw at him. 'I'm also too tall, too skinny, and my feet are too big.'

He said, 'If we're listing faults, my nose is too large, I'm seriously bad-tempered until I get my coffee in the mornings, and I sing in the shower even though I can't.'

She said passionately, 'Don't laugh at me. This isn't a joke.'

He said slowly, 'No, I see that. But even if all those

claims you make are true, why should that stop you making love with me?'

She buried her face in his shoulder. Her voice came to him muffled. 'Because I—honestly can't do it. I'm—useless in bed. A—a freak. I can't bear you to know it, too.'

His breath caught in sheer astonishment. His hand cupped her chin, forcing her to look at him.

He said roughly, 'What is this nonsense? Never let me hear you say such things again.'

'Even when it's the truth?'

'And everything else is an act?' Rome shook his head. 'I don't believe that, Cory. Not when I've kissed you—felt your body come alive in my arms.'

She said with difficulty, 'It isn't the—wanting. It's what comes afterwards.'

He said quietly, 'Didn't you hear what I said just now—that I want to find what makes you happy?'

'But I need to make you happy, too,' she said. 'And I can't.'

Rome stroked the curve of her white, unhappy face with a gentle finger.

He said, 'I'm really not that hard to please, *mia cara*.'

She said on a whisper, 'But I wouldn't want you to be kind either—or to make allowances.' She thought with a pang of anguish, or laugh about me afterwards...

There was a silence, then he said, 'Who was he, Cory? The man who made you like this? Because there must have been someone, and I need to know all of it.'

He felt her shudder again. She said, 'Please, I don't want to talk about it.'

His hand gentled the line of her jaw, traced her throat and shoulder.

He said, 'But you need to be rid of it, *mia*, before it poisons your whole life. So, you must tell me...'

She was quiet for a while, then she said, 'We were going to be married. His name was Rob, and he worked for a merchant bank in the City. I—I'd been at school with his sister. I hadn't liked her much then, but I'd run into her a couple of times in London afterwards, and she was much friendlier. She even invited me to her birthday party.'

'And you met him there?'

'Yes. He spent a lot of time with me. I'm not much of a dancer, so we sat out on the terrace and talked. He—seemed to like all the things I did, but I realised later that Stephanie must have primed him. He phoned the next day, invited me to dinner. It was a wonderful two months,' she added stiltedly. 'We went everywhere together, and then he asked me to marry him. I suppose he—swept me off my feet.'

The arm that held her was like a band of iron.

'Go on,' Rome said tersely.

'But although we spent all that time together, we weren't lovers. Oh, he'd tried, but I—I suppose I wanted to wait until we were married. Then one evening, a few weeks before the wedding, we were having dinner at his flat, and it seemed silly to go on saying no.'

'So, you went to bed with him?'

'Yes.' Her throat tightened uncontrollably. 'I was incredibly naïve, but I just didn't expect it to be like that—so painful and so—quick. I was in love with him, for God's sake, and I didn't feel a thing. I just wanted it to be over.

'When we did it again, I tried to respond—to do what he wanted. I could sense he was disappointed, getting impatient, and that hurt in a different way.' She paused. 'After that I—pretended to be asleep.

'When I woke up in the morning, he wasn't there, and I supposed he'd gone off to make some coffee. I just wanted to leave—get back to my own place and have a shower.

I—I felt dirty somehow—and confused. It was as if Rob had suddenly become a different person—and one I wasn't sure I liked.

'He had a phone extension beside his bed. I picked it up to phone for a cab and realised he was on the line in the living room—talking—laughing to some friend.

'He said, "I tell you, man, bed's going to be a nightmare. She hasn't a bloody clue, and it's like making love to a coathanger anyway. I'll just have to keep my eyes shut and think of all that lovely money."'

She felt Rome move swiftly and restively beside her. She risked a swift glance upwards and saw his face, bleak and set, his eyes staring in front of him as if fixed by some troubled inner vision.

She said, 'For a moment I tried to pretend it wasn't me he was talking about. I couldn't believe he could be so cruel. I knew I hadn't been—any good that night, but he'd told me that I'd learn—and it would get better.'

'Then he lied.' Rome's voice was harsh. 'It would never have been any better for you, Cory. Not with him.'

She said, 'I realised for the first time that he'd never actually cared about me at all. That it had just been an act. I got dressed, and left. I could hardly bear to look at him, but I told him that it was all off. That there would be no wedding and I never wanted to see him or hear from him again.'

She shuddered. 'He got so angry then, and started shouting at me. Telling me I was making a fool of him—of myself, and what made me think anyone else would ever want me, no matter how much money I had. I could hear him all the way down the corridor to the lift. People were opening their doors—staring at me. I—I wanted to die.

'The wedding was cancelled. I told Gramps that I'd changed my mind, but I never told him why. I—I couldn't.

I've never told anyone—until now. Everyone—even my best friend—assumed he'd been unfaithful, and I let them think so. It was—less painful, somehow.'

There was silence, then Rome moved abruptly. Reaching for his robe, he said, 'I need a drink. Can I get you one?'

She shook her head. 'No—thanks.' But her heart cried out, Don't leave me—stay with me.

Even though she knew it was impossible, and that one day soon Rome would go from her life for ever.

Leaving her, she realised, a stifled sob rising in her throat, more bereft that Rob ever had, or could have.

Condemning her to spending the rest of her life alone—and lonely.

CHAPTER NINE

ROME closed the bedroom door carefully behind him and leaned against it, his breathing as hard and strained as if he'd taken part in some marathon.

Saying he wanted a drink had just been an excuse. Suddenly he'd needed to be on his own—to think. To come to terms with what he'd just heard. If he could…

He walked over to the French windows, opened them and gulped the chill rain-washed air into his lungs.

He felt nauseous—sick to his stomach. And dizzy with the kind of shame that no amount of alcohol could cure.

The decent thing, he knew, would be to get dressed and take Cory home before he did more harm.

She might be hurt, but that was inevitable. And it was nothing compared with the wound he would almost certainly inflict if they stayed together.

As he'd listened to her struggling with the quiet, halting story, he'd been possessed with a savage longing to seek out this unknown Rob and give him the beating of his life.

Except, as he'd suddenly realised, he was no better. For wasn't he deceiving Cory just as viciously—and for money?

Cursing under his breath, he leaned against the doorframe, staring up at the scudding clouds.

He was caught in this trap, and there was no escape. Whatever he did, the end result would be the same.

He would lose her.

He wasn't sure of the precise moment when she'd become essential to him, or how it had happened—or why.

He only knew that when he'd gone to her in the Gallery that morning it had been because he couldn't keep away any longer. He'd been drawn to her, instinctively, involuntarily, knowing that he had to be with her, whatever the eventual cost.

He hadn't, he thought wryly, even had a chance to fight it. In too deep before he knew it, and lost for ever.

Yet there was no way they could ever be together. This was the brutal reality he had to face. The anguish that twisted in his gut.

If he told her the truth she would turn from him in hurt and disgust. And even if he could prevail upon her by some miracle to trust him again he would have nothing to offer her. Because Montedoro—his home, his livelihood—would have gone. He would be starting again with bare hands, and he couldn't ask any woman to share that kind of hardship, even if she were willing.

While if he simply continued with his grandfather's plan, let the whole thing run its treacherous course, she would end up betrayed and—hating him.

But no more, he thought wearily, than he hated himself.

He stepped back into the room and closed the windows. He collected a bottle of mineral water from the bar, and two glasses, and took them back into the bedroom.

Cory had not moved. Her eyes were closed, but he knew she wasn't asleep.

And she'd been crying. He could see the marks on her face, and felt the hard knot of reason inside him dissolve into an aching tenderness and, a heartbeat later, into a need that could not be denied any longer.

To hell with the right thing, he thought, shrugging off his robe, letting it drop to the carpet. They would have this one night together. A chance, perhaps, for him to undo the harm that Rob had done and prove to her that she was a woman both desirable and capable of desire.

Maybe his last chance.

While, for a few hours, he in his turn could forget shoddy bargains, threatened ruin, and the inevitability of heartbreak, and think instead of nothing but her. Lose himself completely in the slender paradise of her body.

He slid into bed beside her, and drew her gently back into his arms. Her eyelids fluttered and she looked at him, her eyes wide and bewildered.

She said, 'Rome…' and he laid a quieting finger on her lips.

'Hush, *mia cara*,' he whispered. 'Don't speak. Just— feel.'

And he began to kiss her.

Even as her lips parted beneath his, Cory knew she should resist. But the urge to yield was too strong, too beguiling, she realised dazedly.

His skin smelt cold and fresh, as if he'd been in the open air, and she wanted to ask him about it, only other ideas, other sensations were beginning to press on her, driving coherent thought away.

His hands seemed to drift on her, and everywhere they touched her skin sang. She felt her body lift, arching towards him in a silent demand which was almost pleading.

He pushed away the concealing sheet and caressed her breasts slowly and very gently, making the rosy nipples soar in proud response. He bent his head, worshipping each small, delicate mound in turn with his lips, letting his tongue flicker over the aroused peaks, forcing a small, frantic sound from her throat.

His mouth returned to hers, soothing her. Whispering

softly in Italian against her lips, coaxing her to relax—to trust...

The fingers that stroked her skin were warm and leisurely, exploring every curve, every plane and angle as they moved downwards, and she felt his touch in her veins, quickening her bloodstream.

When his hand reached the silken barrier of her briefs she tensed again, and Rome paused, running a questing finger along the band of lace that circled her hips.

He kissed her more deeply, the play of his tongue against hers a heated, wicked incitement.

His lips moved to the whorls of her ear, and down to the haywire pulse in her throat.

The hot dart of his tongue penetrated the valley between her breasts, licking the salty excited moisture from her skin.

His cheek rested against her ribcage, assimilating the flurried thud of her heartbeat, and his hand moved downwards with exquisite deliberation, his fingertips burning through that final fragile barrier, but so slowly that she thought she might not be able to bear it.

Because she knew where she needed him—where she craved him—and he was making her wait—dear God—so long. So terribly—agonisingly long.

Her thighs were slackening and parting, offering him access in a molten, scalding rush.

He touched her through the silk, grazing softly, intimately against her tiny, excited bud. Then delicately increasing the pressure, using that last covering against her to deepen the delicious friction. Creating a rhythm that she could recognise—that she could respond to.

The breath caught in her throat as she lifted her hips to thrust herself against his hand in open need. To tell him that she wanted that ultimate obstacle gone—to be as naked as he was himself.

Suddenly Cory could feel the velvet hardness of him against her thigh. Her hand cupped him shyly, marking him, measuring him. She heard him groan softly in answer.

He moved swiftly then, stripping away her final defence, his fingers reclaiming her with total mastery. Stroking her, circling on her, drawing her into a sudden breathless spiral of sensation. Bringing her with throbbing intensity closer and closer to some undreamed-of edge where all control would be gone.

This was uncharted territory, and for a moment she was scared, afraid of ceding him too much. Of losing her identity and becoming some mindless creature of his instead.

And, as if he sensed her sudden tension, she heard him whisper against her skin, 'Don't fight me, *cara*. Come with me.'

His hand moved again, and almost at once she was lost, crying out soundlessly, wordlessly, as her body was caught—tossed to heaven and back—in the rippling convulsions of her first orgasm.

And Rome held her close and kissed her, and felt her shocked, delighted tears on his lips.

When she spoke, her voice was husky, dreaming. She said, 'I never knew—I never guessed...'

She felt his smile against her hair as she lay, her head pillowed on his chest.

He said, 'And that's only the first lesson.'

'What's the second?'

'This.' He took her hand and brought it gently to his body again.

'Ah.' Her fingers encircled him, softly, teasingly. Caressed him with new knowledge—new wonder. And, she realised, new confidence, as she felt him stir beneath her touch. 'And only this?'

Rome said thickly, 'No.'

He turned, tangling a hand in her dishevelled hair, bringing her mouth to his powerfully and urgently while his other hand began a long journey down the length of her spine, tracing the curve of her hip and the taut roundness of her buttocks with sensuous greed.

Cory found herself shivering with pleasure under the passage of the long, clever fingers, her body arching—straining towards him—so that the sensitive points of her breasts grazed the hard wall of his chest.

She said breathlessly, 'I want you. All of you.'

'Show me.' The invitation was almost a challenge, delivered huskily.

She felt the heat, the potency of him at the apex of her thighs, and, gasping, driven by pure instinct as her body melted—opened, she brought him into her.

He entered her slowly, his control absolute, the blue eyes scanning hers for any sign of pain or fear. But her gaze was clouded, sultry with pleasure, her breathing quickening with excitement as his strength filled her.

Then, when the union of their bodies was complete, he held her for a long moment, giving her time to accustom herself to this new sensation. Waiting...

Her hands touched his shoulders, revelling in their hard muscularity. Her fingers stroked the dark silky hair at the nape of his neck. She placed her hands flat against his chest, feeling the hammer of his heartbeat, revealingly unsteady, against her palms.

Her finger brushed his lips and he captured it, biting gently at the soft flesh.

Then, gently but deliberately, Cory began to move under him, and he matched her, taking her rhythm, letting her dictate the pace. Carefully reining back his own need for release for her pleasure.

Her body rose and fell, answering his measured thrusts. Glorying in them.

He kissed her mouth, his tongue hot and demanding against hers, then the arch of her neck, and the small eager breasts, suckling the hard pink nipples, making her moan in her throat, her head turning restlessly on the pillow.

He was murmuring to her against her flesh, his voice slurred and heavy.

Nothing existed for her in the universe but this man, in her bed, in her arms, in her body. She buried her face against him, breathing him, wanting to be absorbed into him.

His hand slipped down between them to the moist centre of her, softly and sensually caressing, and she felt the first quiver of rapture rippling like water across her being.

She lifted her legs, clasping them round his lean hips, her hands clinging to his shoulders as Rome began to drive more deeply, more powerfully, inciting her, drawing her on.

She said something—sobbed something that might have been his name—and found herself overtaken, her body imploding, fragmenting into ecstasy.

She cried out wildly, eyes blind, all her senses consumed by pleasure, and he answered her, his body juddering dangerously in his own climax.

Afterwards, when the world had steadied to a semblance of reality, they were very quiet together, lying close, kissing softly.

She said wonderingly, 'I thought I was dying.'

'They call it the little death.' There was a smile in his voice. 'Do you want me to prove that you're still very much alive?'

She looked at him demurely from under her lashes. 'You think you could?'

'Not at this moment, perhaps.' He grinned at her lazily. 'But soon.'

She was silent for a moment. 'Rome—is it—always like that?'

'It was like it for us,' he said. 'Isn't that all that matters?'

'Yes.' Her voice was quiet. 'Thank you.'

'For what?'

'For the lessons—all of them.' She forced a smile. 'I think I've just undergone a crash course. And I'll always be grateful.'

He propped himself on an elbow and looked down at her. He said slowly, 'What we had just now was beautiful, and sensational, and totally mutual—as you must know. So gratitude doesn't enter into it.'

She played with the embroidered edge of the sheet. 'But it's not the same for you. It can't be. You can't possibly pretend it was your first time…'

He took her hand and carried it to his lips. He said, 'It was my first time with you, Cory. And you blew my mind. And if you've got it into your head that I made love to you out of sympathy, I have to tell you I'm not that altruistic.'

She said, not looking at him, 'Would you have made love to me if I hadn't told you about Rob?'

'You hadn't told me about Rob when we walked home from Alessandro's—and I could barely keep my hands off you.' His voice was cool and considering. 'Nor at Blundham House this afternoon. We went up in flames together, Cory, and you know it. We could fight it as much as we liked, but it was really only a matter of time before we ended up in bed with each other.'

He paused. 'But, in the interests of frankness, I'll admit I wanted to make it good for you so that it would drive

that poisonous bastard out of your mind, once and for all.'
He framed her face with his hands, speaking very distinctly.
'He can't damage you any more, *carissima*, do you under-
stand? He's gone—finished with—so forget him.'

He dropped a kiss on her nose. 'Are you hungry?'

A gurgle of laughter welled up inside her. She said,
'That's quite a change of subject.'

'Not really,' he said. 'Because I no longer have to fight
to keep my hands off you, and the time is fast approaching
when it won't be enough for me to simply look at you and
talk to you.'

He kissed her mouth softly and sensuously.

'We have a long night ahead of us, *mia bella*,' he whispered, 'and we need to keep our strength up. So—I'll ask
you again—are you hungry?'

And, to her own astonishment, she was.

Rome ordered smoked salmon sandwiches and champagne from Room Service, and she ate and drank, propped
up on pillows in the crook of his arm, and knew she had
never felt so happy or so much at peace.

The awkward girl, she told herself, had given way to a
woman with her own sexual power.

And then, like a frost to blacken her mood, came another
thought.

How in the world, she asked herself with anguish, was
she ever going to live without him?

He said, 'You're very quiet.'

Cory started slightly, banishing the unhappy reverie that
she'd conjured up some five minutes before. She said
lightly, 'Just conserving my energy.'

Rome took her chin between thumb and forefinger and
tilted her face so he could look into her eyes. 'Truly?'

'Of course,' she lied. 'Try me.'

His face was solemn, but his eyes were dancing. '*Mia cara*, I thought you would never ask. Just let me get rid of these plates.'

When he came back, his expression was oddly brooding, as if he too had been having unpleasant thoughts.

She said, 'Is something wrong?'

'I hope not.' He sat on the edge of the bed, studying her. 'But I don't know.' He was silent for a moment, then said abruptly, 'Cory, *mia*—are you on the Pill?'

'The Pill,' she repeated wonderingly, then grasped the implication. 'Oh.' She swallowed. 'No—no, I'm not. I—I never have been.'

'That,' Rome said grimly, 'is what I was afraid of.' He shook his head. 'Dear God, how stupid—how irresponsible can I be?'

She put a hand out to him. 'It's not your fault. I'm just as much to blame. I wasn't thinking…'

'Nor was I,' he said. 'But I should have been.' His tone was bitter with self-reproach. 'I should have taken care of you.'

She watched him in silence for a few moments. She said, her voice quiet, 'Would it matter so much—if it happened? If I was—pregnant?'

He said roughly, 'Cory—you're not a child. You know it would.'

She'd hoped for comfort, and instead there was pain. He was telling her, she realised, that they had no future together. That sex, however wonderful, was not enough to make a lasting relationship—and a baby would just be an unwanted, indeed an impossible complication.

And you, she thought, are all kinds of a fool to have hoped for anything different.

She found herself praying that she hadn't given herself

away too seriously, and wondering, at the same time, what she could do to retrieve the situation.

One thing she was sure of. If this was all she was to have of Rome, then she would make it memorable—for both of them.

She lay back against the pillows and smiled at him composedly. She said, 'If the horse is gone, there's little point in worrying about the stable door—is there? So why don't we do as we planned and—enjoy the rest of the night?'

He groaned. '*Carissima*—be sensible.'

She said softly, 'Oh, it's much too late for that.' She let the sheet fall away from her breasts. She heard the small sound he made in his throat, and her smile deepened. 'Besides—I'm getting impatient...'

Hours—perhaps aeons—later, she lay beside him as the early-morning light began to penetrate the room and watched him sleep. His breathing was deep and peaceful, his skin dark against the white bedlinen.

He deserved his rest, she thought, colour warming her face as she remembered how one act of love had seemed to flow naturally into the next. As she recalled the things he'd said to her—the things he'd done.

Their bodies had moved together with such harmony, she thought. There'd been laughter too, and, once, tears.

And now it was over.

Moving carefully, she slid out of bed, collected her clothing and went to the bathroom.

She looked in on him again before she left. He was still sleeping, but he'd moved into the space she'd vacated as if unconsciously seeking her.

The porter was not on duty when she went down to the foyer, but there was a friendly girl at the reception desk, who told Cory the nearest station with a direct link to

London, looked up the time of the next train, and ordered her a taxi to take her there.

'There's no need to disturb my husband,' Cory said calmly. 'He's planning to spend the day locally—do some walking. But unfortunately I have to get back.'

'Oh, that's a shame,' the other woman sympathised. 'Particularly as it looks like being a nice day. I hope you'll stay with us again some time.'

Cory made herself smile. 'Some time—perhaps.'

But she knew in her heart she could never come back. That it would be too painful to relive, even at a distance, the crazy beauty of this night, with its tenderness and its savagery.

Now she had to go away, and try to forget.

The journey back was a nightmare. Because it was Sunday, there were engineering works taking place, and the train crawled along in between long pauses in the middle of nowhere.

It was mid-afternoon before she arrived back in London, and took a cab to her flat.

She would change, she thought, and do some food-shopping. Or perhaps even book a table at the neighbourhood French bistro, because it might be better to be with other people.

She paid off the cab and turned towards her door. And stopped, a sudden prickle of awareness edging into her consciousness.

She turned nervously, and saw him walking up the street towards her.

For a moment they stood facing each other. Cory bit her lip, expecting anger—recriminations.

But all he said, quite gently, was, 'Why did you run away?'

'Perhaps because I hate saying goodbye.'

'Then don't say it. Unlock your door and invite me in, and listen to what I have to say.'

'There's no need to say anything.' Bravely Cory lifted her chin. She thought, Don't apologise. Oh, please don't tell me you're sorry, because that I couldn't bear. 'It happened,' she went on, 'and it was wonderful, and now it's over. And we both get on with our own lives.'

Rome shook his head. 'It's not that simple, Cory.'

'If you're still thinking there might be a baby, it's my problem and I'll deal with it.' She gave him a travesty of her usual smile. 'There'll be no paternity suit. I won't ask you for anything.'

'I wasn't thinking that,' he said slowly. 'Of all the many thoughts I had on that hellish, lonely drive back, the prospect of becoming a father didn't even feature. Not that I'm against it in principle,' he added. 'But I feel it would be better for us to have some time just with each other before starting a family.'

She stared at him, her eyes enormous. She said, 'I think one of us must be going mad. What are you talking about?'

He sighed. 'I hadn't planned on doing this in the street,' he said, 'but I'm asking you to marry me, Cory. To be my wife. Will you?'

CHAPTER TEN

SHE said, 'I still can't believe this is happening. We—we've only just met…'

Rome pulled her further into his arms. 'If we're strangers,' he murmured. 'I don't think I'd survive being a close friend.'

They'd almost fallen into the flat on a wave of joy and laughter that had turned in seconds into a passion that would not be denied. He'd lifted her into his arms and carried her into the bedroom, mouths clinging, hands already beginning to tear at zips and buttons.

Now they lay sated and relaxed in each other's arms.

'Anyway,' he added softly, 'I think that in some way we've always known each other. Always been waiting to meet.'

She sighed. 'Then I'm glad I went to that charity ball. I didn't want to, you know.'

'Nor did I.' There was an odd note in his voice.

'And then we kept bumping into each other.' Cory giggled. 'Quite literally at times. I should have known it was fate.'

Rome was silent for a moment. Then he said, 'Cory, can I ask you to do something for me? Something a little strange which I can't explain just now.'

'How mysterious you sound.' She planted a row of tiny kisses on his throat. 'What is it?'

He hesitated again. 'I don't want you to tell anyone about us—at least not for a while.'

Cory looked up at him, her eyes wide with bewilderment.

'You mean—not even Gramps? But he'll be so happy for us, Rome. It's been his dearest wish for me to meet someone and fall in love. And I want the two men in my life to like each other. It's important to me.'

He said, 'It matters to me, too. But I have my reasons, even if I can't tell you what they are.' He grimaced slightly. 'And your grandfather may not be as delighted as you think. I'm no great catch for his only granddaughter.'

Cory was silent for a moment. 'Gramps is quite old-fashioned,' she said at last. 'I think he'd like it if you formally asked his permission.'

'I plan to,' he said. 'But we have to wait for a little while. Will you do that for me?'

'Yes,' she said. 'You know I will.' She gave a wondering laugh. 'Love at first sight, and now a secret engagement. This is all a dream, and soon I'm going to wake up. I know I am.'

'Don't say that, Cory.' His voice was suddenly harsh. 'Don't even think it.'

She looked up at him in surprise. 'Rome—are you all right?'

'Yes.' He kissed her, his mouth tender on hers. 'For the first time in my life, I believe I am.'

'And you really can't share this mystery with me?'

'Soon,' he said. 'I promise. I have some things to sort out first.'

'But I might be able to help.'

'I'm afraid you can't, *mia cara*.' His voice was regretful. 'Not this time.'

Her answering smile was faintly troubled. 'I understand.'

Only, she wasn't sure that she did. Only an hour ago she'd stood on the pavement, locked in Rome's arms, oblivious to everything but the joy opening inside her like a flower. The certainty that this was where she belonged.

She wanted to shout her happiness from the rooftops. But she couldn't. In fact, she couldn't tell a single soul. And she didn't know why.

She was aware that Shelley would say instantly that this was one mystery too many, and demand an immediate explanation before committing herself. That this was the reasonable—the rational course.

But I love him, she thought. And somehow reason and rationality don't seem so important any more.

There were so many things she wanted to ask him, so many gaps in her knowledge, but she supposed she would just have to be patient—and trust him.

He began to kiss her again, his fingers warm and arousing on her breast, and all doubts and vague uncertainties slid away as she turned to him, rapturous and yielding.

Later they had dinner at the bistro, and then watched an old film on television.

Cory had taken it for granted that Rome would be spending the night with her, but to her disappointment he told her he was going back to his own flat.

'I'm going away on business for a day or two,' he said. 'I need to pack and make an early start.'

'Must you go?' She couldn't disguise the sudden desolation in her voice.

He pulled her closer. 'The sooner I go, the sooner I'll be back,' he reminded her.

'I suppose so,' She paused. 'What's your flat like?'

She was hoping he'd say, Come back with me, and help me pack.

Instead, he shrugged. 'Dull—impersonal. Rather like a hotel room. You'd hate it.'

'I've nothing against hotel rooms.' Cory sent him a mischievous look. 'On the contrary. But if you really dislike it, you don't have to stay there.' She paused. 'You could always move in here.'

'Except that would blow our secret to smithereens,' Rome said drily. 'Besides, if you find out too soon that I snore and leave my clothes all over the floor, you might change your mind about marrying me. It's wiser to stay as we are.'

'Who cares about wisdom?'

'I think it's time one of us did,' he said wryly. 'We haven't been very sensible so far.'

'And now you're walking out on me.' She made it jokey, to hide the little pang of hurt. 'And I can't even comfort myself by talking about you.'

He framed her face in his hands, looking at her with heart-stopping tenderness. 'When we're married,' he said, 'you won't be able to get rid of me, and that's a guarantee.'

'I know I'm being really stupid.' She sighed. 'But I don't want to lose you. It's just too soon. I need to have you all to myself for a while.'

'You're not losing me,' Rome said steadily, 'because I'm taking you with me—in my heart, my mind and my soul. And when I come back you'll have the rest of my life—if you want it.'

She pulled him down to her. 'You think there's some doubt?' she whispered against his lips.

Yes, Rome thought, as he let himself into his flat. There was a chasm—an abyss of doubt.

More than once over the past forty-eight hours he'd come within a hair's breadth of telling her everything.

And perhaps, in the end, that was the only way to cut himself out of this maze of deceit he was enmeshed in.

Which, of course, he should have done before he asked her to marry him. He was a fool and more than a fool for that, he thought bitterly, but he hadn't been able to help himself—if that was any excuse.

Her enraptured response to his loving had sent him over the edge into a kind of madness where nothing mattered other than she should belong to him for ever.

And then he'd woken and found her gone.

He'd argued with himself every mile of that headlong drive back from Suffolk, trying to convince himself that she'd done the right thing. That the enmity between their two families was too strong, and there was no way they'd ever be allowed to be together.

Her affection for her grandfather shone out of her. How would she react when she found that he, Rome, was being paid to seduce her with the aim of extorting more money from Arnold Grant? She'd think that every bad thing she'd heard about the Sansoms was fully justified. He'd about been able to see the stricken look in the clear eyes as she turned away from him.

But he hadn't allowed himself to think like that, or he might really have gone mad. His priority—his pressing, urgent need—had been to find her—to talk to her about some of the feelings that were tearing him apart. And to ask her to wait for him while he sorted out the stinking mess his life had become.

But when he'd seen her, standing in front of him, he'd lost his last precarious hold on reality and asked her to marry him instead.

He'd had no right to do anything of the kind, and he knew it. But there was no way he wished the words unsaid.

And now he had to fight to keep her, along with Montedoro. And with no real idea even how to begin, he thought with bitter weariness.

The light on his answer-machine was blinking, and when

he pressed the 'play' button, he got Matt's angry voice, demanding to know where he was.

It was a good thing that he hadn't yielded to the overwhelming temptation to bring Cory back here with him, Rome thought, his mouth twisting wryly as he listened. Because Matt Sansom on the rampage defied explanation.

'You'd better have some good news for me when I call next time,' his grandfather rumbled furiously at the end of his tirade. 'Because I've had enough of this.'

'Which makes two of us,' Rome muttered, and deleted the message.

'You seem very pleased with yourself these days.' Arnold Grant directed a shrewd glance at Cory, who was singing softly to herself as she sat in front of the computer screen.

'I do?' Cory realised she was blushing. 'I—I can't think why,' she hedged.

Arnold glanced over her shoulder. 'Been making a killing on the market?' He sounded amused. 'Since when have you been interested in stocks and shares?'

'For quite a while.' She gave him a sedate smile. 'It's my hobby.'

'You're full of surprises, child. You look different, too.' He gave her a long look. 'What have you done to your hair?'

Cory put up a self-conscious hand. 'Just a few highlights.' She paused. 'You don't approve?'

Arnold said drily, 'I don't think it's my approval you're looking for.' He paused. 'So, who is he?'

Cory studied the screen with extra concentration. 'I don't know what you mean.'

'In other words, I'm to mind my own business.' Arnold nodded. 'But ultimately, my girl, your happiness and wellbeing are my business. Remember that, please.' He paused.

'So why haven't you mentioned him before? Is he someone I wouldn't approve of?'

Cory bit her lip, wishing with all her heart that she hadn't pledged to keep her relationship with Rome a secret. Especially when it was impossible to hide the sheen on her hair, the colour in her cheeks, the swing in her step—all the tell-tale signs of happiness.

And this might have been the perfect moment to enlist her grandfather's support.

'No. And I haven't told you about him because I haven't known him that long, and it's too soon for formal introductions. Besides, he's away at the moment on business,' she added quickly.

'Hmm.' Arnold was silent for a moment. Then he said gruffly, 'Is it serious?'

She said a quiet, 'Yes—I hope so,' and was frankly relieved when he did not ask her to elaborate further.

Rome had called once, leaving an outrageous message on her answering machine which had made her blush to her toes, but giving no clue as to when he would be back.

This was the third day and night, she thought forlornly, and it felt like for ever.

For the rest of the afternoon she was aware of her grandfather's speculative gaze, and was quite glad when he told her that she could leave early. A certain abruptness in his tone told her that he was hurt because she hadn't confided in him more fully.

Up to now, she thought ruefully, her life had been pretty much an open book where he was concerned—and fairly dull reading at that.

But what would his reaction be when he found she was planning to live in Italy?

I'm all he has, she thought, troubled, as she made her

way home. But I'll just have to cross that bridge when I come to it.

Earlier that day, Rome had been on his way back from the North of England, where he'd been following up a list of contacts that Allessandro had given him. And a gratifying number, it seemed, were ready to give the Montedoro vintages a trial.

At any other time Rome would have been well-satisfied. He might even have been turning cartwheels.

But he could not escape from the knowledge that the wine he was selling might soon no longer belong to him.

But if he could demonstrate that his business was prospering, surely he'd be able to attract some independent financial backing somewhere, to ensure that he and Cory would have a life together at Montedoro?

However, nothing was certain in this uncertain world, he reminded himself bitterly, and there were powerful forces stacked against him.

But, as Steve had once told him, if you didn't stake everything, you didn't deserve to win. And he was fighting for his future. And for Cory.

When he got back to his flat, he found several messages from Matt Sansom, angrily bidding him to pick up the phone.

But what he had to say to his grandfather needed to be delivered in person, he thought without pleasure.

Even when the sun was shining Matt's house looked grotesque, he thought, as he parked his car and walked up to the door.

Today, it was answered by a woman in a neat overall. He asked for Miss Sansom, and was conducted through the house to a large elaborate conservatory at the rear. Here, among a welter of large and faintly menacing green plants, he found Kit Sansom, tranquilly engaged with some *petit point*.

She laid it aside when she saw him. 'Rome, my dear.' She held out a hand. 'I didn't know you were coming. Father didn't mention it.'

'He doesn't know.' He sat down on one of the cushioned wicker chairs she indicated. 'I suppose you know why he sent for me originally—what he wanted me to do?'

'Oh, yes.' She sighed sadly. 'He's quite obsessed, you know. Although, to be fair, they both are.'

Rome leaned forward. 'How did it start, Aunt Kit?' he asked quietly. 'Have you any idea?'

'Oh, yes.' Her voice was matter-of-fact. 'I knew a long time ago—even before Sarah left. My godmother told me everything.'

'Can you tell me?'

Kit Sansom folded her hands in her lap, her expression reflective. 'To begin with it was just business rivalry—even healthy competition—although there probably wasn't much love lost between them even then.

'But in those days your grandfather had other things on his mind as well, not just making money. He'd fallen passionately in love, and become engaged to this lovely girl. He was planning his wedding—his life with her.

'He had to go away for a few days on business, and while he was gone his fiancée went to a friend's birthday party. Where she was introduced to Arnold Grant.'

She smiled sadly. 'Apparently, it was the kind of encounter you only read about—the genuine *coup de foudre*. Once they'd met, nothing else existed for either of them. So she broke off her engagement to your grandfather and married Arnold Grant instead.

'My godmother said Matt was like a crazy man. That he went round vowing all kinds of revenge on them both, but everyone assumed that he'd get over it in time and be reasonable. Only, he never did.'

She sighed again. 'From that moment on, Arnold Grant was his sworn enemy. At first he wouldn't retaliate, no matter what your grandfather did, but eventually, inevitably, Matt went too far, and it became mutual—a full-scale feud with no holds barred.'

'*Dio*—it's unbelievable,' Rome said. 'To go on bearing a grudge like that—hating for all these years. Filling the house with it. No wonder my mother ran away.' He paused. 'Why didn't it stop when he met my grandmother—found someone else to love?'

Kit shook her head. 'My father married my mother because he needed a wife, and she was available.' She spoke without rancour. 'The problem was he wanted someone to play hostess when he entertained clients, and Mother was basically shy, and rather timid. I take after her, I think. Also, he wanted a son to inherit his business empire, as Arnold had, and she gave him two daughters.

'I think she loved him,' she added quietly. 'But she couldn't compete with the ghost of the woman he'd loved and lost—Elizabeth Cory. Sarah and I were always aware of—tensions between them. This was never a happy house.'

Rome drew a sharp breath. 'If he loved Elizabeth so much, how could he contemplate destroying her granddaughter?' he demanded roughly. 'Using her as a weapon in this senseless vendetta?'

'To hurt as he was hurt, perhaps.' Her voice was grave. 'It's all so dark and twisted that it's difficult to know. Sarah was lucky to escape—to find some happiness.'

He looked at her. 'Were you never tempted to leave—and not come back?'

'Oh, yes.' She smiled a little. 'So very often. But then

he'd have had no one, and somehow I just couldn't do it.'
She returned his gaze. 'What are you going to do, Rome?'

'I'm going to try and stop it,' he said. 'Because it's gone
on too long. And I won't allow it to damage me—or the
girl I love. Because I'm going to marry Elizabeth's granddaughter, Aunt Kit.'

'Ah, Rome.' Her voice was tired. 'Do you really think
they'll let you?'

He smiled at her. 'I grew up with a gambling man, Aunt
Kit. I just have to take that chance.'

There were sudden tears in her eyes. She said, 'Rome—
be careful. Be very careful.' She paused, looking down at
her hands. 'Was he good to her—the gambling man? Did
he make my little sister happy? Please tell me he did.'

Rome said gently, 'Yes, he adored her. He was kind,
laid-back and humorous, and we both thought the world of
him.'

'I'm so glad,' she said. 'Glad that she found someone to
love her. She hadn't had much luck up to then—either with
her father or yours.'

Rome was very still. He said, 'Aunt Kit—are you saying
you know who my father was?'

'Oh, yes,' she said calmly. 'She needed to confide in
someone—but I'd guessed long before. Guessed—and
feared for her.'

'Will you tell me?'

'If it's really what you want.' She saw him nod, and
sighed faintly. 'His name was James Farrar, and he was a
business associate of your grandfather. Dark and handsome,
but considerably older than she was. I sometimes wondered
if that was the attraction. If she was really looking for another father figure. Someone who wasn't eaten up by his
need for revenge. She knew he was married, but he told
her he was getting divorced.'

'And she believed him?' Rome asked bitterly. 'My God.'

'You mustn't blame her, my dear.' Her voice was kind. 'Up to that time she'd led a pretty sheltered life—we both had. When Sarah told him she was pregnant, he went completely to pieces. Begged her not to tell Matt, or he'd be ruined. Said all the money was his wife's, and she'd throw him out. Offered to pay for an abortion.

'She told him to go, and never saw him again. But she wouldn't identify him to Matt.' She sighed. 'He stormed at her—called her terrible names—but she was like a rock.

'He tried to make her have an abortion, too, but she refused. She told me that she might have messed up her life, but some good was going to come out of it. All the same, she wasn't going to bring her child into a house of hate either—so she ran away.'

There was a silence, the Rome said, 'What became of— him?'

'He died about ten years ago. A car accident. He'd started to drink heavily.' She put a hand on his arm. 'I wish it was a nicer story.'

'I can see why she wouldn't want to remember him.' Rome's face was sombre.

'But she was happy in the end.' His aunt paused. 'I've kept her secret a long time,' she said quietly. 'I hope you'll continue to respect that.'

'I'll tell Cory one day,' Rome said. 'But only her. And— thank you.' He got to his feet. 'Now I'd better go and talk to my grandfather.'

'You've asked her to marry you, and she's agreed?' Matt Sansom released a shout of astonished laughter. 'Well, that's fast work by anyone's standards. You've lived up to my expectations, boy, and more.'

He was dressed today, and sitting in a high-backed chair

by his bedroom window, a rug over his knees, his face alive with malice.

Rome said coldly, 'I hope that's not a compliment, because that's not all of it. The marriage will be for real. When I return to Italy Cory's going with me, as my wife.'

Matt was suddenly very still. The calm, Rome thought, before the storm. But when he spoke his voice was mild.

'You're saying you've fallen in love with her—with the Ice Maiden? How did this come about?'

I have you to thank,' Rome said. 'After all, you brought us together.'

'So I did,' Matt said softly. 'So I did.'

'And she's Elizabeth Cory's granddaughter,' Rome added. 'Things may not be as hopeless for me as you believe. I intend to fight you for Montedoro.'

Matt stared at him. 'If you're hoping that Arnold Grant will give you his blessing, and a handsome settlement, then you're an even bigger fool than I took you for.'

'I'm going to try and persuade him to listen to reason,' Rome returned levelly. 'To tell him what I've told you. That the feud must end. That it's too costly, and too damaging in all kinds of ways.'

'And you think he'll listen?' Matt laughed again, hoarsely. 'I wish you luck.' He paused. 'Have you said all you came to say?'

'Yes.'

'Then you can go, and be damned to you. I need to think.'

Rome nodded, and rose to his feet.

At the door, Rome paused. He said, 'I wish you'd meet Cory—to get to know her. I think it would make a difference.'

'Yes,' Matt said, almost absently. 'Yes, it might. I'll think about that, too. Yes, I'll certainly think about that…'

As Rome reached the foot of the stairs, he heard his name called softly and saw his aunt beckoning to him from the drawing room.

'How did it go?' She closed the door quietly.

Rome shrugged. 'Not well,' he said. 'But he's going to think it over. Maybe it's a first step.'

'Yes,' Kit Sansom said drily. 'But in which direction? However, that's not what I want to talk about.' She picked up a small jeweller's box from a side table, and handed it to him. 'I'd like to offer you this. My mother gave it to me before she died, and I'm sure she'd wish you to have it.'

Rome opened the box and saw a ring, a large amethyst surrounded by small pearls in an antique setting.

He said slowly, 'It's quite beautiful, Aunt Kit, but I can't accept it. It belongs to you.'

She smiled at him. 'My dear, I've never worn it. My hands are the wrong shape. And I don't remember my mother wearing it either,' she added thoughtfully. 'She always said that amethysts weren't her favourite stone. Anyway, I'd like to know it was being put to a proper use at last. It's far too lovely to spend its life in a box. Give it to your Cory—please.'

Rome put his hands on her shoulders and kissed her cheek.

He said, gently, 'I want you to be our first visitor at Montedoro.'

She patted his arm. 'I'd love it. But first you have to win your battle.' Her voice was sober suddenly, almost fearful. 'And, Rome, I say again—do take great care. You may not know what you're up against.'

CHAPTER ELEVEN

CORY let herself into her flat, hung away her trenchcoat, filled the kettle and set it to boil, then kicked off her shoes.

All set, she thought wryly, for another quiet evening at home. But she didn't feel tranquil. She was restless—on edge—prowling round the living room with her mug of tea, glancing through the television listings and finding nothing to interest her, picking up a magazine and tossing it down again, loading her CD player and switching it off halfway through a track.

She switched on her computer, checked the latest share prices, then abandoned that, too.

She supposed she could make a start on her evening meal, but none of the food in the fridge held any great appeal either.

She rang Shelley and left a call-back message on her machine, although it was likely that her friend, who'd had three young men circling round her at the last count, had gone straight out to dinner from work.

She was just reaching for the phone to dial a take-away service when it rang.

She grabbed the receiver, 'Hi…'

Rome said softly, 'Open your door.'

She uttered a shriek, dropped the phone, and leapt for the door, flinging herself into his arms. 'You're back—you're here…'

'I'm also deafened.' Rome pulled her close, kissing her mouth hungrily. '*Dio,*' he muttered when he raised his head at last, 'I've missed you so.'

'Not as much as I've missed you.' She clung to him shamelessly, arms round his neck, legs round his waist.

Rome reached down with difficulty to retrieve a bouquet of long-stemmed crimson roses propped against the wall, and carried Cory and the flowers into the flat, kicking the door shut behind them.

He put her down on the sofa and handed her the flowers. 'For you, *mia cara*.'

'They're wonderful.' Cory luxuriously inhaled the rich dark scent. 'I'd better put them in water.'

Rome took them from her hands. 'I think they can survive for a little while without attention.' He tossed them on to the table, then sank down beside her, pulling off his coat. 'I, on the other hand, cannot,' he added huskily.

Her hands were shaking as they unbuttoned his shirt. She pushed it from his shoulders, then dragged her shell-pink sweater over her head and fumbled to release herself from the folds of her matching wool skirt.

Rome, too, was hastily stripping off his clothes, his eyes fixed on her as if he was afraid she might suddenly vanish.

He threw cushions down on to the floor and drew her down to him, his hands rediscovering her feverishly, his mouth drinking her—draining her—until at last he lifted her over him, his eyes smiling up into hers, to join her body to his.

She took him slowly, her breath escaping in a low, sweet moan as she felt his hardness filling her ever more deeply.

His hands reached up to cup her breasts, his thumbs lightly brushing her nipples as she began to move on him, her eyes half-closed and her head thrown back, exposing the taut, delicate line of her throat.

In a silence disturbed only by their panting breath they established a rhythm—found a harmony together as their bodies rose and fell.

Rome caressed her with words as well as his hands, his eyes darkening sensually as he watched her enraptured face.

He let his hands stray down her backbone, moulding the swell of her buttocks and trailing over her flanks.

He stroked her ribcage and shaped her slim waist, his hands trailing a delicious path over the concavity of her stomach down to the silky triangle between her thighs.

A sob broke from her as his fingers began to tease her with intimate subtlety, moving softly, fluttering on her.

She felt her control slipping as, deep inside, she sensed the first stirrings of pleasure.

And heard him whisper, 'No, *mia cara*—not yet.'

Again and again he brought her to the edge of extinction, then retreated.

And she rode him wildly, her body slicked with sweat, her voice a soundless scream, begging for release.

When it came, it was explosive, and she cried out harshly as her body achieved its fierce freedom. Within seconds Rome had followed her, groaning his delight as his body shook with the force of his climax.

Then they collapsed, breathless, boneless, into each other's arms.

Eventually he said, with a ghost of laughter in his voice, 'Perhaps you really did miss me.'

'I kept thinking that you might never come back—that I'd never see you again.' She couldn't dissemble, pretend prudent indifference. 'Not any more.'

'I have something for you.'

'I know.' She stretched like a contented cat. 'My beautiful roses.'

He reached for his coat. 'No, more than that.' He extracted the little square box and handed it to her.

Cory gasped out loud as she saw the deep mauve of the amethyst, surrounded by creamy pearls.

She said huskily, 'It's—wonderful. And it's my birth-stone, too. How did you know?'

'I didn't,' he admitted ruefully. 'It's a family ring, so this makes you my family for evermore.'

He took her left hand and kissed it, then slid the ring over the knuckle of her third finger. It fitted perfectly.

Her voice shook a little. 'Does this mean we're officially engaged?'

'Almost.' He kissed her gently. 'I still have to get your grandfather's blessing, so it might be better to wait for that. Until then you could always wear it on your other hand, in public anyway.'

'I'd even wear it through my nose.' Cory's smile lit up the world. 'Just as long as I don't have to hide it away in its box.'

They spent the evening doing small, mundane things, content to be sharing them with each other. Cory put her roses in water and cooked some pasta, while Rome made a rich aromatic sauce out of tomatoes, bacon, herbs and garlic.

Afterwards, they went to bed, and slept wrapped in each other's arms.

And, for once, Cory forgot to set her alarm for the morning.

When she eventually opened her eyes, she yelped with dismay.

She was going to be late for work and, granddaughter or no, Arnold was a stickler for punctuality in the mornings.

Rome's arms scooped her back. 'You're running away again,' he muttered sleepily.

'Only to work.'

'Call in sick.'

'I can't.' She wriggled free. 'You want Gramps to like you, don't you?'

'I want you to like me.'

'I will—I do. This evening I'll think the world of you, I swear.' She scrambled out of bed. 'But now I have to rush.'

Even so, she wasn't surprised when he joined her in the shower.

'You shouldn't be here.' Her breathing fragmented as he began to soap her, his hands lingering on her breasts and thighs. 'Oh, God—I don't—I really don't have—time—for this…'

Rome kissed her wet shoulder. 'Really and truly?'

'Cross my heart.' Her pulses were going mad, and her knees were weak, but she spoke with determination and he laughed.

'Then I'll be good, and make you some coffee instead.'

Cory was standing in her robe, drying her hair, when the door buzzer sounded.

'Shall I get it?' Rome called from the kitchen.

'I'd better,' she said. 'It might be the postman, early for once.' And, 'All right, I'm coming,' she called, as the buzzer made another imperative summons.

She went barefoot to the door, pulling the robe more closely round her and tightening its sash.

She'd planned to say, 'I hope this is a seriously interesting parcel.' But all words died on her lips when she opened the door and saw who was confronting her.

'And about time, too,' Sonia said tartly. 'Well, don't just stand there. Ask me in. It's freezing out here.'

'Mother,' Cory said, dry-mouthed, as she spotted a small mountain of luggage piled up in the passage. 'What are you doing here?'

'I was in New York, seeing friends,' Sonia said lightly. 'And I decided to extend my trip and check on my only daughter.' She leaned forward, air-kissing Cory on both cheeks. 'So, I caught the red-eye and here I am.'

Well, there was no denying that, Cory thought ruefully, assimilating the pale blonde hair, artfully coiffed, the immaculate maquillage, the close fitting dove-coloured trouser suit that showed off her mother's slim, toned figure to the best advantage, and the fur jacket draped casually round her shoulders.

As usual, Sonia made her feel as if she'd been swapped at birth.

She swept past Cory into the flat, and looked around her. 'My God, what a small apartment. How many bedrooms do you have?'

'Just the one,' Cory admitted.

Sonia raised her eyes to heaven. 'In that case, painful as it will be for both of us, I'll be staying with your grandfather. Is that coffee I smell?'

Cory felt hollow. 'Yes.'

Sonia made for the kitchen, then stopped abruptly, with a gasp that owed more to genuine surprise than her usual talent for drama.

'And just who are you?' she demanded sharply.

Rome continued to pour black coffee into beakers. 'My name's Rome d'Angelo, *signora*. And I'm seeing your daughter.'

'And she, in turn, is seeing you.' Sonia's voice held a distinct edge. 'About ninety per cent of you, or even a hundred, if that towel slips any further.'

'I'll make sure it doesn't—at least in your presence.' Unperturbed, Rome handed her a beaker.

'Thank you.' Sonia tasted the brew suspiciously, then nodded. 'You make good coffee. Just one of your many talents, I'm sure,' she added waspishly.

'The least of them,' Rome confirmed, unfazed. 'And another is to spot when I'm in the way. I'm sure you both have so much to catch up on, so I'll clear out and leave you to it.'

Cory followed him to the bedroom. 'Will I see you tonight?' she asked unhappily.

He hesitated. 'You may have other obligations. I'll call you.' He dropped the towel to the floor and began, swiftly, to dress. 'I take it this visit was unexpected?'

'A bolt from the blue. My mother,' Cory said with some bitterness, 'is a creature of impulse.'

He slanted an amused look at her. 'Perhaps that's something you have in common.'

Cory gave him a troubled look. 'You realise the cat's well and truly out of the bag? Sonia doesn't have a discreet bone in her body.'

'Yes,' Rome said with a certain grimness, 'I realise, and I'm going to deal with it.' He wrapped his arms round her and kissed her hard, making her senses spin.

'Don't let her get to you, *cara*,' he whispered. 'And I'll see you later.'

As she picked up her ring from the night table and slid it on to her right hand, Cory could hear him bidding Sonia a courteous goodbye.

Steeling herself, she rejoined her mother in the living room.

'My, my, aren't you the dark horse?' Seated on the sofa, legs crossed, Sonia gave her daughter a searching look. 'And just when I thought you'd settled for being an old maid.'

Cory shrugged. 'I discovered I didn't have to settle for anything,' she returned stiffly.

'Hmm.' Sonia studied her frowningly, taking account of her flushed cheeks and reddened mouth. 'What does he call himself—Rome? What kind of name is that?'

Cory lifted her chin. 'His.'

'I see.' Sonia sounded amused. 'Well, don't be so protective, darling. I'm sure your Rome d'Angelo can look after himself, and has been doing so for some years, if I'm any judge.' She paused. 'D'Angelo,' she repeated thoughtfully. 'You know, that rings a bell. Someone I once met in Miami…'

Cory shook her head. 'Rome lives in Italy. He has a vineyard there.'

'How very romantic,' Sonia said. 'And I know it wasn't him that I met. I think I'd have remembered such a—spectacular young man.' She drank some coffee. 'Where did you meet him?'

'At a charity ball, originally. And then we discovered we were neighbours—almost. And it went from there.'

'You can say that again.' Sonia's voice was dry. 'Well, how very convenient, and such a coincidence, too.' She paused. 'And what does Arnold think of him?'

Cory hesitated. 'They haven't met—yet.'

'Is that your choice—or the boyfriend's?'

'Mine,' Cory said shortly. 'And isn't it a little late for *you* to start being protective?'

Sonia looked at her consideringly, then shrugged. 'Maybe you have a point.' She looked at Cory's hand. 'What a beautiful ring. Where did you get it?'

'It was a present,' Cory said quietly. 'From Rome.'

'A love token,' Sonia said brightly. 'How very sweet.' She became brisk again. 'Call me a cab, will you, honey? I'm going over to Arnold's now, before these tiny rooms give me claustrophobia.'

'Give me five minutes to get dressed, and I'll come with you,' Cory offered.

Sonia shuddered. 'I wish you wouldn't talk about getting dressed in five minutes,' she said peevishly. 'I suggest you start paying a little more attention to your appearance—

especially if you want to hang on to a piece of work like Mr d'Angelo. I never let your father see me in the mornings until I'd combed my hair and put on my mascara.'

'I doubt if I'll have time for such niceties,' Cory said lightly. 'Not on a vineyard in Tuscany.'

'Well, you're not there yet,' Sonia said sharply. 'But there's no need for you to come to Arnold's right away. It's going to be quite a reunion after all this time, and we'll have plenty to talk over. So, why don't you take it easy?'

'One of the preferred topics of conversation being myself, no doubt?' Cory's tone was cutting.

Sonia sighed. 'Honey,' she said, 'I may not have made a big success of the role, but I'm still your mother, and, believe it or not, I'm concerned for you. And so is your grandfather—sure you'll be a topic. A major one. So why don't you let us have our discussion, and meet us for lunch at twelve-thirty? We should be all done by then.' She glanced at her watch, and winced. 'My God, this time difference is a killer.'

When she eventually left, in a haze of perfume, Cory sank down on the sofa, curling her legs under her in an unconsciously defensive posture.

Sonia's arrival was a totally unforeseen complication, she thought unhappily. And one she could well have done without.

She'd always known that it wouldn't be easy convincing Gramps that she'd finally met the man she wanted to spend the rest of her life with—especially when she'd known Rome such a short time. Although he of all people should understand, she thought with a sigh. Only it didn't always work out like that.

Still, she'd been sure that she could talk him round. But if he was aligned with her mother…

She shook her head. That was a pretty formidable combination.

Sonia had made it clear she had misgivings about Rome—echoing all Cory's own early doubts, if she was honest.

Why, indeed, should a man like that choose a girl like her?

'Because he loves me,' she said aloud, lifting her head in affirmation. 'Because we love each other.'

But some of the radiance of last night had faded, and, do what she would, she could not summon it back.

She looked down at the amethyst, glowing on her hand.

My talisman, she told herself. And raised it to her lips.

Over in Chelsea, Sonia wasted no time.

'When I got to Cory's apartment today there was a man there,' she said, after the usual greetings and enquiries had been exchanged, and her luggage taken upstairs to the guest suite.

Arnold looked down his nose. 'Suddenly turned prude, my dear? This is the twenty-first century.'

Sonia snorted. 'No, of course I haven't. But how much do you know about this guy?'

'Very little,' Arnold admitted, frowning. 'She's being rather secretive about him.'

'I don't blame her,' Sonia returned. 'If he belonged to me, I'd find a deserted house in a deep forest and chain him to the bed.' She paused. 'He calls himself Rome d'Angelo.'

Arnold thought, then shook his head. 'I haven't heard of him.'

'Then I feel you should make his acquaintance without delay.' Sonia pursed her lips. 'She's wearing a ring.'

'An engagement ring?' He was clearly startled.

'Wrong hand, but what do I know?' Sonia frowned. 'It's a lovely thing—looks antique and expensive—a big amethyst with pearls around it.' She sighed. 'Pearls for tears, they say, but maybe Cory's not superstitious.'

'An amethyst?' Arnold's tone sharpened. 'Are you sure?'

'Those are the mauve stones, aren't they? Why do you ask?'

There was an odd silence, then he said, 'It just seems a strange choice for an engagement ring—if that's what it is. Diamonds are more conventional.'

Sonia leaned back in her chair. 'I don't think,' she said slowly, 'that convention means a great deal to the sexy Mr d'Angelo. I feel we should start making a few discreet enquiries about him.'

Arnold was staring into the distance, eyes narrowed and mouth set grimly.

Lunch in Chelsea was a strained affair. Arnold was silent and preoccupied, and Sonia laughed and talked a little too much.

It was like a dream she'd once had, Cory thought, pushing poached salmon round her plate. She'd found herself on stage with the curtain about to go up—and she was wearing the wrong costume and knew none of her lines.

When coffee was served, Sonia rose from the table, announcing she was off to get a massage and beauty treatment—'Best way to cope with jet lag, honey'—and Cory found herself alone with her grandfather.

There was a silence between them that Cory, for the first time in her life, felt unable to break. She knew that she had to sit and wait for him to speak.

Eventually, he said, 'This man you're seeing—I asked yesterday if you were serious about him. You didn't see fit to mention you were living with him. Why?'

Cory lifted her chin. 'Because we're not actually living together.'

'Ah,' he said. 'You just allow him to use you when the mood takes him. Is that it?'

She stared at him, shocked. 'Gramps—don't. You make it sound so sordid.'

'Perhaps I find it so, Cory. Knowing that my only granddaughter is sharing her body with a man she's apparently known for days, hours and minutes, rather than weeks, months, years.'

She said steadily, 'It's not really such a new thing. We fell in love, just as you did when you first saw Gran. If it had happened now, instead of years ago, you'd be doing the same thing.'

'Don't dare to compare the situations.' His voice was harsh. 'In my day you offered a woman security and respect along with passion.'

He paused. 'What do you really know about this man? Your mother says she now remembers meeting a Steve d'Angelo in Florida some years ago. He was a gambler, a man who lived by his wits and made a living by calculating the weaknesses of others. Are they related?'

'His stepfather.'

'And his real father?'

Cory bit her lip. 'He never knew him.'

'I see,' Arnold said coldly. He looked at her hand. 'I understand he gave you that ring. It's a very unusual design—very distinctive. Do you know how he came by it?'

Cory got to her feet, her face very white. She said, 'Just what are you implying? That Rome stole it?'

'Or won it at cards, perhaps.' There was an odd urgency in his tone.

'Then you're wrong. It's a family ring,' she said huskily. 'Does that satisfy you?'

'A family ring,' he repeated slowly. 'But from which member of the family, I wonder?'

'Does it matter?' Cory shook her head. 'I can't believe I'm taking part in this—interrogation. You've always claimed you wanted me to fall in love. I didn't realise you intended to investigate my lover.'

'You seem to think I'm doing him an injustice.' Arnold seemed to rouse himself, looking at her with eyes that hardly seemed to see her. 'And perhaps I am. But, until we meet, I'm having to rely on hearsay. Maybe you should allow him to speak for himself.'

There was a silence, then she said, 'I love him, Grandfather. I can't live without him.'

'You think that now, child.' There was a note of appeal in his voice. 'But you'll probably fall in and out of love several times before you meet the right man for you.'

She said, 'Would you have got over Gran so easily—and gone on to someone else? I don't think so. And with Rome and I there's no one else involved either.'

There was a wild look in his eyes. 'You don't think so? How can you know?'

'Because I trust him—just as Gran trusted you. You knew she was the only one, and so did she. And I'm your granddaughter, so maybe it's in my genes.'

She went to the door. Turned. 'And please don't call me "child" again. I'm a woman now—Rome's woman.'

His glance was heavy. 'For good or ill?'

She said, 'Yes,' and went out, closing the door behind her.

Arnold Grant sat very still for a moment. Then, moving slowly and stiffly, he reached for the telephone.

CHAPTER TWELVE

'This,' Cory said passionately, 'has to rank as one of the worst days of my life.'

'Thanks,' Rome said drily. 'Shall I get dressed and leave?'

'I'm sorry.' She kissed him repentantly. 'I mean apart from the last couple of hours—which is evening anyway, so it doesn't count.'

I'm relieved to hear it. And I told you not to let your mother get to you, sweetheart. You should have listened.'

'Oh, it wasn't Ma,' Cory said bitterly. 'She cleared out to the beauty parlour and left me to the Spanish Inquisition.' She moved restlessly. 'It was awful. Gramps was like a stranger, staring me down, behaving as if I was on trial—or you were.'

'What did he say?' Rome asked curiously.

'Oh, nothing much. Just that you were a liar, and a con-man, and possibly a thief. Usual stuff.' She shook her head. 'In the end I slammed out of the house. I spent the afternoon in Hyde Park, just walking, trying to clear my head.'

Rome was silent for a moment. 'Darling, I think it's time your grandfather and I had a serious talk.'

'It seems he does, too,' Cory admitted reluctantly. 'When I got home there was a message on the machine. Apparently, he wants us to go to dinner tomorrow night.'

'Did you accept?'

'I haven't replied yet. He doesn't deserve it. Besides, I don't know if I can stand it. More questions over the soup.

Final arguments with the main course. Sentence of death pronounced during dessert.'

'I think we should go,' Rome told her. 'It could be an olive branch.'

Cory pulled a face. 'All the better to beat us with.'

'I really need to see him.' His voice was gentle. 'Get a few things straight.'

'Then I'll tell him yes.' She sighed. 'We didn't have our secret very long, did we?'

'It's not always good,' Rome said, his face suddenly brooding, 'to keep things from people you love. The longer it goes on, the harder they are to explain.'

'You sound very old and wise.' There was sudden laughter in her voice.

'I haven't been very wise at all,' he said. 'Not from the start of all this. As for being old…' The hand that had been curled round the curve of her hip moved without haste and to devastating effect. 'Let's see about that—shall we?'

'Yes,' she managed dry-mouthed. 'Oh, yes, Rome. *Rome…*'

She didn't go to work the following day, and Arnold did not ring to enquire where she was, so it seemed he was not expecting her.

In spite of the harsh words between them, Cory hated being on bad terms with him.

But after tonight, she told herself, everything will be fine.

She put on a new dress for the occasion, a silky jersey in a subtle aubergine shade. And she put her ring on her left hand.

Rome said, 'You look beautiful.'

He was smiling as he looked at her in the mirror, but his face was strained.

'And so do you.' She had never seen him in a formal dark suit before. 'Gramps will be swept off his feet.'

On their way out, she snapped off one of the crimson roses that was still in bud, and tucked it into his buttonhole.

He was on edge all the way to Chelsea, his hands gripping the wheel as if he was drowning.

Cory stole a troubled look at him. 'Rome—are you sure you want to go through with this—seeking his blessing?'

'I've never been so sure of anything.' His voice was husky. 'But, Cory—there's something I should tell you.'

She said, 'I hope this isn't the moment you reveal you're already married. Because Grandfather would not take that in good part. Other than that, we're home and dry.' She paused. 'We're also here.'

As she rang the bell, she said. 'So, what was it you wanted to tell me?'

He shook his head. 'I can't talk to you about it now. I think I should see your grandfather first.' He put his hands on her shoulders. His voice was serious. 'The only thing that matters, Cory, is that I love you. Never lose sight of that—please.'

'Well, it all seems relatively civilised,' she murmured as the housekeeper conducted them to the drawing room. 'No paid assassins lurking. After the way he was talking the other day, I did wonder.'

'He's quite right to be cautious,' Rome said soberly. 'But everything's going to be fine. You'll see.'

And it seemed they had indeed been worrying unnecessarily. When they entered the drawing room Arnold came to meet them, smiling affably as Cory performed the necessary introductions.

As they shook hands, the two men exchanged overtly measuring glances.

'My daughter-in-law I believe you've met,' Arnold said.

'Oh, yes.' Sonia was smiling from one of the sofas. She was elegant in black, with magnificent diamonds in her ears and on her wrists. 'We're quite old friends. I'm glad to see you dress for dinner if not for breakfast, Mr d'Angelo.'

'I haven't invited any other guests to meet you,' Arnold went on. 'I thought we'd have a quiet family party. Sherry?'

'Thank you.' Rome accepted with a smile, but he wasn't fooled. His sixth sense was warning him that the knives were out for him here in this luxurious room, with its wall sconces and brocaded furniture.

He said quietly, 'I hope I can have a private talk with you during the evening, Mr Grant.'

'Oh, there's no need for that,' Arnold said. 'We can say all that needs to be said here, in the open. Among friends.' He handed Rome his sherry. 'I take it there's something you want to ask me? Something of a personal nature?'

Rome's brows drew together sharply, but he kept his voice cool. 'Yes, there is, although I hadn't planned to do it in quite this way.'

'It was to be over the brandy and cigars, perhaps? When I was feeling mellow.' There was a faint smile playing round the older man's mouth. A smile that held neither humour nor warmth. 'Well, say what you came here to say, Mr d'Angelo. I'm listening.'

'Very well.' Rome spoke levelly. 'The truth is, Mr Grant, that Cory and I love each other. I've come to ask formally for your blessing to marry her.'

'The truth?' Arnold said meditatively. 'As in the whole truth—and nothing but the truth?' He shook his head. 'I don't think so.'

'Grandfather,' Cory protested angrily.

'Sit down, my dear.' His voice was marginally kinder. 'I'm afraid I have an unpleasant shock for you. You see, your suitor is not quite what he seems. I'm sure you already know that he's not Italian, but are you aware that d'Angelo isn't his real name—just the one he took from his stepfather?'

'Yes,' Cory said. 'Yes, I am.'

'But did he tell what he is really called—the name he was born to? I think not. Perhaps you'd like to enlighten us now—Mr d'Angelo.'

There was real venom in the older man's voice.

Groaning inwardly, Rome met his gaze, then turned to Cory, who was looking bewildered.

He said gently, 'It's Sansom, *mia cara*. My mother was Sarah Sansom, Matt's younger daughter.' He glanced at Arnold, his mouth hard. 'Is that what you wanted to hear?'

'Part of it.' Arnold nodded. 'And please believe this gives me no pleasure. My grandchild is very dear to me— as of course you know already. I never wanted her to be hurt, but I fear it's unavoidable now.'

The room was overheated, to suit Sonia's taste, but Cory suddenly felt icy cold.

She said, 'I don't understand any of this. What are you talking about?'

'About an illusion,' Arnold said heavily. 'An illusion created by a vengeful man and carried out by his grandson. Your lover was bribed, Cory, to set you up. Matt Sansom gave him a loan for that vineyard of his, and then threatened to foreclose unless he managed to seduce you. And I was supposed to pay him to go away. Isn't that the way of it, Mr Rome Sansom? Wasn't that the unholy bargain you made with that old devil?'

Rome stiffened, but his glance didn't waver. 'Yes.'

'No.' Cory's cry of pain and disbelief pierced the room. 'No, Rome, it's not true. It can't be.'

'Yes,' he said steadily. 'It was true, every word of it, in

the beginning. But not any more. Not for a long time. Not after I fell in love with you. You have to believe that.'

'Believe it?' Her voice broke. 'When you've lied to me from the start? When it was just money—all over again? How can I believe anything about you—now?'

She turned away, her body rigid, covering her face with her hands, and Sonia jumped up, placing a protective arm round her.

'Why don't you go?' she hurled at Rome. 'Why don't you just get out?'

Rome turned back to Arnold Grant. 'I'd intended to tell you all this myself tonight, but not in front of Cory. Not like this. You could have spared her.'

'She has the right to know the kind of man you are. The filthy deception you've practised.'

Rome said quietly, 'You can't call me anything I haven't called myself. But it makes no difference, because the deception stopped a long time ago—and my grandfather knows it. I'm still going to marry Cory—with or without your permission.'

'Over my dead body,' Arnold said with a sneer. 'You'll have to look for another heiress to bale out your sinking vineyard.' His smile was thin. 'You gambled heavily on tonight, I think. You'd won my girl. You hope to do the same with me. To use my affection for her to persuade me to trust you. Only the deck was stacked against you in a way you could never have imagined.'

He walked across the room and opened a door. He said curtly, 'You'd better come in now.'

Matt Sansom walked slowly into the room, leaning on a cane.

Rome stood motionless, his attention totally arrested.

Then he said softly, 'So that was how Mr Grant was so well informed. Congratulations, Grandfather. You've actually managed to surprise me. And had your moment of triumph into the bargain.'

Matt looked at him with contempt. 'Did you really think I'd let the fact that you've gone soft spoil that for me? I wanted to see the look on his damned face when I told him I'd offered my bastard grandson money to seduce his precious girl, and I did.' He laughed hoarsely. 'And it was worth every penny I've got to see all his worst fears confirmed.'

Cory said very quietly, 'Why do you hate me so much, Mr Sansom?'

He swung round, looking for the source of the intervention. She was very white, and there were tears glistening on her eyelashes, but she was in control again, standing straight, her head high. Rome's amethyst glittered on her hand and Matt's eyes went straight to it, and then, sharply, to her face.

He gasped harshly and took a step back, his own face blanching. 'That ring,' he said hoarsely. 'Where did you get it?'

'Aunt Kit gave it to me,' Rome said. 'For the woman I love.'

'She had no right.' Matt was ashen, fighting for control. 'I gave that ring to my Elizabeth.'

'And she gave it back,' Rome said quietly. 'When she decided to marry someone else.'

'It was the ring that gave you away,' Arnold said grimly. 'Beth was wearing it when I met her, and I've never forgotten it. As soon as I saw it I guessed who was behind all this.' He sent Matt a look of frank loathing. 'And he was only too happy to confirm it.'

'But he misjudged his man. You can tell who you damn well please about this filthy plot of yours—if you dare— but you'll not see a penny of my money. And you'll never have anything to do with my granddaughter again. She's going to Miami with her mother.'

Rome was looking at Matt, too. He said slowly, 'You gave the ring to your wife—to my grandmother—but she hated it, didn't she? Because she guessed it had belonged to someone else—someone you'd loved in a way you'd never cared for her.'

'There was never anyone else in the world for me.' Matt's voice cracked. He took a step forward, putting out a shaking hand to where Cory stood, pale and straight in her aubergine dress. 'It could be her,' he muttered. 'Her eyes—her gentle mouth. Beth—oh, my Beth...'

'No,' Rome said, his voice like ice. 'My Cory—the girl I love.'

'You dare to say that?' Arnold almost exploded. 'After what you've done. The way you've treated her.'

'I'm not proud of the way I've behaved,' Rome said curtly. 'When I first saw her I was obeying instructions, and I admit it. But after that I was following my heart, because, with her, I put out my hand and touched paradise.'

He threw his head back. 'I agreed to do what my grand-father wanted in order to keep Montedoro, because it was all that mattered to me then. But everything's changed now. Cory changed it. She means more to me than a thousand Montedoros, and she always will, because my life is empty without her.'

He looked at Arnold. 'I came here tonight in good faith, to ask you for her. To announce our engagement. In spite of everything, I still want to do that.'

Matt sank heavily on to a chair. He said, 'Well, you can forget that. It's over—finished with. You'll get nothing from him—and when I'm done with you you'll hardly be able to support yourself, let alone a wife.' He laughed again, the sound grating. 'I'll strip you of everything.

You'll regret the day that you crossed me.' He glared round. 'You'll all be sorry, damn you.'

Cory shook off her mother's restraining hand and walked across the room. She faced Rome.

She said, 'Is this what you were trying to say in the car?'

He met her gaze unflinchingly. 'Yes. But I thought it would be better to confess my real identity to your grandfather first. Try and explain. Only, I was pre-empted.'

Her eyes were grave. Questioning. 'Why didn't you tell me before? In Suffolk, or when we came back?'

He said huskily, 'Ironically, because I was afraid I'd lose you. And I couldn't bear it. Couldn't take the risk. And now I've ruined everything.'

She drew a deep breath. 'And the rest of it—is that true? Can your grandfather really take Montedoro away from you?'

Rome put out a hand and gently brushed a tearstain from her cheek. 'He can try.'

She nodded. Her voice was quiet. 'Do you love me?'

'Cory,' Sonia almost shrieked. 'The guy set you up. Tried to rip off your grandfather. He'll tell you anything because he's broke and you're an heiress. Where's your pride?' Her tone became cajoling. 'Forget him, honey, and walk away. If you don't want to go to Miami, I'll take you to the Bahamas and show you such a good time. In a month, I guarantee you won't give him a second thought.'

Cory's tired mouth smiled faintly. 'Unfortunately, I don't think I'm that shallow.' She looked into Rome's eyes. 'Please answer me.'

'Yes,' he said roughly. 'Yes, I love you, heart of my heart, and I always will. You're part of me, and nothing can change that. And I want to go on my knees and beg you to forgive me. Only that's impossible now. We can never be together, because for the rest of your life you might look at me and wonder if your mother was right.'

'That will never happen anyway.' Arnold spoke roughly. 'Because I'm telling you now that if she dares to go with you—if she even gives you a second glance—I'll change my will and leave the whole lot to charity. She'll get nothing. See how she likes that. And see how long true love lasts at that rate.' And he laughed scornfully, triumphantly.

Sonia shrieked faintly, and fell back on the sofa.

There was a long tingling silence, then Rome took Cory's hands in his. He said softly, almost wonderingly, 'My God, *carissima*. Do you realise what he's just said? He's set us free. They both have. They've taken everything and left us with each other.'

His voice became urgent. 'Leave with me now, my sweetest love. Come with me. Because if you stay, they'll have won.' He looked into her eyes, deeply, gravely. 'These bigoted, greedy, selfish old men will have won. And the precious thing we've been building together will be lost for ever.'

His hands tightened round hers. 'Don't let that happen, *mi amore*. Leave them to their plots, and their hating, and their precious millions. I'll make a life for you, if not at Montedoro then somewhere else. Anywhere as long as it's with you. I'll dig ditches if I have to. Anything.'

Cory's face was suddenly transfigured, her eyes luminous.

He remembered how he'd thought once that she was enclosed in an invisible circle. Now, somehow, he'd stepped over the perimeter, and the circle held him, too. He was at peace as never before, and could have wept with gratitude and relief.

She said, 'Yes, Rome. I'll come with you.' And went

into his arms, simply and directly, lifting her mouth for his kiss.

'Cory,' Sonia moaned. 'You're crazy. Arnold's not kidding—he means it. And don't look to me to bail you out.'

Cory ignored her. She said, 'But, Rome, you mustn't lose Montedoro. You can't. It's your whole life.'

He said, 'Not any more, *carissima*. You've taken its place. But we'll fight together to keep it, if that's what you want.'

Cory turned in his arms to look at them all. There was a militant sparkle in her eyes, and a new crispness in her voice.

'No one's going to take Montedoro,' she said. 'Because my grandmother left me some money and we'll use that to save it—'

'A nest egg,' Arnold interrupted dismissively. 'A drop in the ocean. It won't cover the kind of debt he's in, so pull yourself together, because I wasn't joking.'

'Nor am I,' Cory said. 'The original legacy wasn't that big, I agree, but it's grown in the past year or so.' She looked steadily back at Arnold. 'Remember my amusing little hobby? Well, I didn't just watch share prices. I started investing in the stock market—buying and selling on my own account. I even found I was good at it. And I've certainly made enough to repay the loan on Montedoro. With interest.'

'Cory *mia*.' Rome's voice was husky as he framed her face in his hands. 'I can't take your money. Surely you must see that.'

'It's our money,' she said, and smiled into his eyes. 'For our marriage. Our life. Our children. And you must take it, my love, if you want me, because all my worldly goods go with me. That's the deal. And we're going to make great wine, because you know how.'

Her voice deepened passionately. 'Oh, Rome don't you understand? If you refuse now, then they'll still have won, but in a different way. Their hate will have won, and not our love. Are you really going to let that happen?'

He said very softly, 'My darling—my precious sweet.' He drew her into his arms, resting his cheek against her hair. 'Together we'll make the finest wine in Tuscany. And the loveliest babies.'

'Cory.' Arnold held out a shaking hand. His face was suddenly gaunt—uncertain. 'You can't do this. You haven't thought it through. You can't leave me.'

Cory looked at him. She said sadly, 'You wanted me to hate Rome, but you're the one I'll find it hard to forgive, Gramps. Can you imagine what Gran would have said if she could have heard you threatening me?'

She shook her head. 'You must do as you wish with the money. I don't want to be an heiress. I never did. And with or without it I'm going to have a life with the man I love.

'As for you—' she turned on Matt '—you lost your daughter, and now you're losing your only grandson. Both of you are going to be lonely and miserable, and you deserve it. You've wasted years of your life in hating each other, and in the end hatred's all you'll have left. Because Rome and I are going—leaving you all behind if we have to.'

There was a silence, then Arnold said with difficulty, 'Cory, you're very dear to me, and I can't bear this. Is there any way I can make amends?'

She said gently, 'Not while you hate Matt Sansom more than you love me. Nor while you won't accept my husband.'

Rome spoke, his voice cool and very clear. He said, 'This feud has got to end if you want to see us again—if you want to hold your great-grandchildren. But that's your decision. Because we've made ours.'

He took Cory's hands and lifted them to his lips. *'Mia bella,'* he said softly. 'My lady. My dear love. Let's go home.'

Cory smiled up into his eyes. She said tenderly, 'Together—and for ever.'

They had reached the door when Matt's voice reached them, halting and barely recognisable. He said, 'Rome—boy—is—is it too late?'

And Sonia said miserably, 'Cory, honey…' then trailed off into silence.

Hand in hand, they turned and looked at the three anxious, unhappy faces watching them go.

There was a pause, then Rome said, 'You know where to find us. And we'll be waiting.' He paused, then added softly, 'See you at Montedoro.'

And he and Cory walked together out of the room, and into the hopeful promise of the night.

THE SWEETEST REVENGE

by

Emma Darcy

Initially a French/ English teacher, **Emma Darcy** changed careers to computer programming before marriage and motherhood settled her into a community life. Creative urges were channelled into oil-painting, pottery, designing and overseeing the construction and decorating of two homes, all in the midst of keeping up with three lively sons and the busy social life of her businessman husband, Frank. Very much a people person, and always interested in relationships, she finds the world of romance fiction a happy one and the challenge of creating her own cast of characters very addictive.

Don't miss Emma Darcy's fabulous brand new novel *The Secret Baby Revenge*. Out in July 2006 from Mills & Boon Modern Romance™.

CHAPTER ONE

MONDAY morning, and as usual, the staff of Multi-Media Promotions was abuzz with the swapping of weekend news before everyone settled down to work. Nick Armstrong exchanged only brief greetings as he strode to his private office, trailed by his friend and business partner, Leon Webster. The moment his door was shut, he released his pent-up anger to the one person who *should* understand his situation.

'You know what Tanya said to me on Saturday, after I'd called off our planned outing *once again?*' he exploded.

'Something undoubtedly designed to cut you off at the knees,' came the voice of experience.

Nick grimaced, remembering that Leon had just been through a nasty break-up with a live-in girlfriend. 'She said what I really wanted was a toy doll whose feelings wouldn't be hurt from being left on a shelf until I had time for playing.'

'Sounds good! A toy doll wouldn't nag.'

'Better still, a fairy princess doll...'

'Yep. Beautiful, glamorous, long blond hair, sparkling eyes, a smile to warm a man's heart...'

'...with a magic wand that would give me the energy to be the kind of lover that even a plastic toy would expect of a man.'

'Oooh… we're getting into kinky stuff here.'

'Leon, this is serious. And we are going to have a serious discussion.'

Eyebrows lifted mockingly. 'About women?'

'About business.' Nick glowered at his friend as he rounded the desk and dropped into his chair. 'Take a seat. And wipe that smirk off your face. This is deadly serious.'

'The man is wounded,' Leon muttered, settling into a chair with a mournful expression. Seeing Nick's irritation, he made an effort to present a suitably serious countenance.

It was dangerous to rile Nick in this mood. He was the darkly brooding type—a creative genius and a computer whiz from way back—and he often needed lightening up, but this was not the moment, Leon decided.

They were opposites in many ways. Even in looks. Nick—tall, black-haired, blue-eyed, had a face and body that were stamped with masculine strength, both physical and mental. Oddly enough, Leon never felt diminished by him. While he himself was only average height and his colouring wasn't so dramatic, having fairish brown hair and brown eyes, he had the gift of the gab and could attract any woman he wanted.

They made a great team—the design king and the salesman—and Leon was not about to allow anything to disturb it. Besides which, his partner's mental well-being was of paramount importance to their success.

'Business!' Nick tapped the desk with a strong index finger for emphasis. 'You know how much the Internet stuff has taken off, Leon. I'm snowed under. I need two more graphic designers to help take the load.'

'That will cut into our profits,' he cautioned.

'I need a life, too,' Nick bit out.

Leon rolled his eyes. 'Just because Tanya got in a snit over not getting your undivided attention? She doesn't own you, Nick, and take it from me...'

Blue lightning flashed straight back at him. 'I take a lot from you, Leon. You're a fantastic salesman and we're doing great, but I will not work to this pressure anymore.'

Hands instantly lifted into a truce position. 'Okay, okay,' he soothed. 'So long as this is *you* talking and not Tanya. You always said if we worked like dogs until we're thirty...'

'I'm thirty next week. Both of us pocketed over five million dollars last year...'

'And may well pocket twice that this year.'

'But we've paid a price for it. You lost Liz...'

'There you go, bringing women into it...'

'Damn it, Leon! I want a life beyond work, even if you don't. I'm thirty next week. Enough's enough. I need more staff.'

'Okay, okay. I'll ask around. Head-hunt someone good for you.'

Nick held up two fingers.

Leon sighed. Two more salaries to pay. 'So we'll get someone good and one out of design school to be trained. How's that?'

'Cheapskate.'

'Not at all. Common sense to train them our way. You know that, Nick.'

Nick privately conceded the point, but was not about to relax his stance on the issue. 'Get right onto it, Leon. And don't be giving me any delay tactics. I don't care what it costs. It will cost a damned sight more if I reach burnout.'

'Don't mention that word!' Horror-struck, Leon jackknifed from his chair. 'Your wish is my command, dear boy. I shall go forth this moment and head-hunt.'

'A trainee, as well.'

'No problem. They'll be storming the portals to get in here.' He strode to the door and paused, looking back with cynical eyes. 'I bet Tanya is still coming to your birthday bash. She likes what our money can buy. Don't forget that when she turns the screws again.'

'Business, Leon,' Nick tersely reminded him, and he went.

On edge, disgruntled with his world, Nick turned to his computer, switched it on, and tried to settle himself to work. But Leon's words stuck in his mind. The flaming row he'd had with Tanya had ended with her saying that the party would be his last chance with her. If he hadn't made some move to reorganise his life…

His lips thinned. She'd gone too far, expecting him to order his life to suit her. It wasn't as if he was being unfaithful, taking out other women on the side.

And she certainly didn't mind him spending the big money he earned, always asking him to take her to the most fashionable restaurants and get the best seats at the live shows she wanted to see. Leon was right about her suckering him for all he could give.

Not that it was an overly disturbing factor. What was money for, anyway, if not to buy life's pleasures? Except Tanya wasn't delivering much in the way of pleasure herself. In fact, she *was* becoming an unreasonable nag, picking fights at the end of the night which inevitably turned him off wanting to have sex with her. It wasn't so much energy he lacked, but desire.

His last chance…

He had a good mind to finish it before the party, which of course she didn't want to miss. Who would? Leon had organised a marquee on Observatory Hill overlooking Sydney Harbour, a hot jazz band, top caterers. All the young successful men who were making their mark in business would be there for her to cast her eyes over.

Let her, Nick thought grimly.

Maybe he would cast his eyes around, too. There had to be someone who'd be more amenable to his needs… who wouldn't mind occupying her own shelf while he dealt with the stimulating challenge of business. He could certainly do without an unreasonable nag.

Leon headed for his own private office, hoping he'd just spiked Tanya's guns with that last comment—

selfish trouble-making bitch. She pumped Nick for all
he was worth and never gave anything back, as far
as Leon could see. Maybe he should rope in some hot
party girls for Nick's birthday bash, show him there
were many more fish in the sea, fish that would only
be too happy to swim with him without kicking up a
storm.

Better still….

Leon smiled.

Why not a fairy princess doll? With a magic wand
that would turn Tanya Wells into an ugly croaking
frog.

The smile broadened to a gleeful grin.

'*Party Poppers,*' Sue Olsen announced brightly, tucking the telephone receiver on her shoulder as she
reached for pad and pen, hopeful of a lucrative booking. 'How may we pop for you?'

'You supply acts for birthday parties?' a male voice
answered.

'Yes, indeed, sir. What do you have in mind? We
have The Singing Sunflowers, The Cuddly Animal
Farm, The Jellybean…'

'I want a fairy princess with a magic wand to sing
"Happy Birthday" and sprinkle some sparkle
around,' came the decisive demand.

Sue grinned at her friend and business partner,
Barbie Lamb, who still felt ragged from yesterday's
clown act for thirty screaming five-year-olds. 'We
have the perfect fairy princess for you,' she answered
with proud confidence.

Barbie rolled tired eyes at Sue. Clearly she needed a sprinkle of magic dust herself to raise some enthusiasm this morning. Four children's parties over the weekend was a heavy schedule and a huge energy-sucker. On the bright side, the fairy princess job would be a breeze for her, much easier to carry off than the clown act.

'What date are we looking at?' Sue inquired of the caller.

'I want to be sure of the goods first,' came the wary reply. 'Perfect, you said. I need beautiful…'

'Absolutely beautiful,' Sue assured him, grinning at Barbie.

'Long blond hair? All loose…like flowing around her shoulders?'

'That describes her hair exactly.'

'It's not a wig? A wig won't do.'

'I promise you it's not a wig.'

'Fine. What about her smile? Good teeth? A big warm smile?'

'A dazzling smile. Any dentist would be proud of her.'

'Dazzling, huh? Well, that fits the bill so far. How tall is she?'

'Tall?' Sue frowned over this requirement.

'I don't want a midget. I mean, we're not talking a dressed-up kid here, are we?'

'No. Our fairy princess is a beautiful young woman, taller than average but not quite model height.'

Barbie pulled a face, distorting her lovely features,

baring her teeth and raking out her hair to produce her Wicked Witch of the West look. Sue poked out her tongue.

'Great!' her caller enthused. 'This is sounding good. Just one more question. How does her figure rate?'

'I beg your pardon?'

'Her figure. You know…curves in the right places?'

'Uh-huh,' Sue said non-committally, waiting to see how far he would go on this contentious point.

'A skinny rake won't do,' he stated emphatically. 'If she's got sexy curves, that's the ticket.'

'Hmm…' *Sexy* set off alarm bells in Sue's mind and raised a nasty suspicion. They did occasionally get weirdo calls. Time to nail this one down. 'Is this booking for a children's party, sir?'

'No. No kids at *this* party.'

'Would this happen to be a bucks' night?' Sue asked sweetly, ready to pour acid on the idea.

'Believe me. Weddings are not in the air,' he answered sardonically. 'This is a big party for my friend's thirtieth birthday and I want this act as a special surprise for him.'

'Will there be women as well as men in attendance?'

'There most certainly will. You could say the bachelors and spinsters of the social-climbing crème of Sydney society will be there. Nothing secret or closeted about this party, I assure you,' he added, catching the wary drift of her questions. 'Very public. It's to be held in a marquee on Observatory Hill.'

'I see.' Opportunity leapt to the fore in Sue's thinking. A bunch of eligible bachelors on the loose was an attractive proposition. 'Well, I would have to insist on accompanying my fairy princess to ensure she isn't subjected to any...shall we say, indignities?'

'No problem. You're welcome to join in the party afterwards,' he offered, striking precisely the bargain Sue had been angling for. 'I take it she *does* look sexy,' he added, wanting confirmation.

Caution dictated Sue's reply. 'Her figure is definitely curvy in all the right proportions. But I wouldn't want anyone to get any wrong ideas about why she's there. This is simply a fairy princess appearance to sing "Happy Birthday." Correct?'

'Spot-on. Oh! Forgot to ask. Can she sing? I mean...*really* sing.'

'She has toured the country as a professional entertainer. Good enough?'

'Fabulous!'

This is going to cost you big, Mister, Sue decided, as she proceeded to get party details and settle on the fee, which she enterprisingly quadrupled for both herself and Barbie since it was an after-hours' engagement...plus danger money. Not that she thought there was any real danger in it but she felt such a consideration was easily justified.

Barbie was stunned at the outrageous fee Sue was demanding for this gig. No problem about making a profit next week, she thought gratefully. Ever since they'd started *Party Poppers,* they'd been battling to make ends meet, but at least it brought in more regular work than their Country and Western act, and they were settled back in Sydney. Travelling around the country-club circuit had been fun but not exactly financially rewarding.

However, listening to Sue talking on the phone, it was clear the engagement she was arranging was not about entertaining children at all. It sounded somewhat dodgy. Admittedly running a car and paying the rent on this two-bedroom apartment in Ryde, not to mention buying food and paying other bills, meant they couldn't look a gift-horse in the mouth, but...

The telephone receiver clattered down. 'Got it!' Sue cried triumphantly, dollar signs sparkling in her wickedly gleeful green eyes. She could do a great pixie or Tinkerbell with her short, ragamuffin red hair and her slim, rather petite figure, and she was definitely projecting a high degree of mischief right now.

'Got what exactly?' Barbie demanded warily.

'He didn't even hesitate over the money. Shows he's really loaded and doesn't mind spending. I just *love* men like that,' Sue bubbled on.

'Sure he's not a dirty old man?'

Sue grinned. 'Could be a dirty young man. Definitely young, thirtyish, and a bachelor. Co-owner of Multi-Media Promotions.' She cocked her head on one side. 'Maybe I could ask him to set up a website for us. Get clients from the Internet.'

'We haven't even got a computer,' Barbie dryly

reminded her. Sue's mind invariably soared with wild dreams and pulling her feet back onto the ground was often a difficult task.

She shrugged. 'Just thinking ahead. This is really good for us, Barbie. All that lovely money and opportunity plus.'

'When you get your head out of the clouds with silver lining, would you mind spelling out what this is all about?'

She did, virtually dancing around their small living room in excitement as she laid out the party details and the invitation to stay on and mix with the crème of Sydney bachelors. Which Barbie had to concede, did sound interesting, given their current dearth of social life.

'What's this guy's name? The one who booked my fairy princess act,' she asked, wondering if there was some way of checking out his *bona fides* before the night.

'Leon Webster.'

It struck a nerve and the twang was highly unpleasant. 'Leon…' Hadn't Nick Armstrong had a friend of that name, a guy full of slick patter whom he'd linked up with in his university years? Compelled to know for sure, she asked, 'And his partner's name? The birthday boy?'

'Nick Armstrong.' Sue broke into mad song. 'Happy birthday, dear Nick. Happy birthday, dear Nick….'

'Stop it!' Barbie yelled, rising from her chair with

clenched fists, so violent was the rush of emotion *that name* had stirred.

Sue stopped dead, gawking at her as though she were mad. 'What's the matter?'

As quickly as shock had drained the blood from her face, the memory of the worst hurt and humiliation of her life poured heat back into it. 'Don't you remember?'

'Remember what?' Obvious bewilderment.

Above flaming cheeks Barbie's silver-grey eyes turned to icy daggers as *she* remembered the man who'd broken her heart into irrecoverable little pieces. 'Nine years ago I sang at Nick Armstrong's twenty-first birthday party.'

Sue still looked non-plussed. 'You did?'

'Yes, I did. And I poured it all out to you at the time…how he…' She bit off the wretched recollection and faced Sue with blazing resolve. 'I will never…ever…sing for him again!'

'But…uh-oh!' The memory finally caught up with her. She grimaced. 'The guy you had the big crush on when we were schoolkids.'

'I was sixteen!' Barbie's voice shook with the violence of feeling the memory stirred.

She'd *loved* Nick Armstrong with all she was, and he'd totally belittled that love by preferring what a sexy tart with a flash car could give him. Which undoubtedly proved he wasn't the person she'd believed he was, but even telling herself he had to be a shallow rat to be seduced by such superficial assets, did not stop her from feeling utterly crushed.

'A lot of water under the bridge since then, Barbie,' Sue pleaded.

True, yet she'd carried that deep misery with her all the way. No other man had even scratched the surface of what she'd once felt for Nick Armstrong. He'd blighted her faith in love and had probably blighted her belief in dreams, too.

'It's only a ten-minute act,' Sue argued. 'It will put us well in the black financially.' Her hands lifted in appeal. 'He probably won't even recognise you. You had braces on your teeth then. Your hair was short and much fairer, almost white...'

Yes, white and crinkly like a baby lamb's coat. *Baa-Baa* Lamb was what Nick's friends had called her in those days, teasing her for following them around. She'd hated it.

'You wore glasses instead of contacts,' Sue rattled on. 'And well...you were a skinny rake when we were teenagers. You're much more mature in your looks now.'

'That's not the point,' she flared. 'I won't sing for *him*. You can if you want, Sue.'

'Oh, ycah...likc I'm blond and beautiful and sexy. Come on, Barbie, the fairy princess act is yours, not mine. Besides which, I promised Leon Webster no wig.'

'Cancel then. Let him find someone else.'

'And lose all that lovely money? Not to mention the chance to rub elbows—and possibly more—with guys on the rise?' She shook her head and advanced on Barbie, the glint of determined battle in her eyes.

'Best for you to sit down, calm down, and think reasonably about this. If the thought of Nick Armstrong can hurt you so much after nine years…you've got a real problem, and it's time you faced it and got over it.'

Barbie sat down, not wanting to fight with her friend but mutinously resolved on sticking to her guns. She would not sing for Nick Armstrong. Never!

'Remember the other side of our business—*Drop Dead Deliveries?*' Sue prompted as she propped herself on the large padded armrest of the chair.

The idea of someone delivering a bunch of dead roses to a party who had injured them had appealed to quite a few clients. It was a relatively harmless outlet for feelings of frustration and anger, a *healthy* outlet, Sue had argued, when Barbie had voiced doubts. At least it stopped people doing worse and gave them the satisfaction of doing *something* instead of just being a victim. Which was probably true.

Nevertheless, Barbie preferred to pass on those jobs to Sue who liked doing them. She didn't. And delivering wilted flowers to Nick Armstrong to demonstrate what she thought of him and his actions was no answer. She wanted no contact with him at all.

'Forget it, Sue. I'd rather face a tiger snake, and you know how I feel about snakes.'

With an expressive shudder, Barbie leaned the other way, resting her elbow on the other armrest and adopting an air of unwearable-down patience. Her friend could rail at her as much as she liked, but on this issue, she would not be moved.

'Forget the dead roses. That's not what I've got in mind,' Sue assured her.

'Then why bring it up?'

'Because there's nothing like a bit of revenge when someone's done the dirty on you,' Sue went on, beginning to wax lyrical with their own advertising copy. 'Having the last laugh is wonderful. You can then get on with your life, knowing you squared the ledger. Clean slate.'

Barbie rolled exasperated eyes at her.

It didn't stop Sue.

'Revenge *is* sweet,' she declared with relish, her eyes beginning to sparkle again as she spread out her hands like a magician about to perform a marvellous illusion. 'Now imagine this, Barbie…'

CHAPTER TWO

BARBIE was literally trembling, her nerves a total jangle as she waited to make her entrance. She shouldn't have let Sue talk her into this. Somehow her friend had plumbed a well of pride, stirring it to the point where Barbie had actually thought that seeing the stunned look on Nick Armstrong's face might mend the scars on her heart. Especially when she sprinkled stardust over him, turning him into *the child,* with her being *the adult,* falsely smiling at him.

Sweet revenge, Sue called it, but right now Barbie seriously doubted that anything about this gig could turn out sweet. She would hate it if Nick Armstrong didn't recognise and remember her and she would hate it if he did. And it was useless to even try to pretend *she* had forgotten him.

Nevertheless, she was here, outside the party marquee on Observatory Hill, and it was too late to call off the promised performance. Someone inside was making a speech—Leon Webster?—to bursts of appreciative laughter and occasional guffaws. About a hundred guests, dressed in very trendy evening gear, Sue had reported, definitely a moneyed crowd.

Since the sides of the marquee were clear plastic for the guests to have an unimpeded view of the harbour and its spectacular coathanger bridge, as well as the myriad night lights of North Sydney, Barbie was standing out of sight behind their car while Sue stood at the entrance, watching proceedings until the vital moment came.

At least she could make a fast getaway, Barbie consoled herself, with the car so close by. Ten minutes— just ten minutes—of being a fairy princess and she could be out of here. Sue, of course, didn't want to leave. She was all dressed up to party in a slinky green satin slip dress—a very sexy pixie tonight—but she'd promised she would find her own way home if Barbie wanted to take off.

A burst of applause made her heart start skittering. Sue held up her hand, the signal to get ready. Barbie briefly closed her eyes and prayed that her wings wouldn't fall off, that the long train of her skirt wouldn't catch on anything, that her vocal cords wouldn't collapse on her, that the stardust mechanism on her wand would work without a hitch. One perfect performance, she pleaded, for this one night.

Leon Webster grinned around at his audience as the applause for his speech died down. 'Please...hold your seats, everyone. We have a special surprise coming up for Nick, just to add a little bit of magic to the big 3-0 milestone.'

He gestured an over-to-you to the bandleader and stepped off the podium, having stirred a buzz of speculation around the tables. Nick watched his friend striding across the dance floor to their table, a slight swagger to his gait. Leon was certainly in top form tonight. He'd pulled off a hugely entertaining speech and now he was about to pull something else out of his hat of amusing tricks.

Leon was a great party guy, Nick reflected, smiling at the high-octane energy still radiating from him as he dropped into his chair at their table. Over the years they'd had a lot of fun together—all through university, setting up the business and running it. Long-time friends and always would be, Nick thought, knowing each other probably better than any women in their lives ever would.

The band started playing something he didn't recognise until the clarinetist came in with the melody. Then Nick burst out laughing at Leon. '*"Somewhere Over the Rainbow"?*'

'The pot of gold is coming, man.'

'A bit childish, isn't it, Leon?' Tanya sniped.

Nick gritted his teeth, biting down on the urge to tell Tanya to take a hike. She'd been in a picky mood all evening—criticising everything—and very soon now he was going to advise her to join another table.

Leon gave her a smile that smacked of sweet satisfaction. 'I'm giving Nick a touch of romance, Tanya. He needs it.'

Nick felt Tanya bristle and braced himself for another snide sling off at him. The surprised exclamations of 'Oh, look!' and 'Wow!' from other guests came as welcome relief, drawing their attention to where everyone else was turning. Swivelling around in his chair, Nick was initially hit with stunned disbelief.

A gorgeous glittering blonde with gossamer wings?

Then he took in the total image and barely stifled a glorious bubble of laughter. Leon—with undoubtedly the most wickedly Machiavellian pleasure—had got him a fairy princess with a magic wand! Tanya, of course, would not appreciate the joke, but Nick no longer cared what Tanya thought. Or did. In fact, if a wave of that wand could make her disappear, he'd have no objection at all.

He smiled at the fairy princess. He wouldn't be leaving *her* on a shelf for long if he had her in his keeping, and he wouldn't need any magic to spark off desire, either. She was the best-looking fantasy he'd even seen in the flesh.

And what flesh!

The gauzy silver evening dress shimmered around hourglass curves and the clingy fabric clearly revealed there was no artful underwear involved in creating the sexy effect. This was all living, breathing *woman,* so perfect she could have emerged from the pages of a fairytale.

Her lovely face was made even more luminous by a smile that could have made gooey mush out of a stone heart and eyes that sparkled through a sprinkling of stardust. A delicate diamanté tiara crowned a long rippling flow of silky blond hair which looked all the more beautiful, framed by the wings with their fine network of silver spokes and loops.

A princess indeed, Nick thought, and hoped she would grant his wish for her to stay on at the party so they could work some magic together.

* * *

So far, so good, Barbie told herself, smiling so hard her face ached. She'd made it up the aisle between the tables from the entrance to the dance floor without a falter or mishap. Her *surprise* appearance was certainly coming off as a surprise and she was intensely grateful that the response from the guests was positive—no cat-calling or anything off-putting, just a buzz of wonder and appreciation and a heightened sense of anticipation for what would happen next.

She spotted Nick Armstrong as she stepped onto the dance floor. Leon had told Sue that he and the birthday boy would be at the table directly opposite where the band was set up, and there they both were, Leon emphatically pointing at Nick to identify him as the guest of honour.

Barbie nodded to show she understood. Nick was happily smiling at her, looking even more handsome than she remembered him, a dark blue shirt enhancing his dark colouring and heightening the vivid blue of his eyes…eyes that were gobbling her up as though she were everything his heart could desire.

For a moment, *her* heart leapt with treacherous joy… Nick loving the image of her. Then her mind savagely kicked in—*lust, not love, you fool.* He'd probably have the same look for a curvaceous bikini girl popping out of a birthday cake.

Her gaze slid briefly to the woman sitting next to him—masses of black hair in a tousled mane, pouty red lips and a red dress with a décolletage that had undoubtedly attracted him—out of the same mould as the scarlet tart he'd preferred to *true love* on his twenty-first birthday.

Barbie hated her on sight. And quite clearly, the woman was making no bones about hating her right back. The fairy princess for Nick was not going down at all well with her.

Unaccountably a sweet sense of satisfaction swept through Barbie. She bestowed an especially warm smile on Nick before turning to walk to the podium where the microphone awaited. Let him lust after her instead of his black-haired bed-pet, she thought wickedly, and put a more seductive sway into her hips to help him focus his attention where she wanted it.

Sue was right about revenge. It would be balm to her wounded soul if Nick ended up panting after her tonight. Of course, it would mean he *was* a shallow rat, but proving that beyond a doubt might help to finally put him behind her. And then she could crush him and walk away. Walk away forever!

She timed her arrival at the podium to the last chords of 'Somewhere Over the Rainbow.' The musicians were grinning at her, thoroughly enjoying the effectiveness of her appearance. The bandleader winked his approval and another wicked idea slid into her mind.

'Remember Marilyn Monroe singing ''Happy Birthday'' to the president?' she whispered.

He nodded, his eyes twinkling with mischief.

'I want that tempo. Okay?'

'You got it, babe.'

She took the microphone and swallowed a couple

of times to moisten her throat. One of her talents was doing a good mimic. She hoped she could pull this one off tonight. It was worth trying, anyway, she boldly reasoned, even if her voice did waver off the note. If it was sexiness that turned Nick Armstrong on, she'd pour it out at him.

The audience settled and hushed. Sue gave her a thumbs up sign from where she still stood at the entrance to the marquee. Leon Webster leaned forward, saying something to Nick at their table. The black-haired sexpot looked furious. Nick flashed a grin at his friend, ignored the woman beside him, turning his back to her as he concentrated his attention on the fairy princess about to sing for him. Not polite attention, Barbie noted triumphantly. Wolfish attention!

The band struck up a vibrant opening chord. Barbie took a deep breath and lifted the microphone close to her mouth so she could purr into it.

'Ha…ppy birth…day…' another big breath '…dear… Nick…'

A ripple of amusement ran around the marquee. It was pure over-the-top candied honey. Nick tilted his head back in delight, a low chuckle emerging from his throat…music to Barbie's ears. He was captivated all right.

She repeated the line, putting a huskier edge on her voice. The band paused for her until the appreciative laughter died down, picking up again as she started the third 'Happy Birthday', soaring with her as she poured more volume into the high note, then dropping softly to the 'Dear Ni…ick,' into which she pumped a load of seductive come-on.

He was not the least bit embarrassed by it. His head was cocked slightly to one side, as though bewitched and bemused, wanting more.

Barbie gave it to him, drawing out the last line and loading it with sensual innuendo as she sang '…to…you-ou-ou,' her lips rounded in a suggestive oval, sending a long, long, visual kiss.

The crowd in the marquee erupted then, guys standing up on chairs, clapping and hooting and whistling, the women laughing and cheering. Leon Webster jumped to his feet, arms up in the air, drinking in the credit of being a magnificent impresario to have brought this off.

But Nick didn't even glance at his friend. Or at his rollicking guests. His gaze was burning up a line that linked him straight to his fairy princess, and Barbie didn't feel her face ache at all as she smiled some sizzling heat right back at him. She replaced the microphone on its stand and stepped down from the podium, all primed for the final part of her act.

'Everybody join in singing now,' Leon shouted, swinging around and waving up more enthusiasm.

The band broke into a more jolly rendition of 'Happy Birthday' and everyone who wasn't already standing, rose to give loud voice in accolade to the one man who remained seated. Hands slid over his shoulders as Barbie walked towards him, her wand benevolently raised—hands with long red nails, claiming jealous possession.

If Nick felt them he showed no sign of it. No appeasing smile was flashed at the woman behind him. His gaze remained fixed on the princess approaching him, feasting on every physical facet of the illusion.

Barbie feasted on the sense of power this gave her. It was more exhilarating than any applause she had ever received for entertaining people. This was real woman-power and she was holding it over the one man in the world she most wanted to hold it over... Nick Armstrong.

Her stomach was contracting in spasms of delight. Her breasts seemed to thrust themselves out more, peaking and tingling. Her hips rolled in voluptuous provocation, her thighs sliding sensuously against each other with every step she took towards him. She was intensely conscious of every part of her femininity, as though it had not only been awakened to a new level of awareness, but aroused to fever-pitch and highly primitive immediacy.

Nick was facing her, still seated, but with his face upturned when she stopped in front of him, barely a step away. It was a miracle she remembered what had to be done with the wand. His eyes were locked on hers, transmitting a blazing quest for more knowledge of her, intimate knowledge of her, and the desire to get it.

'Make a wish,' she invited huskily, smiling as she lifted the wand over his head and pressed the button on the silver rod, opening the star at the end of it to release a shower of silver glitter. It speckled his hair, his nose, his cheeks, and the brilliant blue of his eyes suddenly seemed to become more piercing, magnetic in its intensity.

She bent to bestow a fairy kiss on his cheek. Her heart was drumming in her ears, driving the noise around them off to some far distance. She saw his lips part slightly and temptation seized her. Instead of planting her mouth where it should have been planted to seal the wish-spell, an irresistible force dragged it down to meet his.

The moment the first tantalising contact was made was the last Barbie had any control over. Nick surged to his feet, a thumb hooked under her chin, fingers thrusting into her hair, taking a firm grip, tilting her head back, his mouth dominating hers as his other arm burrowed under her wings and scooped her in to a full body blast of his highly energised masculinity.

It was like no other kiss Barbie had experienced in her whole life—a wild, storming kiss that electrified every nerve, a stampeding kiss that reduced her mind to a whirlpool of fantastic sensation, an ecstatically passionate kiss that taught her that lust had an intox-icating excitement that could not be denied. Enthralled by these overwhelming factors, she was unaware of the removal of the wand from her grasp. Indeed, she didn't even realise where her hands were.

With shocking abruptness, the mouth that had wrought such intense rapture was wrenched from hers. The harsh words, 'What the hell!' rang in her ears. Her eyes flew open just as the star at the end of her wand was slammed down on Nick's head as though it were a flyswatter being wielded with deadly intent. Glitter sprayed from the impact.

'I'll give you magic!' a woman's voice screeched, and the wand lifted, ready to crash down again.

Nick's hand hastily disengaged itself from Barbie's hair and he threw up an arm to ward off its descent. 'Quit it, Tanya!' he grated.

'*You* quit it!' came the fierce retort.

Tanya, the black-haired witch! Dazedly, Barbie stared at the furious attacker, feeling oddly detached from the emotional violence playing across the other woman's face.

'How dare you kiss *her*, in front of *me!*' she snarled as Nick swivelled to grab the damaging wand from her.

Tanya whipped it out of his reach and advanced on Barbie who was now hugged to Nick's side but open to frontal assault. The red mouth was stretched into an ugly jeer as her arm swung back to deliver another forcible blow, this time aimed at Barbie's head.

'And you...you fairy cow...can milk someone else for sex! Nick is mine!'

It was Leon Webster who caught the wand in mid-swing, tore it out of her grasp and tossed it onto the dance floor. 'Cool it, Tanya!' he commanded.

Being de-weaponed, however, did nothing to lower the raging fury. With arms raised and fingers curled like talons, Tanya lunged at Barbie, hissing like a snake.

Nick threw in a shoulder-block. Leon knocked her arms down and pinned them to her sides in a smothering hug from behind. Everything had moved so fast, Barbie was still in a shocked daze, though her body was quivering in reaction to the chaos without and within.

'Let me go!' Tanya seethed.

'Not until you're ready to behave,' Leon tersely retorted.

'Right!' another voice cracked into the maelstrom. Sue!

'No indignities you said, Mr. Webster!' she reminded him in high dudgeon. Her hands were planted on her hips in aggressive mode as she subjected Nick and Leon—still holding the struggling Tanya—to a look of arch scorn. 'The crème of young Sydney society?' she drawled with biting acid.

'Miss Olsen…Sue…' Leon started ingratiatingly.

'My fairy princess gets grabbed and ravished in plain view of a hundred people…'

'I didn't anticipate she'd be so…'

Sue cut him off. 'We delivered precisely what you ordered, sir. Sexy, you said. Indeed, you insisted.'

'I know. I know. But…'

'Control, Mr. Webster, was in your court.'

'I'm doing it. I saved her from being attacked. Tanya, apologise to the ladies.'

'Ladies! They're no better than whores!' she shrieked.

'More indignities,' Sue hammered. She glared at Nick. 'Kindly unhand my fairy princess, sir. I am taking her out of this unsavoury scene.'

His warm, supporting arm was removed, leaving

Barbie feeling chilled and shivery. He gestured a plea to Sue. 'I'm sorry things got out of hand…'

'Perhaps you'll now take them *in* hand,' Sue shot at him, glancing meaningly at Tanya. 'I expect Mr. Webster to escort us out of this marquee, guaranteeing safety for my fairy princess. And may I say, sir…' Her green eyes knifed into Nick's. '…your choice of companion is no lady.'

'Who the hell do you think you are!' Tanya snarled.

Sue ignored her, nodding to Barbie. 'The wand needs collecting.'

Barbie took a deep breath, gathering herself together, then stepped away from Nick, trying to maintain an air of dignity as she set off to where the wand had fallen on the dance floor.

'No, wait!' A hoarse plea from Nick.

Barbie hesitated, still feeling the magnetic pull he'd held on her, but she resisted it, realising Sue was right in her judgement to get them out of here, pronto! Nothing good could eventuate from what had already gone on. Revenge, she decided, was a very tricky thing to play with.

'Please…stay!'

It was an almost anguished cry from Nick this time, curling around Barbie's heart, squeezing it, throwing her into confusion. Before she could respond either way, her wings were grabbed from behind and jerked from the boned slot in the back of her dress. Crying out in horror at the damage that might be done, she swung around to find Nick juggling the wings with an equal expression of horror, babbling apologies. 'I didn't mean… I just wanted…'

'More indignities!' Sue accused hotly. 'Mr. Webster…'

'For God's sake, Nick!' Leon begged. 'Leave her be and take Tanya from me.'

'I don't *want* Tanya!' Nick snapped at him. 'She can go take a flying leap off the Harbour Bridge for all I care!'

'You scum!'

The black-haired witch broke free of Leon and smashed Barbie's wings out of Nick's hands with her fists. They fell to the floor and she jumped on them, stamping her feet all over them like a dervish, her red toenails splayed openly in black stilleto sandals, looking like drops of blood on the silvery gossamer as she wreaked her malicious damage.

Sheer shock paralysed everyone for several seconds.

'No…no…' Barbie moaned.

It shot Nick into action, hauling the hysterical woman off her feet and carrying her to the other side of the table where he forcibly held her to prevent any more harm being done.

Barbie stared down at the broken wings. They'd taken her so many hours to create and they'd been beautiful. Tears welled into her eyes. It was like a desecration…

Someone tapped her on the arm and offered her the wand she'd meant to collect. The star was hanging drunkenly at the end of the silver rod. It was broken, too.

'You're going to get a huge damage bill for this, Mr. Webster,' Sue threatened darkly, folding her arms in firm belligerent style.

'Okay. I'll pay,' he promised on a ragged sigh. 'If we could move now…'

They moved, Leon shepherding both Sue and Barbie through the loud melee in the marquee. The wings were left where they lay crushed. Leon muttered something about a good joke going awry. Sue castigated him for not providing adequate protection. Barbie stared at the battered wand in her hand.

A falling star, she thought.

A wish…

Did wishes ever come true?

CHAPTER THREE

LEON swept into Nick's office for their usual Monday morning conference, hoping his friend had wiped the birthday disaster from their joint slate, only to be faced with incontrovertible evidence that Nick was still obsessed with it!

'What are those fairy wings doing on your desk?' he demanded in exasperation.

Nick lifted a belligerently determined face. 'I'm going to fix them.'

'And just how do you propose to do that? Tanya punched so many holes through them with her stiletto heels, the fabric is irreparable.'

'I am aware of that, Leon.' He glowered dangerously. 'Which is why I need to get the fabric matched so I can replace it. I decided you wouldn't mind lending me your secretary for a while this morning. She'd probably know how…'

'You can't use Sharon for personal jobs.'

One black eyebrow lifted in challenge. 'Can't I?'

'This is ridiculous!' Leon expostulated. 'I said I'd pay the bill for damages and I will. As soon as it comes in.'

'I'm going to fix the wings,' Nick repeated stubbornly.

'Why?'

'Because I want to. Because it will mean something when I give them back to her.'

Leon expelled a long breath. Nick was definitely out of his tree. He lifted his hands in a plea for sanity. 'It was just an act. An act I paid for, Nick. Nothing more. Just a…'

'It turned into something more.'

'Okay, she was beautiful. She was sexy. She turned you on. But you don't even know the woman, Nick. She might be…'

'I don't care who she is!' His hand slammed down on the desk as he stood up. 'I want to feel that again. I have to know. And I *will* know.' He paced around the office, clearly disturbed, his hands moving in agitated gestures. 'When I kissed her… I've never experienced anything like it in my life before. She's different, Leon.'

'Fairy princesses tend to be different, Nick. Kind of like dream stuff.'

That perfectly rational point earned a flash of impatience that said he didn't understand, didn't have the experience to understand.

'I can't let it go,' came the steely resolve.

Totally out of his tree!

Recognising a brick wall when he saw it, Leon asked, 'So, have you tracked her down, arranged to meet under normal circumstances?'

Nick's face twisted with frustration. 'I called and called the *Party Poppers* number yesterday and all I got was an answering machine. Then finally, this morning, I reached that Sue Olsen on the phone, but she flatly refused to give out the name and address of her fairy princess. Against company policy.'

Dead right, Leon thought approvingly. Fantasy and reality didn't mix. Expectations could never be met and it was a stupid waste of time to go chasing them.

Nick grimaced and muttered, 'But I'll get it somehow. Sue Olsen said something about *Singing Sunflowers* before I started in on questions. I'll ask my sister to book that act for her kids. My fairy princess is a singer…right? She might be a sunflower, too.'

The desperate hope in Nick's voice told Leon his friend needed help fast or very little creative work was going to get done on the designs they'd been contracted to deliver. He instantly revised his opinion. The sooner hopes and expectations were blasted, the better.

'No need to go to that trouble, Nick,' he soothed.

'I'll go to any lengths,' came the punchy retort, his eyes flashing unshakable determination. 'I have to find her.'

'Sure you do. I understand,' Leon quickly inserted. 'All I meant was…leave it to me. I'll have the name and address you want before today is out.'

Nick frowned, suspicious of his confidence. 'How?' he demanded.

'I'll call Sue Olsen, ask her out for lunch as an apology for the mess on Saturday night. Restaurant of her choice. Promise to write out a cheque for the damages bill there and then. Butter her up. Piece of cake. As you well know, I am the best salesman in the business.'

'What about her company policy?'

'I'll find a loophole. Trust me.'

Nick expelled a deep sigh. Then his eyes narrowed. 'You won't put her further offside?'

Leon laughed. 'That feisty little redhead wasn't offside. She was making hay while the sun shone. A dyed-in-the-wool opportunist, like me. In fact, I'll enjoy having lunch with her. I have the feeling Miss Olsen and I speak the same language.'

'Okay. Just don't slip up, Leon. This is really important to me.'

'No problem, Nick, I swear. Just shovel those wings off your desk and get to work while I...'

'I'm still going to fix them. If you'd send Sharon along...'

Leon ungritted his teeth enough to bite out, 'Okay. But don't take up too much office time on it. It's bad business getting secretaries to do personal jobs, Nick, and you've got a full schedule, too.'

'I just want to ask her advice,' he insisted.

'Fine! Speak to you later.'

Leon went off fuming.

Women!

He'd got rid of Tanya Wells for good, only to be loaded with another festering problem. There was black irony for you. A fairy princess was supposed to remove trouble not make it. He should have hired a doll, not a real woman. Big mistake, Leon, he castigated himself. Though there was one bright spot.

A very feisty little redhead.

Cute, too.

He wouldn't mind having lunch with Sue Olsen at all.

Yes, that was definitely a bright spot.

Barbie was still trying to mend the broken wand when the *Drop Dead Deliveries* telephone rang. She frowned at it. Sue had gone off to lunch with Leon Webster, assured of getting the damages cheque, while she was supposed to deal personally with any bookings that came in. Except Barbie didn't like answering the *revenge* phone, as she thought of it. Why couldn't it have been the *Party Poppers* one?

'Business is business,' she muttered, putting the wand down with a resigned sigh.

Feeling very, very ambivalent about revenge after the cataclysmic meeting with Nick Armstrong, she reluctantly lifted the receiver and pulled an order pad and pen within easy reach.

'*Drop Dead Deliveries,*' she stated flatly, unable to project Sue's enthusiasm. 'How may I help you?'

'I want you to deliver a dozen dead roses to a guy named Nick Armstrong at *Multi-Media Promotions.*'

Barbie's heart flipped.

Was this the black-haired witch who had attacked them with the wand and smashed her wings?

'Your name please?' she asked.

'Tanya Wells.'

Tanya! No mistake about that. Even the voice was

putting her teeth on edge—like chalk screeching on a blackboard.

'And I want you to write just one word on the card—*Loser!*'

'You don't want to add your name?'

'He'll know who it's from,' came the venomous retort. 'And before we go any further I want to know when you can deliver. It has to be today and the sooner the better.'

The demanding tone raised Barbie's hackles. This was definitely a woman who wanted—and expected—to get everything her own way. Nevertheless, a paying customer was entitled to the service they paid for.

'Just a moment while I check,' she said with surface calm, hiding the maelstrom of thoughts the other woman stirred.

Loser! Well, *she* had tickets on herself that Barbie would never have given her, but maybe Tanya Wells had reason to believe Nick valued his relationship with her. If he did, he'd certainly been a fool to act as he had at his birthday party. On the other hand, maybe all women had only one value for him, and he thought he'd found another candidate to fulfil that requirement better than Tanya. Was that why he was so hot for Barbie's name and address?

'Well? When can you get the dead roses to him?' Angry impatience.

'Possibly three o'clock,' Barbie temporised, feeling distinctly negative about obliging Tanya Wells with anything.

'Can't you do it earlier?'

Not if Sue did the job. But what if she went herself? Dressed in a black suit with her hair tucked up under a hat, dark glasses on…the image she'd present would be a far cry from the fairy princess that had taken Nick's fancy on Saturday night. And if he did somehow recognise her, she could deliver a double whammy of rejection. Serve him right for playing fast and loose!

At least he hadn't identified her as Barbie Lamb, so she felt safe about that. No humiliating trip down memory lane would eventuate from this. And it would be…interesting…just to see him again, in his workplace.

Temptation was a terrible, terrible thing.

'We could manage two o'clock if that suits.' It was almost twelve now. She needed time to get dressed…

'Perfect! That should screw up his precious work this afternoon.'

Again Barbie frowned. Tanya Wells was a malicious piece of goods and it didn't sit well, being a partner to her wishes. Yet how could she judge what had actually gone on between her and Nick? Maybe she had just cause…if he *was* a shallow rat!

'May I have your credit card details, Miss Wells?'

Barbie completed the transaction, her mind moving into a ferment over the wisdom of taking this job. Nick's calls to *Party Poppers* proved he wanted to see her again, but he didn't know who she was and Barbie found herself totally churned up over what his response would be if he found out. A sexy fantasy was one thing, reality quite another.

She'd certainly found out what it was like to be kissed by him—with lustful desire. And she couldn't deny she'd felt swamped by lustful desire herself. But undoubtedly it had been no more than a highly heated moment, generated by volatile emotions on both sides. His angry outburst about not caring if Tanya took a flying leap off the Harbour Bridge surely pointed to their having been at odds before Barbie had appeared on the scene as a fairy princess.

Revenge…

For all she knew, Nick himself might have been taking vengeance on Tanya for something the black-haired witch had done!

Barbie stared at the order sheet she had just written out.

Maybe she shouldn't go.

Sue could do it when she came back from her lunch with Leon Webster. So what if the delivery was a bit late…

No!

She wanted to see Nick for herself, *in the cold light of day!* Sue was right about finishing this…this hang-over from the past. Saturday night was supposed to have achieved that purpose, yet when he'd kissed her…somehow it had just made everything worse, stirring up what she had wanted to put behind her. It would be different today.

Best to go and make absolutely certain there was nothing about Nick Armstrong that was worth har-bouring in her memory.

CHAPTER FOUR

NICK propped the broken wings as best he could against the file cabinet, then moved a chair up beside them. The small swatch of damaged fabric he'd cut out of one of them made them look even more forlorn, but the salesman at the Strand Arcade where Sharon had advised him to go, swore the organza he'd subsequently bought was a perfect match. Not feeling quite so certain, Nick wanted to check it truly was right.

He undid the parcel, shook out the full length of the folded organza and draped it over the chair next to the wings. Moving back a few paces, he looked from one to the other and felt both relief and satisfaction. The salesman did know his fabrics. It *was* exactly the same.

A rather tentative knock on his office door brought a smile to his face. It was sure to be Sharon coming to see if he'd been successful in his lunch-hour quest. 'Come in,' he called, not even glancing at the door, his smiling gaze revelling in the evidence of his achievement.

Barbie took a deep breath. It had been bad enough running the gauntlet of curious stares on her way to this door. The receptionist had looked very doubtful about giving directions to Nick Armstrong's office, and Barbie had been fearful of being called back and more rigorously questioned. But she'd made it to here without being accosted—the all-black funereal garb probably an intimidating factor that had worked for her—and now she was being invited to enter by *his* voice.

She had to go through with it.

Stupid not to, at this point.

Nevertheless, her heart was thumping erratically as she turned the knob and pushed the door open. Her mind was so highly energised, she had the weird sensation of floating as her quivering legs took the few necessary steps to move into the room to face the man and the feelings she'd come to confront.

Except he wasn't facing her at all.

Nor even looking at her.

His attention was trained entirely on…*her fairy princess wings!*

'See?' he said, gesturing to a length of fabric draped over a nearby chair. 'A perfect match!'

Shock held Barbie speechless. Her gaze moved slowly from the silvery organza to the man who had gone to the trouble of acquiring it. Would a shallow rat want to fix her wings? Wasn't Leon Webster in the process of paying the cost of replacing them? What was going on here?

She wished she could read Nick's mind. His expression in profile seemed relaxed into a smile, but what did the smile mean? Was he remembering her as the fairy princess, anticipating more from her? Or calculating how to get more?

A convulsive little shiver ran down her spine as she stared at him. He was so very handsome, even in profile, so strongly male. His thick black hair brushed the collar of his white shirt. He had the broad shoulders of a star swimmer and a taut sexy butt, outlined by the grey trousers he wore. She remembered her thighs being pressed to the hard ungiving muscularity of his, her breasts squashing against the hot wall of his chest...

Her nerves leapt in shock as he suddenly turned, looking directly at her, his vivid blue eyes sharp and probing. The lingering smile was instantly wiped from his face and a frown creased his brow as his gaze raked her from head to foot and back again.

Panic plunged Barbie's mind into a fog of fear and set her heart fluttering in wild agitation. Would he—could he—recognise her, despite the large dark sunglasses and the black hat that covered her hair and dipped over her forehead? Her fingers closed more tightly around the base of the cone of black tissue paper which held the dead roses. She could use it as a self-protective weapon if she had to.

'Who *are* you?' he rapped out.

Relief! He didn't know. Barbie struggled to regather her wits. She was here to do a job, not get shattered again by this man. Every self-protective instinct screamed—*get it right and go.*

'Mr. Nick Armstrong?'

Her voice came out too soft and husky. She should

have swallowed first. He was frowning more quizzically at her now. Had her tone struck a familiar chord with him? Was he matching it to the way she'd sung at his birthday party?

'Yes,' he answered belatedly, his gaze zeroing in on her mouth, studying it with highly discomforting intensity.

Barbie was drawn into staring back at his, remembering how it had felt, how it had aroused such a stampede of wild sensations and needs...

Rattled at finding herself so treacherously distracted from her purpose, she rushed into the set speech for this job. 'I hereby present you with a *Drop Dead Delivery.*'

'What?' he demanded incredulously.

Her nerves jangled at the sharpness of his tone. Somehow she found the strength of will to step forward, holding out the bundle of black tissue for him to take. 'This was ordered for you,' she explained.

'By whom?'

He didn't take delivery. His arms remained at his sides, his refusal to accept her offering an innate challenge to her presence, and by stepping closer to him, Barbie had the overwhelming sense of having put herself in a danger zone. It was as though he emitted an electric charge. Her whole body was tingling with an extreme awareness of his powerful masculinity. She wished she could turn tail and run but knew instinctively he wouldn't let her.

The black tissue paper rustled slightly. She was shaking. Desperate to get past this contretemps with him, she quickly spelled out, 'I understand from our client that you will know who the sender is.'

'Someone who wants me to *drop dead?*' he quizzed sardonically, still not taking delivery. His eyes were like blue lasers, boring through the dark cover of her sunglasses. 'Now who would that be?'

The lenses were impenetrable, weren't they? He couldn't possibly see through them. Barbie took a deep breath to quell the frantic fears and his gaze instantly dropped to the heave of her chest, obviously noting the strain of her full breasts against her figure-hugging suitcoat.

'I am merely the messenger, sir,' she gabbled, appalled by the responsive hardening of her nipples.

His gaze slowly trailed up her long throat, paused at her mouth again, then lifted to her sunglasses. 'I see,' he drawled.

What did he see?

If he did recognise her, what did she want to do about it? What did she really want? How could Nick Armstrong spark so much...*response* in her? This wasn't a hangover from the past. This was here and now!

'A messenger, dressed in mourning,' he continued. 'No doubt emphasising that the gift is a very black mark against me. And you are paid to perform this act. To the hilt, one might say.'

Feeling like a pinned butterfly, Barbie squirmed inwardly at his summing up. 'Yes, I'm paid to do it,' she acknowledged.

His face hardened and there was a mocking glint

in his eyes as he said, 'You obviously take pride in superb attention to detail. Do you carry through all your paid performances…to the hilt?'

He knew.

Barbie could feel it in her bones.

And he didn't like it. He didn't like it one bit.

While she felt trapped in a cage of her own making, he reached out and snatched the cone of black tissue from her, leaving her unshielded from his gaze which once again raked her from head to toe, not so much inspecting the black funereal attire this time but very definitely taking in the shapeliness of her figure, making her burn with the sense he was matching it up in his mind to the memory of another act.

Why did she feel so guilty? She hadn't done anything wrong, had she? This whole thing had started as a need to put a painful memory to rest, simply a means to a justifiable end.

Inexorably, her gaze was drawn to the broken fairy wings, propped against a file cabinet, and the length of organza obviously bought to mend them.

Why?

What was their significance to him?

'A bunch of dead roses,' he drawled. 'Symbolic of the end of love?'

She jerked her gaze back to his and uttered the one word that had driven her here. 'Closure.' Except there could be no closure while such tantalising questions remained unanswered.

'I beg your pardon?'

'*Drop Dead Deliveries* are about closure,' she elaborated, knowing she should go. He'd taken delivery so her job was done. Yet she felt paralysed by her inner confusion.

'Ah!'

He flicked open the card and read what was written inside. *'Loser!'* His mouth curled in irony. 'Typical of Tanya, wanting to get in the last word, wanting to crawl into my mind again.' Again his expressive blue eyes mocked her purpose here. 'As it happens, she's wasted her money on this last little malicious act. It doesn't touch me. At all.'

But the fairy wings did.

They had to or they wouldn't be here.

'Do you get many clients who want this kind of closure?' he asked curiously.

'Quite a few,' she replied, deeply disquieted by his description of 'a last malicious act.' Revenge was supposed to be about balancing justice. An eye for an eye, a hurt for a hurt...

'Can the clients specify *who* does the delivery?'

It leapt into her mind that he thought Tanya had specifically asked for her to bring the dead roses to him and that she was a co-conspirator in malice. Which she was in a way, but she hadn't meant him to recognise her, to put it together...if he had.

Though she had thought of delivering a double whammy. But that was to be a payback for his playing fast and loose, and how could she link playing fast and loose to the time and trouble of buying the organza to fix her wings? Everything about this scene was wrong and Barbie had the sinking feeling there was no way to put it right.

Best to get out of here.

Fast.

'No, the messenger is simply the messenger to both parties. Anonymous,' she replied emphatically, and took a step backwards, testing her legs were steady enough for a quick escape.

'Anonymous,' he repeated, his eyes glittering in a way that shot danger signals through Barbie's entire nervous system.

'Yes,' she answered, barely able to draw breath. 'And since the delivery has now been made, please excuse me.'

She swung on her heel, heading for the open door-way, desperately needing space to rethink this whole situation with Nick Armstrong.

A hand clamped on her shoulder, forcibly halting her flight.

Then to her utter horror, her hat was yanked from her head and she felt her hair spilling from the pins she'd used to fasten it out of sight—hair that Nick was absolutely certain to connect with the fairy princess!

CHAPTER FIVE

SHEER desperation drove Barbie's reaction. It felt as though everything was zooming out of control and she had to hang on to it somehow. Her hands flew up to grab her tumbling hair and she spun around, tearing her shoulder out of Nick's grasp.

'My hat!' she shrieked at him in outraged protest.

His face was set in aggressive determination, his blue eyes blazing a mocking triumph, and he took absolutely no notice of her protest. In a lightning-fast move, he reached out and whipped off her sunglasses, leaving her face totally naked to his view. Naked and hopelessly vulnerable to positive identification. Which he made, beyond any shadow of a doubt.

'So!' His mouth curved into a nerve-shaking smile of sardonic satisfaction. 'We meet again. Quite in-triguing…reincarnation.'

Barbie's mind boggled over his meaning. The shock of being so abruptly and effectively unveiled was still pounding through her. Her hands remained stuck in her hair, though any rescue operation there was now futile. All she could do was stare helplessly at him as he folded her sunglasses and tucked them into his shirt pocket.

'They're mine,' she said, fighting to regain some iota of control.

'Safe-keeping,' he assured her and in another startling action, strode right past Barbie, straight for the door which he not only closed but stood against, blocking any path to freedom. 'Safe from interruption, as well,' he declared, emanating resolute purpose.

Like a powerful magnet he'd drawn her gaze after him, and she stood half-turned, watching him, totally mesmerised by what he intended to do next. Her heart was hammering in her ears. Slowly, without any real decision-making at all, her hands slid from her hair and her arms dropped limply to her sides, defeated in their quest to ward off a moment that had come, regardless of her efforts to stop it. Her hat was forgotten. Nick Armstrong dominated her entire consciousness.

'From heavenly fairy princess bestowing favours…to dark lady of vengeance in one fell swoop,' he commented with a wry twist of his mouth. 'Do you enjoy playing mind games?'

The shock question jolted her mind back into some semblance of working order. 'You weren't supposed to recognise me.'

His eyebrows lifted challengingly. 'So you wanted the upper hand of checking me out while I was under fire from the dearly departed Tanya.'

'Something like that,' she admitted.

'The relationship with Tanya was in its death throes before the party. Neither of us was happy with the other.'

'Then why were you still together?'

'The party was planned some time ago. It

seemed…' He shrugged. '…ungracious to retract the invitation.' His eyes glittered with a surge of desire that encompassed Barbie, stirring a host of ungovernable responses. 'Though I've regretted that mistake ever since,' he softly drawled, raising goose bumps on her skin.

'You didn't care about her feelings,' Barbie shot at him in wild defence, dredging up the nine-year-old memory of how he hadn't cared about her feelings, either. He'd thanked her for the twenty-first birthday gift she had thriftily saved to buy him, then put it aside. But when the sexy tart with the sports car gave him the same gift—albeit worth a lot more money—he'd worn it for everyone to see whose offering he prized more.

'Some feelings can override all others,' he answered.

Yes, like feelings below the belt. Nothing to do with his heart, Barbie thought, fighting to retain some sensible perspective on her experience of his actions.

'They can even reach past a superficial disguise,' he went on, stepping away from the door, towards her, instantly raising her tension and enveloping her in his as he continued talking to her. 'There I was, looking at the broken wings, and suddenly I *felt* your presence in this office.'

He couldn't, Barbie fiercely reasoned, not wanting to believe it. Probably a desire to transfer a lingering fantasy into substance.

'My scalp actually started tingling,' he said, closing the distance between them at a slow deliberate stroll.

Barbie felt her own scalp starting to tingle with the intensity of feeling he was projecting at her. Had she done that to him while she'd stood looking at him, recalling how it had felt when he'd kissed her?

'An extraordinary sensation,' he continued. 'Like a shower of magic setting off waves of intense awareness.'

Her stomach contracted, whether in panicky fear or some treacherous excitement she had no idea, but she was certainly experiencing intense awareness now as he came closer and closer. It didn't occur to her to move backwards. Her whole concentration was wrapped up in watching him. She even forgot to breathe when he gestured at her clothes.

'When I swung around to find seemingly a stranger in black, I thought all my instincts were out of kilter.' He stopped barely an arm's length away and his eyes mocked her belief in being unrecognisable. 'Then you spoke…and the voice was unmistakable.'

Her breath whooshed out on a gust of outrage. If that was true, how come he hadn't recognised it as Barbie Lamb's voice when she'd sung on Saturday night? Hadn't he even bothered to *listen* to her all those years that her family had mixed with his? Or maybe he had a short—a very short—memory span. Either way, Barbie seethed over his *recognition*.

'Angry that your deception didn't come off?'

'I don't believe you. Why remove my hat if you were so sure?'

'To stop you from leaving.'

'And my sunglasses.'

'I hate talking to people who hide their thoughts behind dark glasses. I wanted to see your eyes.'

'You had no right.'

'You walked in here to get at me. You weren't asked to do this job. You chose it, because it involved me. I think that gives me the right to ask why…and see the answer in your eyes.'

Barbie didn't want to answer him.

'You couldn't keep away?' he asked softly, seductively.

'Yes, I could,' she retorted, resenting his power to attract, even against her will. 'This was business. Why should I knock back a job because you're at the end of it? You have no power over my life, Nick Armstrong.'

His eyes flashed a sharp challenge. 'Then it won't matter if you give me your name.'

'I've given you what I've been paid to give you. You have no right to more,' she argued.

'You weren't paid to respond to my kiss as you did,' he shot at her with blazing conviction. 'And yes, Tanya did muddy the situation. But don't tell me it was only business that brought you here today. You thought it was a safe way to see…to know…if what you'd felt then could be felt again.'

Her heart felt as though it was being squeezed. She did want him—had always wanted him—but how could she feel this turbulent desire for a man who'd been so crassly insensitive to her young love? Her gaze flicked to the broken fairy wings.

'I wanted to fix them for you,' he murmured.

More easily fixed than a broken heart, she thought savagely, returning her gaze to his, her inner agitation increasing at the raw flare of need and want she saw. Did *he* have a heart to break?

'Why?' she choked out.

'Because they were part of the magic that happened between us. It was perfect, and to have anything belonging to you, or that moment of coming together, reduced to tatters, feels wrong.'

He certainly hadn't felt that way nine years ago, Barbie told herself, but somehow the reminder was losing its power to armour her against the feelings he stirred. It was different now. He cared. Or was it her own need to believe he did, pressing that view?

He reached out and gently stroked her cheek. 'It was real...what we felt. It's real now, too. Which proves it wasn't fantasy.'

Her skin heated and tingled under his touch. For the life of her she couldn't move. With feather-light fingertips he seemed to be infiltrating her bloodstream, making her pulse beat faster and faster. His voice was drumming through her brain and heart, setting off echoes she couldn't stop.

'And it wasn't one-sided. You kissed me right back. You were *with* me.'

With him...with him...with him...

The yearning welled up in her like an unstoppable tidal wave. The sexy tart with the sports car was sucked away. So was the black-haired witch, Tanya. This was *her* time with Nick...the man she'd loved, hated, dreamed about. Why not have it? Why not?

His fingers drifted into her hair. His head bent, his mouth coming closer and closer to hers. Anticipation zinged through her, blowing all worrisome thoughts away. Her whole body craved the kiss that was coming, everything within her poised to match it with that one previous, sensational experience. Would it be the same? Would it be more?

His lips brushed hers. She closed her eyes, her entire being focused on the soft sensuality of this initial pressure, an intensely erotic caress, lips sliding over hers, changing direction, exploring, tasting, his tongue delicately probing, exciting a compulsion to take some initiative herself, to gather sensory impressions of him and arouse the same excitement she felt. She didn't want it to be like a one-sided dream.

Her tentative assault on his mouth triggered a more aggressive possession of her own and Barbie was instantly caught up in a passionate entanglement that was certainly not the fluffy stuff of dreams. The wild explosion of sensation was like a cascade of fireworks, fountains of brilliant pleasure shooting in every direction, intense bursts of excitement flaring, lingering, overtaken by more and more fantastic effects.

She loved it, revelled in it, exulted in it. Her arms curled around his neck, wanting to hold him close, wanting to feel all of him as she had before Tanya had broken the spell on Saturday night, real flesh-and-blood Nick, hot and hard and male, pressing the unmistakable strength of his desire for her, man and woman surging towards an intimacy that demanded urgent fulfilment, and everything within her craving it, sizzling with need.

'Nick!'

The call of his name was like a whip-crack, slicing through their mounting enthralment, a sharp discordant intrusion on an intensely private togetherness, yet they were so deeply immersed in each other, disengagement was reluctant on both sides.

'Nick! Have you totally lost it?' came the harsh, exasperated demand.

Nick's slowly expelled breath tingled over her sensitised lips as he interrupted their kiss to growl, 'Get out, Leon.'

'Oh, great!' A jeer of fuming frustration. 'I bring Sue Olsen along to check you out personally, and the fairy princess is already history.'

Sue? Barbie's eyes flew open. Her sluggish brain snapped to red alert. Sue could mess up everything!

'I don't need help,' Nick tersely asserted, loosening his embrace, sliding one arm away from her as he half turned to put Barbie in clearer view of his friend. 'I've got her right here with me. So take yourself off, Leon.'

'Barbie!'

Shock horror from Sue, her mouth gaping as she released the fatal name that could link to a memory Barbie couldn't bear to have raised in Nick Armstrong's mind. Barbie Lamb…the horrible childhood nickname, Baa-Baa…it would ruin what they shared now. Totally ruin it. He'd start thinking about her differently, be amused instead of stirred, and he'd remember how she'd felt for him at sixteen…

Panic welled up in Barbie as she stared at her friend who was standing just to the side of Leon Webster and close to the door he'd opened, undoubtedly expecting his partner to be at work. How could she stop any further revelation?

'It *is* her!' Leon agreed in surprise, taking in the tumbling mass of blond hair on top of the very different clothing. 'In black drag?'

'A *Drop Dead Delivery* came in from the harpy who broke my fairy wings,' Barbie shot at Sue, hoping to shut her up. 'I had to come…'

'Business.' Sue caught on, collecting herself enough to glare disapprovingly at Nick. 'And *he* assaulted you again.'

'Looked mutual to me,' Leon declared, turning an arch look on Sue. 'Trying to work damages on this score is not going to wear. She was certainly not fighting, not the slightest sign of struggle. In fact…'

'Do you mind?' Nick cut in. 'This is my private office.'

'Which happens to be for work, Nick,' came the fast and pointed retort. 'Remember work? What we're supposed to be doing here?'

'And I see the delivery has been made,' Sue said, expressing equal disapproval of the current use of Nick's office. 'Come on, Barbie. You're leaving with me.'

'Barbie…'

Nick's softly musing repetition of her name

squeezed her heart. She couldn't let him start thinking about it, possibly making the connection to the girl he'd known when they'd shared the same neighbourhood.

'It's Sue's nickname for me,' she blurted out, feverishly seeking some meaning for it as he looked quizzically at her. 'Like barbed wire. I'm usually very prickly with men who come on to me.'

'And you should be prickly with this one, too,' Sue strongly advised, ever sharp at picking up the ball. 'He's not just coming on. He's charging.'

Nick ignored this remark, ignored both Leon and Sue, focusing entirely on Barbie, his vivid blue eyes eloquently pleading the cause of a here-and-now involvement which he wanted to stretch beyond this moment. To her intense relief, there was no flash of memory clouding that desire, nothing but the need to know, the need to reach out and hold on.

'So what is your real name?' he asked.

Her mind whirled, groping for an answer. She was christened Barbara Anne. Her second name should be easy to remember.

'Anne,' she replied. But what about a surname? Lamb was a dead giveaway. 'Shepherd,' she added, the sheep association popping out. 'Anne Shepherd.'

He smiled both encouragement and satisfaction in her conceding it to him. 'So now we're properly introduced.' And his voice was like warm velvet, caressing her.

'Right!' Leon snapped. 'Having got that settled…'

'Butt out, Leon. I have more to settle.' Nick's expression changed to one of powerful intent as he looked at his partner and Sue beside him. 'If you'd be so kind as to leave us alone for a few minutes…'

'Fine!' Leon agreed on a huff.

'I'll wait in reception,' Sue instructed, giving Barbie a look that asked if she had a hole in her head.

And Barbie briefly wondered if she did as they left, closing the door behind them. Then Nick was turning back to her, lifting the arm he'd freed, tenderly stroking her cheek, her hair, his eyes telling her how very desirable he found the woman she now was. It was like champagne bubbling through her blood, too wonderfully intoxicating to dilute it with any bitter dregs from the past.

'Meet me after work. We'll have dinner together. Is that possible?'

'Where?'

'Where do you live?'

That was tricky with Sue all too ready to mouth off. If she was to keep her real identity a secret—and that was paramount right now—best to keep Nick away from their apartment in Ryde.

'I'll meet you in the city,' she said, showing a reservation about accepting too much too fast.

He didn't argue. He smiled reassurance, probably remembering her claim to *prickliness*. 'Whatever you wish. Do you know the restaurant, Pier Twenty-One, at Circular Quay?'

'I'll find it.'

'Seven o'clock?'

'Yes.'

'You won't disappear on me again?'

'I'll meet you for dinner.'

No promises beyond that, Barbie told herself. She may have embarked on madness, but she could allow this much time with Nick, just to see...

'I'll look forward to it,' he said, a happy grin spreading across his handsome face as he released her and withdrew her sunglasses from his shirt pocket. 'No more disguises?'

Barbie flushed, the deception she was determinedly playing very high on her awareness scale. 'It was my job,' she excused.

'I'd like to hear more about that tonight.' He gave her the glasses then stepped away to scoop up her hat from the floor. 'Sorry about this but I had to take it off,' he said, smiling a rueful apology as he handed it back to her. 'Your hair is too beautiful to hide.'

She was hiding much more than her hair, Barbie thought, as she crammed the hat on. This was a game—a dangerous game—of hide-and-seek. If and when she was caught...would she know how to handle it by then?

'Thank you,' she said. 'I must go now. Sue's waiting.'

'Is she your boss?'

'More a case of mutual interests,' Barbie answered evasively.

He didn't pursue the point. 'Until tonight then,' he said, ushering her to the door.

Just before Barbie made her exit, her gaze flicked

to the broken fairy wings, propped against the file cabinet.

Were they both pursuing a fantasy?

She paused in the opened doorway to take one last direct look at him and was instantly swamped by the sexual awareness he generated. His eyes blazed with a wanting that had nothing to do with fantasy, and her whole body sizzled with a response that was very very real.

'Tonight,' he repeated.

It was like a drumbeat on her heart.

She nodded and left, unable to think, just feeling...feeling what Nick Armstrong did to her...not wanting to let it go.

CHAPTER SIX

'ANNE SHEPHERD?'

Barbie sighed at the caustic drawl from Sue. At least they were out of the renovated warehouse which held the various departments of Multi-Media Promotions, and in the privacy of their own company car. She had known Sue wouldn't hold her tongue for long, but she wasn't ready to answer. She didn't want to explain anything.

How could anyone really explain *feelings?*

'Come on, Barbie. This is going a bit far, isn't it?'

The critical comment stung, yet Barbie hastily reasoned Sue didn't—couldn't—understand how this new thing between her and Nick would be spoiled if the truth of her identity was known. She just wanted to let it run for a while, without those shadows from the past.

The past of Sydney was all around her in this old inner city suburb of Glebe where Nick had his business offices. She stared out at the terrace houses, many of them turned into trendy restaurants and galleries now. Times changed, places changed, people changed. Or at least their views did. Nick definitely saw her differently, very positively *wanting* her in his life.

'A false name,' Sue scorned. 'How long do you think you can fool him with it?'

'Long enough,' Barbie muttered.

'Enough for what?'

'Never mind.'

'If this is an extension of the revenge idea, you're playing with real fire, Barbie, and you may get badly burned,' Sue warned. 'Saturday night's act was harmless, good for your pride, but if you're planning on a closer encounter…'

'It's not revenge.'

This terse statement of fact hung in the silence between them as Sue drove the length of the Anzac Bridge and took the route towards Ryde. Wanting to smooth over the ruction in their usual good understanding, Barbie offered the one piece of proof that Nick was not a shallow rat.

'He bought the fabric to mend my fairy wings.'

It was answered with blistering scepticism. 'Leverage. The guy will try anything to get to you. And he has, hasn't he? I'll bet you right now nothing more will be done about mending those wings, because he's already won what he wanted.'

There was no reply to that argument. Only time would tell the truth of it.

'What's the next step?' Sue went on relentlessly. 'Dinner, bed and breakfast?'

Barbie grimaced over the derision, but at this point she no longer cared what Sue thought. 'Dinner. This evening,' she answered. 'I'll be meeting him in the city so I'll need the car if that's okay with you.'

'Dinner,' Sue muttered, shooting a dark look of warning as she added, 'Well don't kid yourself that wolf hasn't got bed and breakfast on the agenda.'

Barbie's chin lifted, defying the bloom of heat in her cheeks. 'So what if he has? I might want that, too. You said yourself I should get him out of my system.'

'Not this way, Barbie.'

'You opened this can of worms, insisting we needed the business. The lid won't go back on it now. I've always wanted him, Sue. That's the truth of it.'

'You're pursuing a dream.'

'Yes. Why not?'

'Starting it off on a lie, Barbie? Deceiving him as to who you are?'

'A name doesn't mean anything. It's the person who counts.'

'If it doesn't *mean* anything, why hide it?'

Barbie once again retreated into silence, hating the argument, not wanting to listen to her friend. It was *her* business, not Sue's. She was the one whose childhood and teenage years were emotionally entangled with Nick Armstrong.

Once those memories were triggered in Nick, she would shrivel inside and all the good feelings would die. He would look at her and see *Baa-Baa*. Whereas if they connected really well as the people they were today, perhaps they might reach a point where they could both laugh over those old memories.

'Do you expect me to back you up?'

Hearing the strong disapproval in Sue's voice, Barbie had no hesitation in releasing her friend from any responsibility for whatever ensued from this decision. 'No, I don't. Thanks for not blowing my cover back there in Nick's office. From now on I'll do my best to keep you right out of it. It's my play.'

'A bit difficult when Leon has asked me out.'

'What?' Barbie gaped at her in surprise, not for a moment having anticipated this outcome.

Sue shrugged. 'I like him. He's fun. He's invited me to a party this coming Saturday night.'

Barbie sagged back into her passenger seat, closed her eyes and rubbed her forehead, needing to still the whirl of complications that this connection set off in her mind. Leon Webster had been a friend of Nick's since university days, and shared the same business. They were bound to talk together as much as she and Sue did. Impossible to ask Sue to drop him if she liked him. That wasn't fair.

'We'll have to keep these involvements separate,' she argued. 'You with Leon. Me with Nick.'

'Or you could be honest with him. Get it out of the way,' came the salutory retort.

'No. Not yet.'

'I don't want to lie to Leon about you, Barbie.'

'Then don't. Do what you have to do and let me do what I have to do. Okay?'

Sue didn't reply. She didn't say anything more on the subject. Neither did Barbie. But they were both very conscious of the serious difference of opinion between them—an unwanted wedge in their long and close friendship.

Was Nick Armstrong worth it?

Barbie grimly decided she would have to find that out, beyond any shadow of a doubt... before Saturday night.

Having explained the circumstances of the *Drop Dead Delivery* to Leon, and the subsequent unmasking of Anne Shepherd, who'd played the fairy princess, Nick felt no compunction to explain anything else. Anne Shepherd was now his business—his personal, private business—and Leon had no rights over it.

'Thank you for being persuasive with Sue Olsen on my behalf,' he said, winding up the inquisition. 'I hope it wasn't too much of a chore. As it is, Anne and I can take it from here so you can drop it, Leon. Okay? Back to work now?'

'No, it's not okay,' came the sharp retort.

'You did remind me when you broke into my office that we were supposed to be working,' Nick dryly pointed out.

'Sue was right. You're charging like a bull, Nick. I bet you've got Anne lined up to race her off to bed tonight.'

Not *race*. He wanted to savour and revel in every bit of anticipation, then eke out every bit of pleasure he knew was coming with his fairy princess. Impossible to explain how he felt about her to Leon.

'I'm not working tonight so it's no concern of yours,' he said dismissively.

'No concern!' Leon rose from his chair with the rising of his voice, hurling his arms around and gesticulating dramatically as he paced around the office, flinging out a torrent of unsolicited advice. 'So I'm supposed to ignore it while you get into another mess with a woman. Remember, Tanya? You raced her off to bed the first night you met her, then spent the next four months finding out what a bitch she was. You're too fast on the draw, Nick.'

This was different. No way was Anne Shepherd in the same ring as Tanya Wells and he didn't like Leon linking them, either. Irritated by his friend's criticism he shot him a quelling glare. 'Look who's talking?'

'Sure I've done it, too,' Leon whipped back. 'Taking what's there whenever I've felt the urge. No harm done with willing parties. But the break-up with Liz taught me something. Great sex peters out when you find you've got nothing in common and you're pulling against each other's interests. Like with you and Tanya. Right?'

Nick leaned back in his chair and visually quizzed the reformed character Leon was supposedly demonstrating. 'When did this wisdom descend on you?' he asked. 'I didn't notice it in play at the party on Saturday night. Seems to me I remember…'

'There was no one *important* there,' Leon cut in emphatically. 'You said this Anne Shepherd is important to you.'

'So?'

'So treat her right. Get to know her.'

'I intend to.'

'It didn't look that way to me when Sue and I came

in,' Leon reminded him, sounding like a preacher pushing some righteous path.

Nick frowned at him, wishing he'd mind his own business. 'I appreciate your concern. Now let's drop it, shall we?'

Leon stopped his pacing and took a stand, glaring vexed disapproval. 'She and Sue are friends. Long-time friends. And business partners,' he stated curtly.

'I gathered that.'

'Sue is very protective of her when it comes to pushy guys.'

'I gathered that, too.'

'I like Sue Olsen. She's in tune with me. We might become a big item.'

Understanding dawned. His friend and partner fancied the little redhead. 'Each to his own, Leon.'

The usual agreement between them was not forthcoming. Leon did not relax. If anything, the tension he was emanating increased, his hands clenching and unclenching as though he wanted to throw a punch.

Bemused and rather unsettled by the aggressive flow from his friend, Nick waited to be enlightened further.

'We've got wires crossed here, Nick,' he stated with an underlying throb of vehemence, quite uncharacteristic of his usual easy-going manner. 'I'm counting on you not to give them a negative charge.'

'Right at this moment I don't see any problem,' Nick assured him confidently. All the signals with Anne were very positive.

'Well, think about this.' Leon wagged an admonishing finger. 'Sue wouldn't be so protective of Anne without a damned good reason. I figure there's some bad history that might need soothing over. Better find out what that reason is before you charge, Nick. Or we may find ourselves in major conflict.'

He made his exit on that sobering challenge, closing the door with a bang that telegraphed very serious concern.

It gave Nick considerable pause for thought.

Leon must *really* fancy the redhead.

And he was right. There were crossed wires here.

A strong sexual interest could break up friendships. He'd seen it happen many a time, women coming between men, men coming between women. It could mess up family relationships, too, when an interest wasn't approved, severely testing loyalties.

Nevertheless, he couldn't see why it should happen here. Sue Olsen had certainly been protective of Anne, and clearly there was some hurtful history he didn't know about. The signposts had been spelled out.

Barbie—barbed wire—prickly with men who came on to her.

But he hadn't *come on to her*. It was she who had initiated the kiss at his birthday party. And today, she had known what he was about to do. There'd been no protest, either verbally or physically. Remembering the touch of her tongue on his…nothing unwilling about her desire to taste him, to explore the wild exhilaration of arousing more and more excitement… Nick felt himself stirring, needing what she could give him.

There was no doubt in his mind.

She'd wanted to satisfy herself, as much as he'd wanted to satisfy himself.

Mutual wanting.

Where could it go wrong?

CHAPTER SEVEN

'YOUR table, sir.'

'Thank you.'

'And you're to be joined by?'

'I'll see her coming.'

'A drink while you wait, sir?'

'A jug of iced water will be fine.'

'I'll be right back with it.'

The waiter was as good as his promise, bringing the jug and pouring Nick a long glass of iced water before leaving him alone to wait for Anne. Normally he would have ordered a beer to relax over, smoothing away the tensions of the day, but he didn't have work on his mind, and the tension he felt was exciting, not to be diminished.

Tonight of all nights, Nick didn't want his senses blurred by alcohol. He would order wine when Anne came. A glass or two spaced over dinner wouldn't dull his mind from concentrating on everything about her. As he settled back in his chair and looked around him, taking in the colour and movement of the quay, he realised he had never felt so *alive,* waiting for a woman.

A glance at his watch showed it was still five minutes short of seven o'clock. Having reserved this out-of-doors table, under the huge marble colonnade that led to the opera house, Nick was in the ideal position to watch for Anne, and he found himself enjoying the passing parade of people and the coming and going of harbour ferries. Usually he was in too much of a hurry to take notice of what were familiar sights but this evening even the air smelled sweeter.

It had been a warm day for mid-November and the warmth still lingered. With daylight saving in force, tourists were still milling around, happily clicking cameras. Theatre-goers in evening dress strolled past, heading for their choice of entertainment; a concert, a play, a ballet performance. Nick's interest wasn't captivated by any of the stylish women. None of them held a candle to the one he was waiting for.

His wandering gaze picked her out of the promenade of people when she was still some fifty metres away, coming past the newspaper and magazine stall that served ferry passengers. His breath caught in his throat at sight of her. She shone. And the whole scene he'd been watching receded into grey nothingness.

Her glorious hair was loose, its gleaming mass rippling down over her shoulders. She'd discarded the black suit, an unpalatable reminder of his aborted relationship with Tanya. The dress she wore was like the rising sun—pale bands of soft yellow and orange—a clingy, filmy creation that flowed lovingly over and around her curvy figure and ended in a fluid flare well above her knees. A creamy wrap hung around her arms. A small gold bag dangled from one hand and at the end of her long golden-tanned legs flashed cream-and-gold sandals.

She was beautiful, utterly, heart-mashingly beautiful. She was also so vibrantly *female,* every sexual instinct in Nick started sizzling, demanding primal satisfaction. He rose from his chair with the mindless speed of a lemming rushing towards a cliff, and barely stopped himself from striding out to sweep her into his arms.

Charging like a bull...

Leon's warning punched through the body grip of desire. Nick forced himself to relax. Take the time to get to know her, he sternly told himself. It was important. Yet everything within him screamed it didn't matter. Only this feeling mattered.

The abrupt movement of a man standing up from one of the tables outside the Pier Twenty-One restaurant instantly caught Barbie's eye. Her heart flipped. It was Nick. Nick, waiting for her, watching her come to him.

Keep walking, she fiercely told herself, determined not to let her feet falter, thereby revealing some uncertainty about a meeting which should seem perfectly welcome to a woman who was attracted to a man. She should look eager, pleased to find him waiting for her. Anne Shepherd would. It was the sixteen-year-old Barbie Lamb who shrank from facing him.

But this was nine years down the track.

Barbie had the eerie sensation of a tunnel opening up between them, with Nick Armstrong at the other end of it, a powerful magnet tugging on the woman she was now, tugging inexorably on the most primitive depths of her sexuality, arousing needs that confused any sense of romance she'd ever had.

The bustle of people around her faded from her consciousness. It was as though only she and Nick were real. Nothing else mattered. She wasn't even aware of her legs moving anymore, only of getting closer and closer to him, her whole body zinging in anticipation of making contact.

He had changed out of his business suit. He wore an open-necked dark red shirt with black trousers and somehow the more casual clothes amplified his very male physique, projecting a dangerous dominance that both thrilled her and stirred a tremulous vulnerability. She dragged her gaze back to his face, the darkly handsome face that had haunted many dreams. He smiled at her and it was like a burst of sunshine chasing away the miseries of the past.

I'm Anne, she thought, and smiled back at him… Anne Shepherd, letting the ghost of a broken young heart melt away under the brilliance of being smiled upon.

He stepped around the table and pulled out a chair ready for her, a gentlemanly courtesy that was all too frequently overlooked these days in the dubious name of equality. 'You look wonderful,' he said, his voice slightly furred, sending a sensual shiver down her spine.

'Thank you,' she replied, her mind too fuzzy with pleasure to produce any other words.

He gestured to the chair and she sat, helping him adjust its position for comfortable access to the table.

He hadn't offered his hand in greeting—no body contact at all—yet his closeness behind her emanated a warmth that seemed to stroke her skin and he lingered there for moments after she was settled.

Was she imagining it or was he touching her hair? Perhaps the light breeze off the harbour was ruffling it. Yet her pulse quickened at the thought of him feeling it, liking it, wanting to touch.

She was about to look up when he moved, stepping around the table, back to his own chair. His smile seemed to simmer with sensual satisfaction as he sat down and Barbie was instantly certain he had run his fingers through her hair.

'It's a lovely evening,' she remarked, trying to ignore the wild catapulting of her heart inside her chest.

'Perfect,' he answered, his vivid blue eyes focused directly on her, making the comment intensely personal.

'Is this a favourite restaurant of yours?'

'It's good and it's handy. I live close by.'

'Oh?' Her stomach fluttered. Was Sue right about bed and breakfast being on his agenda? For all her bravado about possibly wanting that, too...did she really? This fast?

He gave her a quizzical look. 'Does that disturb you?'

She shrugged. 'Why should it? You have to live somewhere. Though it must be expensive to rent anything in this part of the city.'

'I don't rent. I bought one of the apartments built above the colonnade.'

'*This* colonnade?'

Impossible to hide her shock. She remembered his family being financially sound—a large, double-storeyed brick home at Wamberal, two not overly expensive cars, living well and wanting for nothing— but she'd never thought of them as in the millionaire class. To own an apartment at Benelong Point, overlooking the harbour…had Nick achieved so much in partnership with Leon Webster?

He frowned. 'It *does* disturb you.'

'It's just…you're talking very serious money here. I didn't realise…' The party on Observatory Hill should have told her. Plus the renovated warehouse at Glebe. Did he own that, too?

'Realise what?'

'How…how rich you are,' she blurted out.

His mouth quirked. 'Is that a black mark against me?'

It sounded absurd. How could wealth attained by hard work and talent be a black mark against anyone? Yet it put him on a level far above her own situation where she and Sue were struggling to make ends meet. She wondered who and what Tanya Wells was—a high-flying career person, a socialite?

All this time she'd been thinking of Nick as the Nick she had known, wanting him to love her, while he…how was he thinking of her? Bed and breakfast?

'What's the problem, Anne?' he asked quietly, caringly.

Anne…

She had changed from the person she once was.

He had changed, too.

This was, indeed, a new ball game, and it had to be accepted as the current day reality it was. Pursuing a dream—an old dream—suddenly seemed very foolish. Yet looking at Nick, she felt the same drawing power he'd always had on her. More...

She took a deep breath and spelled out one undeniable truth. 'I'm not in your league. I'm a professional singer but it's never been what I'd call steady work and I've never cracked the big time. I love singing and I make a living out of it.'

'Nothing wrong with that,' he slid in. 'Not many people can make a living out of doing what they really enjoy doing. It's great that you've been able to in what must be a tough, competitive field.' He leaned forward earnestly, his eyes warmly approving. 'I admire you for going after it, taking it on.'

Smooth words, persuasive words...sincere words?

'I share the rent for a very ordinary, two-bedroom apartment at Ryde. Hardly high class,' she stated brusquely, needing to clear up this issue of status.

He smiled ironically. 'When I first came to Sydney, I rented a room in a dump of a place at Surrey Hills. It was all I could afford. I do understand living within one's means, Anne. And I respect it.'

'But it's different for you now, and you're obviously accustomed to its being different,' she argued.

'Yes. And I won't say I'm not glad to be in a position where I can buy most things I want.'

Did he think he could buy her?

Had his money attracted Tanya Wells?

'*Things,* Anne,' he went on, a more urgent intensity in his voice. 'Like having dinner here whenever I want to. Driving a classy car. Taking a trip overseas. Living in luxury. And all of that is good. I like it. But it doesn't answer all the needs I have.'

His eyes burned into hers as he asked, 'Would it answer all yours?'

She flushed. 'I'm not a gold-digger.'

'And I'm not looking for a cheap thrill from you.'

'What *do* you want with me?' The challenge sliced off her tongue, laced with the cynicism Sue had fed her.

'To know you.'

'There are all sorts of *knowing,*' she flashed back, her eyes nailing her meaning. 'What sense are you talking about?'

'Every sense.'

She stared at him, desperate to believe he spoke the truth. He held her gaze unflinchingly, beating down any scepticism over his intentions. The tightness in her chest slowly eased. Sue had to be wrong. Nick looked truly genuine in his desire to know more of her than a one-night stand would give him.

'Did some rich guy hurt you, Anne?' he asked quietly.

Again she flushed under his directness. 'Why would you think so?'

'Firstly, you are quite stunningly beautiful. Having you would be an ego boost to many men, and rich guys generally see beauty in a woman as a reflection of their success in life.'

'Do you?'

He shook his head. 'I want more in a woman than skin-deep beauty. I guess you could say I've been taken in by that a couple of times,' he added wryly. 'We all make mistakes. I was just wondering if you'd been taken in, too. It was the idea of my being rich that upset you.'

Her hands fluttered an agitated appeal. 'I hadn't thought about you in those terms. It came as a shock. I felt…foolish.'

He reached across the table and took one of her hands, pressing it into a stillness that was meant to soothe fears, yet the feel of his flesh encasing hers sent a wave of exhilarating warmth through her bloodstream and set off deep tremors of desire for a more intimate touching.

'Give us a chance, Anne. You and me. Is that asking too much?'

'No,' she whispered, barely able to catch her breath. He was gently stroking her palm with his thumb, sparking off electric tingles. The effect was mesmerising. She couldn't shake her mind free of it.

His whole expression emanated a fervent need to convince as he said, 'I feel…'

A waiter interrupted, offering them menus. The moment was lost and Barbie could barely curb her frustration, sensing Nick had been about to reveal something important to her. As it was, he withdrew his hand and turned his attention to the waiter, who proceeded to rattle off 'The Specials' for tonight.

She was too distracted to hear them properly and

when Nick asked, 'Do you fancy any of those?' she had to ask the waiter to go through them again.

Even then the food combinations he listed were confusing, unfamiliar. Haute cuisine had not featured largely in her life. Fashionable restaurants like this one were too expensive and she'd never had the time to take an interest in fancy cooking. Rather than reveal her ignorance, she looked to Nick for help.

'What do you recommend?'

'Do you like seafood?'

'Love it.'

'The barbecued calamari in oregano, coriander and lime, and the sole grilled with lemon grass butter are both excellent here.'

He rattled them off, obviously having no problem at all in remembering the ingredients and accepting them as a good mixture without question. He also clearly expected her to choose a starter and a main meal, regardless of cost.

'Is that what you're having?' she checked.

'Yes.'

'Then I'll have it, too.' She just hoped the herbs and lemon grass stuff didn't turn her stomach.

'Wine, sir?'

'The Brown Brothers Chardonnay,' Nick answered without even glancing at the wine list. He smiled at Barbie. 'If that's all right with you.'

'Fine,' she quickly replied, though the Brown Brothers were a complete mystery to her. She and Sue bought wine in a cask from the supermarket. 'I won't be drinking much,' she warned. 'I'm driving.'

'I understand,' he replied, not voicing even the slightest protest or showing a trace of frustration.

Which relieved Barbie's inner turmoil over the bed and breakfast agenda. If seduction had been on Nick's mind, he would surely have said something like, 'A glass or two won't hurt.'

The waiter collected the menus they hadn't even glanced at, and departed, leaving them to themselves again. Relieved to have the meal-ordering over and done with, Barbie could once more think about what had transpired before the interruption.

She wished she could ask Nick what it was *he felt,* but decided it was up to him to continue the conversation. It might appear too forward, too *anxious,* to pursue it herself.

'Would you like some iced water?' he asked, picking up the jug on the table.

'Yes, please.'

He filled a glass for her, adding to the impression he would respect her wishes about the wine-drinking and not try to push her into doing anything she didn't really want. It served to make Barbie feel more comfortable with the situation, certainly less tense about his motives for pursuing a relationship with her.

They sat back, studying each other, assessing where they were now. Nick looked satisfied, content for them simply to be together like this. He wore self-assurance as though it were ingrained, which it probably was, given the success he'd made of his business.

Maybe he'd always had it, an innate part of his character, Barbie thought, remembering how he'd been a natural leader even when they were children in the old Wamberal neighbourhood. Everyone had taken notice of what Nick suggested, what Nick decided, what Nick did. He created games. He was clever and brave and exciting to be with.

Was this just another exciting game to him?

Give us a chance. You and me.

It was silly to let doubts and fears get in the way.

You and me... magic words.

Even this much was a wish come true. She had to try for more, wherever it led.

Occupied with her inner thoughts, she hadn't noticed his expression change until he spoke. His words instantly shattered any peace of mind Barbie had attained.

'You remind me of someone I once knew.'

Light, musing words, but she caught the tension in his stillness, the concentrated weighing in his eyes, and an iron fist squeezed her heart.

CHAPTER EIGHT

NICK saw the shock hit her…the tightening of her face, the flare of angst in her eyes, the swift struggle for control…and any possible doubt was wiped from his mind.

Anne Shepherd *was* Barbie Lamb.

He should have put it together sooner—the deep-down sense of knowing her, the physical instincts she triggered, the intensity of feeling she projected, the passion, Sue Olsen calling her Barbie.

The passage of so many years had pushed his memory of her into the far background and the physical changes wrought by those same years had dazzled his vision. On top of which, the circumstances of their meeting again hadn't helped him see straight. But he was seeing straight now and he knew he was about to walk a tightrope where the wrong step might well mean death to any hope of the relationship he wanted with her.

He had to know what she was thinking, feeling, whether he had a real chance with her. *Bad history,* Leon had said, and he'd been spot-on. Except the bad history, in this case, was personal to him, not some anonymous rich guy. *He* was the one who had inflicted the hurt that needed soothing.

Her lashes swept down, veiling her telltale eyes as

she leaned forward and picked up her glass of water, playing for time, struggling for composure. Her hand shook, lifting the glass to her lips. He watched the convulsive movement of her throat as she sipped, and knew she felt sick, as sick as he did at what he had done to her, while telling himself it was for the best.

He didn't need to be told why she'd played the fairy princess as she had to him…the burning desire to interest and excite, to make him wish for what he had rejected, to tantalise him with the promise of it, then walk away. Was tonight about teasing him more before she slapped him in the face with it? When she put that glass down, would she be Barbie Lamb or Anne Shepherd?

Barbie sipped the iced water, using the glass to hide her face and its contents to cool the fever of uncertainties that gripped her. Was he beginning to recognise her? Reminding him of someone was not positive identification, she sternly told herself, forcing down the sick, panicky feeling. It might not be Barbie Lamb he was thinking of at all.

Everything within her recoiled from confronting the past. Not yet, her heart screamed. She couldn't bear it. She had to have this chance with him, free and clear of spoiling memories. Play for more time, need dictated. He couldn't know for certain who she was.

Feeling slightly more composed, she lowered the glass and attempted a wry little smile. 'I'm not sure any woman likes to be told that.'

He was silent for a moment, seemingly slow in digesting the comment. Her nerves jangled, fear whispering he'd been waiting for some admission. Then to her intense relief he laughed and shook his head. He leaned forward, resting his forearms on the table, his eyes bathing her with warm reassurance as he answered her.

'I wasn't comparing. You shine alone, Anne. Believe me, I feel incredibly lucky that our paths have crossed.'

The fear of recognition receded. Her smile relaxed into pleasure at his compliment. 'Then how do I remind you of someone?' she teased, confident now that he hadn't made the connection.

'It's the eyes,' he said, nodding in confirmation of his observation as he looked directly at them. 'Such a clear light grey. Mostly there's a bit of blue or brown—hazel. I've only seen eyes like yours once before.'

Hers? Had he ever really noticed them back then? The need to know forced the question. 'So who shares them with me?'

He shrugged dismissively. 'It was a long time ago. The memory just struck me. Where I grew up, there were lots of kids in the neighbourhood and we hung around together. One of the girls had eyes like yours.'

That girl was me! she almost screamed at him. It was a struggle to contain the sudden violent surge of emotion as the hurt of being referred to as just a girl in a neighbourhood gang seared every bit of common sense in her brain.

A wise person would probably let the matter drop, move on. After all, there was nothing to be gained by raking over the past and much to lose. Anne Shepherd was not *one of the girls.* She shone alone in Nick Armstrong's eyes.

But an old, old devil of torment writhed inside her, insisting on some release. The opening was there to probe exactly what Nick had thought of her in those days, without him even suspecting who she was. Painful it might be, but she couldn't let it go. The words tripped out, taking a dangerous path that was loaded with pitfalls.

'You must have a very clear memory of this girl. Was she special in some way?'

He smiled reminiscently. 'Yes, she was. It didn't matter how often the guys tried to chase her off, she determinedly stuck to joining in whatever we did, regardless of how tough the challenge was. She wouldn't get left behind and never once cried or complained if she got hurt in the process. She followed us everywhere.'

Baa-Baa Lamb.

Her chest tightened. Still she persisted on the path of knowledge, recklessly bent on filling out the picture of Nick's memory of her.

'Did you find her a pest?'

'No.' His expression became more seriously reflective. 'It's strange, looking back. She was fearless. Yet there was a terrible innocence in her fearlessness. She made me want to protect her.'

'I can't imagine the character you've drawn would want protecting.'

His eyes flicked appreciation of her understanding. 'You're right. She had a fierce pride. But I was five years older so a certain weight of responsibility fell to me.'

'Why to you?'

'I guess because…' His mouth twisted with irony. '…she looked to me. Rightly or wrongly I felt I was the one influencing her.' He paused before quietly adding, 'In the end I had to stop it.'

Barbie's mind staggered at this totally unexpected admission of a *deliberate* act of rejection, a weighing of the situation she had never ever suspected. The question tumbled out, impossible to hold back.

'Why?'

'It became too personal.'

The provocative reply goaded her into pursuing the point. 'How too personal?'

He made a rueful grimace. 'She didn't even see that my younger brother, who was more her age, had a crush on her.'

Barbie's mind reeled. Danny? Shy Danny with the stutter who had never discussed anything but school-work with her? She'd always tried to be kind to him, mostly because he was Nick's brother, but she'd never thought of him as anything else but Nick's brother.

'Are you saying she saw only you?'

'Something like that. It upset Danny. He'd rage at me…but I hadn't made any moves on her. She was too young for me anyway. It would have been wrong all around.'

'So how did you put a stop to it?'

He sighed. 'I made it obvious I was attracted to someone else.'

'Were you?'

'Enough to make it stick. It got Danny off my back.'

'And the girl? It got *her* off your back, too?' Again the question tumbled out, on a rush of bitterness this time, and she could only hope he didn't notice a change in her tone.

For a moment there was a pained expression in his eyes and Barbie registered that he took no pleasure in the success of his manoeuvre. 'It was effective in that sense,' he acknowledged. 'But she didn't take up with Danny. I didn't think she would. She simply dropped out of our lives, kept to herself. A year or so later, her family moved away, up the coast some-where, Byron Bay, I think.'

'But you still remember her…very clearly,' Barbie commented, hiding the terrible twist of irony in her heart.

'She was part of a big chunk of my life.' His eyes warmly invited *her* memories as he said, 'You must have had people in your growing-up years who col-oured your life, one way or another.'

He'd coloured it black. Totally black in that act of rejection. Only now did she realise there had been greys. He hadn't been a shallow rat. He'd cared about his brother's feelings... Danny, who'd meant nothing to her...

'Where does your family live, Anne?' Nick prompted.

She shook herself out of the dark reverie brought on by these revelations. Later she would think about them, put them in perspective. Dealing with *now* had to take priority. She had Nick here with her and she didn't want to lose what might be between them this time.

'Queensland. On the Sunshine Coast,' she answered truthfully. Her parents had moved on from Byron Bay.

'You're a long way from home.'

'I've been travelling around the country since I was eighteen. Pursuing a career in singing meant I had to.'

He smiled his understanding. 'Of course.'

'What about your family?' It was less dangerous ground.

'My parents still live at Wamberal. That's on the Central Coast.'

So nothing had changed there.

'The rest of the family has scattered,' he went on. 'I have a sister who lives in Sydney. She's married and has a couple of children.'

Carole...two years older than Barbie and very fashion-conscious from the moment she hit her teen years. It was a safe bet she'd married well. 'And your brother...the one you've mentioned?' she pressed.

'He's currently in San Diego. Danny is into yacht racing. He always was mad about boats.'

She remembered the small catamaran the Armstrongs had owned, Danny sailing it on Wamberal Lake. He'd asked her to go with him and she had a couple of times, more to show she was game for the experience than to share it with Danny. She'd really wanted to sail with Nick.

It was good to hear Danny was so far away and mad about something else. At least he couldn't interfere with this relationship.

Three waiters descended on them, one with the bottle of wine, another offering a selection of bread rolls from a basket, the third setting down the calamari starter. Barbie was grateful for the little flurry of activity which took Nick's focus away from her. She hadn't realised how difficult it would be, pretending to be a stranger, carrying the emotional strain of monitoring every word she said, trying to make her questions sound like natural curiosity.

She took a bread roll, smiled at the food waiter who said, 'Enjoy!' nodded to the wine waiter who held the bottle hovered inquiringly over her glass. By the time all the business of serving was done, she had almost convinced herself Nick could not be blamed for the decision he'd made to *end it,* although it was impossible to end *feelings.* They might be buried, twisted, transformed, but they didn't end.

At least his memories of her held some admiration, mixed with the conflict his brother had caused. Perhaps some regret, too, for what had been lost in the action he had taken. Nevertheless, she didn't want to revisit that old humiliation by talking about it openly. She needed the balm of his current admiration to heal that re-opened wound.

'Something wrong?'

Nick's query jolted her gaze back to his. 'No. Why?' she spilled out, hoping he hadn't sensed any disturbance in her thoughts.

'You seemed to be looking dubiously at the calamari. Would you like to order something else?'

'No. It's just that I've never seen it presented like this.' She smiled to alleviate any concern. 'It's so artistic it's almost a shame to dig into it.'

He picked up his cutlery to encourage her. *'Bon appetit.'*

She followed suit and began to eat, concentrating on the taste of the food, finding the calamari beautifully tender and the subtle flavourings interesting.

Nick's mind was in hyper-drive, trying to assess what was going on in Barbie's head. And heart. She was still sticking to Anne Shepherd. He had no idea if the answers he'd given to her quiz on the past had satisfied her quest to know how he remembered her and what had driven his actions. He could only hope she now understood there had been mitigating circumstances to the denial he'd chosen.

She was the one choosing denial now, he realised, and if he was to have any chance with her, he had to respect her choice. She didn't want to tell her side.

Too hurtful? Too revealing? Would it make her feel too vulnerable?

Which led him to ponder protection. She had thought herself protected today when she'd come to his office. And Anne Shepherd was now protecting the girl he had once known. But was it protection…or deliberate deception feeding a deep, vengeful streak that would lash out at him when she judged *he* was at his most vulnerable?

He instinctively recoiled from this scenario. It was too dark, suggestive of a more disturbed mind than he cared to deal with. Nine years had gone by. He could understand her being wary of him, wary of letting herself be attracted to him, but to deliberately set him up for a fall at this point…no, he didn't want to believe that.

The Barbie Lamb he remembered had been straight and true in everything she'd done. People's characters didn't change. Pride might make her cover up the past, but he was sure there'd been nothing false in her response to his kisses. No pretence. No deception. It had been too real, too giving of herself to the passion that had exploded between them.

Mutual desire.

Or was he fooling himself?

She put down her knife and fork and smiled warmly at him. 'That was delicious. A great recommendation. Thank you.'

An electric charge hit his groin.

'Glad you enjoyed it,' he returned just as warmly, any concern about her motives totally obliterated.

He *wanted* her, regardless of what she called herself, regardless of where the wanting led. He was not about to let this feeling go. Not about to let her go, either.

CHAPTER NINE

HIS smile made Barbie tingle all over. Even when she was young it had invariably made her feel happy, generating bubbles of joy through her whole bloodstream. Then it had seemed to say he really liked her. And perhaps he had, although other things had been more important to him.

Focused on her now, a woman who was not too young for him, it had a far more powerful impact, loaded with the message he found her infinitely desirable and emanating an intense level of sexual intimacy, his eyes reflecting the knowledge of how she'd felt in his arms, how her mouth had moved with his, and the wanting to savour the experience again and again.

She found herself squeezing her thighs together, capturing and enclosing the excitement he stirred. Her nipples were tightening into hard little buds. Never had she reacted so physically to a man before and she marvelled at the difference between wanting someone from afar and having the desire actively returned at close quarters.

What would have happened if he'd looked at her like this when she was sixteen…if he'd kissed her…?

Barbie shook her head. She had to stop thinking about *then*.

'What's going through your mind?' Nick asked.

'I'm amazed that here we are…you and me,' she answered with more truth than he could possibly know.

'Fate smiled on us, bringing us together.'

She laughed. 'Do you really believe in Fate?'

He shrugged, smiling whimsically. 'Fortuitous circumstances are sometimes uncanny, things falling into place at the right time. Who knows how that works? Is it blind luck or are there energy forces that somehow guide meetings and outcomes?' He paused, his eyes probing hers very personally. 'Perhaps we were always meant to be here at this time and place…you and I.'

Goose bumps ran over her skin at the suggestion of something preordained. 'I could have said no to your invitation.'

'But you didn't.'

The pull had been too great to resist, Barbie silently acknowledged.

He didn't wait for a reply. His eyes still engaging hers with compelling intensity, he softly stated, 'I have the strong sense that I've been waiting for you a very long time.'

It hit a chord that throbbed painfully. He could have found her if he'd wanted to. Though he didn't know who she was, reason dictated, flooding her with confused emotions. Should she tell him now, have it out in the open? And see his expression change to one of shock, embarrassment?

No. She didn't want that.

'Perhaps we were connected in some previous life,' she said with considerable irony.

'And something drove us apart,' he added, his eyes glittering in a way that made her feel uneasy, as though he could see into her soul.

'A very romantic fantasy,' she remarked dryly, picking up her glass of wine, defensively breaking eye contact with him.

There was a momentary silence. Then he laughed, relaxing the intensity he had built up. 'I guess I like the idea of people getting a second chance. We don't always make the right decisions the first time around.'

'That's true,' she agreed, happy to leave it at that…a second chance. 'Though you must have made a lot of right decisions in your business for it to have gone so well.'

'Oh, Leon and I saw the openings, particularly with the Internet developing so fast,' he answered off-handedly.

She set her glass down and leaned forward, eager to know more of his current life. 'I'm sorry to be so ignorant, but what does Multi-Media Promotions actually do?'

'Every form of advertising. Whatever we win a contract for.'

'You mean you design promotional stuff for other companies.'

He nodded. 'We do our best to present their products in a sales-winning format.'

'Give me an example.'

A waiter arrived to take their empty plates and refill

their glasses. The momentary distraction did not deflect Barbie's intent to understand precisely where Nick was now and how he'd got there. Under her pressing interest, he revealed he was the head designer at the company, responsible for all the artwork they produced for their clients.

This, Barbie, was fascinated to hear, was computer-generated, able to be structurally altered or differently coloured by the stroke of a key. Of course, Nick had been known as a whiz at computers in his school days, but he'd never talked about what he did on them to her. Now it seemed he manipulated this technological world at will.

It was obvious he liked his work, enjoyed the challenge of keeping up what he called street-edge designs, and took immense satisfaction in the results he achieved. She listened to the warm enthusiasm in his voice, the passion for getting everything just right and putting his vision across to others, winning their commitment to his concepts. She felt the inner fire and drive that made him the success he was and knew this was a deep part of his personal magnetism.

He believed in himself.

He was a born leader, the kind of man who forged a path that others followed.

And in her heart of hearts she wished she was attached to it, attached to him. Although she'd only been on the edge of his world in her growing-up years, she'd missed the excitement of it, missed the involvement in something special because he was there, making it happen.

He'd left a hole in her life with his driving her away from him, and the desire to have that hole filled now—filled to overflowing—was so intense, she hung on his every word, drank in his every expression, revelled in his sharing all that he was. In many ways, opening his mind to her like this was more intimate than a kiss. It was an acceptance she was his equal in understanding.

The fish course they'd ordered was set in front of them, interrupting the magical flow of communication. Nick drew back in his seat, offering an apologetic smile. 'I've been talking too much about myself.'

'No,' she quickly denied. 'I wanted to hear.'

He quizzically studied the warm sincerity in her eyes. 'It's hardly your scene.'

'Should I be limited to mine?'

He shook his head. 'It's just that I don't usually talk about my work outside of the office.'

'Then I'm honoured.'

'No. *I* am. You really did want to know.'

'It's a big part of you.'

'Yes. But not a part many people care to understand.'

'You mean…like Tanya.'

She wished the acid little comment unsaid the moment it was out of her mouth. It was stupid to bring that woman up when she was no longer in Nick's life. Yet Barbie could not stifle a welling of resentment at his choice of companion during the long years of supposedly *waiting for her.*

Tanya Wells was a horrible person with a really mean, vicious streak. Surely he should have picked that up in her character, or had the sex been enough for him? Take it while the urge was on and walk away when the physical attraction was whittled away by other differences? Was enjoying a new and exciting sexual partner all he was seeking with her now?

'I realise you have no reason to be impressed by Tanya,' he answered ruefully. 'But she could be fun when she was in a good mood.'

'Fun,' Barbie repeated, thinking fun and games in bed.

'Relief from the pressures of work,' he added.

'Perhaps I shouldn't have brought up the subject of work then.'

'It's different with you,' he assured her, his smile playing its powerful havoc again.

Barbie took a deep breath, picked up her knife and fork and purposefully attacked the sole grilled in lemon grass butter, needing something to settle the flutters of excitement in her stomach.

Different... the word was like a wild intoxicant, making her feel giddy with pleasure. Whatever Nick had shared with Tanya—and other women—didn't matter. After all, she'd tried a few relationships herself, wanting more from them than they'd ever given. Sometimes need drove people into making mistakes. Why blame Nick for his?

This was different.

Their second chance.

And everything within Barbie craved to take it, wherever it led.

Nick ate the fish course mechanically, not even tasting it. That crack about Tanya had suddenly left him with the sense of being on trial and he didn't like it, not one bit. He'd explained why he'd acted as he had in the past. Surely any reasonable person would accept the explanation. He'd given her time to digest it, given her another opening to admit who she was, couching it in words that should have reassured her as to how he felt about meeting her again.

Why had she bypassed it?

What more positive signals could he have given her?

The memory of his twenty-first birthday night started plaguing him—the cut-off night for a too young and innocent Barbie. She'd sung the birthday song as the cake had been carried in, a solo effort his mother had arranged because Barbie had such a sweet, true voice. Except the way she'd sung it…he'd been so discomforted by her obvious feeling for him, when she'd presented him with her gift afterwards, he could hardly bear to accept it, shoving it quickly aside.

Only later did he discover it was a watch, the back of it enscribed so endearingly, it had made him feel rotten, even more so because Jasmine Elliot had also given him a watch which he'd worn that night. It had been an unwitting cruelty to Barbie's feelings, although he had ultimately argued to himself, an effective one in pushing her away from him.

She had been far too young.

It couldn't have worked.

Now was their time.

Or hadn't she ever forgiven him that brutal hurt?

Was she priming him for a fall, in revenge for how he'd dealt with her? The avid interest in his work…was it genuine or a ploy to make the high he'd been riding even higher before she walked away, leaving him as flattened as he must have left her all those years ago?

But she had been too young, damn it!

Whereas now…

He surreptitiously watched her eating the meal he'd ordered, daintily loading her fork, lifting it to her mouth. Her hands were steady—finely shaped, long-fingered hands—and he yearned to have those hands stroking him, softly, sensually, lovingly. Even how she slid the fork into her mouth and out again was intensely sexy, the way her lips closed over it then slowly released it.

Her long lashes veiled her eyes, keeping her thoughts a taunting mystery. Her glorious hair shimmered, a silky flow of temptation that teased his imagination and conjured up erotic fantasies…how it would feel on his pillow, his naked body, brushing over his skin.

She finished the meal, her gaze lifting to his as she set down the cutlery. 'You certainly eat well if you come here often,' she remarked appreciatively. 'That was delicious, Nick.'

Her distinctive grey eyes seemed clear of any artifice, yet she had to be taking him for a ride. Why else would she hide her identity? How long did she intend to string it out? How much would she give before turning her back on him?

'There are many fine restaurants around the quay,' he remarked, smiling as he pushed away from his own emptied plate. 'I'd like to introduce you to all of them.'

She blushed. From guilt or pleasure?

'I'd like that, too,' she said simply, her eyes telling him he was the main attraction, not the food.

It made him burn with a torment he couldn't bear. A wild recklessness seized him, demanding he push her to the limit right now, testing how much she wanted to be with him.

'Do you fancy a sweets course?'

She shook her head. 'I've had enough, thank you.'

'Then let me show you where I live. I'll make you coffee in my apartment.'

Her blush deepened. She stared at him, an agony of indecision in her eyes.

Nick sat still, returning her stare, a relentless challenge beating through him in fierce waves. If her wanting him was real, let her prove it by coming with him. If this was some vengeful game, let her reveal it now, excusing herself from the prospect of being alone together in a private place with the risk of a more dangerous intimacy developing between them.

He might be charging like a bull, but the red rag was out, waving through his mind, and he couldn't ignore it.

'All right,' she said in a breathy little voice.

Relief and excitement brewed a heady cocktail. In coming with him she was giving up a certain control, gambling more than any game-player would. Or was she recklessly upping the stakes, driving the ride higher? Whatever her thinking, the ball was now in his court and he instantly determined on playing it hard.

'Have you had the apartment very long?' she asked.

'Two years.'

'Time enough to make it your home.'

She was curious about him, he realised, wanting to see. Wanting to judge? Putting him on further trial?

'It's furnished to my taste, if that's what you mean,' he answered, wondering if she'd make it into his bedroom, wanting her there, resolved on testing *her* wanting.

'Did you use an interior decorator?'

'No. I looked around, bought what appealed to me.'

She nodded. 'I guess you wanted to please your own artistic eye.'

His heart thudded with the realisation that she understood him even more than Leon did. His friend had declared it a waste of time hunting for furniture. Let the experts do it, was his motto, and Nick couldn't deny they'd done a classy job on Leon's apartment.

Still, he preferred his own. It gave him a deeply personal pleasure, living with his own choices.

'Style isn't so important to me,' he acknowledged. 'I like to feel comfortable.'

And more than anything he wanted to feel comfortable with her—nothing hidden between them. He *would* push her to the limit, force her to reveal what was in her mind.

Their waiter came to whisk away the plates. 'The menu for sweets, sir?'

'No. We're finished here.' He took out his wallet and handed over a credit card. 'The bill, please.'

'Be right back, sir.'

'Some more wine?' he asked, noticing her glass was empty.

'No, thank you.' Her eyes were nervous but there was a hardy glint of determination in them, shining through the flickering uncertainties. She didn't want to back off…yet.

The bottle of chardonnay was still half full. Normally he would ask the waiter to cork it for carrying home, but he didn't care about the waste tonight. Anticipation was a fire in his veins. He could barely wait to touch her.

She picked up her glass of iced water and sipped from it. Were her thoughts feverish? Did they need cooling down? Or was the fire of desire in her veins, too?

Well, he'd soon find out.

The waiter returned with the bill. Nick quickly signed it, slid the copy and his credit card into his wallet, then stood up, burning to move this game onto his ground. Before he could reach her chair it was scraping back. She was on her feet, clutching the little gold handbag. For a tense few moments Nick had the impression she was poised for flight—panic in the air—car keys in her bag, people still around them, safety in numbers.

He picked up her creamy wrap which had fallen onto the back of the chair and draped it around her shoulders. There were goose bumps on her arms. 'Cold?' he murmured.

'A bit.'

The admission was slightly choked, breathy.

'You'll be warm in my apartment,' he promised, lifting her hair out of the wrap to let it swing free, taking the opportunity to run it over his hand, revel in its softness.

Her head jerked slightly, skittishly, but she made no protest at the liberty he was taking. Her shoulders squared. She was not going to back off, not at this point. A surge of triumph sizzled through him. He moved, picking up her hand to draw her with him, lacing his fingers through hers to lock her into *his* game plan.

They fluttered before settling into his grip. He heard her suck in a deep breath as she fell into step at his side. His sense of winning was slightly marred by these poignant little signs of vulnerability. Leon's warning flashed into his mind.

You're too fast on the draw, Nick. Treat her right. Get to know her.

Which was all very fine, Nick thought caustically, if she was treating him right.

She'd made the game, closing doors he'd given her more than one opportunity to open. There could be no real knowing of anyone when deliberate deception was in play. Nick felt he had every right to smash those doors down. He had to know where she was at, where she was coming from, where she wanted to be. There could be no going forward until that was settled and Nick wanted a future with her.

Barbie Lamb…the girl…the woman…lost and found.

Not to be lost again.

Not without a fight.

CHAPTER TEN

'IT'S not far,' Nick said encouragingly.

Barbie's heart was galloping. Sue would undoubtedly say she was mad, accompanying him to his
apartment. Too far, too fast. But he was holding her
hand, taking her on his path, and she couldn't let go,
couldn't break away, however far he intended to take
her. The need to hold on to him was more compelling
than any common sense arguments about how best to
handle relationships.

Besides this was different.

It would be impossible to keep her real identity
hidden much longer. Since Nick had said Anne
Shepherd shone as a uniquely special woman to him,
it seemed paramount to use every possible minute in
his company, finding out if he really meant it. Only
then would Barbie have the confidence to emerge as
one and the same woman.

Seeing the home he'd chosen would also tell her
more about him, she reasoned, although reason had
little to do with the journey she was now taking. The
hand gripping hers was irresistible, its warm, possessive strength belonging to Nick... Nick, wanting her.
Never mind for what purpose, or for how long. The
wanting felt so good, Barbie would have walked anywhere with him.

'Do you ever cook for yourself?' she asked, trying to sound natural, not so affected by his closeness and the invitation to even more closeness.

'Not much. The occasional breakfast.'

Bed and breakfast...

She clamped down on the spoiling thought, but lost the will to pursue any trivial conversation. The nervous excitement of being with Nick consumed her and his silence seemed to transmit the same inner intensity of feeling...an urgency to be alone with her, only with her.

She had no idea how far they walked along the colonnaded promenade, nor was she aware of anything they passed. It was as though she had stepped into a dream world where wishes could come true, and she refused to consider a reality which might be different.

He steered her through a huge marble archway into a rotunda-like foyer that featured a grand staircase winding upwards.

'Do we climb that?' she asked, her voice echoing around the high emptiness, seeming to emphasise the abrupt cut-off from a public place.

'It only leads to floors of offices,' he answered briefly, drawing her towards an elevator set in the side wall.

The doors slid open the moment he hit the Up button. They stepped inside. Nick produced a security card from his shirt pocket and inserted it into a slot on the control board before pressing the number 8. The action indicated an exclusivity that only the very rich could afford. An eighth-floor apartment, directly overlooking the harbour, would indeed be fairyland for her, Barbie thought.

Would Nick treat her like a princess…or would she be coming down to earth with a thump?

Again she pushed the question aside, determined on following his lead. She recalled him saying he'd felt protective of her, except that had been Barbie, not Anne. All the same, she did instinctively trust him not to do anything she didn't want. If there was any problem it probably lay in her own wanting.

Which hit her forcibly when they emerged from the fast-track elevator and he released her hand to unlock and open the door to his apartment. The loss of that small physical contact with him left her oddly bereft, as though it were vital to her sense of well-being.

For a moment the disconnection aroused a tremulous uncertainty about what she was doing. Then Nick opened the door and his eyes blazed at her, seeming to dare her to step inside.

Her heart turned over. It was like the old days…was she brave enough to keep up with him, do what he did, share the thrills and the spills?

Pride and the long-held desire for his approval compelled her feet forward. Lights were switched on and the vista of his spacious living area diminished the sense of entering dangerous ground. The immediate impact was warmly inviting and she walked on without any prompt, eager to see his private world, to match it to the man who now wanted her in his life.

'This is lovely, Nick!' she cried, eyeing the two long sofas which dominated the lounge area, relieved and happy to feel real pleasure in his choices.

There was nothing intimidating here. The sofas were upholstered in a forest-green velvet with a tiny brown sprig pattern which lent more interest. Scatter cushions in gold and brown and green dressed the thickly rolled armrests, and beautiful gold lamps stood on side tables, giving a lovely mellow light.

A large square coffee table with a polished parquet surface provided easy service for anyone seated on either sofa, and floor-to-ceiling curtains beyond it obviously hid a magnificent view. As she tried to imagine it, Nick strode past her and operated the cord that pulled the curtains apart.

Even at night, the sheer scope of it was breathtaking, the lights of the city climbing upwards from the harbour shores, the island of Fort Denison floodlit, the moving lights of boats on the water.

'Oh!' she breathed in awed delight, instantly walking forward to see more. 'It must be marvellous to look out on this every day.'

'Yes. There's always something interesting happening on the harbour, liners coming in, yacht races, navy ships on the move.'

He was on the move, too, coming towards her, and his vibrant masculinity hit her anew, kicking her pulse into a faster beat. Suddenly he looked very aggressively male, the strong planes of his face gleaming more sharply in the lamplight, his eyes hooded, his body emanating deliberate purpose.

'I don't think you'll need this now,' he said, removing her wrap and dropping it on the end of the closest sofa.

His arm replaced it, curving around her shoulders and turning her as he gestured towards the dining area and the kitchen which had a bar separator from the rest of the living area and high stools where people could sit and converse with whomever was working behind it.

'The open plan allows the view to be enjoyed from everywhere,' he pointed out. The fingers stroking her upper arm stilled and tensed as he added, 'You get a similar outlook from the master bedroom. Come and see.'

She glanced up, sensing another underlying dare, a test of courage he would judge her on. His eyes briefly met hers, simmering with a challenge she didn't understand. Before she could sift it through her mind, he was propelling her along with him.

Hugged to his side, acutely conscious of his body heat and the muscular strength she was brushing against with each step they took, Barbie stopped seeing anything. She moved in a blur, the word, *bedroom,* pounding through her mind.

Wild fears and hopes leapt through her, causing nervous havoc. She didn't need to see the view again, but there was a terribly intimate attraction about being shown *his* bedroom, and somehow halting what was happening was not an option.

Another door was opened, lights switched on, and having swept her into this most private of all rooms,

Nick left her near the bed while he moved to the table on the other side of it and pressed a button on a console. The wall-length curtains on the far side of the room whooshed apart but Barbie was too distracted by the bed to look past it. She stood transfixed by the richly sensual temptation in front of her.

The top bedcover seemed to be made of softly glowing rows of sable fur, lushly inviting her to stroke it. Underneath was obviously a doona encased in stone-coloured raw silk. Piled against the bedhead were pillows in the same silk as well as of the dark brown fur, and even more stunning cushions in embroidered red velvet bordered by a leopard print.

'Is it real fur?' she asked, unable to stop herself from reaching out and running her hand over the thick, luxurious softness.

'No. Fake.'

'It feels real.'

'Yes, it does. A high-quality fake.' He walked back towards her, an ironic twist to his lips, his eyes glittering with a savage kind of mockery. 'It looks right. It feels right. Good enough to fool anyone that it's real. But it is an artificial simulation. Like you…'

'What?'

'…being a fairy princess. For children, you would seem very real, though in actuality you're a fake fantasy.'

She straightened up, jolted by the comparison, feeling as though her integrity was being attacked.

He rounded the bed, hands out, expressing an appeal. 'So I'm wondering…how real are you, Anne?'

Did he suspect some deception? How could he? Barbie struggled to collect her scattered wits. 'I don't know what you mean.'

He was close now, close enough to lift his hand and stroke her cheek, close enough for his eyes to burn into hers, seeking, demanding. 'You come to me in different guises, playing roles.'

'Just dress-ups,' she defended. 'I'm the same person underneath.'

He slid an arm around her waist and scooped her into full body contact with him. Her hands flew up, pressing against his upper chest, giving her some breathing space. She didn't understand what was going on here, only that she seemed to be on trial and Nick was fiercely resolved on not being fooled by her. Had his recent experience with Tanya scarred him?

'You *feel* right,' he said with a low throbbing vehemence that thrummed into her heart. His fingers slid into her hair, his thumb lightly fanning her temple as though wanting to infiltrate her secret thoughts. 'Do I feel right to you?'

Her body was quivering inside, whether from fear or excitement she didn't know. Her mind was a mess. The intensity of feeling pouring from him made any thinking difficult. She remembered how it had felt when he kissed her...no conflict then.

'Kiss me,' she whispered, the need to set everything right between them so urgent, she couldn't think further than that.

For a moment his eyes darkened with turbulent emotion. Panic increased Barbie's turmoil. It wasn't the answer he wanted. What was? What did he need from her?

Then his mouth crashed down on hers, hot and wild, and Barbie's panic surged into an equally heated response. It was not a kiss of sweet exploration, nor one of sensual pleasure. It was a passionate plundering, intent on smashing any barrier between them, a tempestuous testing of how far desire went, how *real* it was.

There was anger in it, frustration, the need to rip into each other, taking instead of giving, as though this was their one chance to get what had been missing from their lives and there was no other source for it. They were greedy for each other, feverish in their need to know, to prove the *rightness* they craved.

On some sane level Barbie knew she was being insanely reckless but didn't care. There was no turning back. Nick Armstrong was not in the lead now. She was not a little lamb following him. She was holding him to her and revelling in the feel of him, his hard maleness pressed against her, wanting entry to the woman she was, his mouth exploding into hers again and again, needing the essence of her, determined on having it.

His hand burrowed under her hair and scooped it off her back, hooking it over her shoulder, out of the way, as he found the head of her zipper and opened her dress. A leading advantage to him, she thought, and instantly dropped her hands to his shirt, tearing at the buttons. *I can do whatever you do,* was racing through her mind. *You won't leave me behind. Not this time.*

Clothes hit the floor. Shoes were kicked off. Strong hands almost encircled her waist, digging into her naked flesh, lifting her off her feet. She was tossed onto the bed, landing sprawled across the sable fur, sinking into its thick softness, the fibres caressing her bare skin with sinful sensuality.

And Nick stood there like a primitive caveman, his chest heaving, his eyes glittering over the prize he'd brought to his lair. 'You really want to go this far?' he demanded.

Echoes of the past rocketed around Barbie's mind, the doubt that little Baa-Baa Lamb could go the distance.

'I'm already this far,' she fiercely retorted and a woman-devil inside her drove her to stretch out provocatively. 'It's up to *you* to join *me.*'

He certainly had the superior strength. His magnificent body rippled with taut male muscles. But she had power, too, the power of being a woman he wanted, and his very evident erection made that undeniable. It was good he had to come to her. It was great to be the one he followed for once, had to follow because *he* needed to be with *her.*

She gloried in the sizzling flare in his eyes as he moved, one knee sinking into the fur beside her. He nudged her legs apart with his other knee, taking a subtle mastery over her position. A flood of vulnerability suddenly attacked her sense of power, but Barbie wouldn't let it win. She was not going to show any fear to Nick. Even when he kneeled over her on all fours, threateningly dominant, her eyes held his in fierce challenge—no surrender in this game of games.

Come and get me, she silently dared.

No more hide-and-seek.

They were down to absolute basics, a man and a woman coming together.

He took her mouth, invading it with such erotic passion, her body instinctively arched for the more intimate invasion. But he withheld it, resisting the pull of her arms, tantalising her with the simulated promise of what was to come. She clawed his back. He lifted his head. For a moment she saw the gleam of savage satisfaction in his eyes, the triumphant knowledge of her frenzied need.

In the very next instant it meant nothing. He moved, his head dipping down to her breasts, taking their extended peaks in his mouth in turn, and all she knew were the sweet bursts of pleasure he evoked with the wild suction of his mouth, the exquisite lashing of his tongue, pleasure she violently wanted prolonged, wanting more and more of the intense excitement he aroused. Her fingers raked through his hair, grasped his head, intent on seizing control, moving him to match her ravening need.

Again he eluded any submission to her will, tearing himself out of her grasp, trailing his mouth over her stomach, leaving kisses of pulsing heat, moving lower, lower. A hand slid down the soft, moist folds between her legs, fingers stroking, circling, caressing…mesmerising sensations. Her own hands stopped scrabbling to hold him. The distraction was so intense she instinctively closed her eyes, her whole being drawn to concentrate on inner feelings.

Unbelievably, the enthralling touch was suddenly accompanied by a kiss so shockingly intimate she almost jerked away from it. An arm across her hips held her still and the shock melted away under the sweet flood of sensation his mouth wrought, delicious waves of it, peaking and spilling through her, gathering a rhythmic momentum that ultimately begged for a truly mutual mating.

'Stop!' The cry ripped from her throat, driven by a need she couldn't hold back, couldn't control, couldn't help herself. 'Come to me now, Nick! Now!'

She threshed against his hold, wild for him to do what he should. His arm lifted and burrowed under her. She reached for him, feverishly primed to fight for what she wanted. It wasn't right yet. It had to be right. But she didn't have to fight. He surged up and over her, making the entry she craved, the blissful joining, a deep penetration that filled her with rightness, a stunningly ecstatic rightness.

'Yes…' she breathed on a burst of relief, all her inner muscles squeezing him, hugging the wonderful pleasure of him.

'Open your eyes.'

A raw need gravelled through his command and Barbie instantly complied.

His eyes blazed into hers. 'Don't close them. I will not be a fantasy. This is very…' He pulled back, leaving her momentarily devastated by the loss of the deep connection. '…very real,' he harshly asserted, and drove forward, emphatically proving the power of his reality.

'Very real,' she agreed, exulting in the proof.

Slowly, tauntingly, he repeated the withdrawal, leaving her quivering in anticipation until he came again, filling the emptiness, taking possession of it, setting off convulsive ripples of intense excitement.

'It feels good?' His eyes glittered, demanding her admission, or was he mocking her need for him?

'Yes, yes…' she cried. 'You must know it does. Why are you asking?'

'Because I want to hear you say it.'

Was this about winning for him? Being on top?

'Don't play with me, Nick.' She lifted a hand to his face, urgently stroking an appeal. 'Just be with me. Don't you want that?'

He closed his eyes, expelled a long deep breath, and without another word, moved them both into an all-consuming rhythm, their bodies pulsing to the drumbeat of their union, a deep pounding of flesh within flesh that was totally exalting, primal, power-ful…fulfilling a long-dormant sense of destiny that had lain in Barbie's mind and heart for years and years and years.

Nick and her.

She loved the feel of him, loved the thought of him loving the feel of her. She didn't know how many times she climaxed around him. It was wonderful that he didn't stop, that he wanted to go on and on. She used her hands to transmit her sense of wonder and pleasure in him, caressing his beautiful body, adoring it, revelling in it, delighting in the excitement she stirred, the faster tempo of his driving into her.

It was only right that he should come to climax, too, the exquisite release of tension it brought, and she urged him towards it, using her whole body in a voluptuous tease, wanting to give him all he had given her.

And when he finally came, it was a magical sensation, the hot explosive injection of himself so deeply inside her, the intimate melding she could feel taking place, Nick relaxing, hugging her tightly to him, letting it be, the two of them joined as one...at peace.

What bliss to lie together like this! Even when he rolled onto his side, he carried her with him in close entanglement, and her head ended up resting over his thundering heart. Contentment seeped through her and she wished this lovely sense of well-being could go on forever.

Or was that a fantasy?

The thought brought back the memory of what Nick had implied earlier. She frowned, not liking what they were sharing linked to anything that wasn't real. Impulsively she spoke, wanting to clear any misconception he had about what she was doing here with him.

'This isn't a fantasy to me, Nick. More like a dream come true.'

The words filtered through his absorption in her glorious hair, the heady scent of it, the silky texture, the sensual pleasure of its soft flow over his skin.

What dream?

He frowned, remembering how she had continued to evade admitting who she really was, inviting him to kiss her, challenging him to take her, pleading for him to finish what he'd started. And the finishing had blown all the disturbing sense of wrongness out of his mind.

It was a struggle even now to focus on it when he felt so good with her. But she still wasn't telling him the truth about herself. He didn't want to think about the girl he'd turned away from him. He wanted to immerse himself in the pleasure of the woman in his arms, but he couldn't stop himself from wondering what dream Barbie Lamb might have nursed…a dream that had now come true.

Had she imagined taking him as her lover, showing him what he had missed all these years?

What was the next move?

Slapping him in the face with who she was, then leaving him with an unforgettable taste of what he could have had if he'd acted differently?

The buzz of torment in his mind was abruptly obliterated as her mouth closed over the nipple closest to his heart and she began licking and tugging at it. The unexpected burst of erotic tingling had his fingers winding tightly around her hair, pulling her head up. She looked at him, a joyful teasing dancing in her clear grey eyes.

'You did it to me, Nick. Now it's your turn.'

'Tit for tat?'

She grinned so openly, he couldn't believe she was taking him for a ride. 'Let me. I want to,' she replied, her voice a soft siren call that promised pleasure.

He let her.

Her kisses sent out streams of hot excitement and the delicate feathering of her fingers traced erotic paths all over him as she moved down his body, her soft female flesh pressing, sliding, arousing and inciting more sexual desire. Then her hands were cupping him, encircling him, stroking, lightly squeezing, making him swell with urgency.

He started to move, and she stopped him, laying an arm over his stomach as she took his re-erected length into her mouth and seduced him into stillness with the utterly exquisite sensations she delivered, not only internally, but externally with her long hair fanning his thighs and groin.

His muscles tensed. He knew he couldn't contain himself for long. She was taking him to the edge of control and suddenly he didn't want it this way. It was too one-sided. He jack-knifed forward, hauled her up and set her astride him, burying himself inside her to the hilt, loving her slick velvet heat.

'Ride me,' he invited, recklessly uncaring of any fall she had in mind for him.

She was a golden goddess, and she could steal his soul for all he cared at that moment. Her eyes sparkled with the power he gave her but she didn't flay him with it. She rode him slowly, savouring each long slide, and it was incredibly sexy, like a waltz designed to revel in secret intimacies. Like knowing her breasts were bare and accessible behind the veil of hair that had fallen forward over her shoulders, the thick silky tresses swaying, giving glimpses of dark areolae.

He reached under the veil, filling his hands with the lovely soft weight of them, feeling them move to the rhythm she chose, a secret pleasure, hidden from his vision but there in his hands. And any concern over where this night was leading was lost in the need, the compulsion to feel everything there was to feel with this woman.

It went beyond sexual gratification. The desire for more of her didn't stop at climax. Her body was end-lessly exciting, her mouth a feast of sweet passion, her sense of sensuality more erotic than anything he'd known. She gave the much ill-used words, *making love,* real meaning, and it was that very loving which eventually soothed him into sleep, imbued with the feeling that nothing had ever felt so right.

It was a deep, peaceful slumber and nothing dis-turbed it. There was no sense of anything changing, no alarm signals slipping into his subconscious, no awareness of being left alone.

At six-thirty, the clock-radio beside his bed came on, signalling the beginning of another workday, mu-sic playing, bringing him awake. Barbie, too, he thought, not yet aware that she wasn't beside him.

With a smile already gathering from a flood of memories, Nick opened his eyes…and found she was gone from his bed, gone from his apartment…and there was nothing to say she would ever be with him again!

CHAPTER ELEVEN

NICK slid his Porsche into his parking slot behind the warehouse just as Leon was stepping out of his BMW. Bad timing. He wasn't in the mood for any personal chat with Leon and it was a dead certainty what the hot topic would be.

He switched off the engine and sat brooding over whether to get out or not. The urge to drive over to the Ryde apartment and confront Barbie Lamb face to face had been burning through him ever since he'd woken up and found her gone. It was still burning. But would such action achieve what he wanted?

If this was the fall she'd intended all along, nothing was going to change her mind, and he'd just be asking for more punishment. Alternatively, if she needed more time…time to think, to re-appraise, to decide she really did want him…time might be his friend. Either way, he hated the feeling this was Judgement Day.

Leon knocked on the window, mugging a comical query. Expelling a sigh of deep frustration, Nick opened the door, determined not to answer his friend's curiosity. He had no answers anyway, none that he liked.

'Well, did the beauteous Anne live up to your expectations?'

Nick glowered at him. 'Why don't you mind your own business, Leon?'

'I'm an interested party, remember?' came the quick retort.

Caught up in his own dilemma, Nick had forgotten about Leon's interest in Sue Olsen. He closed his door, locked the car, thinking Barbie's partner had to be well aware of the deception. And just where did that place Sue Olsen?

'She wasn't what you wanted after all?' Leon persisted.

'She's everything I want,' Nick declared, wanting an end to the inquisition. He needed more time to sort things out himself.

Leon glanced sceptically at him as they fell into step, heading indoors to their offices. 'So how come you're not bursting with happiness?'

'Because I'm not sure where she's at,' he shot back. 'Now drop it, Leon.'

'You didn't rush her, did you?'

'I said *drop it!*'

'Yeah. Right. Just so long as I don't cop any fallout from Sue.'

The feisty little redhead was in on Barbie's game. She had gone along with the Anne Shepherd cover-up yesterday. Maybe both women were taking him and Leon for a ride. Nick held his tongue, though he didn't care for the taste of these thoughts. No point in warning Leon until he knew what the play was. He certainly wouldn't be thanked for it.

'I hope you can give your full concentration to the interviews today,' Leon sliced at him.

'What interviews?'

Some under-the-breath muttering preceded a biting reminder. 'The ones where you decide on the two extra graphic artists you insisted you needed. Of course, I realise the pressures you're currently feeling have nothing to do with work, but…'

'Okay! I'll be ready for them. Roll them into my office when they arrive.'

'First one is ten o'clock.'

'Fine!'

'Take time to check their résumés again, Nick. We don't want misfits on the team.'

'I know how to look after my side of the business,' he snapped.

'Fine!' Leon snapped back and sheered off to his office, leaving Nick in no doubt about the friction he'd stirred.

He grimaced and carried on to his own office, boiling with resentment over being caught in this awkward situation. Why couldn't Barbie have been straight with him? And how in hell could she just walk away from what they had shared last night? Even on the most basic level, did she think that depth of sexual harmony could be found with anyone?

By the time he settled behind his desk, Nick knew he had to force a resolution, one way or another. It wasn't just himself affected here. Leon was involved, too. He picked up the phone book, found the number he needed, and jabbed the buttons on his telephone with grim determination. He heard the buzzing at the other end and fiercely willed it not to be followed by an answering machine.

'*Party Poppers,*' Sue Olsen's perky voice announced. 'How may we pop for you?'

Right out of the cake you and Barbie have baked, Nick thought, hellbent on having the sweet icing of deception burst asunder. It was on the tip of his tongue to ask for Barbie Lamb, tempted to surprise some relevant reaction out of her friend and partner in crime, but he really wanted the admission to come from Barbie herself, and freely given, not forced out of her.

'Nick Armstrong here. May I speak to…Anne Shepherd, please?' The false name almost stuck in his craw.

'Anne,' Sue repeated, as though it tasted sour to her, too. 'Could you hold please? I'll just go and get her for you.'

'Thank you.'

No *Drop Dead Delivery* from Sue Olsen. If that was on the agenda, she intended Barbie to do it herself. It could be that she didn't like this deception any more than he did. If Sue was truly attracted to Leon, it was certainly a complication she wouldn't welcome, with Nick being Leon's partner. She might be pressing Barbie to tell the truth right now.

Nick geared himself to play the conversation carefully. If there was a chance of winning, he didn't want to blow it.

*   *   *

'Wake up, sleepyhead! Rise and shine!'

Sue's adamant command penetrated Barbie's peaceful slumber and jerked her head off the pillow. 'What's up?' she asked groggily.

'*You* should be,' came the terse reply from her friend who was propped against the doorjamb, eyeing Barbie's bleary confusion without the slightest trace of sympathy. 'It's almost nine o'clock and lover-boy is on the *Party Poppers* phone.'

'Lover-boy?'

'Nick Armstrong. Let's get the personal stuff out of the way before business hours begin. Okay?'

'Nick… on the phone…' Her heart started to flutter.

'Asking for Anne Shepherd so I take it you didn't 'fess up.'

Barbie flung off the bedclothes and scrambled to her feet, struggling to clear her woolly head. Nick may well want answers to why she had left without telling him. How could she say that in the end, she hadn't quite trusted him to keep wanting her? After all, he didn't know who she was, and leading her into his bedroom so soon after meeting…was that his habit with any woman he desired?

Once he'd gone to sleep, the *bed and breakfast* thing had started haunting her, leaving her very uncertain about what the night had meant to him. She couldn't stay, couldn't handle being faced with…less than she wanted from him.

'I can't imagine what you managed to talk about until three o'clock in the morning,' Sue drawled.

'Couldn't have been about Barbie Lamb. And I doubt any restaurant stays open to that hour, either.'

'Three?' Was it that late when she'd left Nick's apartment? She hadn't looked at clocks. Too much else jamming her mind.

'It was almost four when I heard you come in,' Sue dryly stated. 'Did he take you on to a nightclub?'

'He's waiting on the phone,' Barbie reminded her, cutting off the inquisition. 'And we agreed this was my business, Sue.'

'Right!' she mocked, stepping back from the bedroom doorway to let Barbie out to the living area. 'Go ahead. Make a mess of things.'

She winced, knowing she could look for no understanding or helpful advice from her friend. 'Thanks for waking me up.'

'I wish you would wake up,' Sue muttered darkly, swinging away to go into her own bedroom, respecting Barbie's right to privacy with this personal call, despite strongly disapproving the relationship as it stood. 'And don't forget we've got a gig at the line-dancing club tonight,' she tossed over her shoulder. 'So no making other plans.'

On a beeline for the telephone, Barbie raised a hand to indicate she'd heard. Her mind was feverishly playing through what to say to Nick. This call had to mean he wanted to continue the relationship with Anne Shepherd.

Or have more sex with her.

Had it been a terrible mistake to go to bed with him? The memory of her madness in wantonly goading him into it burned through her as she picked up the receiver. Swamped by a rush of self-consciousness, 'Hi!' was all she could manage.

'Hi to you, too,' Nick replied. Then after a pause she didn't know how to fill, he added, 'I missed you this morning.'

Her cheeks bloomed with heat. 'I thought it best I go,' she gabbled. 'I wasn't sure…I mean…I'd parked the car in the street and…and I couldn't remember how long that was legal for, once it was morning and the traffic started up…and I knew Sue would be expecting me home…and…'

'And you didn't want to wake me to say goodbye,' he helped her somewhat dryly.

She sighed, relieved he seemed to be accepting her explanation. It was impossible to go into the emotional conflict he stirred because much of it was related to a history that still made her feel extremely vulnerable where he was concerned. More so after abandoning herself so utterly to him in bed.

'I did wonder if last night was as special to you as it was to me,' he went on after another pause she didn't know how to fill.

'Yes. Very special,' she said feelingly, unable to help herself from admitting she had been a very willing partner in their intimacy, revelling in it as long as it lasted.

'So there's nothing…troubling you?'

About a thousand things, but none she could bring herself to speak of. 'I'm fine, Nick,' she assured him.

'I'm sorry I left without a word but…it was late…and…'

'Yes, I understand. It simply occurred to me that talking was…limited…after we…connected in other ways. If there's anything you want to say…any concern… I do want to be with you again. Very much.'

'I want that, too,' she rushed out, recklessly squashing the doubts about the path he was treading with her. Time would tell, she told herself. She needed more time.

'Then what about tonight?'

Sue's warning stopped an eager assent. 'I'm booked to work tonight, Nick. I'm free tomorrow evening if that suits you.'

'Fine! I'll pick you up from your place at seven.'

'Here?' Barbie frowned, imagining Sue in the background making smart cracks. 'I don't mind meeting you in the city.'

'Better not to have problems with your car. I'm happy to take you home whenever you want to go. All you have to do is tell me.'

'Oh!' Guilt squeezed her heart. It had been wrong to sneak off as she had, leaving him wondering how she felt the morning after. 'I'm sorry, Nick. I should have written you a note. Come Wednesday night, I'll be ready on the dot of seven.' *And be off before Sue could get a look in.* 'You've got the address?'

'Yes. From the phone book. What apartment number?'

'Four.'

'Thank you. I'll look forward to seeing you.'

'Me, too,' she said warmly, and was smiling as she heard the disconnection and lowered her own receiver.

Nick was not smiling. He'd just given her another chance to open up to him but the deception ride was still on and he still did not know if it was a vengeance trip or a trial run towards a judgement on him. Now he had to wait two more days for the next move.

Just how far did she want him to commit himself before the truth came out…or before she cut him off at the knees? Had that been an act on the phone—the embarrassed apology and the warm pleasure in hearing from him?

Nick shook his head, the only certainty slicing through the pummelling of doubts was that he couldn't bear to carry on with her in this false way. It was dishonest on both sides, with him hiding his knowledge and her pretending to be someone who'd never entered his life before.

It had to stop.

It would be impossible for him to act naturally towards her tomorrow night. He'd be grinding his teeth at her duplicity if she persisted with it, and she'd just indicated she intended to. Nevertheless, directly facing her with the fakery was tricky business.

It might make her feel a fool, realising she *had* been recognised. She might even hold last night's plunge into intimacy against him, regardless of how it had turned into something…incredibly good… totally unique in his experience. Surely in hers, too.

He didn't want that twisted into something bad.

Though he was so twisted up inside at the present moment, he had to find some resolution that would work positively and get him out of this mess.

What he needed was some outside intervention that would force her hand, make her reveal the motivation that was driving her decisions. Once he knew precisely what he was dealing with, he could win her around to trying a future together. He couldn't believe she had done what she'd done last night, without feeling genuine pleasure in him.

So what outside intervention could he bring into play?

Leon?

He instantly dismissed the idea of confiding *this* problem to his friend.

Sue Olsen knew, but she had no reason to help him.

His sister popped into his mind. He had intended asking her to help him find the fairy princess. If she booked *The Singing Sunflowers*... yes, Carole would certainly remember Barbie Lamb. The secret would have to come out, because Carole might blab to her brother and there'd be no evading the truth any longer.

Nick reached for the telephone again.

He didn't stop to question the wisdom of the plan evolving in his mind.

He wanted Barbie Lamb, not Anne Shepherd.

And he wanted her tomorrow night.

CHAPTER TWELVE

'I DON'T see any preschoolers whooping it up,' Barbie said, eyeing the beautifully landscaped grounds that were totally empty of children. 'Are you sure you've got the right address, Sue?'

'I double-checked. She's probably rounded them up and put them inside for *the big surprise*.'

Barbie wasn't convinced. The exclusive little cul-de-sac in the high-class suburb of Pymble reeked of expensive privacy, not the place for young families. 'It doesn't feel right. And with the call only coming in yesterday…such short notice. Maybe it's some black joke.'

'Who cares? The fee was paid upfront. We're here. We go in,' Sue declared, dismissing Barbie's doubts. She checked her watch. 'Ten fifty-seven. Three minutes to showtime. Let's get our hats and cuffs on.'

They were already wearing their green bodysuits and yellow petal skirts. Barbie reached over to the back seat of the car and collected the rest of their costumes.

'There's a woman coming out of the house now,' Sue informed her. 'Probably been watching for us to arrive. Better be quick, Barbie. It's bound to be Mrs. Huntley. Looks the right age to be the mother of tod-dlers.'

The brown cuffs with the flare of yellow petals were easy to shove on, but the hat was tricky, positioning it just right for the full sunflower to circle their faces. In her haste to get fully costumed, Barbie didn't even glance at the woman. She was only too relieved that no mistake had been made and the party call was genuine since they were expected by the home-owner.

Sue was out of the car first, ready to greet their client. Barbie hurried to line up with her, pausing to pick up the portable sound system which they needed for their act. The music for the action songs little children loved was all prerecorded, ready to play, and Sue had said the client had agreed to activate it on cue, no problem with having a power-point handy.

'Hi! So glad you're on time,' the mother was saying. 'I have the children packed into the family room downstairs with the other mothers looking after them. I wanted you to be a surprise for them.'

It must be a split-level house, Barbie thought, although that wasn't obvious from the street. The sloping block of land disguised it.

'Mrs. Huntley?' Sue prompted.

'Yes, I'm Carole Huntley. Stuart and Tina are my children.'

'I'm Sue Olsen and this is my partner…'

Barbie quickly swung around to join Sue and smile at the client.

'…Barbie Lamb.'

The smile froze on Barbie's face as recognition hit. Carole Huntley was Carole Armstrong—Nick's sister! She'd been stylish at eighteen. She was even more stylish now, her thick black hair brilliantly cut in a short bob and her boutique clothes perfectly co-ordinated.

'Barbie Lamb?' Carole repeated incredulously. 'You're not...?' Her bright blue eyes stared search-ingly at the face that was encircled by a sunflower. 'Yes, you are. Those eyes are unmistakable. Barbie Lamb, after all these years...' She shook her head in amazement. 'I was Carole Armstrong. Remember? Two years ahead of you at school? Danny's and Nick's sister?'

'Carole...' Barbie repeated numbly, her heart sink-ing like a stone.

'My goodness! It must be...nine years. The last time I saw you was at Nick's twenty-first birthday. You sang.' Her face beamed with pleasure in her rec-ognition. 'And you've made a career of singing?'

'A career of sorts,' Barbie mumbled, barely able to speak over the shock of being confronted by a mem-ber of Nick's family, her identity made certain by Sue's introduction.

'How fantastic!' Carole burbled on, delight and avid curiosity in her eyes—the same vivid blue as Nick's. She laughed, taking in the whole of Barbie's appearance. 'I must say you make a beautiful sun-flower.' Her gaze slid to Sue in sparkling pleasure. 'Both of you.'

'Thank you,' Sue quickly returned. 'Hope the chil-dren think so, too. If you'll show us the way...?'

'Yes, of course.' Carole flashed an apologetic smile. 'No time for memory lane right now.' As she turned to usher them down the path to the front door, she looked appealingly at Barbie. 'Perhaps afterwards you'll stay for coffee? I'd love to catch up on your news.'

'We…we have another gig this afternoon,' Barbie lied, desperate for any excuse to get away.

'Not a good idea anyway, Mrs. Huntley,' Sue chimed in. 'It would spoil the illusion for the children. Best that we come and go.'

'Oh! I guess so.' Carole looked disappointed.

'You didn't say whose birthday it was, Stuart's or Tina's,' Sue rattled on, taking the heat off Barbie.

'Neither. Stuart is three and a half and Tina's not quite two. Stuart broke his arm last Saturday and hasn't been able to go to play-school. I thought I'd throw him a party to cheer him up.'

Which explained the short notice, Barbie thought dazedly, still plunged into turmoil by the terrible co-incidence of coming face to face with two Armstrongs through the *Party Poppers* business, both within *a week* of each other. And this meeting with Nick's sister could very well blow her cover as Anne Shepherd. Carole was always the gossipy kind.

The discomforting blue gaze targeted Barbie again. 'The accident stopped us from going to Nick's thir-tieth birthday party. Which reminds me…'

'These things happen,' Sue cut in sympathetically, waving to the front door. 'Now before we go in, and since the children are in the family room out of sight…perhaps the best idea is for you to take our music box, Mrs. Huntley, and go ahead of us, plugging it in all ready to play. That way we can really make a surprise entrance.'

Barbie was intensely grateful for the timely distraction. She offered the player to Carole who took it and looked down at the control panel as Sue explained what had to be done.

'Yes, fine,' she agreed. 'It's okay for you to wait in the foyer for a minute while I go ahead and switch on. They can't see you from there.'

Finally accepting the focus on business, she ushered them inside the house, leaving them to watch the direction she took to the family room—straight ahead, down the stairs, along a lower-level foyer and through an archway from which the noise of a lively party drifted.

'Get yourself together, Barbie,' Sue whispered warningly. 'I can't do this act by myself.'

She took a deep breath, needing the oxygen to clear her whirling head. 'Thanks for taking the flack off me, Sue.'

'You looked like a stunned mullet. Just forget her and concentrate on the toddlers. The show goes on.'

'I won't let you down.'

'You'd better not. If the fat's in the fire, it's of your own making and it's not fair to burn me, too. If you don't perform, I'll kick you.'

'I'm ready.'

'Then let's do it and get out of here.'

They did it. From the moment they showed their sunflower faces in the archway, a dozen or so under-fives were goggle-eyed, then enthralled by the act that followed, repeating phrases of the songs when urged to, following the simple dance steps, clapping in time with the sunflowers, and beaming joy in the wonder of it all.

With her energy fiercely channelled into connecting with the children, Barbie was barely aware of the mothers who sat watching. She couldn't risk a look at Carole for fear of being put off her stride, and the other women present were simply blurs in the background. However, they did come in useful, keeping the children from following them as she and Sue bowed out after forty minutes of highly concentrated entertainment.

Carole, of course, had to follow them, bringing their sound system with her. 'That was absolutely marvellous!' she enthused, once they were outside with the front door safely shutting the children in the house. 'My friends thought so, too.'

'Great!' Sue replied, whipping out a small bundle of business cards she'd tucked in her sleeve. 'Please pass these around. It's lovely to work from recommendations.'

As Carole took them, Sue deftly relieved her of their property. 'Thanks so much for your help with the music. Perfect timing. Why not go back to Stuart and Tina now? Enjoy their excitement. We'll see ourselves off.'

'Yes. Nice seeing you again, Carole,' Barbie quickly put in, desperately hoping Nick's sister would take the hint and let her escape reminiscences which were not welcome in any shape or form.

Unfortunately the dismissal didn't work. 'No, I'll walk up to the car with you. I understand you have to get on your way, but I've just been thinking, Barbie…'

Please don't!

Somehow she stretched her mouth into a polite smile as they started walking up the path, but she wished Carole Huntley onto another planet.

'It's Mum's fiftieth birthday this coming weekend,' she went on, 'and my husband and I are throwing a party for her on Saturday night. Danny's even flying home from San Diego for it. A big family and friends get-together. Like Nick's twenty-first. It would be lovely if you could come…'

The reminder of Nick's twenty-first set up an instant and violent recoil. Words spilled out before she could even begin to relate the invitation to her current situation with him.

'That's very kind of you, Carole, but I'm not free.'

'Oh! What a shame! It would have been a great surprise to have you sing ''Happy Birthday'' to Mum. She always said you had a beautiful voice.'

The sheer insensitivity of that comment had Barbie grinding her teeth. 'I get paid for doing that now, Carole,' she bit out.

Carole instantly looked stricken by her blunder. 'I didn't mean for you only to come for that. I'm sorry if it sounded…' She heaved a mortified sigh, her eyes begging forgiveness. 'Our families used to be close. I just thought it would be nice to…'

'Perhaps another time.'

'Barbie, I honestly wasn't asking for a…a professional freebie. I wanted your company. The whole family would, I'm sure. And there'd be other old friends from Wamberal for you to catch up with.'

It took a huge effort to stretch her mouth into another stiff smile but Barbie managed it as her hand reached for the handle to the passenger door of the car. 'Well, it sounds like your mother will have a wonderful fiftieth. I hope you all have a marvellous time together.'

Hearing Sue open the driver's door—the cue for a fast getaway—Barbie nodded a farewell. 'Thanks again for the invitation. I'm afraid we must go now.'

'Yes, we must,' Sue echoed across the hood of the car. 'And may I say, Mrs. Huntley, you're very lucky to have such beautiful children. They're a delight.'

Which was a better exit line than any Barbie had given. It held Carole silent while they got in the car. Sue gunned the engine, and they were off, but not quite away. They had to use the turning circle at the end of the cul-de-sac, which brought them back past Carole who hadn't moved.

She stood on the verge of the road, her hands interlacing worriedly, her face obviously troubled. Barbie lifted her hand in a last salute, wishing she hadn't taken such quick offence at the tactless invitation. It would make the next meeting with Nick's sister awkward…if there was a next meeting. One thing was certain. She couldn't spin out the Anne Shepherd cover much longer with Nick. If brother and sister were in contact over plans for celebrating their mother's fiftieth…

'I take it Nick hasn't asked you to this big family do?' Sue inquired sardonically.

'No. Not yet.'

'Didn't even mention it in all the hours of talking you had last night?'

The mocking emphasis on *talking* goaded her into a heated defence. 'Why should he? To all intents and purposes Nick has only just met me. He doesn't know I know his family.'

Sue slanted her a derisive look. 'He's been stringing you along, probably to get what he wants, and I'll bet you spent more time in bed with him than anywhere else.'

'That's my private business!' Barbie grated, her hands clenching at her friend's cynical attitude.

'Then at least get the blinkers off your eyes and see it right,' Sue sliced back at her in exasperation. 'By the end of your night with him, it wasn't Anne Shepherd Nick Armstrong had in his head or anywhere else. He knows who you are. Or suspects strongly enough to put it to the test. What do you think that gig with his sister was about?'

Thrown into confusion by Sue's certainty, Barbie lost the final line of logic thrown at her. 'I don't know what you mean.'

'The booking came in from Carole Huntley just an hour after you talked to Nick yesterday, still pretending to be Anne Shepherd. If you can't put two and two together, I can. Before today is out he'll have confirmation from his sister that Sue Olsen's partner *is* Barbie Lamb.'

'It could have been a coincidence,' Barbie cried, trying to hold back the sickening wave of humiliation stirred by Sue's interpretation of events.

'And pigs might fly.'

'Nick couldn't have told her,' Barbie argued frantically. 'Carole wasn't expecting me. It was your introduction that triggered recognition.'

'Unmistakable eyes,' Sue tossed at her. 'How long did Nick gaze into them over dinner, Barbie? And don't forget I did call you Barbie in his office before you suffered a rush of blood to the head and gave yourself a false identity. You think he's slow at putting two and two together?'

Her stomach started churning at the memory of his comment on her eyes…a vivid reminder of the girl he'd once known.

'Face it!' Sue bored on relentlessly. 'The game is well and truly up. He used his sister as a check on your real identity and she's probably on the phone to him right now, reporting the outcome. So, for pity's sake, don't make a fool of yourself by trying to continue this crazy deception when he turns up tonight!'

A fool of herself?

Sue didn't know the half of it.

Nick's probing questions, his comments on fakery…her own behaviour in asking him to kiss her, ripping his clothes off and…none of it bore thinking about in the light that he had known—or suspected—

she was the very same Barbie Lamb he had once put out of his life.

She wished she could curl up and die.

'You know, that party Carole Huntley was going on about could be the party Leon invited me to,' Sue muttered. 'It's this Saturday night.' She shot Barbie a worried look. 'What are you going to do?'

She shook her head in hopeless distress. 'I don't know, Sue.'

'Well, I don't suppose you want to hear *I told you so*. At least you've got the rest of the day to work it out.'

Barbie closed her eyes, feeling too sick to talk.

'I hope you can work it into something good,' Sue said in a softer voice.

The sweetest revenge, Barbie thought, was also the path to hell.

CHAPTER THIRTEEN

NICK held his impatience in check until two o'clock to call his sister, knowing the children would need time to wind down from the excitement of the party and settle into their afternoon nap. He didn't want Carole distracted. He needed to pick her brains of every impression she had of Barbie Lamb.

The buzz of the call-signal grated on his nerves as he waited and waited for it to be answered. Finally the receiver was picked up and a breathless Carole said, 'Hi!'

'It's Nick, here. Where were you?'

'Cleaning up downstairs.'

'How did the party go?'

'Oh, Nick! You'll never guess…'

'Guess what?' His skin prickled with anticipation. It had to have happened… Barbie forced into facing that the deception couldn't work any longer.

'The party went fine. It was a great idea. The children loved it. And your suggestion to call *Party Poppers* and hire an act was brilliant. *The Singing Sunflowers* had them entranced…'

Get to the main point, Nick silently urged.

'But when the two performers turned up… Nick, one of them was Barbie Lamb! Remember Barbie?

The girl Danny had a big crush on back in our school days?'

'Yes, I do.' *The cat was definitely out of the bag.*

'I was so surprised. I had no idea she'd made a career with her singing. And she is good at it, Nick. Terrific, really. I would have loved to have a chat with her but...' A deep sigh.

'But what?' Nick prompted, uneasy with Carole's sigh.

'I don't think it was a nice surprise for her...seeing me again, I mean.'

'Why do you think that?'

'Well, she didn't enter into any reminiscences with me. You know how people do when meeting again after a long gap and our families *had* been close. It was all strictly business, cutting off any personal stuff.'

Shock, Nick thought, understandable in the circumstances.

'Which I didn't mind,' Carole rattled on, 'because I could see they were all keyed up to give their performance. And they certainly delivered marvellous entertainment.'

'I'm glad to hear it,' he encouraged.

'Anyhow, I thought what fun it would be for Barbie to come to Mum's party...you know, sharing old times and new...and I really put my foot in it, Nick. It's quite upset me actually.'

A nasty feeling crawled down his spine. 'Want to tell me about it?'

'Well, first off she stated flatly that she wasn't free

to come. And I must say it was a late invitation, so fair enough. Though she didn't even pause to consider if she might drop in for a bit. Even late if she had some work commitment. But I didn't notice the lack of any interest then.'

Nick frowned. There should have been interest if Barbie was seriously interested in him. Maybe she was just thrown at the prospect of having to confess to him beforehand. And *he* hadn't mentioned his mother's fiftieth birthday when they'd been talking families. His mind had been on trying to draw her out.

Carole took a deep breath and continued. 'I was wishing she could come and I made the mistake of saying how lovely it would be if she could sing for Mum, like she did for you at your twenty-first.'

Nick barely stifled a groan. Talk about triggering a bad memory!

'She gave me a look... I tell you it could have killed me stone-dead, Nick...and said she was paid for doing that now. Like I was presuming on her professional life, using her...it was awful. I just shrivelled up inside.'

'That was...unfortunate...to say the least, Carole.'

'I tried to recover, explaining how I felt...that it was a friendly thing...and she was frigidly polite...but I was left feeling like the lowest worm, Nick. And I really would have liked to get to know her again.'

'Perhaps you'll get another chance.' Nick hoped.

Was the power of attraction strong enough to override the damage done?

'No,' Carole came back, answering him very decisively. 'She couldn't get away fast enough. It's kind of sad. We were all close once. I didn't mean to make her feel I was just using her…like her friendship wasn't of any value except for how well she can sing.'

Using her… No, Barbie couldn't think he'd been using her for sex. She'd asked for it. Wanted it. Had she been using him? *A dream come true*…

Nick shook his head, realising he was veering off his sister's line of thought. 'You might have hit a raw nerve, Carole,' he said. 'Like with doctors being asked for medical advice when it's supposed to be a social occasion.'

Another deep sigh. 'You may be right. I guess people do get exploited in the entertainment world. And who knows what her life has been like since the Lamb family left Wamberal? It's been a lot of years. Maybe for her there's no going back.'

'No, we can't really go back.' Can't change anything we've done, either, Nick thought grimly.

'I've never been…*wiped*…so completely…'

The nasty feeling increased. 'I'm sorry you felt that, Carole.'

He hadn't foreseen this outcome. He'd wanted Barbie to come clean with him. The confrontation with his sister was telling him that any future with Barbie Lamb would be hard won, if it wasn't a complete fantasy.

'My fault…being so tactless,' Carole said glumly.

'There may be more to it than that,' he soothed, only too sharply aware of his guilt in creating this situation.

'Like what? She just doesn't want us in her life?'

'Could be.'

'That kind of blanket rejection is awful, isn't it?'

'Yes.'

And he was right back to how deeply his actions had wounded Barbie Lamb nine years ago. Deliberate actions...*like her deliberate action of provocatively inviting him to join her on his own bed.* The sweetest revenge of all? Nick Armstrong finding her irresistible, wanting her...wanting her beyond any doubt...*was that the dream come true?*

Carole gave a skittish laugh. 'Not that you'd know much about rejection since you're such an eligible bachelor.'

Nick had a gut-wrenching feeling he was about to know. In spades!

'My life isn't all a bed of roses,' he said with black irony. *It was more a bed of thorns. Or barbed wire.*

'Things not going so well with Tanya?' Carole teased.

'That's finished.'

'Oh! Are you bringing someone new to Mum's party?'

'My love-life is somewhat up in the air at the moment. Not a subject for discussion.'

'Okay. Well, thanks for listening, Nick. And Stuart did stop feeling sorry for himself. No grumpiness at all. The entertainment was a wonderful suggestion.'

'I'm glad to hear it worked for him. Give him a hug from me. Tina, too. Must go now.'

'Thanks for calling. It was good, talking to you.'

Good...

Nothing was *good!*

Nick put down the receiver, fighting the sense that at seven o'clock tonight, the woman who could have been everything he wanted, would proceed to deliver her ultimate revenge—wiping him out of her life.

But could she?

Maybe she had meant to drop him after the absolute proof of his wanting her on Monday night, except their coming together had been so special, she'd been tempted by the promise of feeling more of it.

He had that to fight with.

And fight he would.

On every level.

It was time she started seeing straight. And tonight he'd set her straight. The past was past and she had to let it go. For her own sake, as well as his.

Revenge didn't lead anywhere!

Not anywhere good.

And Nick wanted *good.*

For both of them.

CHAPTER FOURTEEN

'I'M OUT of here!'

The terse announcement from Sue sliced through the dark maelstrom of Barbie's thoughts. She lifted her head from the pillow where it had been buried for some time and tried to focus on her friend. 'Where are you going?'

'To a movie. Anywhere.' Her eyes flicked over Barbie's dishevelled state. 'It's obvious you don't plan on going out with Nick, and I'm not sticking around to be hit by flack from the showdown. The Anne Shepherd thing was your idea, not mine.'

'I can't go out with him. Not with this between us.'

'He's coming here,' Sue tersely reminded her. 'What are you going to do? Shut the door in his face?'

'I don't know. I don't know what I'm going to do,' she cried in anguish.

'Well, Nick Armstrong didn't strike me as the kind of guy who accepted having doors shut in his face, so I'm out of here. It's almost a quarter to seven, Barbie. You'd better start shaping up.'

Having delivered this last admonition, Sue was on her way, leaving Barbie to conduct her *private business* strictly on her own.

A quarter of an hour to go...

Pride forced her off the bed to tidy up her appearance. She exchanged her crumpled clothes for freshly laundered jeans and a blue-and-white checked shirt which she deliberately left hanging loose instead of tucking it in. She didn't want to emphasise her curvy figure, didn't want to look the least bit sexy to Nick's eyes.

She brushed her hair but didn't apply any make-up. Barbie Lamb, *au naturel,* she thought mockingly, staring at her reflection in the mirror. Nick couldn't say she was coming to him in different guises and playing roles tonight. Nothing fake about a bare face.

The doorbell rang.

Her heart, which had been a dead weight all afternoon, leapt to painful life, catapulting around her chest. The unconscionable rat, who'd knowingly given her enough rope to hang herself with, had come for another bite of her, loaded with the certainty she was here for the taking.

He'd known, before he'd swept her into his bedroom, that she was Barbie Lamb. Nothing that had happened there had anything to do with Anne Shepherd—a woman he'd just met and strongly desired. The admissions he had ripped from her in the heat of intimacy had been cold-bloodedly calculated to give him the upper hand in any further encounter with him.

She'd wanted him.

She'd begged for him.

She'd made love to him.

Burning with these humiliating memories, Barbie forced her legs to carry her through the apartment to the door Nick Armstrong was standing behind. She didn't want to open it, but Sue was right. He wasn't going away. And she was bitterly curious to know how he would explain his behaviour this time around.

There was no younger brother Danny lurking in the wings, providing some excuse for playing his game how he'd chosen to play it. And why he'd brought his sister into it today made no sense at all. He hadn't needed Carole's confirmation of her identity. It had been a cruel ploy, like a cat playing with a mouse before he pounced. Just as he had on Monday night.

On a burst of seething anger at his duplicity, Barbie unlocked the door and pulled it open, determined on blasting Nick Armstrong's confidence in manipulating what *he* wanted. Her grey eyes were as hard and as lethal as silver bullets, but the bullets hit a totally unexpected shield before they reached their target.

Her wings!

He was holding out her fairy princess wings…and they were fully restored to their former glory…no trace of damage at all!

One look at Barbie was enough to tell Nick there would be no playing happy families tonight. Tension whipped through him at the obvious evidence that all the female tools for generating sexual attraction had been abandoned. No makeup. Not even a dash of lipstick. And her clothes were more suitable for housework or gardening than for greeting a man whose interest she wanted to keep.

Wipe-out was telegraphed to him loud and clear.

Which meant she had been stringing him along to deliver the hardest, punch-in-the-heart rejection she could.

Anger pumped into a fierce wave of aggression.

He didn't deserve this.

And he wouldn't stand for it.

'Open the door wider so I can bring these wings in for you,' he instructed, determined to catch her off guard long enough to get inside. 'Don't want them damaged again.'

Apparently stunned by seeing them fixed, she stepped aside and let him in. Nick carried them right through the small living area and propped them against the wall next to a hallway which obviously led to bedrooms. He was now in the heart of her private territory and he wasn't about to give up the ground he'd made.

Barbie closed the door automatically, standing against it as she watched the unbelievable proof that he had cared enough to actually follow through on his declared intention. But when had he had the time to mend the broken wings? She felt as confused as she had at seeing them in his office on Monday.

'How did you do it?' she demanded, still seized by a sense of disbelief.

He swung to her with an ironic little smile. 'I contacted a fancy dress costume-maker on Monday afternoon and passed everything over to her.'

Her confusion flattened out. 'Someone else did it.'

'I wanted them to be perfect again.'

'Cost no object,' she muttered, remembering Sue's cynical attitude towards his fixing the wings. 'I guess you've found that money smooths the way to anything you want.'

His chin lifted slightly, his eyes narrowing into slits at her unappreciative reception of his effort. 'I simply wanted to give you pleasure.'

'Take it, you mean,' Barbie snapped. 'A whole lot of secret pleasure in leading Barbie Lamb up the garden path and seeing how far she would go.'

His head jerked in surprise at that accusation.

The fury that had been forcibly stored up inside her all afternoon, broke its banks and spilled forth, her eyes blazing contempt for his trickery. 'Don't think you can fool me anymore, Nick. I know you know who I am. I can pinpoint precisely when you realised who I am. Your comment on my eyes over dinner…'

'So why didn't you come out with the truth then?' he shot back at her. 'Why lie in the first place, and why continue the lie, despite every opening I gave you to admit who you are? Seems to me I was the one being set up as the fool.'

She folded her arms protectively, armouring herself against any firepower he thought he had against her. 'I didn't want you to connect me to any memories you had of *Baa-Baa* Lamb.'

'I never called you that, Barbie.'

'You thought it of me, always following you around whenever I was given the chance. So much so I caused a problem for you and you had to put a stop to it.'

His mouth thinned, biting back any further denial.

'Anne Shepherd let me be *me now,*' she cried, hating the knowledge he'd hidden to pursue his own way with her. 'It let me meet you without you thinking of me like that. *Me now,* Nick, and when it stopped being *me now,* you should have told me. Instead of which you chose to play your own secret game.'

'It was *your* game,' he retorted, anger blazing into his eyes. 'And I didn't know what the hell you were up to.'

'If it worried you, why didn't you come straight out with it?

'And have you walk away from me?'

'As you did from me? Bit of guilt there, Nick? Did you decide I was out to get you and dump you?'

Heat speared across his cheeks. 'It was a possibility,' he answered tersely.

'So instead of risking that possibility, you set out to colour the past differently, spinning me that story about Danny, making yourself out to be the noble older brother, standing aside for him to step in.'

'It was the truth,' he asserted emphatically.

She tossed her head in scorn for his truth. 'Well, you certainly weren't standing aside for anything this time. It was straight up to your apartment, into your bedroom…'

'You could have stopped it anytime,' he sliced in, the air between them sizzling with a ferment of crosscurrents.

'So could you,' she hurled back, and out poured the tumult of bitter feelings his deception had stirred.

'You were getting too much of a kick out of it, weren't you? Remembering I'd once had a crush on you, and here I was, all grown up enough to whisk off to bed. Did it feel great, getting me to admit I wanted you, driving me to the brink, then holding off to make me beg for you…'

'Damn it!' he exploded, his hands whipping up in an emphatic gesture of frustration. 'You're twisting everything around. I just wanted you to admit who you were. I wanted it to be real between us.'

'How much more flesh-and-blood *real* can you get?'

'I didn't think you'd go that far and when you did, still without identifying yourself—and I gave you every chance to, Barbie—' He started walking towards her, his hands spreading in appeal.

'You stop right there, Nick Armstrong!' she commanded, her eyes flaring a fierce warning. 'I'm calling the shots now!'

He stopped, his hands falling to his sides, clenching. 'You were calling them all along, Barbie. The fairy princess act you played was designed to stir me up, and don't you deny it.'

'Yes.' Her chin went up in belligerent pride. 'I wanted to get a different reaction from you than I got at your twenty-first birthday party.'

'A sweet slice of revenge.' He nodded as though he'd known it all along, his eyes glinting accusingly as he read more into it. 'Did it give you a kick, doing the walking away after you'd sung to me this time around?'

Barbie refused to feel guilty. He'd made her pay for what little vengeance she'd taken on him. 'That was the intention,' she frankly acknowledged. 'But when you kissed me…' The memory of her response caused a rush of hot blood to her cheeks. '…it stirred everything up for me and I wished I hadn't done it.'

'Until you had second thoughts and came to my office to see if there was more *reaction* to be had,' he bit out grimly. 'And when there was, you carried it further…and further…taking me where you *wanted* it to go. And don't you deny that, either.'

'I didn't know you had Barbie Lamb in your mind,' she flung back at him in a fury of resentment.

'But you had *me* in *your* mind.' He started walking towards her, seething with the accusations he continued to hurl. '*You* were remembering. All the time you were remembering. Questioning me. Putting me on trial. Do you think I didn't feel it?'

'I didn't mean you to feel it,' she countered, although what he said was true, making her feel uneasy about her own private agenda and prompting a defence. 'I just wanted to find out where I stood with you.'

'Without letting me know where I stood with you,' he mocked. 'And just how long was that to go on for, Barbie? When was Anne Shepherd going to turn into you? When you'd had enough of me so you could do what you meant to do in the first place? Leave me wanting you and walk away?'

'I wasn't out for revenge. Not after the fairy princess thing. I just wanted to be sure I wasn't some fly-by-night affair to you before I laid myself on the line. I would have told you once I felt safe with you,' she defended, drawing herself up tautly, unfolding her arms, ready to fight as he closed in on her.

He came to a halt directly in front of her, using the power of his physique to make her feel she was on the judgement stand. His eyes glittered a savage challenge as he continued his cross-examination.

'So why treat my sister as you did…if you really wanted some future with me? You rejected her attempt at reviving an old friendship and her invitation to a family celebration.'

'I was in shock. The coincidence…except it wasn't a coincidence,' she threw at him bitterly. 'You shouldn't have dragged your sister into it.'

'It was the only way I could think of to make you stop hiding from me. And to flush the truth out of you. I needed to know what was in your heart…hope for some future with me or vengeance for what you obviously perceived as my rejection of you.'

It had been hope. But it was painfully obvious there was no hope of any understanding between them now. The situation was irreparably damaged by her deception and his reaction to it, making it impossible to see where the truth lay anymore.

His eyes raked derisively over her clothes. 'Seeing you dressed like this, the answer is clear. You're even standing by the door to show me out.'

Was this the end of what had started so promisingly on Monday night? Was this the end she wanted? Her sinking heart screamed no. Her mind scrambled to find some saving grace. Before she could say or do anything he moved. His hands fell on her shoulders, curling around them as though he was going to shake her.

'But not quite yet, Barbie. Before I leave…I'll give you the sweetest revenge of all.'

His face was so close to hers, his eyes were like magnets, drawing on her soul. Her mind was torn, wanting to deny she'd ever set out to be vengeful, yet guiltily aware that she had secretly revelled in scoring off him.

His grasp loosened and his hands slid along her shoulders, up her throat, cupping her face as he spoke with an intensity that gripped her heart and squeezed it. 'I want you, Barbie Lamb. Even knowing you're intent on twisting the knife and turning me out of your life, I still want you.'

His fingers stroked slowly up her cheeks, into her hair above her ears, raking it behind her lobes. 'Is that sweet to hear?' His eyes burned into hers. 'Let me make it even sweeter for you. Much better to taste the wanting, feel the wanting.'

Her heart was pounding so hard she couldn't think. Couldn't move, either. His head was bending and she knew he was going to kiss her. The sizzle of challenge was in his eyes, heating her blood, stirring needs she couldn't repress, memories of how it had been together.

Then his mouth was covering hers, his warm lips grazing seductively, igniting tingles of excitement, his tongue tantalising, not forcing an opening but holding out the tempting promise of deeply plummeting passion surging between them.

Would it happen again? Even now? With so much negative turmoil still churning away inside her? Helplessly distracted, Barbie couldn't resolve what was right and wrong. And her mouth craved a deeper kiss, a more telling kiss. No conscious decision was made. Her lips parted of their own accord and let Nick Armstrong in.

Instantly sensation swamped her. From the top of her scalp to the extremities of her toes every nerve came alive with excitement and the anticipation of more excitement. His kiss was so powerfully invasive, so passionately penetrating, resisting it was utterly impossible. Any such thought didn't even enter her mind. There was no thought, only a wild surge of need to possess him just as pervasively. It triggered a fierce response.

Her hands flew around his head, fingers clawing through his hair, holding him to her. He dropped his arms, wrapped them around her back and hauled her body into hard-pressed contact with his. There could be no mistaking his arousal, his desire for her. The wanting was not a lie. She *could* taste it, feel it, and again Barbie revelled in it, exulting in his taut masculinity, every bit of him straining to satisfy his need to capture and possess the whole sense of her.

She felt his hand move under her shirt, sliding up her bare back, unclipping her bra, and the instant loosening of her clothing shot a spear of alertness through the haze of her own urgent wanting. Was this right…this mind-blowing drive for sexual release?

Her breasts were aching for his touch. She was acutely aware of his hand gliding under her arm, reaching the soft swell of her flesh, nudging aside the unfastened bra, fingers encircling, softly squeezing, thumb fanning her nipple which was so hard and sensitised, the shock of pleasure had her moaning for more. She didn't want to stop it, didn't want to pause to consider anything.

Until he stopped it, dropping his hand to the waistband of her jeans, seeking to pull open the stud fastening. The realisation that he meant to take her right here, up against the door, shook Barbie out of her complicity in the intimacies that were fast leading to absolute commitment to the desire raging through her. Was this the only level of *wanting* Nick felt for her? Was he using sex in a last drive to keep her with him...for more sex?

The sudden pain in her heart eclipsed the needs pounding through the rest of her body. Her hands shot from his hair and slammed against his shoulders as she wrenched her mouth from the passionate persuasion of his.

'No!' It was a raw gasp. She threw back her head, gulping in more air. 'No!' It was an anguished cry, vehemently denying the physical upheaval pleading against this enforced parting.

'This is the you now, Barbie. The me now. You feel it. I feel it. Give it a chance,' Nick pleaded hoarsely, his eyes blazing conviction.

His arms wrapped around her again, hands curling around her buttocks, lifting her into an intimate fit with his erection, blatantly reminding her of what they had shared before. 'What we have together is very special,' he declared, his voice throbbing in her ears. 'You know it is. And I won't let you walk away from it, just because I did what I thought was best for you nine years ago.'

Best for her!

The cruellest cut of all…without so much as a word of kindness to soften it?

He was lying!

The wanting now was no lie, but he was trying to manipulate her feelings, just as he had manipulated them on Monday night. Today, as well, arranging the confrontation with his sister. This was Nick wanting his own way, getting his own way, never mind what she felt. Just like nine years ago.

She slammed her hands against his chest and pushed with all her strength. 'Let me go! Get away from me!'

The violence of feeling in her voice and action effected separation from him. He stepped back, releasing her and lifting his hands in vehement appeal, his face expressing angry bewilderment at her rejection. 'Why?' he demanded. 'You were with me. Just as you were when we made love on Monday night. I wasn't forcing myself on you.'

'No. But sex doesn't override everything else. Not for me it doesn't,' she cried, her eyes accusing him of taking unfair advantage of her vulnerability.

'It's been the most honest thing between us,' he claimed, and counter-accusation simmered through every word.

'You've got that right. But I want more honesty than straight-out lust. *Best for me,*' she mocked. 'All you've ever cared about is what was *best for you.* You didn't care about my feelings nine years ago and you haven't cared about them now...trapping me with your sister...not allowing anything to run any way but yours.'

His face tightened as though she had physically slapped him. He shook his head. When he met her gaze again, his eyes were bleak, no longer fired up to fight her. 'I did think it was best for you, Barbie,' he said quietly. 'You were a very special person. Too special to let your life be so singularly focused on me. At sixteen, there was so much more for you to discover, to explore.'

His calm reasoning flicked raw wounds. It felt as though he was the wisely objective adult explaining something to a child and she was no longer a child. She hadn't been a child for many, many years. Stung unbearably by this lack of emotional involvement with her, she picked a flaw in his condescending logic and lashed him with it.

'If I was so special, why didn't you ever look me up, Nick? After I'd had time to discover what you thought I should discover.'

It didn't sting him. He shrugged. 'Life happens. You moved away. I got involved with business.'

The flat statements goaded her further. 'The truth is you never gave me another moment's thought until I entered your life again.'

'No, that's not true.' He dragged in a deep breath and grimaced as he sighed. 'I can't change the past. I am sorry you were so hurt by my decision. I know I didn't handle it well.'

The old devastation of that night came flooding

back…the need to show him, to see appreciation and understanding in his eyes. Only it wasn't there. He'd decided it couldn't be. She searched his eyes now, wanting evidence of feeling for her, some caring warmth, even the heat of desire. There was not so much as a spark in them…dull, lifeless, defeated.

'After that…' he went on, his voice softer, a sadness in it that galvanised her attention, freezing her resentments. 'Well, I thought your life would have grown a long way away from me. And it has. Too far for me to reach you. I wish it were different…but there is no second chance.'

He reached into his shirt pocket and brought something out, his gaze dropping to it as he turned it over in his hand. A watch! An old watch! Barbie's heart lurched as recognition hit her. Surely she was mistaken. It couldn't be the watch she'd given him…

'Take it,' he commanded gruffly.

She did, in a daze of disbelief, turning it over to see. There on the back was the tiny lamb she'd had etched on it—the silent promise to follow him anywhere. He had kept it all these years…

'I may not have looked for you, Barbie, but I never forgot you.'

Before she could even lift her head, or think of a word to say, he stepped around her, opened the door, and walked out of her life.

CHAPTER FIFTEEN

ONE more chance…

Barbie willed it to be so as she carefully sprayed the silver glitter over the long gleaming waves of her hair. It was important to get her appearance absolutely right…as well as everything else. The fairy princess had to work real magic tonight. This was going to be the most critical performance of her whole life. Any possible future with Nick hung on it.

Surely he would realise it was hope driving her, not vengeance. Yet as she put the spray can down on her dressing-table and her gaze fell once more on the gift watch he'd returned to her, fear gripped her stomach. Had she killed hope…rejecting his explanations, rejecting his inner angst over her motives, rejecting the sexual attraction between them, rejecting everything he was?

She picked up the watch and rubbed her thumb over the etching of the tiny lamb for luck. She had meant what it had once promised—to follow him anywhere. If only she had carried that through this time— trusting instead of judging so badly—the terrible outcome with Nick might have been avoided. Following him tonight had to work. *Had* to.

She slipped the watch into her handbag. Nick had kept it for nine years. He hadn't thrown it away.

Maybe it would act as a good-luck charm, not letting Nick throw her away tonight.

Her mirror reflection told her she was as ready as she was ever going to be. If she made a total fool of herself, it didn't matter. It was impossible to lose more than she had lost, and if she won... Her heart quivered at the thought of having Nick look at her again as though she was the most desirable woman in the world to him.

She took a deep breath and set off on the journey that would settle her future with him one way or another. Leon Webster had picked up Sue two hours ago so the party for Nick's mother should be in full swing by now. Her appearance would be as much a surprise to them as it would be to everyone else, and Barbie could only hope Sue would understand.

Confiding in her friend might have triggered quarrelsome discussions and to Barbie's mind, there was nothing to discuss. Only this action could give her another chance with Nick. And she had the excuse that Carole Huntley had asked her to come and sing. If Nick didn't respond...well, she could leave straight afterwards and the performance should have no bearing on Sue's involvement with Leon.

The mended fairy wings and magic wand had already been carefully placed in the car, along with the music she needed. Barbie double-checked she had everything before settling herself in the driver's seat. From Ryde to Pymble was a relatively easy trip, yet it seemed nerve-rackingly long to Barbie, having to concentrate on traffic lights and being in the right lanes for turns.

When she finally reached her destination it was to find the cul-de-sac crowded with parked cars. To her deep relief, there was enough space left on the Huntleys' driveway to get her car off the road and close to the house. It blocked other cars from leaving but that was of no concern right now.

She fumbled with the fairy wings, fumbled with the wand, fumbled with the tape recorder. It was a major effort getting the necessary items out of the car without dropping them, even more difficult to position the wings to slide into their slot on the back of her dress. She wished she had Sue to help her, but even now she felt it was wrong to involve her friend in what was—as Sue said—her private business.

Having settled the wings properly, and fiercely focusing her mind on carrying through what she'd determined to do, Barbie managed the walk down the front path without mishap. The party noise seemed to be emanating mainly from the back of the house, which, she told herself, would make her entrance easier. Silently reciting her set speech about being a hired professional act, she rang the doorbell and hoped whoever answered the summons would accept her explanation without question.

What if it was Nick?

Her heart stopped with the shock of that thought. Dizziness clouded her mind. She stood in a state of total paralysis until the door opened and she was faced with a blessed miracle.

Carole Huntley.

'Barbie…?' she queried in astonishment.

Words rattled out. 'I've come to sing for your mother. You asked me… I can fit it in after all and I thought…you said it would be something special for her…'

'Oh! What a lovely surprise!' Carole instantly enthused. 'I'm so glad you could make it. And coming from some other professional engagement…' Her eyes were busily taking in the fairy princess costume. 'You look wonderful, Barbie.'

'It's all right then…'

'Fantastic!'

'Will you put the music on for me, Carole?' She held out the tape recorder. 'All you need do is press Play.'

'Of course.'

'Are they all downstairs?'

Carole's vivid blue eyes sparkled with conspiratorial pleasure. 'Wait here a minute and I'll herd everyone into the family room. Where Stuart's party was, remember? We can make it the same kind of surprise you gave the children.'

Relief poured through Barbie. 'That would be perfect, Carole.'

An anxious frown suddenly appeared. 'I'll pay you for this, Barbie. I never meant to…'

'No. Please…let's just do it. If you leave this door open a bit so I can come in when I hear the music…'

Carole hesitated a moment. 'Well, we can talk about it afterwards. Can you stay?'

'Yes,' Barbie said with a hope and a prayer.

'I'm so glad!' Her smile was all delight. 'Five minutes maximum to get everyone in place and quieten them down. Just slip in and close the door behind you when the coast is clear and you can be at the head of the staircase ready to make your entrance when the music starts. Okay?'

'Fine! Thanks Carole. There'll be two songs and "Happy Birthday" is second, so don't think you've got the wrong tape.'

'This is fabulous, Barbie. Mum's going to love it.' Excitement beamed from a wide grin. 'I'm off to set the scene.'

Luck *was* with her, Barbie feverishly assured herself as she waited, hearing Carole ordering around everyone inside, footsteps obeying her bidding, heading downstairs, the party noise lowering to a mood of expectancy. She peered around the door, and seeing the coast was clear, carefully manouevred herself into the foyer. Her fingers gripped the fairy wand hard as she wished for more luck, all the luck in the world.

It was quiet below.

She stepped to the head of the staircase and willed her legs not to start trembling on the way down. She swallowed hard to moisten her throat. The music started, providing the right backing for her voice. She took a deep breath. This was it! No retreat. The cue came…and she sang, pouring all the hope and longing from her heart and soul into the words…

'"*Somewhere over the rainbow…*"'

Never had her voice been so true, so powerful…but

Barbie didn't know it. She sang because she had to, and she walked down the stairs with all the majestic dignity of a fairy queen on the mission of a lifetime, not hearing the mutterings of surprise and appreciation, nor the hush settling as she descended to where the party guests were gathered.

Carole had obviously ordered them to circle the family room and those standing across the open entrance to it shifted aside to give Barbie a clear passage. Furniture had been moved back against the walls, probably to leave plenty of space for dancing. The centre of the room was completely empty.

As Barbie glided past the circled guests, she saw Nick's parents, Judy and Keith Armstrong, seated in armchairs at the far end. Beside them stood their family, Nick and a grown-up Danny near their mother, Carole and presumably her husband next to their father. All of them—except Nick—were smiling broadly, enjoying *the surprise*.

Barbie did her utmost to block his grim look out of her mind as she proceeded to the centre of the room, though she was conscious of her heart skipping into a faster beat. She couldn't let fear unfocus her. The song had to be sung without falter. She caught sight of Sue, and it was some relief to see her friend nodding approval and giving a thumbs-up sign.

Would Nick accept that after the most dreadful, damaging rain, a rainbow *could* appear, and he was the dream she was chasing tonight?

Barbie's whole being pleaded for that outcome as she halted and faced his mother to deliver the last poignant lines of the song, starting with the fantasy promised in the word—'"*If...*"' pouring faith and hope and optimism through her voice, needing to reach him, offering the chance—another chance—*if* he wanted to take it. She spread out her arms in a gesture of giving, willing him to understand, and the last line was a cry to him, if only his heart was open enough to hear it.

Loud applause erupted after the final note faded into silence. Judy Armstrong's face was crumpled with emotion, smiling through tears. Keith passed her a handkerchief, nodding benevolently at Barbie. She smiled back at both of them and risked a quick glance at Nick. He was not smiling, but his head was cocked to one side, his eyes narrowed on her, and his expression had subtly changed to a weighing look.

Barbie's heart skittered with wild hope. She wasn't facing a steely wall of resistance. He was receptive. At least a little bit.

Carole called for quiet, waving her arms to warn there was more. The introductory chord for the next song broke over the hub-bub, bringing a quick silence. It was not the sexy musical treatment Barbie had requested for Nick, more the sentimental traditional version of 'Happy Birthday,' and she gave it a lot of warm heart as she sang it to his mother, moving slowly forward, lifting the wand to release a sprinkling of magic glitter as she completed the song.

'Make a wish,' she softly urged as she bent to kiss Judy Armstrong's cheek and murmur her own personal, 'A very happy fiftieth birthday.'

'Thank you, Barbie,' she replied huskily. 'You've just made it extra special.'

'It's our song, *Over the Rainbow*,' Keith said gruffly. 'You sang it better than Judy Garland, Barbie. Wonderful to have you here.'

'My pleasure,' she mumbled, touched by his pleasure.

'Carole…' Keith turned and signalled his daughter. 'Play that music again. Your mother and I are going to dance to it.'

'Okay if I rewind the tape and play it again, Barbie?' Carole asked eagerly.

'Go right ahead.'

Stepping aside to allow room for Keith and Judy to rise from their chairs and take the floor, Barbie found herself lined up next to Danny who instantly caught her free left hand and squeezed it, drawing her startled attention to him. There was nothing shy in his face now. He grinned at her, his eyes sparkling the open appreciation of a mature young man who was very confident with women.

'Great singing!' he complimented, not the slightest trace of his old stutter marring his speech. 'Great homecoming for me, too, meeting you again, Barbie. You sure have grown into a stunner.'

And very desirable…

But it was the wrong man telegraphing that to her. She had never been interested in Danny. She wasn't now. Her gaze darted anxiously to Nick. Did he care that his brother was claiming her like this?

He was watching her, his eyes burning with questions that seared her soul. *Why are you here? What do you want? How much is real? Is it hope or vengeance?*

The music started again.

'How about dancing with me, Barbie?' Danny asked.

'No!' It was a hard, vehement negative.

Danny's head jerked in surprise to his older brother.

Nick glared at him, his whole body tense, emitting a fierce aggression. 'Not this time, Danny. Barbie is not yours to have. She never was. And I'm claiming this dance. Just step aside and go find yourself another woman.'

Danny gaped at him, stunned by the violent feeling he'd stirred in his older brother. He released Barbie's hand to raise both of his in an appeasing gesture. 'Hey, man! Take it easy! I was only…'

'Butting in, as you did nine years ago, wanting all Barbie's attention.'

'Hell!' His face flushed at the memory. 'That's ancient history, Nick!'

'Not to me it isn't,' came the savage reply. 'Back off, Danny. Now!'

'Okay! Deck's clear. Your play,' Danny babbled as he backed off, still wide-eyed and red-faced at his older brother's hostile reaction.

Nick stepped forward and scooped Barbie into a dance hold, his eyes blazing into hers, commanding acquiescence. Her heart catapulted around her chest as the arm encircling her waist pulled her closer, very firmly possessive in its strength of purpose.

'Hold it right there, you two!' Sue's voice whipped in. 'I'll take that.' She snatched the wand out of Barbie's hand. 'Leon…' She passed it to him. '…I've got to remove the wings and hook up the train of her dress so nothing gets torn.' Which she proceeded to do at lightning speed, Leon standing by to be handed the wings as well as the wand for safe-keeping.

'Sue's right. No more damage,' Leon admonished them.

'You can dance now,' she granted them. 'Or fight. Or carry on like lunatics if you must.'

'Are you quite finished?' Nick growled, the tension flowing from him wrapping around Barbie and holding her still and silent, everything within her tautly aching for positive responses from him.

'Quite!' Sue assured him. 'Leon, now that we've rescued the fairy princess costume, let's get out of the danger zone.'

'I'm with *you,* babe!'

Off they sailed in happy harmony with each other—twin souls who knew how to order *their* world, leaving Barbie and Nick to sort out whatever needed sorting in their very private business.

Her hand now freed of the wand, Nick took it, interlacing his fingers with hers to seal his grip. 'Tell me this is no game, Barbie,' he demanded, the intensity of his gaze brooking no attempt at deception.

'It's no game, I promise you,' she answered fervently.

His parents twirled past. 'Are you two dancing or what?' his mother asked in amusement.

Rather than draw more curious and interfering attention, Nick pushed his feet into dancing, gathering Barbie closer as he moved her to the slow beat of the song. She was acutely conscious of his thighs brushing hers, her breasts pressing against the warm wall of his chest. Her heart seemed to be thumping in her ears. She barely heard the music.

He bent his head beside hers and she heard the words he spoke, although they were barely above a soft murmur. 'Are you holding out a new start for us?'

Did he want it?

Panic seized Barbie. She had to give him the right opening, make this chance different to the last one.

'I did it all wrong, using a false name. I know I did. And I'm sorry I messed everything up between us,' she pleaded anxiously. 'My only excuse is…as Barbie Lamb, I felt so…so vulnerable, Nick.'

His chest rose and fell and she felt his sigh waft warmly through her hair. Then came the low, regretful words— 'I moved too fast. I cursed myself for it afterwards. If I'd let you go on as Anne Shepherd, you might have learnt to trust me.'

He was thinking back, not forward. She didn't hear hope in his voice, only sadness for mistakes made, and Barbie felt a dark weight descending on her heart. He didn't believe they could recover what had been lost.

The music stopped.

Nick released her from his embrace, and for one terrible moment, Barbie felt the most devastating despair. It was over. There was no chance. Then he grasped her hand again and into her shattered mind swam his command, 'Come with me!'

He pulled her with him, weaving past the party guests who were now responding to the second music track, loudly singing 'Happy Birthday' to Nick's mother. He slid open a glass door which led onto a patio and drew her outside, quickly shutting the door behind them. They walked to the end of the patio, around a corner of the house, into a pool of darkness.

'We should be private here,' he muttered, dropping her hand and moving away a few paces, establishing distance between them before turning to face her.

Barbie was beyond knowing what his actions meant. A fragile hope whispered he was still with her, though standing apart. He wanted to talk, if nothing else, and talking might help. But her mind was incapable of producing anything to say.

'The issue was always one of trust, wasn't it?' he declared, shaking his head as though in torment. 'I broke it so badly nine years ago…'

'Let's not revisit that time, Nick,' she begged, craving only a future with him.

'I have to make you understand, Barbie. We can't paper over this,' he said vehemently. 'I need you to know you *were* special to me. Even when you were just a little girl, you had this way of looking at me…your eyes so full of innocent trust…like you believed nothing bad could happen to you because I was there to look after you.'

'It's called hero-worship, Nick,' she said derisively, wanting to stop him from looking back, frightened that it couldn't lead anywhere good.

'No, it was more. No one else ever gave me that sense of…a pure love. It made me want to live up to it. I guess you could say I fed on it, Barbie, until I came to realise how selfish that was. I convinced myself I was giving you something—a broader life— when I forced the break. But what I broke was your trust in me.'

It was *true love,* Barbie wanted to cry, but she bit her lips, not brave enough to speak that truth.

'I hated having done it, having lost it,' he went on. 'And I knew it could never be recaptured. So when I recognised Barbie Lamb in Anne Shepherd…it hit me hard, the knowledge of breaking your trust. I wanted you to give it to me again, and when you didn't, I began not to trust you instead of facing up to what I'd done and the repercussions of it.'

He spread his hands in an urgent gesture of appeal. 'I swear this is true, Barbie. I've been in a kind of wilderness of the heart these past nine years. None of the relationships I've had ever felt really important or vital to me. Then, just a week ago…'

He moved back to her, slowly, his hands lightly curling around her shoulders, his eyes darkly watchful, seeking, wanting to know her heart. '…I met a fairy princess,' he continued gruffly. 'And when she kissed me, it was like magic pouring through my whole body.'

'Mine, too, Nick,' she whispered. 'That's why I came dressed like this tonight, hoping it could be so again.'

'Barbie…'

He sucked in a quick breath and kissed her, and she responded with all the passionate urgency of wanting everything to be right between them, for the magic to burst forth and dispel the shadows that had plagued both of them. The past didn't matter. Only now mattered. Now with Nick. And the journey they could take from here.

It was so good…feeling him wanting her, feeling free to want him right back, knowing she was as special to him as he was to her, the glorious sense of a long, long wilderness ending at last for both of them.

'I'll do everything I can to earn your trust again. Just give me the chance, Barbie,' he breathed into her ear.

'Hold on to me, Nick. Don't let me go.'

'Never!' he swore. 'Never!'

And he kissed her with that vow on his lips, in his heart, and her own heart pounded in unison with his, swelling with the love that had always been there for him.

'Nick?… Barbie…?' Carole's voice calling.

Nick ended their kiss on a ragged sigh. 'Yes…what?' he answered reluctantly.

'I'm about to bring in the cake for Mum. I want you in here with the rest of us.'

'Be there in a minute,' he promised. He eased back, lifting his hands to gently cup Barbie's face. 'Are you okay with this…facing my family with me?'

'Are you?'

'No problem for me. I'm only too happy to have you at my side and let everyone know it's where I want to be.'

'Then I'm happy with that, too.'

His thumb tenderly fanned her cheek. 'I *will* look after you, Barbie.'

'I do trust you to do that, Nick,' she assured him.

His smile was loaded with joyful relief. 'This is the start of us being really together.'

'Yes,' she agreed, smiling her own joyful relief.

And together they walked back into the house— arm in arm—leaving the darkness behind.

There was no place for darkness in their hearts.

They carried magic with them.

CHAPTER SIXTEEN

'HAPPY days, Nick.' Leon grinned at him as he lifted his glass of champagne. 'And nights.'

Nick grinned back. 'You've got that right.'

They stood outside the marquee on Observatory Hill, taking a short breather from the crowd of family and friends within. Barbie and Sue had gone to 'freshen up' and Nick didn't want to circulate amongst the wedding guests without his bride at his side.

'Right woman, right time, right place,' Leon went on approvingly, then cocked a teasing eyebrow. 'Don't know about the date though. You do realise this is the Ides of March, the day that Julius Caesar fell.'

Nick laughed. 'Big Julie was after the crown of Rome. Me... I'd give up any crown to have Barbie as my wife. This was the first available date we could get to have the wedding here and I wasn't waiting any longer.'

'It's only been four months,' Leon reminded him.

Nick shook his head. He'd been waiting all his life for her.

'Sue keeps muttering you charge like a bull, rushing everything.'

'Well, I don't notice the grass growing much under

your feet, my friend,' Nick tossed back at him. 'That's some emerald Sue is flashing on her engagement finger.'

'I don't aim to lose that lady. But there's a lot to be said for a long courtship. I'm relishing every minute of it.'

'Each to his own, Leon.'

'Can't disagree with that. We're both coming out winners and we're not even thirty-one yet,' Leon declared with immense satisfaction.

Nick laughed at his friend's habit of always crunching numbers. Age had nothing to do with how he felt about Barbie. She lit up his life in so many ways, he could only marvel at how lucky he was she'd taken her vengeance on him on this very hill four months ago—the sweetest revenge, reviving as it had the unique bond between them. It was indeed fitting to have their wedding here, Nick thought, because magic *had* been wrought that night and this would always be a special place to both of them.

'Hey! What are you doing out here?'

They both turned to Danny who was proudly carrying out his role of groomsman to Nick.

'Waiting for our women,' Leon answered. 'They've left us to powder their noses.'

'And very pretty noses they are,' Danny commented, grinning at both men. 'Got to say you guys have won prizes with Barbie and Sue.'

Nick suddenly felt impelled to ask, 'No hard feelings, Danny?'

He looked startled. Comprehension dawned slowly and moved into a quizzical frown. 'Over Barbie?'

'You *were* very stuck on her.'

'Youthful obsession,' Danny dismissed as though it were nothing. 'I've fished in many waters since and I'm sure as hell not ready to settle down.'

That wasn't exactly the point, Nick thought, but didn't want to make an issue of it.

Danny picked up on the doubt and gestured an appeal for understanding. 'Fact is, I'm really glad you two have got together. Wish I hadn't been such a pain about Barbie only having eyes for you back in the old days. I didn't realise I was mucking up something special. But I can see it is now, Nick, really special, and I truly am happy for both of you.' He stepped forward, smiling and offering his hand, 'Peace, brother.'

Nick clasped it warmly. 'Thanks, Danny.'

Barbie and Sue came around the corner of the marquee and spotted the three men together. 'Leon,' Sue called, pointing to the entrance, 'the band is playing a great rock beat. Can we dance?'

'We sure can, babe.'

He thrust his glass of champagne into Danny's hand and rock-and-rolled straight over to Sue, who shimmied seductively, the silvery green bridesmaid's dress emphasising her femininity. Leon swung her into the marquee with great panache, and their pleasure in each other left the other three smiling.

'Do you want to dance, too?' Nick asked as Barbie resumed walking towards him.

'I'd rather steal a few quiet moments with you,' she answered.

'Right!' said Danny, plucking the champagne glass out of Nick's hand. 'A good groomsman knows how to look after the bride's and groom's needs. I shall see that you're left alone.'

And off he marched, pausing only to say to Barbie, 'Best thing Nick's ever done, bringing you into the family. You two really belong together.'

'Thank you, Danny.' She watched him enter the marquee, then looked inquiringly at Nick.

'Just clearing up where he stands. No problem for Danny. He's happy for us,' Nick assured her.

She sighed. 'He only ever was, and is, your brother to me.'

'I know.'

The sense of how very, very lucky he was swelled through him as he watched her come the rest of the way where he stood waiting for her...so breathtakingly beautiful in her wedding gown, like the fairy princess dress, soft and gauzy, clinging to her curves and glittering with silver bugle beads, and her hair like gleaming silk, rippling down over her shoulders. But what shone out of her eyes was more wondrous to Nick than anything else...the love she held for him in her heart...and the trust he'd won back.

He held out his arms and she walked straight into his embrace, curling her own arms around his neck. 'You're wearing the watch I gave you,' she said, a whimsical question in her eyes. 'I didn't notice it until the speeches and you made a toast to my parents.'

'It felt right to wear it today. I love you, Barbie. There never will be anyone else for me.'

'Nor me,' she murmured. 'You were always the one...the love of my life.'

And that was the most magical thing of all, Nick thought as he kissed her, that she'd still been waiting for him when Fate crossed their paths and gave him the chance to realise that she was the one for him.

The only one.

His wife...his soul mate...the love of his life.

A SEDUCTIVE REVENGE

by

Kim Lawrence

Kim Lawrence lives on a farm in rural Anglesey. She runs two miles daily and finds this an excellent opportunity to unwind and seek inspiration for her writing! It also helps her keep up with her husband, two active sons, and the various stray animals which have adopted them. Always a fanatical consumer of fiction, she is now equally enthusiastic about writing. She loves a happy ending!

CHAPTER ONE

JOSH PRENTICE lifted his head and looked blankly at his agent. 'I've changed my mind.' He accompanied his bombshell with a languid smile that made Alec Jordan want to tear out what little hair he had left.

Josh wasn't just his most successful client, he was also his friend, and Alec knew he didn't have a languid bone in his well-built body. The older man regarded his friend's long-limbed, athletically built frame for a moment with wistful resentment.

'I've got a TV interview lined up for tomorrow night,' he explained for the third time with tight-lipped patience. 'The timing is perfect; your exhibition opens next week. The last interview you did after that art festival went down really well—apparently they love your cute French accent.' He gritted his teeth as his lavish flattery failed to make any impact on the younger man. 'I've already re-scheduled once because of Liam's birthday party.' He was unable to keep the sense of misuse from his voice. This was all the thanks he got for busting his butt rearranging things for an infuriatingly dedicated single parent!

'Thanks for the gift; Liam loved it.'

Alec sighed, seeing no hint of concession in those hard grey eyes, eyes which rarely softened these days for anyone other than his son. He allowed his thoughts to drift longingly in the direction of hungry artists starving in attics—how much more malleable, he mused wistfully, they must be than the likes of Josh, who, to add insult to injury didn't even have to rely on the healthy income from his

chosen career—it went against nature for an artist to also
have business acumen.

'The flight to Paris is booked,' he persisted stubbornly.

'Then unbook it.' Josh remained unmoved as, with a
deep, agonised groan, his agent slumped theatrically into
the opposite chair, his head in his hands.

'Would it be too much to ask where you're going if it's
not to Paris?' Alec enquired in a muffled voice. 'And don't
give me any guff about artistic temperament because we
both know you don't have any!'

Josh's lips quivered faintly at this hoarse accusation.
'Actually I'm not entirely sure yet...' He got to his feet
and absent-mindedly tugged at the zip on his jacket, pulling the cloth taut across an impressive chest. He moved
restlessly around the room before meeting Alec's interrog-
ative stare.

His friend barely repressed the shudder that crawled up
his spine at the detached, bone-chilling expression in those
half-closed pale grey depths. Volcanic emotions, intense
and fierce, were there simmering just below the surface.
He hadn't seen Josh look like this since just after Bridie's
death—during those bleak black days Josh had been totally
consumed by a deep, smouldering rage and the only person
brave or foolish enough to voluntarily expose himself to
all that raw emotion had been his twin brother, Jake.

'It depends...I'm following someone.' Josh's firm,
wide, unmistakably sensual lips compressed into a grim
line as he contemplated the task ahead.

'Did you say f...following...?'

'A woman...' Josh tersely supplied, bringing to an
abrupt halt his friend's incredulous stuttering.

'A woman!' A slow, relieved smile spread across Alec's
face. At last—to hell with Paris, he decided magnani-
mously, this really was great news! 'About time too,' he

boomed approvingly. It just wasn't natural, a man like Josh living like a monk. If he had half as many offers…! It wasn't as if anyone had expected the man to jump into bed with the first female who came along…but *three years* and he hadn't even looked… 'Why didn't you say? Who is she?'

'Flora Graham.'

Alec gasped, his florid complexion growing pale. 'You don't mean *the* Flora Graham. The daughter of…the one who…?'

Josh gave a wintry smile. 'The one who killed my wife?' He ignored Alec's agonised clucking sounds of denial, and wondered why everyone seemed so anxious to make excuses for David Graham—everybody but him, that was. 'The very same,' he confirmed calmly.

Alec, who'd half expected Josh to launch into a furious tirade at his own ill-advised protest, relaxed slightly. As unlikely pairings went, this one had him reeling.

It had taken Josh a long time to come to terms with the fact the young wife he'd adored had died during childbirth. The wounds had been dramatically reopened when it had come to light earlier that year that the much-respected doctor, Sir David Graham, who had been Bridie's obstetrician, was facing drug charges.

Actually the more lurid charges, which, it transpired, had been instigated by evidence supplied by a disgruntled employer who had tried to blackmail the surgeon into supplying her and her shady friends with drugs, had eventually been dropped. This hadn't stopped the media interest; the case had really caught their imagination.

The response from the legal community to Josh's accusations remained sympathetic but firm: their exhaustive enquiries hadn't revealed proof that any of his patients had ever suffered because of Sir David's problem. This attitude had exacerbated Josh's burning feelings of injustice and fuelled his desire for revenge.

Given Josh's feelings, Alec had been surprised at his lack of response when the details of the Graham court case had recently been plastered across every tabloid and broadsheet. Of course, if he'd fallen for the daughter that would explain…

'Stunning girl, of course.' The ice-cold blonde wasn't someone he'd personally like to spend a cosy evening with, but each to his own. Women like that could make him feel inadequate with one look; fortunately feelings of inadequacy were not something that kept Josh awake nights. 'Very…very…blonde,' he managed lamely. 'Had no idea you even knew her! How did you meet?'

'We haven't—*yet*—that's why I'm following her,' Josh explained patiently.

Alec suddenly had a cold premonition in the pit of his belly. 'What are you going to do when you do meet her?' he enquired, suddenly fearful of the reply.

On several occasions Flora Graham had had the opportunity to publicly condemn her father but she'd steadfastly refused to do so. Josh could still hear the beautifully modulated voice, which fairly shrieked of privilege, defending her parent as she'd responded with clinical precision to her public interrogations; his smile deepened. The father might be out of circulation, having chosen to spend time in a rehabilitation centre rather than serve an equally derisory prison sentence, but the daughter was still around, and, according to his sources, about to leave town.

The drug-dealing doctor whom weeks before the tabloids had hated had suddenly, with the typical fickleness of the popular press, become a pitiful figure, a victim, who'd harmed nobody but himself and had actually acted honourably when it had counted. It was the final straw!

Normally Josh was extremely tolerant of weaknesses—at least in others—but this case was a notable exception.

The heavy eyelids drooped over his silver-shot eyes. 'The details are a bit hazy as yet, but making her *deeply* unhappy is the general theme I'm aiming for.' And if that meant sleeping with her, so be it.

It was over an hour after she'd left the motorway before Flora knew for sure she was being followed—as scummy rats went, this one was quite efficient. She glared at the image of the red coupé in the rear-view mirror and something inside snapped. The voracious media had made her life a misery for the past months...wasn't it enough that she was reduced to sneaking out of town like some sort of criminal?

Enough was definitely enough! She braked sharply as the lay-by, half hidden from the winding road by a copse of trees, came into view. She wasn't exactly overcome with surprise when the flashy red car, its wheels sending up a flurry of loose chippings, pulled in a little way in front of her.

Knuckles white on the steering wheel, she took a deep, steadying breath—it was about time she stopped acting like a victim and gave them a taste of their own medicine! To hell with reticence and diplomacy! Her heels beat out a sharp tattoo as she marched purposefully towards the car. She made no attempt to confront the driver, instead she knelt beside the rear wheel and, after a moment's adjustment, heard the satisfying hiss of air escaping from the tyre.

Revenge might just have something to recommend it, she decided with a smile. She was rubbing her hands together in satisfaction when the driver of the vehicle emerged.

'What the hell?'

She recognised the thickset figure as one of the most persistent amongst the pack of journalists who had camped on her doorstep for days on end. It was the sheer incredulity in his face as he stared at the slowly deflating tyre that made Flora laugh, though in retrospect she swiftly acknowledged that the laugh probably hadn't been such a good idea—he was a big man and in a very ugly mood.

Why hadn't she sensibly driven to the nearest police station to get rid of her unwanted companion? What she'd been too angry to take into account earlier now struck her with sickening force—this was a very lonely road in a fairly remote area. At that moment, as if to emphasise the sinister implications of the situation, the wind gave an extra strong gust causing the tall trees to whisper menacingly overhead. She could almost hear them snigger, Talk yourself out of this one, Flora.

'You little cow!' The driver seemed to have recovered from his catatonic state and he was walking slowly towards her.

Flora found her feet stupidly wouldn't move from the spot as the big bulky figure approached her.

'That's criminal damage.' The words sounded so much like those of a sulky, thwarted child that Flora's moment of panic vanished.

'So is going through someone's dustbins,' she corrected with some feeling, 'and if it isn't it should be! Take your hands off me!' She gasped in outrage as the big ape wrapped one beefy paw around her forearm; his grip didn't loosen when she pulled angrily away and the stylish felt cloche she wore on her head slipped over one eye.

He wasn't going to hurt her, but it gave Tom Channing a sharp thrill of satisfaction to know that under that haughty façade Miss Ice Cool might be scared. All those weeks under the cruel light of public scrutiny and her composure hadn't cracked—not even once! People in her situation were meant to feel out of control and vulnerable but somehow this stuck-up little cow managed to act as if she didn't notice the flashing bulbs wherever she went—it just wasn't natural!

To add insult to injury even her friends had turned out to be untraditionally tight-lipped and stubbornly loyal. They'd closed ranks and to a man had refused to dish the dirt! She'd grown to represent everything about her class he detested. In a brief moment of rare honesty he realised that the fact probably had a lot to do with his reluctance to let the story die a natural death even though public interest in the scandal had waned. This was a crusade of a deeply personal nature now.

'What you going to do about it if I don't, Miss Graham?' he taunted, revelling in the heady feeling of being in control.

'Is there a problem here?'

The man holding her turned around with a frustrated snarl on his face. If Flora had been looking at her stalker she might have appreciated the comical speed with which his combative glare became a weak, conciliatory grin. Only Flora wasn't looking at him, she was looking—well, actually, to be strictly honest, which she tried at all times to be—she was staring. Staring at the owner of the rich deep voice, riveting long-lashed slate-grey eyes, and sinfully sexy mouth.

There was quite a lot of him to stare at—he must be six-four or six-five, she estimated, paying silent, stunned homage to the sheer perfection of this athletically built specimen. His shoulders wouldn't have looked out of place competitively employed in an Olympic swimming pool and she could almost see those sprinter's legs eating up the track…everything in between looked just about perfect too. He broadcast raw sex appeal on a frequency every female with a pulse would have picked up at fifty yards. On second thoughts, maybe there wasn't a safe distance from this man!

Flora let out a tiny grunt of shock as her breath escaped gustily past her slightly parted lips. She wasn't the sort of girl who made a habit of mentally undressing men, especially a married man as this one obviously was—the cute little boy beside him was too much of a carbon copy not to be his son, and then there was the little matter of the wide gold band on his left hand!

Fantasising about married men was not a pastime Flora indulged in—in fact, considering that she'd been very publicly dumped by her ever-loving fiancé, she ought not to be capable of anything so frivolous! I'm probably just a disgustingly shallow person, she concluded, reviewing her worryingly resilient heart critically.

'Just a little misunderstanding…' Her stalker saw the direction of those narrowed grey eyes and his hand dropped self-consciously away from Flora's arm. Although the tall guy was smiling—the curve of his mouth didn't soften those chiselled features or spookily pale eyes an iota—and he had a grubby-faced toddler glued to his leg, didn't lessen the fact he looked a dangerously tough customer. There was something vaguely familiar about him too…

Flora fastidiously gave a disbelieving snort and flicked her fingers against the invisibly soiled area of her sleeve. Angrily she straightened the drunken angle of her hat. Next he'd be saying he'd *accidentally* followed her.

She bit back the scathing retort on the tip of her tongue—once you started acting spontaneously it was hard to stop—and summoned a tight smile. More detailed explanations would inevitably mean the handsome stranger getting a potted version of the whole sordid saga. It struck her as perverse that she suddenly felt so squeamish about such a small-scale exposure after what she'd managed to survive.

'I might take issue with the "little"—' her deep blue eyes swept scornfully over the persistent journalist's face '—but I'm fine, thank you.'

Happily the stranger, despite his unconvinced expression, didn't take issue with her lie. He turned to the hack who was nudging his flat tyre with the tip of his boot.

'Flat…?'

The journalist jerked his head in response and shot Flora a murderous glare. 'I'm not carrying a spare,' he realised with a groan.

'Bad luck,' Josh responded blandly. His natural inclination was to assume that anyone giving Flora Graham and her family a hard time couldn't be all bad, but in this case he was prepared to modify his views; he had disliked the guy on sight—a real sleaze bag!

As he turned his head he caught Flora's violet-blue eyes and winked. Dazed by the blast of charm aimed in her direction, she helplessly grinned back at him.

Josh froze and didn't catch what his son said in his urgent infant treble. He was mega unprepared for the transformation from cold goddess to warm, vibrant woman. The faint wrinkles around her suddenly warm blue eyes and the conspiratorial crooked little smile were bad enough, but it was the slight indentation in her porcelain-smooth left cheek that was the real clincher. A dimple! He found he really objected deeply to the fact Flora Graham had a dimple; neither the glimpses he'd had of her outside the courtroom or the image of her impassively enduring television interviews had even suggested such a thing.

Flora was accustomed, even before her face had been plastered across the front page of several tabloids, to men looking at her—this definitely wasn't *that* sort of look! Which was a relief because the pleasure of being admired for something as superficial as the neat arrangement of her regular, and to her mind somewhat insipidly pretty, features, or the tautness of her slim, athletic figure had palled years ago. She knew to her cost that none of these would-be admirers gave a damn about what sort of woman lay beneath the attractive window-dressing.

Whilst she didn't mind this hunk not being bowled over by her beauty—a small ironic grimace flickered across her features at the notion—something about that stare did trouble her. A small frown puckered her smooth forehead, and distant warning bells sounded in her head. She closed her mouth and surreptitiously explored with her tongue the possibility she had some unsightly remnant of her lunch stuck in her teeth.

'My phone's not working, mate. Have you...?' The journalist tentatively approached the silent couple.

'No reception up here...probably the mountains,' Josh elaborated, gesturing with a strong, shapely hand towards the breathtaking but forbidding scenery. 'I seem to recall there was a garage about half a mile back...'

Flora had followed the direction of his hand, registering automatically the strong, shapely part, and she found herself comparing this stranger with the landscape—more rugged and dangerous than pastoral. She dismissed the instinct of moments before that had suggested something wasn't quite right; after all, if her instinct was so reliable what had she been doing engaged to Paul, the ratbag?

'I don't suppose there's any chance of a lift...?' The sardonic quirk of one dark brow brought a rush of colour; it was clearly visible even through Tom Channing's care-

fully nurtured designer stubble, which was meant to under-
line, along with the single gold ring in one ear and the
scuffed shoes, his hard-man street credibility. It narked him
no end that this big guy had buckets of the stuff and he
didn't even try. 'That's a no, I take it,' he concluded bitterly.

Flora had to bite her lip to prevent herself from grinning
as she watched the burly figure flounce off to his car muttering—carefully not loud enough for her companion to
hear—under his breath.

'I think you hurt his feelings.' It was hard not to gloat
so she gave up trying; she was due a bit of gloating.
'You're not meant to drive with a flat tyre, are you?' she
added innocently as the red car bumpily drew away.

'No.'

'I thought not.' Flora gave a contented sigh.

'Daddy!'

This time the urgent tugging at his trouser leg got Josh's
attention.

'What is it, champ?'

'I think I'm going to be sick!'

Stunned at the speed with which this prediction came
true, Flora stared in fascinated horror down at the unpleasant mess congealing over her pale biscuit trousers and favourite soft, handmade loafers.

'I feel better now.' Liam sighed and looked up happily
at his father.

Josh smiled back, silently congratulating his son on his
unerring aim. He produced a tissue to wipe the toddler's
mouth and glanced surreptitiously towards the tall, wil-
lowy blonde, fully expecting her to be close to a state of
complete collapse by now.

In his experience women like her, the sort who never
ventured out into public without the full works—make-up,
smooth, impossibly shiny hair and the season's latest in

designer gear—had a problem with the less picturesque aspects of life. And a kid throwing up fell safely into that category! He had to concede that a kid throwing up so comprehensively over you would have been enough to throw even those women of his acquaintance *not* totally preoccupied with their own appearance.

'I'm glad you feel better. I must say I feel rather yucky!'

Josh gave a disgruntled frown. There was a rueful twinkle in Flora's eyes as she smiled sweetly at his son. Damn woman, he didn't much like having to throw his script out of the window.

'You smell,' Liam told her frankly.

Flora's nose wrinkled. 'I'd noticed that too,' she admitted drily.

'You need a bath. Doesn't she, Daddy?'

Josh gave a noncommittal grunt. He suddenly had a very clear picture in his head of water sliding over satiny skin, gliding slowly down the slim, supple line of a naked female back. Her buttocks would be high and tight, you could tell by the way—his head snapped up so sharply a jarring pain shot all the way down his stiff spine. *Hell!* What a time for his libido to come out of hibernation.

But it wasn't the content of his lustful thoughts that made his guts tighten with a guilty repugnance, it was the person responsible for inciting those lustful thoughts. The whole situation suggested to him that someone up there had one twisted sense of humour!

A warm bubble of humour escaped from Flora's throat. 'Or, failing that, a change of clothes,' she agreed solemnly. She shifted her weight and her shoes squelched rather disgustingly. 'Also I have a pack of Wet Wipes—a *large* pack.'

Josh scooped his talkative son up into his arms. 'I'm sorry about this, Miss…?'

He fixed on his best guileless-stroke-helpless smile. It was the one that had females of all ages stampeding to help him with his son and he wasn't above using it if the occasion warranted it. He'd gone past the period when he'd needed to prove he could cope alone; now he wasn't so averse to making life easier.

She sighed—blessed anonymity! 'Flora,' she supplied, meeting the tall stranger's eyes and feeling inexplicably shy.

'I'm Josh, Josh Prentice, and this is Liam who, as you have probably gathered, isn't the world's best traveller.' He held out his hand towards her. 'You must bill me for the clothes.'

Flora grimaced and wriggled her less-than-clean fingers a safe distance away. 'For your safety I think we should pass on that one. As for the clothes, I'd say we're even.' She gave a sigh as she contemplated the sticky situation he'd rescued her from. 'When I'm around creeps like that I *really* wish I were a man. Don't get me wrong,' she added swiftly, just in case he imagined she was a bit of a wimp, 'I can handle men like that. You just have to be more subtle,' she explained to her rather startled-looking audience.

She'd learnt early on that men could be intimidated by the combination of cut-glass beauty and brains, and some-times that combination allied with a cutting tongue was the only weapon she had or needed—*usually*.

Friends who knew she was a bit of a softy thought it a hoot when they saw her turn on the 'deep freeze' but this ability had come in really handy recently when, trauma-tised deeply by the unkind public scrutiny, not to mention the fact the father she'd worshipped all her life had been exposed as a drug addict—life really was stranger than fiction—she'd retreated behind a mask of aloof disdain.

Firmly repressing the troublesome urge to continue to stare up at him, she transferred her gaze to a far less complex pair of grey eyes fringed by lashes just as preposterously long as in the older version.

'Ever tried ginger biscuits for travel sickness, Liam?' The kiddy looked predictably interested at the mention of food. 'They work for me. In fact, I've probably got some in my car. They might help settle his tummy…?' she suggested tentatively to Josh.

Some people donned dark glasses and wig to escape notice; it seemed Miss Graham donned a different personality—she was behaving like a girl guide! Still, he'd be around when she showed her true colours. At that moment she swept off her hat and he saw the disguise didn't stop there!

The long, waist-length shimmering mane of silvery blonde hair was gone, replaced by a short feathery cap that followed the elegant shape of her skull. The style might lack the impact of long, swishy blonde tresses, but the gamin cut did make her eyes look bigger, her patrician features more delicate, and emphasised the long, graceful curve of her neck. Let's face it, with bones like hers the girl could shave off her hair and still look stunning!

Flora lifted her hand to her head and felt an instant's surprise when her fingers made contact with the short, wavy strands. Just contemplating how much Paul would dislike it made her feel cheerful about her rebellious gesture. Her ex-fiancé had once confided, in one of his rare moments of honesty—did *all* politicians lie?—that he thought women with short hair were unfeminine, and probably a bit confused about their sexuality.

Now she could see what had been blindingly obvious all the time: he *hadn't* been joking; this comment was typical of the man; Paul was a first-class narrow-minded

bigot! And I was going to bear his children! She shook
her head slightly as she considered her criminal lack of
judgement when it came to men.

'Have you got far to travel, Flora?' Josh hoped not—
another half-hour in the car with Liam and he might go
completely gaga. It had afforded him dark amusement
when the car following Flora had been so busy trying not
to be noticed that the driver had failed to suspect that
someone else had the same quarry in mind.

It had made his own task easier, but not that easy.
Liam's low boredom threshold and dislike of car journeys
were two things he foolishly hadn't taken into account
when he'd set out to follow Flora Graham out of town.

Flora got a nice warm glow as she watched Josh jiggle
the little boy from one narrow hip to the other, absently
kissing the toddler's nose as he did so. He seemed not to
notice that the child's grubby hands had comprehensively
mussed up his glossy dark hair. After Paul, who had been
almost pathological about neatness—and still was, no
doubt—it was quite a contrast.

She was off men permanently, because they were more
trouble than they were worth, but she couldn't help thinking... Her eyes moved covetously over his long, lean
frame. This other woman's husband was so spectacularly
delicious, and great with the kiddy. Nice, incredible-
looking and oozing daddy appeal—why don't I ever meet
men like that? she wondered indignantly.

He wouldn't have to be *that* good-looking. In fact, perhaps it might be better if he wasn't, she concluded wryly,
then hungry single women wouldn't be lusting after him
when my back was turned. Women like me! A guilty flush
mounted her cheeks and she replied a little stiltedly.

'A friend has a holiday cottage not far from here.' She
named the little village. 'Do you know it?' The stranger

inclined his dark head in confirmation and she blithely chattered on. After being forced by circumstances to be discreet to the point of dumbness in front of strangers, it was something of a relief to talk normally—well, not totally normally, she felt impelled to admit.

The man was just too damned gorgeous to be able to do anything in front of him totally unselfconsciously. She was ruefully aware that a very unsolicitor-like girly giggle—the one she had to repress if she didn't want him to think she was a brainless bimbo—was only a heartbeat away.

'That is not far; but far enough to make a change of clothes a must.' Her nose twitched in an attempt to avoid the sour smell emanating from her person. 'I need to change. I don't suppose you could…?' She stopped midrequest with a self-conscious grimace. 'No, of course you couldn't…'

'It has been known for me to answer for myself.'

She grinned. 'I bet it has,' she responded, examining his determined angular jawline; doting dad or not, he looked like the opinionated type to her. 'Actually I was hoping you could act as lookout for me whilst I change. It could be a bit embarrassing if I'm stripped off down to my undies when some family pulls up complete with picnic basket…'

'I'd have thought you'd have been more concerned about lone males, but I was forgetting you can handle men…*subtly*…'

Was there a strand of mockery in his deep voice? Flora felt vaguely uneasy as she watched him put down the child and brush his hands against his strong, muscular thighs. There was nothing remotely sexual about the gesture—the sex, she told herself sternly, was all in her own mind—but that didn't stop her body temperature hiking up several notches. This entire weird overreaction was probably all part of the winding-down process. After the last few months that wasn't going to be an overnight thing.

'Realistically I don't suppose there's much chance of *anyone* coming along here.' A cooling-off period was urgently required, so she allowed her eyes to drift around the rather bleak landscape before coming to rest once more on his face.

'I did.'

'It's probably lucky for me you did.' She didn't think she'd been in any actual physical danger from the journalist, just the sort of unpleasant scene which she would much rather avoid.

Lamb to the slaughter, Josh marvelled as she looked up at him oozing trust and lack of suspicion. He ought to be feeling pretty pleased with how things were going, but somehow her trusting disposition was irritating the hell out of him.

'I wouldn't want you to risk indecent exposure charges.'

Flora's eyes widened, a hard laugh was wrenched from her throat. 'Wouldn't they have loved that!'

'Pardon…?'

Flora gathered her wits. Small wonder he was looking at her blankly. 'It's a long story.'

'And none of my business.'

Flora flushed, aware that at the first hint of the conversation growing remotely personal she had automatically reverted to cool disdain. 'Actually it's not something I want to talk about.'

'And I'm a stranger.'

'But a very kind one,' she told him warmly. She couldn't understand why his handsome face hardened.

'And if I wasn't—if I was a dangerous, marauding lone

male with evil intentions—you could deal with me…
right?'

Flora laughed a little uneasily and tried not to notice the
way her stomach lurched when she visualised how it might
feel if that horrifying scenario were true.

'But you're not alone, you're with Liam…you're a *father.*'

'And being a father places me above suspicion…and
temptation?' He silently reviewed the lists of world-class
baddies who'd been doting dads, but resisted the impulse
to point out the obvious flaws in her argument. 'I must
admit I've never quite looked at it in that way before. I'm
overcome by the confidence you place in me.'

Flora didn't think he sounded overcome, just irked.
Perhaps even happily married men preferred to think they
could still be considered dangerous.

'There's nothing wrong with being domesticated,' she
told him kindly. Actually she didn't think half a dozen kids
could make this particular specimen appear domesticated.
She was a sensible, mature woman—*mostly*—with her feet
firmly on the ground, and even her stomach showed a dangerous tendency to go all squidgy when she looked into
those hooded silvery eyes.

'And it's nothing to do with paternity as such.' She
frowned earnestly. 'Don't you ever just get a gut feeling
with some people that you can trust them?' She closed her
mouth with an audible snap…where the hell did that come
from?

Squirming with humiliation, she gazed at the dark colour that stained the sharp, high angle of his achingly perfect cheekbones. Now I've embarrassed him—small wonder! You don't go around telling total strangers you have
gut feelings about them—gut feelings suggest a degree of

intimacy! He probably thinks I'm making a pass at him or something. It was true about the gut feeling, though…

Josh broke the awkward silence. 'Liam's been cramped in the car all morning; he needs a chance to stretch his legs.' To her relief he was acting as if she'd said nothing out of the ordinary. 'If you want to change I'll keep an eye out for coach parties.'

'Well, if you're…thanks…'

Josh kept one eye on his son who was building a tower with the stray rocks he'd gathered and the other on the wing mirror of his four-wheel drive, which kept him up to date with the state of play of Flora's contortions in the back seat of her small car.

Now wasn't the time to be worrying about the general scumminess of such behaviour. He couldn't afford the luxury of scruples if he was going to make Graham pay. He was going to hit him where it hurt and Graham's Achilles' heel was his daughter—he adored her. The moment Josh had seen the interview of the two of them together he'd known that this was the way to make him pay. As for the girl, she hadn't even been willing to admit her father had done anything wrong. As always when he needed reminding of why he was doing this, he brought the picture of Bridie's sweet, laughing face to mind—or he would have if what was going on in the car hadn't distracted him.

Any travellers seeking a respite from their journey at that moment wouldn't have been treated to the sight of Flora's underwear. She wasn't wearing any—at least not from the waist up, which was the bit he could see. Her breasts were fairly small, pointed and high. They bounced energetically as she stretched upwards, pulling a thin cashmere polo shirt over her head. With a muffled curse of self-disgust Josh tore his eyes away.

Who was he kidding? This had nothing to do with revenge; it was pure voyeurism. That was bad, but not so bad if all he'd wanted to do was look!

He heard the sound of her feet on the rough ground but didn't turn around. He watched as Liam carefully selected a stick and knocked down the tower of rocks he'd so lovingly constructed.

'I worry about his aggressive instincts sometimes.'

'I wouldn't, it's perfectly normal,' Flora comforted. She smiled as the youngster laughed out loud before he started to rebuild his destroyed creation. 'I'm sure you did the same.'

'No, my brother Jake built them and I knocked them down, then he knocked me down. These days people pay him a lot of money to build things and nobody knocks them down.'

'He's a builder?'

'No, an architect.'

'And what do you do?' She bit her lip. 'You don't have to answer that—once I get into interrogation mode there's no stopping me,' she babbled in embarrassment.

'So what does that make you?' He responded to Liam's pouting plea by producing a sweet from his pocket. 'Only one,' he warned before handing it over. 'A police woman…?' he suggested, straightening up from his crouched pose and brushing his hands against the seat of his well-worn denims.

'No, a solicitor.'

'Pity…'

She looked enquiringly at him.

'I've always had a soft spot for a girl in uniform.'

His smile and the way her heart started to beat wildly filled her with panic. 'Is Liam an only child?' A swift diplomatic change of subject was urgently required.

Josh didn't reply straight away; when he did his grey

eyes held a shadowy expression that disturbed her. Was she imagining the tenseness in his greyhound-lean body?

'Yes, he is.'

He was young, maybe thirty; he and his wife could produce a lot more children all as enchanting as Liam. Flora, who had never been aware of any strong maternal instincts, felt a surge of envy and a deepening sense of dissatisfaction with where her life was going.

'So am I.'

A nerve throbbed in Josh's lean cheek. 'That must make you all the more precious to your parents.' His eyes were curiously intent on her face.

'Father; my mum died five years ago.'

He touched her hand—hardly even a touch, more a brushing of her skin; the gesture seemed unpremeditated. Flora didn't move. She continued to stare at the busy, happy child, aware all the time of an invisible web of nerve-endings she hadn't even known existed surge to zinging life all over her body. Her skin felt so alive it hurt—pleasure bordering on pain. She found herself completely unprepared for this raw, sensual awakening.

The symptoms dissipated but didn't vanish when his hand fell away. Way out of proportion or what? Her puffily exhaled breath turned white in the chill of the lengthening autumnal afternoon.

'I better be going,' she said, swallowing hard and stirring the loose ground with the toe of her casual flat shoe.

Josh noticed the replacement was just as expensive and exclusive as the one she'd worn earlier. Daddy's indulged little girl...it didn't work; his rage only responded sluggishly to the prod.

'Thank you,' she began with a frank, open smile. 'For everything.' If she drew this out much longer he was going to realise she felt reluctant to leave...it was quite absurd.

His mental preparations hadn't prepared him for this. Making love to Flora Graham wasn't something he was supposed to *want* to do. It was supposed to be a means to an end, a 'close your eyes and think of revenge' sort of situation! It was easy to exploit someone who obviously didn't have a heart or feelings. This stupid woman didn't only have them, she didn't even keep them decently disguised.

This could be so easy; she'd been shaking like a nervous thoroughbred when he'd touched her. The sexual chemistry was a bonus to be exploited, he told himself. She trusted him, her father had just been publicly disgraced, her fiancé had dumped her, she was vulnerable, seduction would be a walk in the park. Telling her the truth would be a pleasure. All he had to do was go gently...

Nobody had ever accused Josh Prentice of taking the easy option!

He had a mouth which knew exactly what to do to reduce his victim to a state of helpless and humiliating co-operation. The searing onslaught of his clever tongue and lips went beyond the physical.

Flora staggered backwards when the pressure ceased and the big hands that had held her face fell away. She continued to stagger until her spine made contact with a convenient tree; the rough surface abraded her back through the thin, hooded top she now wore over a polo shirt. Breathing shallow and fast, she reached behind her to clutch the comforting solidity of the bark in what had become an almost surreal world.

'Why,' she asked in a voice which hovered on the brink of tremulous, 'did you do that?' Good, her voice was beginning to get back to normal.

Kissing her didn't seem to have put him in a mellow frame of mind, although at the time it had seemed to her he'd been enjoying himself! She was humiliatingly aware of the ache in her taut, peaking breasts.

'I had to see for myself if you were as stupid as you look!' he snapped cuttingly.

The outrage on his voice made her blink. 'And am I?' she enquired in a dazed voice.

'With bells on, woman!' he raged. 'Don't you have *any* sense of self-preservation? I could have been anyone and you come out with all that airy-fairy crap about trust. *Trust!*' He choked. 'I could be Jack the bloody Ripper for all you know and all you can do is look at me as if I...' With a snort of disgust he broke off. 'Just because you like the way someone looks, it doesn't make them all the things you want them to be.' He was warning her, you couldn't get fairer than that. Or more stupid, a quiet inner voice sighed.

Two spots of dark colour stained the soft contours of her pale cheeks. Was I really *that* obvious?

'What makes you think,' she snapped with cold precision, 'that I like the way you look?'

He threw back his head and laughed; it was a bitter sound. 'Like you don't like the way I kiss?' One dark, strongly delineated brow shot satirically upwards. 'I noticed the way you *hated* that.'

Flora's face was burning with mortification at his soft, derisive jibe—so what if she might have co-operated for a split second? 'Most men wouldn't be complaining,' she said, glaring up at his hatefully handsome face. She bit her lips as she realised it was too late now to dispute the claim she'd in any way enjoyed being kissed by him. 'But then you only kissed me out of the goodness of your heart to show me how foolishly trusting I was being...teach me a lesson...'

There was more than a grain of truth in her sarcastic

jibe, but it wasn't the entire story. He ran an exasperated hand through his dark hair. 'I kissed you,' he hissed in a driven voice, 'because I wanted to.' Abruptly he turned away from his contemplation of the trees; his deep-set eyes burned into her.

The air whooshed out of her lungs. 'Oh!' Her eyes searched his face. Given the circumstances, it wasn't very flattering that he looked as if he were trying to digest something particularly bitter and unappetising.

She smiled distractedly at Liam, who opened his grubby little hand to offer her a smooth black stone. 'Black,' he explained patiently.

'It's his favourite colour,' his father elaborated tersely.

'Lovely, Liam.' She smiled, pocketing the gift. 'Thank you.'

She stiffened. Am I slow or what? How could I have forgotten a *minor* detail like the ring on his finger, especially when the physical proof of the wretched man's unavailability is playing around my feet? What is wrong with me? I've had better kisses than that and not ended up with mush for a brain. It was a mistake to think about the kiss…stop hyperventilating, Flora.

'Does your wife know you go around doing things because you *want* to?' she enquired with icy derision. Her cold pose slipped. 'I think you're the most disgusting man I've ever met!' she told him in a quivering voice.

The pain that swept across his face made Flora's voice fade dramatically away. It occurred to her that she could never despise him half as much as he did himself.

'My wife's dead.' His voice sounded the same way.

Flora didn't know how to respond and he didn't appear to expect her to.

'I haven't wanted to kiss a woman since…'. The harsh explanation emerged involuntarily.

Flora closed her eyes against a sudden rush of hot, emotional tears and wished he hadn't told her that. She'd come out here to regain a bit of inner peace, not get mixed up with some moody, brooding type who was way too good-looking. He'd got a kid, and—hell!—even more unresolved angst than she had. He was the one that introduced the subject of self-preservation.

Flora's heart ached as she watched them go, but she made no move to prevent them. She had troubles enough of her own without courting the extra ones a man like this one represented.

CHAPTER TWO

'NIA didn't say you were coming.' Megan Jones handed her husband, who was sitting with his heavily plastered leg propped up on a footstool, a fresh cup of tea.

'No.' Josh helped himself to another slice of his brother's mother-in-law's excellent *bara brith*. 'It was a spur of the moment thing.'

Megan Jones nodded understandingly. 'You need a break; Nia says you work far too hard.'

'Does she…?' He suspected his sister-in-law said far too much entirely. The next statement from one of her brothers confirmed this suspicion.

The kitchen door swung open. 'Nia says you need a woman, Josh. Like the haircut,' he added. 'Not so girly, makes you look nearly respectable.'

'Geraint!' his mother exclaimed, slapping her large, burly son's hand as he filched a slice of cake and crammed it whole into his mouth. 'Josh *is* respectable!' She flashed Josh a worried look and was relieved to see her guest didn't look offended by the slur. 'And look what your boots are doing to my nice clean floor,' she scolded her big son half-heartedly.

'I'll be back from Betws before milking, Mam,' her grinning son promised unrepentantly. He winked at Josh and ruffled Liam's hair before he departed just as speedily as he'd arrived.

'Now there's someone who is *definitely* working too hard,' his mother announced with a worried frown.

'I've told you I'd take on another man if we could afford

it.' Geraint's father gritted his teeth in frustration. 'You'd
think with five sons there'd be more than one around the
place when you need them,' he complained.

'Yes, well, I'm sure Josh doesn't want to hear us grum-
bling,' Megan said, pinning a bright smile on her face.

No wonder Megan was looking strained; Josh suspected
that energetic Huw Jones was not an easy patient.

'I don't suppose there's ever a good time to break your
leg, Huw…?'

'But some times are worse than others,' Huw rumbled,
'you've got it right there, boy.'

'Where are you staying, Josh?'

'I was hoping you could recommend somewhere
nearby.'

'You couldn't do much better than The Panton,' Huw
responded. 'Though it'll cost you an arm and leg.'

'The Panton, Huw, really!' Megan chided indignantly.
'Josh and Liam will stay with us, of course. Just like they
always do. I miss having a child about the place.' She
smiled fondly at Liam.

Since Jake had married Nia, Josh, a keen climber, had
joined his brother here at Bryn Goleu for several weekend
climbing expeditions in the rugged Snowdonian mountains. Megan Jones's hospitality was as warm as her smile.

'I think you've got your hands full without extra guests
right now, Megan. We wouldn't dream of imposing.' Josh
saw his hostess looked inclined to press the issue and a
workable compromise occurred to him. 'I will stay, on one
condition: you let me work for our board. I don't know a
cow from a sheep,' he warned them with a grin, 'but I'm
a willing pair of hands.' He held out his hands to demonstrate their willingness.

'We wouldn't dream…' Megan began politely.

Huw put aside his newspaper. 'What do you mean,

woman? Of course we'd dream. Beside, a bit of honest sweat'll do the boy a world of good, build up a bit of muscle.'

Josh took the scornful inference he was some sort of seven-stone weakling in his stride.

'If you let him talk much longer, Josh, he'll convince you you ought to be paying him for the privilege of letting you break your back!' Megan threw her husband a withering glance, but Josh could see she felt just as relieved as the reluctant invalid. Their gratitude made him feel guilty because his offer of help wasn't entirely altruistic. He hadn't been able to believe his luck when Flora had named the village she was staying in as one a mere mile from the Jones farm—it suited him very well to stay for a while at Bryn Goleu.

Flora's walking boots had never actually seen a puddle before; the country experience was proving a baptism by fire for her and them both. The boots seemed to be coping better with water than she had with the mouse in the house last night. Fortunately the village store stocked mousetraps, but Flora wasn't sure which horrified her most: the idea of coming face to face with a live mouse or a dead one.

She consulted the map in her pocket; if she was reading it correctly this footpath would cut her return journey by half. It seemed to go directly through a farmyard. Right on cue a farmyard came into view around the bend. She'd heard tales that suggested all farmers weren't exactly welcoming to ramblers; she hoped these natives, if she came across any, were friendly. Still, she reasoned, they couldn't possibly be as bad as tabloid journalists.

She did see one—it was hard to miss him—a large, shirtless specimen wheeling a barrow piled with fencing posts out of one of the stone outbuildings. His back was turned to her; it suggested he would make short work of driving those heavy wooden posts into the ground. She tried not to stare too obviously at the sculpted power of those rippling, tightly packed muscles; she had limited success.

She cleared her throat to let him know she was there. 'Good morning,' she called out politely. The figure turned slowly.

'*Bore da*, Flora.' Josh exhausted the limit of his Welsh.

She must have walked into the shop and bought it all up, he decided, giving her a quick once-over from her sunlit hair to her shiny new boots. All the stylish, squeaky new clothes were top-of-the-range mountain gear which showed off her lovely long length of leg and neat, incredibly small waist. A light crop of freckles had emerged across the bridge of her nose and her cheeks were healthily flushed, whether from exertion or from the shock of seeing him he wasn't quite sure...but he had his suspicions.

'*You!*' Flora, who had forgotten to breathe for several stupefied moments, took a deep noisy gulp to compensate.

'It's enough to make a man believe in coincidence,' he drawled, lifting a hand to shade his eyes from the sun.

She nodded in a dazed sort of way. Looking at her with a clear-eyed sardonic grey gaze, he was displaying none of the awkwardness she, because of the way they'd parted, felt—he didn't even seem surprised to see her. Willing her eyes not to make any detours over his naked torso, she kept them firmly trained on his face.

'Or fate.' Now why, she wondered with a silent groan, did I say that?

'And do you?' he enquired, unexpectedly expanding on the theme. 'Believe in fate?' He speared a pitchfork into the ground and leaned on it to casually watch her. Flora found the unblinking scrutiny uncomfortable.

Her curiosity reached boiling point and she succumbed to growing temptation and risked a quick, surreptitious peek at his leanly muscled chest and flat belly. Her stomach muscles did uncomfortable and worrying things. The earthy image hadn't done anything to soothe her jangled nerves or hot cheeks.

It was the little details like the line of hair that disappeared like a directional arrow beneath the waistband of the worn blue jeans he wore that got her especially hot under the collar. She wondered what he'd make of it if she picked up the discarded plaid shirt she'd spotted and begged him to put it on—*too much* is what he'd make of it, she told herself derisively.

'*Fate!*' she hooted robustly. 'Of course not.' Her tone was laced with a shade of indignation. What sort of silly woman did he think she was? 'You live here, then?' She recalled he never had got around to telling her what he did for a living. He didn't look much like her idea of a farmer, but then what did she, the ultimate townie, know?

'No, just helping out for a few weeks.'

A casual farm labourer! This possibility seemed even more unlikely than the first option. She'd had him pegged as someone who, even if he didn't give orders, *definitely* didn't take them off anyone. To her there seemed something of the maverick about him.

Her own father had always been proud of his humble beginnings as the son of a coalminer and it struck her forcibly that he'd be ashamed if he knew his own daughter nurtured snobbish preconceptions about manual labourers. Just because a man used his muscles to earn a crust didn't mean he didn't have a brain, and if she needed proof she only had to look as far as this man. Those extraordinary eyes of his held a biting degree of intelligence.

If her friend's reports were anything to go by, babies

were expensive creatures, and most of those households who were frequently pleading poverty brought in two hefty professional salaries. This man had a child to bring up alone and, it seemed, no professional qualifications. Under the circumstances he couldn't afford to be picky about work. It must be hard worrying about money and coping with parenthood, she reflected. He faced problems every day she couldn't begin to understand; her soft heart swelled with empathy. It made her feel guilty when she considered her own comparative embarrassment of worldly riches.

'*Helping!* Is that what you call it?' A large young man with a lilting accent and a head of shocking red hair jeered as he came up behind Josh and thumped him good-naturedly on the back. 'Slacking more like, man.' He laughed. He looked with interest at Flora, his bold eyes admiring. 'Fast worker, aren't you?' he added slyly to Josh in a soft voice.

Flora fell back on her frozen routine, but frustratingly neither man appeared to notice. Josh gave a tolerant, unembarrassed smile.

'Geraint, this is Flora.' He casually performed the introductions. 'She's staying in the village. Flora, this big bull is Geraint Jones.'

'The heir apparent,' Geraint told her, swaggering in an inoffensive way. 'You going to actually do any work to-day, Josh?' he added sarcastically, jumping into a tractor and revving up the engine. 'See you later, *cariad*,' he called to Flora. 'And remember, if you want any real work done I'm your man,' he boasted. 'Now, if you want a bit of sissy painting...' he taunted, driving noisily off.

It was similar to an encounter with a bulldozer. 'Is he always so...?'

'Always, but a bit more so when a beautiful woman is around.'

She'd been called beautiful so often it didn't even register now, so why were her lower limbs suddenly afflicted by a debilitating weakness?

'You paint? I mean, that's your real trade?' An idea, probably not a good one, was occurring to her. It would be foolish to blurt anything out before she'd considered the implications of her inspiration.

'You could say that,' Josh confirmed a shade cautiously.

Flora was so excited by the brilliance of her idea that she decided that she'd throw caution to the winds.

'Well, I don't know what your schedule's like at the moment...?'

'Flexible,' he responded honestly.

'Well, I might be able to put some work your way. My friend Claire,' she explained hurriedly, 'the one who is letting me use her cottage—she asked me to find someone to redecorate the small bedroom in the cottage while I'm here. It's really dark and poky and she's just had a baby...Emily...' On anyone else Josh would have called that soft, fleeting little smile sentimental. 'And she wants the room redone before she comes up at Christmas. If you're interested...'

'You're offering me a job?' He was looking at her oddly.

'You wouldn't be working for me,' she informed him, anxious to make this point quite clear from the outset. 'I'm only acting as an agent for Claire.'

'Decorating a bedroom? You want me to decorate a bedroom?'

Flora glared. Was it such a revolutionary notion? Hadn't he decorated a bedroom before? Anyone would think she'd said something funny. She hadn't expected or wanted gratitude but he looked as though he was about to fall about laughing.

Maybe it was a male pride thing, she pondered. He might not like people, especially a woman, to know he was strapped for cash. She tried to see it from his point of view and had to concede it was possible she was coming over a bit lady bountiful.

'If you're too busy...'

'Aren't you afraid I'll kiss you again?'

She didn't see the question coming until it hit her dead centre; it completely threw her off balance. Aren't you more afraid he won't? the sly inner voice silkily suggested.

Taking a deep breath, she made emergency repairs on her shattered poise. Her slender shoulders lifted casually. 'I hardly think that's likely,' she scoffed laughingly. 'I'm aware it was just a...'

One dark brow quirked enquiringly as she searched for words. Flora flushed.

'A momentary impulse,' she choked resentfully.

'Aberration, even,' he agreed soothingly.

She frowned at him with irritation; she knew deliberate provocation when she heard it. She needed to knock this kissing thing on the head once and for all.

'For your information, I've just broken up with my fiancé; kissing isn't on my agenda.'

'Why did you do that?'

Flora looked at him blankly.

'Break up with your fiancé, that is.'

Flora glared at him. 'None of your damned business,' she declared hotly.

'Sorry,' he sympathised with a patently false sincerity that set her teeth on edge. 'Sensitive subject.'

'Not at all sensitive!' she snapped immediately. 'Paul asked me to make a choice and I didn't make the one he expected.' Paul had been astonished when she had failed to see how imperative it was for her to distance herself from her disgraced father. His astonishment had eventually turned to anger at what he perceived as her selfishness. 'Also,' she added with feeling, 'he was a prize prat!'

'In fact,' Josh drawled, his eyes on her mutinous, flushed face, 'it was a normal, mutually amicable parting.'

'I'm just trying to explain why kissing isn't high on my agenda just now, so you can rest easy,' she told him, regretting her outburst.

She couldn't help recalling that kissing her had not exactly made him happy the first time, so he probably wouldn't want to again. She remembered the bleak expression in his eyes as he'd made that extraordinary statement. If he really hadn't kissed anyone for some time that meant he had a whole lot of sexual frustration to get rid of. She didn't want to be his therapy. Although, she conceded, letting her eyes roam at will for one self-indulgent moment over his sleekly powerful body, there would be fringe benefits! It was almost enough to make a girl sorry she wasn't into shallow and superficial relationships.

'Ah, you're afraid of the rebound thing…?'

Her teeth clenched. Was he jumping to all the wrong conclusions deliberately? She met his eyes—you bet he was, she concluded instantly. There was no mistaking the fact he was enjoying her discomfiture. He'd probably taken delight in depriving flies of their wings when he was a little boy.

'There's absolutely no prospect of me rebounding in *your* direction!'

'You mean you don't encourage the hired help to take liberties. This isn't actually about being off men in general, just a particular category of men, for which read those without the fancy cars, fancy clothes and fancy salaries to match.' His voice was coldly derisive.

He made her feel so guiltily defensive that she almost began searching her conscience until she realised that, whatever other faults she had, she had never judged people by their bank balances, although she knew plenty of people that did.

'Are you implying I'm a snob?'

He considered the heated accusation. 'I don't know you well enough to imply anything—yet,' he qualified.

Flora didn't like that little contemplative smile that accompanied the qualification one little bit. For starters it made her pulse-rate do slightly scary things.

'Do you want the job?' she snapped, already regretting her silly altruism. The man had got by before she'd come along; it wasn't as though he looked malnourished or anything—far from it!

Josh looped his thumbs in the loops of his waistband and looked thoughtful. 'What's it pay?'

'Pay!' she echoed in a startled voice.

'You didn't expect me to do it for free, did you?'

Her lips tightened at the sarcasm; he really did have a knack of making her feel embarrassed and just ever so slightly stupid. If anything, she normally played down her intellect in front of men; for some reason this one made her feel positively inadequate!

'Of course I didn't. I just hadn't thought...' God, what happened to detached and businesslike? I sound like a real pea brain! She cleared her throat and tried to retrieve the situation. 'What's the going rate?' she enquired briskly.

He named a figure and she nodded sagely.

'That sounds fair,' she agreed gravely. She didn't know what she was talking about and she suspected he knew it. If he was trying to rip her off she'd have to make up the excess from her own pocket; she couldn't make Claire suffer financially because she wasn't prepared to admit her ignorance in front of this man.

'That's a deal, then.' He approached her, hand extended.

Flora stared at the strong hand as if it were a snake. As she tentatively placed her own in his the scent of his warm body reached her nostrils. She tried not breathing but the faint musky smell still made her stomach muscles twang like the entire string section of an orchestra. The unseasonally hot day wasn't entirely responsible for the sweat that trickled slowly down between her breasts.

He didn't shake her hand, instead he raised it to his lips in a gesture that should have been absurd, only she felt no desire to laugh at all…melt, well, yes…that was another thing entirely!

He lifted his head and looked directly into her eyes; the expression in those silvery depths was explicitly sensual. It was at that second that she knew exactly how big a mistake she'd made in virtually inviting the man into her home!

Calm down, Flora, she told herself firmly as her heart-rate rocketed. Think worst scenario: you bump into him—not literally, of course—occasionally. She stubbornly worked around images that wouldn't quite clear from her head of several interesting varieties of collisions she could have with Josh Prentice. She bit back a horrified whimper.

Cope, of course she could cope! She hadn't reached her advanced years without being able to survive mentally and emotionally intact the odd bit of sexual craving. She could cope with anything. She was going to fill her lungs with gallons of fresh country air! Wholesome, emotionally untaxing pursuits like walking the hills and talking to the odd sheep were going to fill her days, not steamy daydreams.

'If you have other commitments,' she began hopefully,

putting her tingling hand behind her back and rubbing it against the soft wool of her sweater. 'It might be more convenient for you to decorate the nursery after I've left.'

'And when would that be?'

'I'm not entirely sure yet.' Dad didn't want her to visit while he was in the programme.

'You must have very understanding bosses.'

Flora smiled vaguely and didn't explain that since she'd been made a partner last year she was one of the bosses. Actually her colleagues had been incredibly supportive throughout the ordeal of the trial.

'There's actually no hurry or anything.'

'It's very considerate of you to worry about my welfare.'

Flora didn't feel considerate, she felt cornered!

'But I'm quite adept at juggling more than one task.'

This boast drew a small, wry grin from Flora. 'Not like any men I've met, then,' she snorted.

'No,' he mused with an arrogantly confident smile. 'I think you'll find I'm actually not like any other man you've met.' His voice flowed over her like warm, rich molasses.

Flora swallowed nervously and dabbed the tiny pin-pricks of sweat that beaded her upper lip with the tip of her tongue.

His grey eyes zoomed in on the nervous gesture; his nostrils flared. 'Besides,' he continued hoarsely, 'we won't be here long.'

'You mean you and Liam don't live here? I assumed… Do you move around a lot?'

'A man has to go where the work is.'

His hard, emotionless statement confirmed her initial suspicions concerning his finances and she was glad she'd been able to put some work his way, even though he was a very hard man to relax around.

'That must be hard with a child,' she sympathised softly.

'You disapprove.' His lip lifted in a faint sneer as he pounced on this evidence of her judgemental nature with relish.

'I'm no judge of such things—' and never would be if her track record so far was anything to go by, she thought gloomily '—but Liam looked a pretty happy, well-adjusted child to me.'

'You'll find out when you have one of your own that all kids have a little bit of the Jekyll and Hyde in them.'

The idea of having a child of her own brought about an odd, achy sensation—had her biological clock swung into action early? she wondered. At twenty-seven she'd always considered she had plenty of time to think about children.

'That presupposes I want some of my own.'

'And you don't.' His expression seemed to suggest he wasn't surprised.

'I didn't say that,' she countered crossly. 'I just don't like it when people make assumptions. Besides, call me an old-fashioned girl, but I think it sensible to think about babies after I find a suitable father for them.'

'Paul the prat wasn't keen on kids, then,' he sympathised.

'Paul,' she felt goaded into rashly revealing, 'requires *all* the proper accessories in his life.' Her lips acquired a cynical twist as she considered Paul's priorities. He'd probably have expected her to time the pregnancies to coincide with election years; a baby or a pregnant wife must be good for the odd vote or two.

'It sounds like the perfect match to me. You look like an accessory sort of lady yourself.' He was looking appraisingly at her very expensive clothes.

'You do insults amazingly well, Mr Prentice.' Flora's nostrils flared. 'Strangely, I don't feel inclined to discuss my shallowness just now.'

'You remembered my name…eventually, and it's Josh.'

Truth be told, she remembered everything about him including the expert way he kissed. 'Your name, but not how offensive you are, obviously,' she hissed, 'or I wouldn't have offered you the job.'

'I wondered how long the "I'm not the boss just the agent" line would last,' he fired back with a cynical sneer. 'I suppose you're going to be watching everything I do, stifling my artistic freedom…'

The sheer bloody-minded silliness of this accusation ought to have made her laugh, but it didn't. Did he take his shirt off indoors too? Perspiration prickled over her entire body as for the duration of a single heartbeat she contemplated what watching this man at work would do to her indiscriminate hormones. It made her bones ache just thinking about it.

'Nothing,' she told him, her voice shaking with sincerity, 'could be further from the truth and you can let your artistic inclinations run wild,' she promised recklessly.

'Every man has his price,' he admitted solemnly. 'That sounded suspiciously like an offer I can't refuse.'

He made it sound as though she'd been begging for his professional services. 'That's…that's marvellous,' she responded weakly.

'I'll make a start tomorrow.'

'That soon!'

Her spontaneous dismay made his lips twitch. 'Before you change your mind.'

'I wouldn't go back on a deal, despite provocation…' she told him, angrily defending her integrity. The man somehow managed to twist everything she said to his own advantage. With that marketable ability combined with his indisputable physical attributes—which, sad though it was, *did* make a difference—she was amazed he hadn't found a lucrative niche somewhere. 'I think you're in the wrong job,' she reflected drily.

'You're not alone there.' He grinned wryly, recalling how horrified his family had been when he'd turned his back on the academic avenues open to him and announced his intention of becoming an artist. They'd come around now, of course; success made a lot of things acceptable.

'You should use your natural talents.'

He looked struck by the idea. 'Like kissing, you mean,' he suggested with a hungry-tiger smirk.

'Why,' she ejaculated, 'do you keep bringing that up?' Her teeth hurt as she ground them yet again.

'Because it's on your mind, not to mention mine…? Yes,' he confirmed, giving the subject some thought, 'that's it. I keep thinking about kissing you.' His jaw tightened. It was true and unforgivable: when he ought to be concentrating on other more vital issues his mind kept returning to that single brief, unsatisfactory kiss.

His resentful glare suggested it was all her fault—the cheek of the man—and typical of men, full stop!

'Why? Do I look like your wife? Do I remind you of her or something?'

Flora was so shocked to hear the words leave her lips she gave a horrified gasp and pressed a belated silencing hand over her mouth. True, this question had been nagging away at her since yesterday, but, assuming she'd never see him again, she hadn't thought she'd ever have the opportunity to ask him, or for that matter the lack of judgement to do so!

Josh had gone very still. Flora started when he slowly began to move towards her. Her attention was riveted by the graceful, lithe way he moved, beautiful but almost menacing. His blank expression told her zero about his intentions, but as he came closer she could see the slashing angle of his chiselled cheekbones seemed more pronounced and a solitary muscle pumped in his lean cheek.

He stopped just in front of her and, reaching out, took her chin in one hand and swept it upwards. His eyes swept dispassionately over her beautiful oval face; he seemed to be unmoved by what he saw.

Flora didn't move; she couldn't. Sexual anticipation mingled with mind-numbing apprehension inside her, creating sheer havoc. Wide-eyed, she watched as he slowly shook his dark head firmly from side to side, never for one instant releasing her from the merciless grip of his gaze. Despite the relentless intensity of that stare she couldn't shake the conviction that he somehow wasn't actually seeing her, perhaps it was the face of his lost love, little Liam's mother, he saw.

'No, you're nothing like her.' His voice was harsh. *'Nothing!'* he added as if he couldn't emphasise this point too much.

Flora felt a shaft of relief quiver through her. It mattered, she wasn't quite sure why, but his reply had mattered a lot to her.

'She wasn't a blonde.' His eyes touched the silver strands clustered around her face. 'But then who's to say you are?'

'I think I'm the definitive expert on that subject.'

His hand dropped away and a sudden devilish grin abruptly banished the brooding shadows from his expression. 'You have no idea how tempted I am to say prove it,' he suddenly confessed.

'Restrain yourself!' She sniffed, wondering how she ought to go about distracting him from this ticklish subject.

'If I kissed you now would it constitute a sacking offence?'

Flora's heart turned over in the confined space of her
tight chest. As shock seeped steadily through her she
caught her breath raggedly and her hot colour faded of its
own accord, leaving her pale.

The expression *perfectly pale* flitted through Josh's head
as he feasted his eyes on the delicate symmetry of her
clear-cut features, resting the longest on the full curve of
her softly sumptuous lips. His bold, sensual survey made
the blood pound noisily in her ears.

Some dim memory of self-preservation told Flora she
ought to summon some cutting witticism that would cool
his ardour and cut him down to size. After all, didn't she
have enough in her repertoire to suit any occasion?

As she met the smouldering intensity of his speculative
gaze the memory flickered and died. Truth told, there was
nothing in the world she wanted more than to be kissed
by and kiss Josh Prentice. The admission cost her what
little sense of what was appropriate she had left. Honesty,
even with yourself, *especially* with yourself, wasn't always
the best policy!

'You can't get sacked from a job you haven't started
yet,' she breathed huskily.

'You've a fine legal mind,' he admired, placing his
hands on her shoulders.

'You're not looking at my mind,' she felt impelled to
point out.

'You noticed that, did you?' His thumb made a backwards sweeping movement over the generous curve of her
full lips. Her lips parted under the gentle pressure.

'It's hard to miss.' His dark face was swimming in and
out of focus; the desire to be kissed was so intense she felt
actually faint.

'So are your lips,' he rasped throatily. 'They really are quite, *quite* perfect. Very sexy,' he added, brushing her lips lightly with his own. 'Very sensual.' Another butterfly caress accompanied his observation. 'Very kissable,' he rasped, his voice dropping to a soft, sexy whisper.

'*Josh,*' she almost whimpered his name as his tongue flickered out to touch the moist softness of her inner lip. Her hands grasped helplessly at empty space before finally clutching at his broad, bare shoulders. His skin was warm, faintly moist and satisfyingly smooth. She could feel the faintest quiver of tightening muscles under her hands.

'Yes, angel...?'

The scent of his body made her senses spin and increased her growing sense of frustration. 'Will you kiss me properly?'

His breath whistled in a low sibilant hiss. 'Try and stop me,' he growled.

Such a thing never even entered her head. If she hadn't responded to the pressure of his lips with such spectacular enthusiasm the kiss might have stayed controlled. As it was she plastered herself against him in an entirely wanton manner, aided and abetted in her task by the steely arm that snaked around her just beneath her ribcage.

She automatically opened her mouth fully to intensify the erotic exploration of his thrusting tongue. Her cooperation became almost frenzied as her fingers sank deep into his luxuriant dark hair. With growing urgency her trembling fingertips moved over the strong contours of his face. He turned his head and caught one finger in his mouth. Holding her eyes with his smouldering gaze, he began slowly to suckle.

It was all too much. Flora's knees buckled. She would have stumbled and fallen if he hadn't supported her.

The cold nose of a curious farm dog pressed against her

leg made her start. She looked down into the liquid brown eyes of the Border collie and groaned. 'Oh, God,' she gasped, 'this is stupid!' She pulled free of his arms and he didn't try and prevent her.

'On a spectacular scale, probably,' he conceded. 'But who gives a damn?'

His light-hearted response drew a reluctant laugh from her. 'Call me hemmed in by convention, but me, actually. Also I wouldn't want to be responsible for you getting the sack.' Feeling painfully awkward, she tucked the hem of her shirt back in the waistband of her trousers.

She couldn't quite get her head around her swift and total surrender; it made her pulses go haywire just thinking about those wildly erotic moments. Josh had kissed like a starving man, which wasn't surprising considering he must have been repressing the sensual side—and he did have a *very* sensual side—of his nature since his wife's death.

Obviously she'd be a fool to read anything deeper in his desire for her. She half wished she were into self-delusion—it would be quite a nice illusion to imagine there was anything remotely resembling a future in any relationship she embarked on with this man. How could it…? He was still in love with his wife!

'What time is it?' he suddenly asked sharply.

Still distracted, disorientated and plagued by all manner of mystifying aches, she glanced at the slim face of her wrist watch. 'Almost three.'

'Hell!' Josh cursed. 'I promised I'd do the fencing before teatime. A rain check, then,' he suggested casually.

Flora found she resented deeply his self-composure when hers had deserted her totally. She wasn't used to men who automatically took her compliance for granted and it was pretty obvious it hadn't even occurred to him she'd refuse. Flora forgot she no longer had a mane of hair to swish and made the flicking motion with her chin that would have sent the swirling mass backwards. I'll have to come up with an equally effective distracting gesture to give me breathing space or people will start thinking I've got a nervous tic.

'Tomorrow, then.'

Flora blinked. It was a masterly dismissal; she was having a bigger problem than ever seeing him taking orders.

'Maybe, I'll leave the key under the doormat if I'm not home.'

'Sure.' His smile seemed to say he knew full well she'd be home but he was prepared to humour her.

The spectacular scenery was totally wasted on Flora during the rest of her walk back to the cottage.

CHAPTER THREE

'IS ANYONE home?' Josh pushed open the ajar kitchen door.

'Thank goodness!' Flora breathed thankfully. She gestured urgently with her tightly balled fists. 'Don't just stand there, come in…come in!' she hissed.

Josh had been prepared for a cosmetic display of coolness—just at first, of course; he was fairly confident that Flora would thaw quite quickly—but *this*! He walked over the threshold and saw immediately that her urgency had very little to do with a compelling desire for his body.

'Well, don't just stand there!' she told him in an agonised whisper. 'Do something!'

'*Me!* You've got the…' Brows raised, he looked at the metal implement clenched in one white-knuckled fist. 'What is that, anyhow? A poker?' Whatever it was it looked lethal and more than up to the task of disposing of a rodent a lot bigger than the small defenceless one she had cornered—or was it the other way around…?

It made quite a picture. He strove to maintain a solemn expression; if Fleet Street's best had only known what it took to shake the cool and collected Miss Graham.

His bland tone made Flora want to scream. Why wasn't the stupid man responding with the urgency the situation demanded?

'I hardly think that's relevant,' she told him, still without taking her eyes off the small, frozen figure of a field mouse. Her toes curled with disgust in her blue furry slippers.

'Bash it or something,' he suggested.

50

Flora gave an exasperated sigh. 'If I could have,' she pointed out witheringly, 'don't you think I already would have? I just can't kill things.' She confessed this failing with a wail from between clenched teeth.

'Then let it go,' he suggested. One glance told him the little rodent wasn't going anywhere while they were here. It was literally frozen with fear, half a breath away from heart failure—and it wasn't alone, he thought, his scrutiny switching to Flora who was giving a good impression of a statue if you discounted the odd tremor or two. He had to concede she made quite a striking statue; she reminded him of one of those long-legged impossibly graceful Degas figures, except her skin wasn't cold bronze, it was creamy white, soft and... He cleared his throat noisily and transferred his attention to the intruder.

'What?' she yelped. 'And stay awake another night hearing it scratching under the floorboards—not on your life!'

'You want me to bash it, is that it?'

She looked at him for the first time, her big blue reproachful eyes screaming heartless monster. 'No...no!' she responded miserably.

'Well, make up your mind.' Female logic was enough to drive a man to drink.

Flora suddenly had an inspirational thought. 'Couldn't you put it outside...? Not near the house, though.'

'Let me get this straight. You want me to remove the mouse, pat it on the head and tell it to go find another residence.' So what if the heartless woman had a soft spot for furry things and children? He wasn't going to let that influence him. It was possible Lucrezia Borgia used to get mushy about babies. It was essential he didn't start getting sucked in by her act; he had to remember why he was here.

The popular theory amongst those who knew him well was that when they handed out the obstinacy Josh had got a second helping.

'In essence, yes, and sooner would be better than later.'

Flora couldn't look as he bent over to scoop up the tiny terrified creature. Her entire body sagged with relief as she heard him leave the room. It was gone. She sank down into a cheerfully painted kitchen chair and let out a long, shuddering sigh. It was only a few minutes before he returned and Flora was already geared up to defend her pathetic behaviour.

'I know it was more scared of me,' she assured him, determined to get the first word in before any of that mockery in his eyes could find its way to his lips. Her stomach went into a clenching routine she was getting familiar with by now. *Why does every thought I have about this man have to include his mouth?* 'I know it was a stereotypical female reaction...' she croaked.

'I don't know, you didn't climb on a chair,' he conceded.

Only because my knees were shaking too hard. 'Thanks for that,' she responded drily. 'I already feel a complete idiot.'

'I can't imagine why,' he drawled.

'I don't actually have a thing about mice.'

'I'm glad you explained that or I might have gone on thinking you were phobic.'

She gave him a frosty glare. 'It's that horrid scratchy noise they make—' she gave a tiny shudder '—and they're dirty.' He couldn't argue that point. 'Speaking of which, hadn't you better wash your hands?'

'You've not got some cleanliness fetish too?' he enquired suspiciously. His eyes skimmed the cluttered work surface and he shook his head. 'I see you've not.'

'It's hardly kind to call someone a slob when they're in a traumatised condition,' she informed him severely. 'I was in the middle of making my breakfast when that...'

'Wild beast leapt out at you.'

'You can laugh!' Her pout quivered into a reluctant grin. 'If you hadn't come along I'm not sure what I'd have done next.'

'I was wondering that myself,' he admitted. 'In a war of attrition the tough survive; I suppose it depends on how tough you are?'

Flora's expression hardened as her mind automatically drifted back over the last weeks. 'Tough enough when necessary,' she assured him grimly.

'I believe you.' He turned from the sink and, shaking his wet hands, looked expectantly at her.

Flora got to her feet, extracted a clean towel from a drawer and handed it to him. 'Well, thanks, you may be a sarcastic pig, but you were handy.' She sniffed.

His comprehensive scrutiny of her person recalled her a little belatedly to the fact she was still dressed only in a light robe which gaped revealingly down the front to display a large quantity of her short silky slip nightdress and an even larger quantity of bare leg. Trying not to act as if his eyes didn't make her want to crawl out of her hot skin, she casually belted the robe around her middle—perhaps *too* casually because he looked mildly amused by her action.

He was wearing jeans as he had the day before but this pair was more disreputable with large jagged tears in the knees, his white tee shirt was clean and nicely pressed but permanently stained with large multi-coloured blotches of paint. The thin fabric clung, giving more than a mere suggestion of his muscle-packed torso. Overalls would have been more professional, she decided disapprovingly. A tent might be even better, an acidly derisive voice in her head added, and a lot less revealing. If she was honest with herself Flora knew that even if he wore a paper bag over his head it wouldn't deter her lustful and lurid imagination.

'What are you doing here at such an ungodly hour?' she grumbled, unhappily acknowledging that all the determination in the world couldn't prevent her reacting at some basic instinctual level to this man—in short she fancied him like hell! Unfortunately, an equally strong gut instinct told her, it would all end in tears, as her granny, had she had one, might have said.

'Ungodly!' he echoed derisively. 'The day's half over, woman. At least,' he qualified, 'it is if you've been up since five.'

'Who looks after Liam while you work?' she wondered out loud.

'Oh, he's having a whale of a time. Megan dotes on him—for some mystifying reason she can't get enough of him.'

Did that go for the father as well as the son? Flora wondered darkly. Could this mysterious Megan, whom he hadn't seen fit to mention before, be just as keen to get her hands on Josh? She didn't like the sound of this Celtic temptress one little bit.

'*Megan*…?' She heard the sharp tone in her voice and had no trouble detecting a shrill thread of pure, unadulterated green-eyed monster! What made this mortifying discovery even harder to swallow was the strong probability that Josh too had heard and was even now drawing the exact same conclusion she was—it wasn't as if he was exactly slow or unaware of his own charms!

Determined to bluff this out if she died in the effort, she lifted her chin up and pinned a suitably disinterested expression on her face. If he *dared* to suggest she was doing anything other than making polite chit-chat…! She could fake it as well as anybody; at least, she could normally. The fact that Josh Prentice's presence seemed to seriously inhibit certain essential social skills increased her panicky feelings.

'What a lovely name,' she gushed insincerely.

'I think so,' Josh murmured pleasantly. He bit back a complacent grin as her sickly smile slipped slightly. 'You must meet her—I feel sure you'd get on.'

'I can't wait. But actually I didn't come here to socialise.'

'Why exactly did you come here?'

Josh saw wariness slide into her blue eyes before they slid away from his completely.

'I thought I'd already told you my fiancé and I recently split up.'

He struck the side of his head with his open-palmed hand. 'How could I forget? Paul the prat! So you're here to lick your wounds and recover from your emotional devastation,' he drawled sarcastically.

She ground her teeth and glared at him in open dislike. Why doesn't he just come out and say I'm a hard cow!

'Not everybody parades their feelings for the world to see!' she snapped.

He carefully folded the towel and handed it back to her. When she went to take it he didn't let go. 'Not everyone *has* emotions to parade,' he taunted softly.

Her eyes sparkling with temper, Flora snatched the towel free after a short and undignified tussle.

'You don't expect me to believe you were actually in love with this guy! Oh, I'm sure he had a lot to recommend him, like moving in the right social circles, and call me intuitive or just plain psychic, but was he by any chance loaded?' His languid smile grew closer to a sneer as her bosom continued to heave dramatically and her eyes filled with tears of anger.

'I don't give a damn what you believe!' she gritted back defiantly.

He made her engagement sound shallow and calculating—he obviously thought she was both. In fact Paul had never actually proposed, so there had been no specific moment when she'd had to come to a decision; it had just been something he and their family and friends had taken for granted would eventually happen. And Flora herself, when she'd thought about it, hadn't been able to come up with a single reason why they shouldn't get married!

She wanted children eventually, and she'd never enjoyed the meat market that passed for the singles scene, and as for waiting for the *one true love thing*, she was far too old and worldly wise for such nonsense. Besides, she'd seen close to what loving someone too much could do if that special someone was taken from you. If that sort of loss could destroy someone as strong as her father, what chance would she have?

'Well, what am I to think? You didn't exactly fight me off with a stick, did you…? Hardly the actions of a woman who loves someone else.'

No, she hadn't, and in not doing so she'd laid herself wide open to this sort of derision. She silently cursed the hormonal insanity responsible for her wanton behaviour. 'That's because sex has nothing to do with emotions.' Here's wishing…she thought wistfully.

'That's a very masculine point of view.'

Flora found the creamy skin of her throat where his eyes had touched was tingling. She resisted the temptation to lift a hand to protect that vulnerable area from his gaze.

Happily her breathing had returned to something that would pass for normal; Flora gave a sigh of relief. 'It's a man's world,' she reminded him calmly. 'I find a girl gets on much better if she lives her life by their standards,' she claimed brazenly.

'In fact, you're one of this new breed of female who can drink as hard and curse as hard as any man. *Impressive!* I'm not knocking it; I can see the advantages. Seduction would be so much simpler, not to mention cheaper, if a man could dispense with flowers and romantic dinners, if he could just say do you fancy a...'

'You're about as romantic as a hole in the head!' she flung angrily at him. Her eyes narrowed and she threw the towel still clutched in her hands in the linen basket, wishing with all her heart that this infuriating man could be disposed of so easily. The man had a positive genius for misrepresenting *everything* she said.

'I suppose *you* think nature arranged it for men to have fun spreading their oats while women stay at home darning their smelly socks.' She looked on resentfully as he threw back his head and laughed; it was a rich, deep, uninhibited sound. 'What,' she enquired frigidly, 'is so funny?'

He wiped the moisture from the corner of his eyes, which she discovered crinkled in a deeply delightful way when he laughed.

'The idea of you darning a sock, that's what,' he told her. 'In fact, I'd eat mine if you even knew what a darning needle looks like.'

'It was a figure of speech; nobody darns socks these days.'

'Megan probably does,' he mused thoughtfully.

'Then she sounds the perfect mate for you,' she snarled back nastily. 'A doormat.'

'I know it brings out the matchmaker in most people to see a single father, but I'm not actually interested in finding a mate.' He was gambling that she was the sort of woman who couldn't resist a challenge and hopefully not him either. He firmly quashed unspecific feelings of unease. It wasn't as if there was any law that said you couldn't enjoy revenge!

'Does Megan know this?' she hissed unpleasantly.

'Megan's already married,' he admitted sadly. 'To Huw.'

'Huw?'

'Geraint's father. You remember Geraint—the young farmer, big bloke, very eager to sow his share of oats. Megan is his mother.'

'Oh.'

'I don't know why you're jealous, you know you're the only woman I want to kiss.' Self-loathing darkened his deep-set eyes and robbed the statement of flattery. Even so, Flora found his words tugged at her senses, producing a dangerous drowsy dreaminess.

Now his libido had come out of its grief-induced coma, Flora doubted he was going to be satisfied with one woman for long. She might be the first but she had no illusions about being the last. This was one good reason not to go any further down this particular path. In theory the uncomplicated 'sex of the safe variety is harmless' line worked fine! In practice the whole thing was an emotional minefield she didn't want to negotiate.

'I'm not the jealous type, never have been.' She gave a happy carefree trill of laughter—at least, it was meant to be carefree; unfortunately it emerged as shrill. 'Don't let me hold you back if you want to get on with your work,' she told him pointedly. She proceeded to make loud bustling noises with the crockery messily spread out on the work surface.

'It's traditional to offer tradesmen a cup of tea before

they actually commence work,' he remonstrated mockingly. 'Don't you know *anything*?'

'Apparently not,' she responded drily. The kitchen was too small to contain such a large man without inducing a strong feeling of claustrophobia. She wiped her damp palms along the sides of her wrap. 'Any other rules I should know?'

'The tea should be supplied at regular intervals throughout the working day.' He bent his head and she felt the warm brush of his breath against her earlobe. 'The next is just a little personal foible of mine…' His intimate husky whisper trickled over her like warm honey.

Weak-kneed, her body swayed slightly and he stepped forward to provide the support she needed. The fit was remarkably snug, she decided as their respective curves and angles slotted neatly together. She couldn't help imagining how it would feel if they got even closer. Her aching breasts felt heavy and swollen as they chafed against the thin fabric of her nightdress.

'What would that foible be?' she enquired huskily. Actually, she thought maybe she knew; standing this close it was impossible not to notice that he was in an aroused state. A bone-deep excitement rose up from some secret, previously untapped reservoir within her. The ferocity of her response to his arousal was almost frightening. Her busy hands slowly stilled; the sexual tension in the air around them was so thick she could have taken a knife and still had trouble slicing through it.

Turning around might constitute encouragement, but what the hell? she decided recklessly! There was only just so much a woman could take!

Josh looked down into her expectant, delicately flushed face; there was nothing coy about the way she was looking at him. There was no banner saying, 'Take me!' but that slumbrously sexy invitation was just as explicit. She was quite simply breathtaking in her tousled, not-long-out-of-bed state. Thinking of her in bed set off a train of thought that exacerbated the persistent ache in his groin.

His throat muscles visibly worked overtime as he swallowed hard. 'Biscuits,' he told her flatly. 'Preferably chocolate. If the old blood sugar takes a nosedive I'm worse than useless.'

One second she could almost taste the kiss, the next all she could taste was the bitter bile of humiliation. One shocked blink and the sexual glaze cleared from Flora's eyes. She gave a tiny gasp and, cheeks burning with mortification, tried to turn away.

'Whoa!' Josh soothed. Taking her by the elbow, he restrained her bid for escape. 'I was joking.'

And since when couldn't I take a joke or rejection? she asked herself. Maybe since the joke included not being kissed by Josh—is that desperate or what? Tiny pinpricks of blood dotted her lower lip as she released the pressure of her teeth. Her hectic breathing gradually slowed. Soothed slightly, and feeling deeply embarrassed, she stopped struggling and stood passively.

'Poor joke?' he suggested woodenly.

Either he had got cold feet at the last minute or he got his kicks from seeing women squirm; if so he must be a very happy man... A quick upwards glance told her he didn't look happy.

'I think maybe I'm the joke. I came onto you like a...' She found there was a limit to how far she could take the brutal honesty route, even though it seemed a bit late to act as if nothing had happened, but if she was being strictly accurate she supposed nothing had. Perhaps that was why she was hurting so much...? She cleared her throat. 'But you did do your share of encouragement.'

'Did you come here to torment me or decorate the nursery?' she wondered bluntly.

A maverick nerve leapt in his cheek. 'The torment is a two-way thing,' he responded with equal candour.

Her expression softened. His shadowed eyes suggested he had an inner conflict at least as great as her own, and small wonder! She was so caught up in what she was feeling, she hadn't really paused to look at it from his point of view.

Did he feel he was betraying the memory of his wife by wanting another woman? This was what you got for getting involved with a man with emotional baggage.

'Call me shallow, but part of me is glad to hear you say that,' she confessed. 'It's nice to have company when you're suffering.' The self-mocking smile died from her lips and her forehead pleated in an earnest frown. She didn't want to come over as some sort of bleeding heart, but she felt she had to let him know she understood, as much as anyone who hadn't been in his shoes could, that was...

'But you mustn't feel bad about...about...' She struggled to find a word which covered the almost kiss and the high-voltage sexually charged atmosphere. She gave up. 'Sexual feelings are perfectly normal.'

Josh looked startled by her solemn announcement. The hand that had been raking his dark hair fell away.

'You really ought to talk about these things, you know,' she told him kindly, 'not bottle them up. We all have needs; it was bound to happen some time.'

Josh had been clinically pondering her sexuality since he'd met her. Well, he'd been able to fool himself it was clinical interest—at least up until this point. There was nothing intellectual about the savage impulse that made him contemplate discovering Miss Flora Graham's needs—he'd like a leisurely day or so to explore all the possibilities of that particular subject.

The savage feelings he was fighting to control seemed all the more crude because she appeared to ooze sensitivity. It was getting harder by the second to reject the possibility that she actually was sensitive, compassionate— you got exactly what you saw!

Not that he'd be getting anything if that was the case, he reminded himself heavily. The 'sins of the father' line only worked up to a point, and not at all when the son in question was a beautiful daughter who had eyes that shone with integrity, when they weren't shining with lust for him! Not just lust, there was warmth and affection there too. God, what a mess!

'Perhaps you're just not ready…emotionally speaking, for…' Hell! He'd felt pretty ready in every other way.

Thinking about the imprint of his big, sexually primed body up against her sent a gentle wave of carnation pink over her fair skin. It occurred to her that being plagued with lustful thoughts as she was made her unbiased advice a bit suspect.

'Or maybe I'm not the right person to…' she suggested bravely. 'Is it long since your wife…?' she fished delicately.

'Three years.'

'Three!' She was startled. 'But Liam must have been…'

'Bridie died during the birth, some sort of embolism.' His face could have been carved from granite as he provided the basic details.

Flora didn't wonder at the dark anger in his eyes; there was no way to rationalise such a cruel twist of fate. She thought of Liam and swallowed the emotional lump in her throat. Silently she pushed Josh down towards a kitchen chair. He co-operated and folded his big body into the inadequate seat. Flora shuffled her bottom onto the table beside him; she maintained the physical contact of her hand on his shoulder.

'That's very rare. My father's a doctor,' she added to explain the depth of her lay person's knowledge. She could feel the tension that tied his muscles in knots through her fingertips.

'I was told that it's uncommon.'

'You've brought Liam up since he was a baby?'

'We've spent one night apart. I decided on that occasion that he'd be better off without me. I ran away.' The self-recrimination in his voice was vicious. 'I sometimes think that he'd have been better off in the long run if I'd left him with Jake, he'd have a more normal family life... siblings...two parents...' In his blackest moments he still occasionally wondered if he was just being selfish...if he wasn't putting his needs ahead of Liam's.

An instinctive sound of protest escaped Flora's throat. Hadn't she seen with her own eyes what a great father Josh was? She decided she didn't like the sound of this *perfect* architect brother one bit. He probably never lost an opportunity to remind Josh how successful he was, she decided, endowing this unseen figure with an ego to match his insensitivity.

'That's rubbish!' she suddenly announced. Her outraged tone drew Josh's startled attention to her indignant pink-cheeked face. 'If it was only one night you couldn't have run far,' she concluded logically. 'Nobody expects you to behave sensibly when your world has just fallen apart!' She clasped his hand and firmly pulled it onto her lap.

'Just because your brother has a well-paid job and nice house, it doesn't mean Liam would be better off with him, so don't even think like that. You're a great father!'

Josh could have mentioned that his twin would have

been the first to agree with her. 'You think so?' What the hell? Jake's reputation could take the odd knock or two; besides, it was rather enjoyable to have Flora defending him.

'You and your wife were obviously very…I've never had that with someone,' she told him awkwardly. 'I don't know whether that makes me lucky or unlucky,' she reflected in a soft undertone. 'But I do know someone who lost his wife and he…' Her voice cracked and she swallowed hard.

Josh stared at her fingers wrapped around his and then lifted his gaze to look long and deep into her blue eyes. They were soft and misty with compassion.

'Your parents?'

She nodded. 'Mum was such a quiet person, you wouldn't think someone like that could leave such a great gaping hole in your life… I felt it, but not like Dad did. He's the strong, reliable sort, who always copes. I suppose that was the problem: everyone thought he was coping—but he wasn't. If only I'd been…'

Suddenly aware that his attention matched the intensity of her outpouring, Flora made a self-conscious meal of clearing her throat. Her eyelashes flickered downwards to shield her eyes from him.

'The point is, Josh, that he didn't cope—you have and you've brought up a beautiful boy.' There was no mistaking the depth of her admiration. 'You shouldn't knock yourself if you make mistakes, or have doubts.'

'I can't do this!' he ground out abruptly as he surged to his feet.

Flora was bewildered by the strength of his unexpected and mystifying declaration. 'What…?'

'You're definitely not the right person,' he explained harshly.

It gave Flora a brutal jolt to recognise her own words. 'Oh!' Well, she had asked. Hell! She'd even put the idea into his head to begin with. 'Well, that simplifies matters, doesn't it?' She felt physically sick with the suddenness and finality of the rejection.

A rational part of her knew she should be glad he'd saved her from making a bad mistake. How could you feel you'd lost something that had never been yours to begin with? she wondered. Ironically, she hadn't felt anything approaching this awful when Paul had announced he couldn't marry her.

Josh gave a terse nod. 'Where's the room?'

'You're still taking on the job, then?'

'Do you want me to?'

Having him around would be a kind of refined torture, but she must have some hidden masochistic streak—it was the only explanation, she concluded miserably as she found herself nodding. 'I've told Claire I found somebody and she was delighted.' Flora continued to look at some point over his left shoulder.

'Lead on, then.'

Flora gestured towards the door that concealed the narrow stairway. 'I'll leave you to it, if you don't mind. There's only two bedrooms; you want the one at the back.'

She waited until she heard his footsteps on the wooden boards above her head before she permitted the tears to seep from beneath her eyelids. Silently she allowed them to stream down her cheeks for a couple of minutes before she dashed her hand angrily across her damp cheeks. She splashed water from a cold-running tap over her no doubt blotchy face, then for good measure ducked her head under the cold stream.

She was giving a good impression of a wet dog shaking the moisture from her dripping head of hair when she became aware that Josh was standing there watching her. His quiet, still presence sent a shiver up her spine. His expression was sombre.

'In lieu of a cold shower.'

Her bluntness made him blink. 'I upset you.'

'Something like that,' Flora confirmed wryly. She wiped the excess moisture from her face with a slightly unsteady hand. 'A bit of sexual frustration never did anyone permanent damage,' she announced briskly. 'Don't look so shocked,' she snapped. 'It's not as if we both don't know what just happened.' He'd said thanks, but no, thanks, that was what had just happened and she felt a lot more than humiliation. She felt…bereft, she acknowledged wonderingly. *Why…?*

'That can't happen to you very often…you're a very desirable woman,' he added gruffly, by way of explanation.

So desirable he'd had no trouble saying no. 'I think you made the right decision,' she told him with serenity she was far from feeling. 'You've obviously got a lot of unresolved emotional issues to deal with before you take the plunge, so to speak.'

Plunge. Josh had an intense mental flash of himself plunging deeply into her receptive body. His body responded vigorously to the erotic image. His breath expelled in an audible hiss as he dragged his eyes away from her face.

Her ablutions had left a pool of water on the flagstoned floor and dotted her nightgear with dark damp patches. Josh's roving gaze was drawn irresistibly to one prominent patch which covered the uptilted peak of her left breast.

Responding belatedly, Flora wrapped a protective arm across her chest. 'This isn't a wet tee shirt competition,' she informed him icily.

A laugh was wrenched from him. 'Do you always say things like that?'

'I can't say I've ever had the occasion to make that particular accusation before.' She sniffed. 'Actually,' she conceded, 'Paul did make a passing reference to my indelicate mind when he asked for his ring back...'

'He asked for...?' Josh's expression grew openly contemptuous. 'What a...'

'Prat?' she suggested with a half-smile and a sniff. 'Paul's a politician, so he's not big on straight talking. Actually, I can be circumspect with the best of them when the occasion warrants it.' She knew she was good at keeping people at a distance and she was slow to make friends, but those she had she valued. 'But not with my friends. Not,' she added hastily, 'that you're...' She broke off, colouring uncomfortably.

'A friend?'

'I really wouldn't have made a very good politician's wife, would I?'

'Did you want to be one?'

Her shoulders lifted. 'It seemed like a good idea at the time.'

'In other circumstances I think we might have been friends...' He sounded as though he'd made an amazing discovery. 'Maybe more,' he continued in the same dazed tone. His expression hardened. 'But the circumstances...' With a snarl of frustration he turned away, giving her a fine view of his magnificent profile.

'You don't have to explain, Josh.'

Which was just as well because he couldn't. 'Believe you me, Flora, you're better off without me.'

Flora would have liked to dispute this, but that just might have constituted grovelling and so far she'd stopped short of that—*just*. She'd like it to stay that way. She had never chased a man in her life. What was it, she wondered as he closed the door firmly behind him, that made her want to alter the habit of a lifetime for this one? If there was a remote possibility he could make it any clearer that he didn't want her, she didn't think she was up to hearing it!

CHAPTER FOUR

It was after three in the morning before Flora finally reached the cottage. She'd taken at least three wrong turnings on her journey back from the Holyhead ferry, which at a conservative estimate had probably added a good forty miles to her trip.

Well, at least she could be sure she wasn't going to stumble across Josh and that, after all, had been the idea behind her day trip to Dublin. He'd worked on the nursery for several hours the day before, but all they'd exchanged before she'd taken herself off to walk the rain-soaked hills had been a few polite nothings. She hadn't returned until he'd been safely off the premises.

Her crop of blisters—curse the expensive new boots— had made a similar retreat today a painful prospect, though not as painful as being in close proximity to Josh all day! The day trip to Ireland had been the perfect solution, and Dublin always had been one of her favourite cities, though she'd not really been in an appreciative mood today. Hopefully Josh would have almost completed his task now and soon there would be no reason in the future for their paths to cross, she concluded. The thought failed to produce the philosophical smile she'd been working towards.

She kicked off her shoes as soon as she got through the cheery brick-red front door of the cottage. She dropped her purchases on the floor—for once retail therapy had failed to produce its usual soothing effect—and wearily began to climb the narrow stairs. Halfway up she turned back and, searching through the pile of bags she'd dropped, she extracted a large plush teddy bear with a particularly appealing face. She hugged him to her chest as she retraced her steps. She'd thought of Liam the instant she'd seen him. She just hoped Josh wouldn't read anything untoward into this spontaneous gesture—untoward such as she was being nice to the son because she wanted the father—and *how* she wanted the father! She noticed a light still shone from under the nursery door; Josh must have forgotten to switch it off.

'Oh my!' she breathed as she glanced around the door. The bare electric lightbulb revealed the most extraordinary transformation. An entranced expression on her face, she entered the room fully. The dark, poky little space had been transformed into a magical place by a series of stunning murals. Even she, a cynical twenty-seven-year-old, could almost believe she were under the water. The creatures peering out from behind rocks, emerging from seashells and peeping out of a wrecked galleon were all so vivid and real. It would give any child hours of delight just discovering all the hidden surprises in the vividly depicted underwater scenes.

She pulled back her hand when her fingers encountered slightly tacky paint. 'What a waste, teddy,' she breathed. 'He ought to be an artist,' she concluded admiringly.

'An interesting thought.'

Flora started violently and spun around. One arm braced against the doorjamb, Josh was standing there as large as life and twice as exciting; he was watching her. His powerful body blocked the entrance, or exit, depending on how you looked at it, completely. Flora was thinking exit in a big way and had been from the instant she'd heard his voice.

'I...I didn't know you...' she stuttered. 'What are you still doing here? Do you know what time it is?' Her heart was hammering so loudly he must hear it in the small silent room. Amidst the conflicting emotions his fixed stare was communicating, one remained constant: hunger—raw hunger! It sent neat toe-curling electricity surging through her tense frame and tied her stomach muscles into tortuous knots.

'I had nearly finished the job so I came back after Liam went to bed,' he explained. 'It's easier to work without distractions.' His lips curled in a thin, self-derisive smile.

Flora frantically tried to decipher this cryptic utterance. Does he mean I'm a distraction, and if he does am I a pleasant one...? Or were distractions by definition nasty? Panic had set in in a big way and her poor, beleaguered brain wasn't up to sorting out this sticky question.

'I'm sorry if I got in the way yesterday.' Flora listened to her meek little girl voice in exasperation. Why not just apologise for breathing and have done with it?

'Are you?' he ground out. Abruptly he lowered his smouldering eyes from hers and dragged a hand through his already tousled dark hair; the gesture was intensely weary. 'Brought back a friend—strange, I didn't have you pegged as a fluffy-toy sort of girl.'

Awkwardly Flora stopped clasping the teddy to her bosom; as a protective device he was pretty useless anyhow. 'I bought it for Liam,' she said, holding the toy out towards him. 'I just thought...' She gave an offhand shrug. 'I hope you don't mind...'

'Why should I mind?' He took the bear from her nervous clasp and placed him on the middle rung of a stepladder. 'Liam will love it. I've put the spare paint pots in the shed,' he told her prosaically.

The dangerous undercurrents that had had her on a knife's edge of anticipation were absent from his voice. A silly self-destructive part of her came close to regretting this. 'Is this what you had in mind?' he enquired, glancing casually at his handiwork.

'No,' she replied bluntly. 'My mind couldn't have come up with anything half as creative, it's incredible,' she confessed ruefully. 'You're obviously very talented!'

Josh watched as she slowly performed an admiring three-hundred-and-sixty-degree turn, pausing occasionally to chuckle spontaneously over some witty little detail.

He wasn't just talented but original too. Her face alight with enthusiasm, she turned back to Josh. 'Have you ever considered doing anything like this for a living?' she enquired tentatively. 'Not necessarily just murals...pictures and things.'

'My family wouldn't consider that a proper job for a grown man.'

Flora frowned disapprovingly. 'My father didn't think criminal law was a proper job for a woman,' she recalled drily. He'd sung the praises of house conveyancing to her on many an occasion; anything was preferable in her parents' eyes to their only child mingling with the criminal classes. 'But it didn't stop me.' She stopped, aware that her words might well have come over a bit self-congratulatory. 'Not that the two cases are similar, of course...' She hastened to assure him she could see his dilemma. 'I mean, obviously I didn't have a child to support.'

'Actually my family have been a lot of help in that direction.' Josh sent a silent apology to his nearest and dearest for creating the illusion they were a load of ignorant oafs. 'And I have imposed upon them shamelessly— once, that is,' he conceded drily, 'I got past the stage when I had to prove I could do everything a mother could only better, with one hand tied behind my back for good measure. I think they call it overcompensation,' he concluded

His flippant words obviously covered what had been a hard time. If she contemplated for too long the poignant picture in her head of a bereaved and hurting Josh bringing up a baby all alone she'd be in floods of completely uncharacteristic tears.

Anyone would think she'd never encountered a hard luck story in her life; as it was her heart felt as if an iron fist were slowly squeezing the life from it. What was it about this man that turned her all squidgy and sentimental…and, yes, *protective*? He was big and bold enough to get by without her misplaced maternal instincts. But then there was nothing remotely maternal about the way Josh Prentice made her feel, she acknowledged unwillingly.

'How is Liam?'

'Asleep, I hope. As we all should be…I'm on the rosta for milking in the morning, which according to my watch isn't very long away…'

Flora noticed for the first time the faint bluish smudges under his eyes. 'Early mornings like that would kill me.'

'I got used to "Liam" hours some time ago and I've never needed much sleep, although I must admit…' He glanced once more at his watch.

His restlessness suddenly made sense; he wanted to be going and he hadn't bargained on a lovesick female giving him career advice in the wee hours. She was being incredibly thick—the man had chosen to sacrifice his sleep in order to avoid her. That did kind of hint that he didn't want her company.

'You want paying…of course. Will a cheque do?' She froze; her entire nervous system went into shock mode. Her eyes slowly widened in horror. *Lovesick!* Of course! It's taken you long enough! a small mocking voice in her skull informed her.

'Is anything wrong?'

Flora forced her mouth into a stiff smile. She shook her head. 'No, nothing.' If you discounted discovering you'd fallen in love for the first time. 'I just thought for a minute I'd lost my handbag, but I left it downstairs.' His cue to precede her down the narrow stairs—frustratingly he didn't move. 'Will a cheque do?'

'Cheque...?' Sleep deprivation seemed to be fuddling his normal mental dexterity. His eyes were moving in a distracted manner over her tense figure.

'You've finished the job,' she pointed out.

'I don't want your money,' he announced in a bewilderingly belligerent manner.

'What? Oh, it's not my money really,' she assured him earnestly. 'Claire will reimburse me.' Actually she'd decided the nursery make-over would be a nice thank-you for her friend, who had come up with the offer of this convenient bolt-hole in her hour of need.

His jawline still stayed steely and inflexible despite her assurances. 'No.'

Flora's exasperation reached new heights. When she thought of all the nice, *easy*, manageable men she might have fallen for she could have wept. No, *I* had to fall for this stupid, stubborn, incomprehensible man who doesn't even like me! Nice one, Flora!

'What's your problem?' she enquired spikily.

'I don't have a problem. I enjoyed doing this...' His expansive gesture took in the entire room. 'It was therapeutic.'

Flora wasn't sure she believed this unlikely claim. Therapy implied relaxation and he didn't look like a man who was relaxed; in fact he looked almost as strung out as she felt.

'Well, some people might think getting paid for something you enjoy is what it's all about. I enjoy what I do, but I have no problem with the pay cheque at the end of the month.'

'Shall we just call it the start of a whole new career and leave it at that?'

Tears of frustration formed in her eyes and she blinked them back. 'No, we won't!' she cried, bringing her shoe-less foot down hard on the boarded floor. 'Silly, misplaced pride won't buy Liam new shoes,' she reminded him angrily. 'It's not charity, you earned it...' she glanced in the direction of his handwork '...and more.'

'I'm not taking money off you, so the subject's closed.'

'You're so obstinate!' she breathed. 'But I can't accept your generosity, it's not...not appropriate.'

'I'm not being generous!' he growled. One angry, spontaneous stride brought him to her side.

They stood chin to chin or, rather, chin to chest; Flora lifted her head to rectify this situation. His physical presence, the sheer magnetism of the man was the most exciting and intimidating thing she'd encountered in her life. She felt burningly hot and teeth-chatteringly cold simultaneously, a situation which probably broke all known laws of science, but then the way she felt about him broke all laws of logic so why not? Giddily she met his seething grey eyes; they were filled with a depth of smouldering anger that she couldn't understand.

'Do you really want to know what I'm like?' His deep voice reverberated with disgust. His chest was heaving as he drew in air in great gulping breaths. '*Shall I tell you...?*' he challenged.

Flora didn't respond—she couldn't. His grip on her shoulders made her wince, but it was the only thing keeping her upright and had been since her knees had responded to the musky masculine scent of him and stopped offering her shaking body any support at all.

The sound of the phone sliced through the stark silence that followed. Josh's eyes went automatically to the mobile clipped on his belt.

'It must be mine, I left it downstairs.'

'Are you going to answer it?' he asked tersely.

'I should…' she admitted quietly. The anticlimax was extreme.

He stood to one side and she shot past him.

At some point during the conversation he had come into the room; Flora wasn't sure when that was. She looked up in surprise when he came over and took the dead phone from her limp grasp.

'What's happened?' His eyes assessed her blank, bruised-looking expression.

'My father's dead,' Flora explained, her brow furrowing in confusion because he couldn't be…how could he be? 'It happened this evening; he had a heart attack.' She raised her eyes to his face. 'Isn't this the part where you say you're very sorry?' The numbness was complete; it encased her like a strait-jacket of ice.

Josh didn't express his sorrow, but his eyes were warmly compassionate. He'd stopped confusing what he felt for the father with what he felt for the daughter. In fact he'd already come to the conclusion that he couldn't destroy the father if that meant hurting this young woman. Which meant what…? Josh thought he knew, but he wasn't ready yet to face the answer.

'Sit down,' he suggested.

She shook her head and began to pace the room, lifting a distracted hand to her blonde head every so often. 'He'd lost everything, his status, his job. They weren't going to strike him off the register, but he'd lost the respect and trust of his patients so what was the point carrying on?

That's what he said,' she told him dully. 'What's that?' she mumbled as he thrust a glass into her hand.

'Brandy.'

'It's Claire's.'

'I don't think she'll mind,' he encouraged softly.

Flora screwed up her nose and shuddered as the alcohol hit her taste buds, but dutifully she swallowed.

'Apparently it started in a pretty benign sort of way after my mother died.' Her eyes were closed when she spoke. 'Tranquillisers, that sort of thing.' Josh didn't think she was even talking to him in particular—she was just talking.

'I don't think he even realised he was hooked, but she did, the new secretary.' She lifted bitter blue eyes to his face. 'She tried to blackmail him into supplying her and her friends with drugs. He said that was when he realised how low he'd sunk.' Angrily she brushed the tears from her face. 'He went to the police and confessed, only she had been there before him. She was determined to take him down with her, you see. The court threw out the charges because there wasn't enough proof. Of course there wasn't enough proof—Dad wasn't a drug dealer, he was a sad, lonely man!' she cried. 'The damage had been done though; the press had latched onto the story.'

Her eyes suddenly opened; they blazed with self-condemnation. 'If I'd spent less time building up my career and more… If I'd been there when he needed me…it wouldn't…! He was lost without Mum. I don't ever want to do that,' she told him wildly, 'love someone so much I can't function without them.' She gave a wild hiccough. 'At least there wouldn't have been a chance of that with Paul.' Her face crumbled as the tears began to fall in earnest.

Josh took the glass from her hand before it was dropped to the floor and pushed her down into a convenient chair.

He laid a soothing hand to the back of her head and drew it towards him.

Flora stayed with her head pressed against his stomach, her arms looped around his waist, until the violent outburst abated. Finally she lifted her head, sniffing and dabbing her blotchy face with the back of her hand.

'I'm sorry.'

'No need, my shoulder is well known for bawling purposes, or, in this case—' he pressed a hand to his flat midriff '—my belly.'

'I have to go back to London.'

Visibly the threads of her self-control knitted smoothly together. It was almost as though the distraught young woman of moments before had never existed, he marvelled. For the first time since he'd met her she bore some resemblance to the ice-cool woman who'd treated the media circus with mild contempt.

'You should get some rest first.'

She shook her head dismissively. 'I need to make…' Josh saw her throat muscles spasm '…I need to make arrangements, and I mean *need*,' she told him fiercely. If you were doing something practical you couldn't think— thinking was painful. She gave a brisk smile; she wanted to dispel any fears he might be harbouring that she was going to start leaning on him either physically or any other way!

'Well, you can't drive,' he announced flatly. She opened her mouth to deny this claim when he nodded significantly towards the open brandy bottle on the dresser.

'Hell!' She set her mouth determinedly. 'It'll have to be the train, then. I need a taxi to take me to Bangor.'

'I'll take you.'

'*You!*'

'Yes, me. You pack or whatever, and I'll let Geraint

know what's happening. The express doesn't leave until five-thirty,' he added, when she looked impatient enough to start walking if they didn't leave immediately.

'Are you sure?' she fretted.

'Absolutely.'

True to his word, Josh returned by the time she had flung a few personal items in an overnight bag. 'I could drive, you know,' she said as he led the way to his four-wheel drive. 'I only swallowed a mouthful.'

'You could also fall asleep at the wheel and cause an accident,' he informed her sternly.

Flora lapsed into silence as she could hardly deny this accusation. Josh didn't attempt to make conversation or cheer her up on the way to the station and she was glad to be left alone with her own thoughts.

Her father's death still didn't seem real; she'd only spoken to him last night on the telephone and for the first time since the court case he'd sounded almost optimistic about the future. As the conversation they'd had replayed in her head over and over pain lodged as a solid, inexpressible ache in her chest.

'The last thing I wanted to do was hurt you, Flora.' He'd returned to this theme several times. Nothing she'd said had been enough to ease his bitter self-recrimination.

Josh passed her her overnight bag as she stepped into the first-class carriage. 'I do know how you feel, you know, and it probably won't help me saying it, but it does get easier.'

Rigid with contemptuous anger, she rounded on him, but she bit her lip to hold back her snarling response as it hit her that he was speaking the truth—he *did* know how she was feeling. She ventured a small noncommittal nod.

'I didn't pay you for my ticket!' she exclaimed, recalling suddenly that she'd stood passively by whilst he'd paid her fare. She began scrabbling feverishly in her bag, knocking several items on the floor in the process. Tears of frustration began to form in her eyes and she angrily brushed them away. 'I can't find...'

'Forget it!' Arms folded across his chest, he stood there on the platform acting as if he had money to burn, and it was first class! She didn't know what she wanted to do most: strangle him or kiss him.

'Don't do this again!' she pleaded. 'It's a lovely, kind gesture but you can't pay for me, Josh, you don't have any...' She bit her tactless tongue.

'You can owe me,' he offered calmly, apparently not put out by her reference to his financial circumstances. 'Will you be coming back?' The question was casual, but the intense expression in his eyes suggested otherwise.

Flora's agitated efforts abruptly ceased as she squatted there on the carriage floor. Her heightened emotions told her that something momentous had just occurred.

'I...I...will you be here?' she wondered huskily.

Eyes still sealed with hers, he nodded slowly. 'I will if you want me to be.'

She gave a shuddering sigh; she instinctively knew that Josh wasn't a man to make promises lightly. 'I do want that,' she told him simply. She got shakily to her feet and gripped the edge of the open window.

Josh could see the tears in her eyes shimmering as the train drew out.

It was a little thing perhaps—Flora didn't know yet—but the knowledge that she'd be going back and he'd be there, waiting, somehow sustained her through the next few days. She didn't know how much she'd been longing to return until she arrived back at the cottage almost a week later in a state of feverish anticipation.

I'm probably making one hell of a fool of myself, she

mused wryly as she tramped along the footpath that led to the farm. All the logic and common sense in the world couldn't stop her heart racing in anticipation as the cluster of whitewashed buildings that composed Bryn Goleu came into view.

She was almost running when she came across Geraint, who was gently chastising a young dog in his native tongue.

'He's young and has a lot to learn, doesn't he, girl?' he said, switching to English as he rubbed the ears of the patient older dog beside him. 'You after Josh, then?'

I suppose I am! Boldly she nodded, refusing to be intimidated by the amused glow in the young man's eyes.

'You'll find him in the barn, *cariad*.' He gestured down the hill.

'Thanks.'

Already striding out across the rocky ground followed by the two dogs, he waved a casual backward hand in response to her gratitude.

The barn was dim and filled with the sweet, earthy scent of hay bales which were piled high all around. Flora saw Josh before he saw her. Stripped to the waist, his olive-toned skin gleamed with a fine sheen of sweat. As she watched he paused in his labours and slowly rotated his head, stretching the tight muscles in his neck and shoulders. She caught her breath sharply, covetously watching the play of lean, rippling muscle over firm smooth flesh.

Josh looked around instantly.

'Hello!' she mumbled stupidly.

'How was it?' he asked, his eyes greedily taking in every detail of her appearance.

A shadow passed over her face and her mouth quivered

as her rigid control momentarily slipped. 'Pretty terrible,' she confirmed huskily.

'When did you get back?'

'About fifteen minutes ago.' Her cheeks flamed. Why be coy, Flora? Just go ahead and tell him you were so pathetically desperate to see him you didn't even unpack the car! 'I'm disturbing you...'

'Always,' he confirmed huskily.

'Your work...'

'I was about to take a break, do you want to...?'

'Yes, please!' she rushed in quickly. 'Dear God!' she groaned, covering her blushes—the visible ones at least—with her hands. 'I don't believe I'm doing this!'

'What are you doing, Flora?'

The gap between her fingers widened and she peered out. 'It's very nice of you to act like you haven't noticed, but I'm acting like...I'm coming on to you like a hussy,' she told him with a very unhussy-like blush.

'A very beautiful hussy,' he qualified, gently peeling the last of her fingers away from her face. 'Welcome home, Flora.' His bold glance was warm and intimate as he locked her startled eyes to his so tight she couldn't even blink.

'Home,' she echoed thickly. Her body was screaming out in need.

'Isn't that where the heart is...?'

'I think it might be, Josh...?' A deep shudder ran through her body as the tension inside her reached a critical level.

'Come here,' he instructed, his voice rough velvet.

The dam inside her broke and she didn't need asking twice. She walked into his arms, which happened to open just at the right moment. His head lowered towards her and she sank her fingers possessively into his thick glossy hair—she wasn't taking any chances; if he changed his mind about the kiss she might go quietly bonkers. He didn't change his mind.

Slowly her blue eyes flickered open and she made a small sound of deep contentment as his head finally lifted. In that moment her selective senses were only aware of things which were directly connected with him—things like the warm, musky male smell that came from his body, the damp, satiny texture of his glorious skin, the impression of controlled strength in his embrace. She took in with primitive pleasure all the things that were part and parcel of this man she'd fallen in love with.

The hand which had rested on the slender curve of her waist slid lower, testing the firm, taut curve of her bottom. His exploration caused him to groan deeply. He pulled her hard against him to show her the urgency of his desire and his face contorted in a grimace that was almost agony as he gazed with raw desire at her flushed face.

'This probably isn't too clever,' he admitted reluctantly. 'Someone might come in.'

Flora trailed a finger down his lean cheek and shivered when he turned his head to kiss the tip. She ran the same slightly damp finger along the sensual outline of his lips.

'Isn't that traditionally the girl's line?' she asked huskily.

'I don't think you're like any traditional girl I've ever met.'

'Is that good?' she enquired softly, stretching up on tiptoe to chew softly at his lower lip. She gave a sigh and rubbed the tip of her nose against his. 'I adore your mouth,' she told him without a shred of overstatement or self-consciousness. 'It's utterly *utterly* perfect.' She scrutinised with hungry reverence the sternly sexy outline of his lips.

'I wish all my critics were like you.'

'You got any problems, point them in my direction.'

His lips twitched as she made her throaty declaration of war. 'That's mighty generous of you, little lady,' he drawled.

She cleared her throat. 'I hate to spoil a beautiful moment…'

'It is, isn't it?' he agreed smugly. The lure of her luscious lips proved an irresistible temptation to Josh. He plunged headlong into all that sweet, soft taste of heaven.

A breathless Flora tenaciously rediscovered the thread of her complaint. 'But I do have a slight problem with the ''little lady'' thing.' In truth, the patronising term made her feel kind of small and delicate, as if he could pick her up and put her in his pocket in a nice, cherishing sort of way.

Then just as she was puzzling over this evidence of a hitherto unexpected character trait—a desire to feel cherished—Josh quite suddenly did pick her up. He didn't put her in his pocket though, just in a snug, sweet-smelling cavern tucked away amongst the hay bales.

Far more promising than a pocket, she decided as his hip nudged hers with delicious familiarity as he lay down beside her. Resting on one elbow, he brushed a few soft strands of bright hair from her face.

With a slow, languorous smile she stretched like a cat. 'This puts a whole new slant on a roll in the hay.' Despite the lightness of her words there was a raw throb of emotion in her voice as she gazed up at him.

'Forget rolling,' he advised thickly as he reached down to dextrously flick open the top button of her shirt. He paused a moment to admire the curve of her collar-bone and the creamy flawless perfection of her skin before moving on to the next button. 'Conserve your energy.'

Flora didn't think she had an energy problem; every time he touched her she generated enough electricity to power the national grid! He watched her small breasts rise and fall in their light, lacy covering as he finally pulled aside her shirt. The expression in his eyes robbed her of breath.

Her head had fallen to one side. When he pressed his thumb to the point of her chin her face fell bonelessly against his supportive hand. He could feel the heavy vibration of the pulse spot at the base of her lovely throat.

'Flora? Are you all right?' he asked, his voice rough with sudden concern. The concave hollow of her flat belly deepened as her ribcage rose and fell rapidly. Her waxy pallor began to alarm him.

Her eyes, deep, drenching blue eyes, flickered open and relief shot through him.

'Never felt better,' she assured him, putting her heart into each syllable.

'Perhaps this isn't a good idea,' he said slowly, doubt beginning to cloud his eyes. 'You've had a traumatic time...'

Flora reached up and, grabbing the back of his hair, yanked his head down. 'Not half as traumatic as you'll have if you try and weasel out of this!' she hissed. 'I'm in full possession of my wits. I know *exactly* what I'm doing!' she told him fiercely.

Josh grinned, his teeth flashing white in his tanned face. 'I'll come quietly,' he promised, holding up his hands in mock surrender. 'Ouch!' He winced as several strands of hair came away in her fingers.

Flora examined the dark strands wrapped around her fingers. 'Sorry.' She grimaced. She levered herself upright. 'It's not as if you haven't got plenty to spare,' she felt impelled to point out as she examined the lush crop of hair that still clung firmly to his head.

'Just now I'm not interested in my follicle count.'

'Really? Most men when they reach your age get very interested. Why, I know…*oh*!' she mouthed silently as he pressed her back down into the hay and covered her with his body. A nudge of his knee had her thighs parted to provide just enough space for him to fit his long legs in between.

'Isn't this cosy?' he purred, running an exploratory hand down as far as her quivering flank.

Not the first description that sprang to Flora's mind, but she wasn't in the mood to argue with him about anything whilst he carried on doing all these deliciously wicked things to her.

He kissed her and carried on kissing her until she forgot to breathe, forgot her own name…but not his…never his. His name was etched on her soul in letters a mile high, because she loved him. She'd never dreamt that submission could feel so wonderful.

She never could figure out how or when he'd removed her shirt and bra without her noticing. It was his ragged gasp and the direction of his stark, needy stare that eventually drew her attention to her nudity. Always at ease with her body, she experienced a fleeting moment's concern, so great was her need to please him. His next throaty words dispelled any fledgling doubts.

'I wanted you since the moment I saw you. I didn't know how much until now…' he rasped. 'You're incredible.'

He couldn't take his eyes off her. Her nipples were small, yet plump and pouting. And surprisingly dark against her creamy skin like sweet, ripe berries. Taking hold of each soft, firm mound expertly in his big hands,

ιe bent his head to suckle first one and then, when he'd
ιad his fill, the other.

Flora's back arched as she gave herself up totally to the
ιensual pleasure of his touch. He was curved over her, and
ιis mouth moved from her tingling, aching breasts, up the
ιulnerable line of her graceful throat until he reached her
ιenderly swollen lips.

Fingers splayed, Flora let her hands glide over the broad,
ιair-roughened expanse of his chest down his washboard-
ιlat belly. She felt him suck in his breath and saw the
ιuiver of muscles beneath his smooth skin respond help-
ιessly to her touch.

Breath coming in short, anguished gasps, her tongue
ιirmly tucked between her teeth—nobody looked at her
ιest drooling—she began to unbuckle the leather belt that
ιvas looped through the waistband of his washed-out den-
ιms. Her co-ordination was shot to hell!

The basic skill seemed to be beyond her clumsy capa-
ιility. Sweating with effort, she suddenly gave a sharp cry
ιf frustration and pulled hard until his braced knees col-
ιapsed and he was on top of her. Feeling ever so slightly
ιrantic, she pressed herself against him, glorying in the
ιard impression of his erection against the softness of her
ιower belly.

'I want…I want,' she babbled brokenly.

'Hush, honey, I know,' he soothed with indulgent
ιoughness. Displaying none of her incompetence, he
ιwiftly divested her of her jeans and shoes. A wolfish grin
ιased the tension stamped on his face as he contemplated
ιe final item, a tiny lacy scrap, before he let it drift to the
ιround.

'A natural blonde.'

She opened her mouth to remonstrate him for ever
ιoubting it, but her vocal cords didn't respond.

The air felt cool on her overheated skin, but it did noth
ing to reduce her inner temperature, which continued to
boil. Her eyes felt heavy as she raised her slightly startled
eyes from her own state of undress to Josh.

He had stood up to slide his jeans, closely followed by
his boxer shorts, over his narrow hips. Inhibition was ob
viously a term he didn't understand. He made an intimi
datingly erotic picture as he stood there naked, and obvi
ously...*very* obviously aroused.

'Don't just stand there, man!' Her words started as an
imperious command and ended as a desperate breathy plea.
That was exactly how Flora felt: desperate and totally out
of control.

Just watching him move turned her insides hotly molten.
He touched her body; his hands and lips seemed to know
exactly how to drive her sweetly out of her mind. She cried
out in feeble hoarse protest as he located her most sensitive
area and was relieved when Josh ignored her. As the mois
ture from his marauding mouth evaporated it left burning
trails over her flesh.

'So wet for me,' he moaned brokenly, lifting his head.

Kneeling between her thighs, Josh cupped her bottom
in his hands. Eyes like molten metal melded with hers, he
thrust himself with agonising slowness into her, and the
intensity of the febrile tremors which shook her body in
tensified even further. The breath fled her lungs in a series
of fluttering gasps as he filled her.

Josh felt the tight, delicious resistance of her body as he
obeyed the elemental compulsion to thrust deeper into her
slick, receptive heat.

'Dear sweet...' An almost feral groan was wrenched
from his dry throat as her ankles locked in the small of his
back.

She hadn't known *wanting* could be like this. Nothing

in her life had prepared her for the raw intensity of this degree of sheer *feeling*. Every nerve in her body was screeching for a gratification she suddenly felt sure existed, she just wasn't sure how it happened. The idea of not fulfilling the expectation that held every muscle in her body rigid made her frantic.

'Yes, oh, yes, I want all of you, Josh...' She sobbed as her fingers clutched at the distended corded muscles of his shoulders and forearms.

Josh responded with fervour to her plea. Delirious with delight, Flora matched his rhythm move for move as the intensity of his measured strokes grew increasingly frenzied, increasingly desperate. She cried out in startled pleasure as it hit her, her teeth closed over the damp skin of his neck as a shocked hoarse cry emerged from her dry throat.

'*I didn't know!*' She sobbed as she felt the last hot, pulsing surges of his body within her before he stilled, breathing hard.

His big, wonderfully sweat-slick body felt deliciously heavy against her. One long leg remained looped over his hip as he rolled to one side. She could feel his heart still pounding hard. The situation was deliciously intimate, just as much in a different way as their frenzied coupling of moments before.

'It's never happened to me before, you see,' she explained in a distracted manner. 'If I'd married Paul it might never have,' she realised, her eyes widening in horror in her flushed face. No longer orgasmically uneducated, she knew *exactly* what she'd been missing. 'That would have been...'

'A terrible waste,' Josh completed softly. He tucked a stray damp strand of hair behind her ear before running a gentle hand down the soft contour of her cheek. His eyes were quite extraordinarily tender.

Paul the prat had certainly earned his name, he thought scornfully. Before Bridie he'd had a series of casual liaisons which he was neither ashamed nor proud of, but even though the emotions involved on both sides had been shallow he had got as much satisfaction from providing his partner with pleasure as taking it himself. When he'd eventually fallen in love, adding an emotional element to the equation had only intensified this need to give pleasure and he felt deeply scornful of men who missed out on this enjoyment.

His response made Flora blush—how could you blush with a man you'd just done *that* with? It probably was quite terribly bad taste to discuss a previous lover with your current lover, she pondered worriedly. She didn't want Josh to think she was the sort of girl who went around bitching about male inadequacies—not that he had any! Flora found she didn't like thinking even briefly about a day when Josh would be an ex.

'Never?' he persisted, a note of incredulity entering his deep voice. She showed an inclination to bury her face in his shoulder but a finger under her chin wouldn't permit this cowardly retreat.

'I guess I've been doing something wrong…?' she mumbled.

'Not so that I noticed,' he responded warmly. 'You know what this means, don't you…?' A small worried frown pleated her smooth forehead. 'It means you have a lot of time to make up,' he explained cheerfully. 'But don't worry—I'm prepared to put some overtime in on the job if you are.' He gently extracted several odd stalks of hay from her hair.

Flora smiled slowly. She was, she definitely was! This

hadn't felt like a one-night stand, but it was good to hear him say something to confirm this.

'Unfortunately, now probably isn't the best time to start. Megan produces afternoon tea about this time and if I'm not there she'll probably come looking.'

'Oh!' Flora gasped, glancing down at their intertwined naked bodies, and realised it might prove a bit embarrassing if they were discovered like this. A bit was probably a massive understatement! The fact she had made love in a barn in the middle of the afternoon was growing more extraordinary with each passing second—talk about out of character! But then, she mused, reflecting thoughtfully on the dramatic contrast between shockingly aggressive aspects of her behaviour during their love-making and the compulsive need to relinquish control...surrender to him...maybe she was just getting acquainted with parts of her character which had been submerged.

She watched from under the protective sweep of her lashes as Josh got lithely to his feet. He really was awesome. Maybe the answer was even simpler—she'd just not met Josh Prentice before!

It took her longer than it should to dress because Josh, who'd donned his clothes almost as fast as he'd shed them, stood there watching every move she made. Consequently every move she made was incredibly clumsy.

'Do you want to join me for tea? Megan would love to meet you, Liam still remembers his "smelly lady"—you made quite an impression...'

'On Liam...?' she enquired, shamelessly fishing.

'On us both,' he remarked, a somewhat grim expression flickering across his face. 'We could go out to dinner tonight if you'd like? Somewhere we can talk.'

'A date?'

A date, dear God, Josh, what the hell are you doing?

What was he thinking? Hell, he'd already done it! 'Yes, a
date,' he confirmed recklessly.

So much for not going anywhere with this until he'd
explained the situation! Problem was he hadn't been thinking with his head when he'd turned around and seen her
staring at him—staring at him with those big, hungry 'kiss
me' eyes. All the prepared explanations had vanished on
the spot. How did you go about explaining to a woman
that the original motivation for seducing her had been revenge? Candlelight and a romantic atmosphere—not to
mention a lot of wine—might make the task easier, but
somehow he doubted it.

'I could cook if you like, it might be more...' she coloured prettily '...private.' She really liked the idea of having him to herself but she was also worried about the state
of his bank balance. She didn't want him to feel obliged
to make an extravagant gesture. 'Claire left the freezer
crammed with food and *she's* a very good cook.'

'That would be good.' A public place might not be a
good idea if she started throwing things when he told her

CHAPTER FIVE

'IT'S instinct, you know.'

Josh squinted against the glare of the sun as he emerged from the barn. A man moved out from the shadows of the outbuilding closely followed by a Border collie who growled warningly at the intruder.

'Nice boy,' the stranger said as he nervously edged away from the dog.

Josh called the animal to his side with a click of his fingers. 'What can I do for you?'

The stranger gave a grin and rocked cockily on the balls of his feet. 'You don't remember me, do you?'

'Actually I do,' Josh contradicted.

The grin wilted but he made a swift recovery. 'Came to you straight like a little homing pigeon, didn't she?' His lascivious leer brought Josh's temper to simmering point in a heartbeat.

Where was his telephoto when he needed it? the journalist wondered, blissfully unaware of the homicidal stirrings seething in the younger man's breast. He was pretty sure that whatever had been going on in that barn would have made very good copy.

'I've not lost the old gut instinct,' he congratulated himself out loud.

'Or the gut,' Josh drawled unkindly.

Tom Channing automatically sucked in the belly which spilled gently over his belt. He smiled tightly; he could afford to be generous. 'No need to be nasty, Mr Prentice. Does she know?'

'Was that meant to take me off guard?' Josh enquired in a mildly bored voice.

'Then she doesn't.' The journalist smirked triumphantly. 'I knew I'd seen your face somewhere before, I'm good with faces. Then it came to me—you were that artist bloke they all rave about. On the off chance I looked up your bio and up popped the stuff about your wife snuffing it, and lo and behold her surgeon just happened to be Sir David Graham...you know, I don't believe in coincidence.'

'You know,' Josh commented languidly, 'I guessed you didn't.'

'You were following her too, weren't you, that day?'

'This is your story.' Josh's casual gesture invited the journalist to continue.

'I don't know what your game is exactly, but I can guess.' His smirk made Josh wonder how long he would be able to stop himself rearranging those sickeningly smug features. 'Have you thought how much more satisfying your little vendetta would be if it became public knowledge?' He paused to let the idea sink in. 'How I slept with the daughter of my wife's killer. How do you like that?'

'A little ambitious syllable-wise for the sort of newspaper you work for, isn't it? It is the *Clarion*, isn't it?'

'How do you know that?' With a puzzled frown the thickset man produced a rolled-up tabloid sheet from his pocket and proudly displayed the lurid headline to Josh. 'One of mine.' He gave a philosophical shrug when the artist type remained stubbornly unawed. 'Partners...?'

Josh's lip curled as he looked at the extended hand and his face hardened. Tom Channing realised for the first time that the big guy wasn't going to play the game; his friendly air faded abruptly leaving the older man looking just plain mean and spiteful.

'Well, it's up to you,' the journalist told him in an off-hand manner. 'I'll write it with or without your help,' he warned.

'Tell me, do you like your job?'

Tom was beginning to feel a bit edgy. He could predict the way people acted in this situation and this guy wasn't doing any of the predictable things. He didn't look angry or panicked. He just wasn't acting the way people did when they realised he held all the cards.

'Sure I do.' And truth to tell, with his track record with the bottle and a couple of minor disasters that had occurred before he'd dried out the last time, he was lucky he had it, because no other national was going to look twice at him these days. What he needed was a really big story: *this* story!

'And of course you were really lucky when they didn't sack you after the Manchester debacle, weren't you? It probably helped that the editor back then was an old drinking buddy from way back—though he's retired now, hasn't he? Tell me, do you get on with the new broom?'

'How do you know about Manchester?' There was a slight tremor in the hack's hand as he wiped away the sweat from his gleaming forehead with the cuff of his shirt.

'You're not the only one who can do a bit of research, and I have to tell you mine was more thorough than yours. I wanted to know what sort of man gets turned on by scaring a woman, and I found out.'

A dark flush travelled up the older man's thick neck. 'She wasn't scared!' he protested.

'Just as your ex wasn't when you put her in hospital the last time.'

The blustering journalist coloured unattractively.

'If Flora Graham had been scared she wouldn't have

shown it.' An admiring light flickered briefly in Josh's grey eyes.

'All this moral outrage is rich coming from you!' Tom Channing sneeringly hit back. 'She was a hell of a lot safer with me than she is with you. My motives are positively *pure* by comparison!'

Josh's nostrils flared as his mouth compressed into a savage white-rimmed line. 'If you want to keep your job,' he advised grimly, 'forget you ever met Flora Graham, forget you even know her name. The only reason you want to hurt her,' he continued in a soft, controlled voice that really shook Tom—shook him almost as much as the ferocious expression in those spooky pale eyes, 'is that she is untainted by the sordid world you live in. You hate it because you can't bring her down to your level, because she's simply a fine human being.'

'My, you've *really* fallen for her!' Mentally he was rewriting those headlines; this got better and better, he decided gleefully. His grin faded dramatically as Josh's fists clenched. This was not your typical effete arty type he was dealing with, he reminded himself. This guy might be greyhound lean but he gave the impression he could cause serious damage if he wanted—and right now he looked as if he wanted! Time to leave…he had his story.

'Got a phone on you?'

The journalist blinked at the unexpected question.

'Of course you have. Got your boss's number?'

'Listen, friend, there's no point you bleating to Jack Baker. He won't…'

'I don't mean your new editor, I mean the proprietor, David Macleod, the bloke who owns the whole stinking rag. Ring David and tell him you want to write this story, then tell him Josh Prentice isn't happy.' Under the circumstances he felt no qualms about employing a little judicious blackmail; to protect Flora he'd go a hell of a lot further.

'You're bluffing.' He stared incredulously at the stony-faced guy in front of him. 'There's no way you could have that much clout.' A shade of uncertainty had entered his voice.

'You of all people should know that money talks and I have serious money,' Josh explained casually. 'And good friends. There was a time when David needed some financial backing and I like to help my friends out... You see, your bio on me left out a few very important details, like I made my first million before I was twenty-one.'

Tom Channing went pale. 'You're having me on!'

Josh shrugged. 'Take the risk,' he suggested generously. 'I don't give a damn, but let me tell you one thing—you print a single derogatory syllable about Flora Graham and I'll take you apart slowly, piece by piece.'

Tom Channing saw no reason to disbelieve him. It seemed to him that the prospect of this dismemberment seemed to make Prentice very happy. This guy, he decided, was an animal and that contrast of the friendly voice and that Grim Reaper glare really chilled his marrow good and proper!

'Freedom of the press...' he objected weakly.

Josh snorted derisively. 'Principles from you! You sold out any principles you had twenty years back and we both know it. And please don't give me that "the public have a right to know" bull, or I'll crack up!' Josh snarled, showing no immediate inclination to laugh. 'There's no national interest involved here. There's just a vindictive little has-been hack, inventing lurid details to do a hatchet job on someone who's never done anyone any harm! Try selling this one on the open market and I'll be forced to reveal how I saw you assaulting Miss Graham after you'd followed her to a lonely secluded spot.'

'I hardly touched her…' The journalist protested as he saw plan B slip down the toilet.

'You *did* touch her though, and she didn't like it; that's enough to constitute an assault. You're not the only one who can be economical with the truth,' he admitted ruthlessly. 'Her father's dead, the story's dead. Do yourself a favour and stop working on your headlines.'

'I don't need to work on them, fact is one hell of a lot more entertaining than anything I could dream up here, mate.' The journalist choked.

Josh's lip curled. 'I'm not your *mate*.'

There came a time when a man had to cut his losses and make an exit with as much dignity as possible—in this case that wasn't very much! Tom automatically reached for the packet of cigarettes that lived in his breast pocket. His scowl deepened when he came up empty. He rolled back his sleeve and ripped off the nicotine patch with an expression of loathing. He'd quit next week.

'You haven't heard the last of me!' he yelled back over his shoulder.

The threat didn't bother Josh but the element of truth in some of the sleaze's jibes had. Soberly he made his way towards the farmhouse.

Josh knew the instant the cottage door closed behind him that something was seriously up. Flora stalked back into the small sitting room, without saying anything to him. Her slender back was screaming rejection. He glanced at the flowers in his hand expecting to see the blooms withered on their stems—it had been that sort of look she'd given him and his gifts. He placed the champagne and the flowers on the dresser.

'Sure you could *afford* them?' she snapped sarcastically as he entered close on her heels.

There was a faint tremor in her fingers as she picked up and replaced with exaggerated care a pretty gingerpot decorated with a traditional blue and white design. It was incredibly hard to control her destructive impulses. When she thought about how he'd deliberately misled her she wanted to break things—preferably parts of his highly luscious body!

She shot him a sideways glance of loathing and saw with growing resentment that the luscious part was still disturbingly applicable. Black suited him, she concluded, taking in the tailored black trousers that suggested the muscularity of his thighs. If she hadn't discovered what a lying rat he was she'd probably already have unbuttoned that crisp cotton shirt to reveal...she closed her eyes and swallowed convulsively.

Josh closed his eyes too; knowing he deserved whatever was coming didn't make this situation any better. Dear God, he *had* to salvage something out of this mess. 'I meant to tell you earlier, Flora, but I...'

'Were having too good a laugh at my expense?' she suggested, placing a hand on one slender hip and thrusting the other out.

He doubted she even suspected how sexually provocative he found the pose...he wished he had his sketch-book with him...but then drawing things had always been his way of delaying the inevitable. After Bridie's death he'd painted himself into the ground before he'd stopped still long enough to let the grieving process kick in, and then he hadn't touched a paintbrush for a long time.

'You must have thought it *very* amusing when I offered you career advice. *Have you ever thought of painting?*' she cruelly caricatured her own starry-eyed enthusiasm. At the back of the drawer were a pile of prospectuses from various art colleges. She supposed she ought to be grateful she hadn't given him those yet!

With a dry-eyed sob of disgust she flung the incriminating colour supplement at him with such vigour the staples gave way and sheets of glossy paper scattered around the room.

'Although, compared to some of these critics, my admiration was pretty tepid!'

'You've found out what I do?' he said blankly, picking up a torn sheet of paper that bore a reproduction of one of his earliest efforts. Impatiently he screwed up the paper and dropped it on the floor.

Flora folded her arms and pursed her lips. 'Why, how many other secrets do you have?' She held up her hands. 'Don't tell me,' she pleaded contemptuously. 'I already know too much about you. You're nothing but a cheap fake...! Though maybe not that cheap, it seems your paintings go for a small fortune!' She made this sound like the worst insult of all.

A thin, ironic smile curved Josh's lips. 'It's not my artistic ability you object to, then, just the fact I'm not starving in some rat-infested attic!'

How dare he make it sound as if *I'm* the one being unreasonable? He couldn't begin to imagine how stupid and humiliated she'd felt when she'd realised who and what he was. It had all been a game for him. Had he ever been going to tell her? she wondered.

'I don't care if you're a bloody millionaire! I'm glad you find this funny!' She sniffed, furiously blinking away the tears of self-pity that stung her eyelids. Her determination to treat him with bland indifference had been long forgotten; in fact she'd forgotten it as the first pang of longing had hit, about the same instant he'd walked through her door. 'The thing I object to—' she choked as abject pity squirmed horridly in her stomach '—is being laughed at and lied to.'

'Did you let me make love to you because you thought I was a penniless decorator?' One darkly delineated brow rose enquiringly. 'Or were you just sorry for me, perhaps?' he suggested thoughtfully.

'Of course not, no, no on both accounts!' she hissed, outraged that he could even suggest such a thing. 'I did that because…' *No!* Under the circumstances that explanation was better left unsaid; she'd had a gut full of humiliation for one day! To her intense relief no sarky prompt was forthcoming.

'Then why does what I do for a living make a difference one way or the other?' he asked instead with infuriating logic.

'It's not what you do for a living, it's what you do by way of amusement which makes you a ratbag first class!' she informed him with lofty disdain. 'You lie…why, you do it so well, you could lie for Britain!' Her voice rose shrilly in volume as her contempt mounted. 'As liars go, Josh, you are world class! And I'm a world-class sap for falling for it. Do you always adopt a fake personality when you're away from home? Does it make it more difficult for your little local conquests to pursue you when you leave?'

'You're not a local,' he pointed out, watching with some fascination the undulations of her heaving, unfettered bosom. It seemed that at some point this evening she'd dressed to please someone—in all probability him—in a discreetly slinky misty blue number that clung in all the right places. 'And if you want to pursue me I'll draw you a detailed map; better still,' he offered extravagantly, 'I'll drive you myself.'

Flora's rapid breathing slowed a little. He sounded flatteringly sincere, but then he did sincere awfully well, she reminded herself.

'As for conquests, you and I both know that I hadn't slept with anyone for a very long time.'

Flora felt the colour fade from her overheated cheeks. She suddenly found it impossible to maintain eye contact… 'I'm no expert,' she gritted. In fact he must now know that compared to his her sexual repertoire was strictly limited. The sizzling spectre of his raw hunger rose up to add to her wretched confusion. He introduced the subject deliberately to confuse me, she concluded with irrational resentment.

'*You know,*' he contradicted confidently. 'Do you think you could give me a minute without throwing something at me or screaming abuse?'

If he thought this was abuse he'd led a very sheltered life! 'Miracles do happen,' she told him nastily. 'Even to the undeserving.'

'If you recall, I didn't say I was a decorator…did I?'

Flora's disgruntled sniff acknowledged this. 'But you didn't disillusion me!' Which in her book amounted to the same thing.

'True, but round about the time I should have straightened things out you'd just invited me into your home, Flora, and I wanted an excuse to be there—any excuse.' The look of stark hunger that flickered over his handsome face was too rawly genuine to be faked.

Flora caught her breath and blinked, the anger abruptly fled her body and, call her criminally susceptible, but the feelings that eagerly rushed in to fill the vacuum were dreamily sensuous.

'You did?' she whispered huskily.

He nodded and his lips quivered to form a faint wry

smile. 'Not that I admitted why I wanted to be there to myself at the time.' His confession held a savage inflection.

'No...?' She tried to stiffen her weakening resolve and fan the flames of her fury. 'What are you doing milking cows anyhow?'

'My brother is married to Nia, Geraint's sister. That makes me family...sort of. I was up here—' he paused slightly '—visiting.' Flora was too interested in discovering how he came to be acting as farm labourer in the middle of nowhere to notice the odd, almost belligerent inflection in his voice as he offered up the explanation for his presence on the farm.

'Huw, Geraint's dad, broke his leg, which makes them one man short at one of the busiest times of the year. I offered to extend my stay and help out a bit...mind you, I didn't intend to stay this long...'

'You didn't...?' It was hard not to sound smugly pleased.

He shook his head. 'Are you still mad with me, Flora?' he asked with a cajoling smile.

'I suppose you think that grin will get you everywhere.'

'It's worked so far.'

'I just bet it has,' she growled sourly. 'Well, you'll find I'm not such a pushover.' If only! Josh appeared to accept her strictures meekly—too meekly probably, she concluded suspiciously.

'I offered to cook for you because I thought you couldn't afford to take me out, and I didn't want to injure your masculine pride by offering to pay.'

'I know,' he admitted frankly. 'It made me feel like one hell of a heel.'

She sniffed; his remorse was a bit late coming. 'Not enough of a heel to tell me the truth,' she observed acidly.

'I *hate* cooking,' she added so that he'd appreciate the enormity of her sacrifice. 'I've thawed enough to feed an army.'

She'd read the article before she'd started preparing the meal so at that precise moment all the thawed food was dripping on the kitchen table. There must be some deep-buried sex-linked gene, she mused, that had suddenly made her feel she had to feed her man. Well, he wasn't hers in any strictly technical sense, but, she admitted to herself with a rush of honesty, she'd like it if he were! Such proprietorial instincts were alien to her; everything tonight was conspiring to unsettle her.

'It'll all ruin now,' she fretted.

'I'm not fussed about eating.'

'Aren't you hungry? All that physical labour mending…things…' Her technical knowledge of farming was seriously limited.

'The most physical thing I did today left me feeling amazingly invigorated,' he explained glibly.

If Flora had needed further elaboration the bold, bad gleam in his eyes was enough to confirm her initial suspicions.

'Me too,' she asserted huskily.

'I make a mean omelette, we could eat later…?' His deep, throaty voice trailed suggestively away. His burning eyes ignited a fire all of her own; it was inside—deep inside.

She shrugged. 'I suppose,' she conceded gruffly, 'that might be all right.'

'How all right?' he persisted.

Flora gave a disgruntled grunt of irritation and glared at him. 'All right,' she informed him spikily. 'It would be *very* all right. In fact, if you must know, it would be a hell of a lot more than all right, and in case you didn't get the drift I can't stand omelettes,' she added on the one-in-a-million chance he still had any doubts about what part of the evening's timetable she found attractive!

Josh's startled, delighted laugh was a low, sexy rumble that made her toes curl. 'My repertoire extends beyond omelettes.'

Just thinking about Josh's no doubt extensive repertoire made her stomach muscles cramp. A troubled light entered Flora's blue eyes. 'Mine's a bit limited,' she confessed; they both knew she wasn't talking culinary skills.

The memory of Paul's spiteful accusation was draining her confidence reserves—it wasn't as if she'd actually believed him at the time, not really... What made her think she could please a man? Especially one like Josh. Maybe Paul had been right—maybe she was frigid! She hadn't felt very frigid in Josh's arms; in fact she hadn't acted frigid either. The memory of how she'd acted brought a blast of colour to her cheekbones. Flora didn't look at him but she could feel Josh staring at her.

A firm hand on the angle of her jaw forced her reluctant head up. 'I don't have a little book filled with set game play, Flora.'

'I'm sorry,' she mumbled, embarrassed by her obvious plea for reassurance. She shook her head and missed the heavy swish of long hair; it had always distracted attention from her face very satisfactorily. Right now she needed some help with distractions; she felt wretchedly exposed. 'I'm not usually so *needy*.'

His eyes darkened. 'Me neither,' he told her throatily.

Flora's eyes grew round and a startled, 'Oh!' escaped her parted lips.

'You don't always have to stay in control of a situation,' he insisted.

'I think I do. Maybe I don't trust...'

He stiffened and she rushed in to mend any damage her careless comments had done.

'Not you, I don't distrust you.' She was so anxious to reassure him. 'It's me...I don't trust feeling this way. People do crazy things when they let...lust get out of hand...'

'*Lust.* I suppose that could be considered progress,' he murmured drily.

Flora was bewildered by the spark of anger in his eyes. 'I mean, think of what we did this afternoon...' she began worriedly.

'I am.'

An inarticulate moan escaped her lips. 'Funny man, you slay me,' she croaked. The irony was he did just that! 'Haven't you realised we didn't use...? I'm not taking the pill, you know...the contraceptive pill, that is,' she elaborated stiffly. 'I don't think there's *too much* danger of anything happening.' Her frown deepened. 'But that's not really the point...'

'It's very much the point,' he contradicted harshly. 'By "anything" I'm assuming you mean pregnancy?'

Flora nodded uncomfortably. 'I'm not really ready to get pregnant.'

'I'm not ready for you to be pregnant—*ever*,' he ground out white-faced and grim. His vehemence shouldn't have hurt her—it was only natural a man didn't want a child from a casual liaison—but it did! The sheer depth of his anger confused and wounded her.

'It wasn't just me being foolish and reckless,' she reminded him bitterly. You could mess around with euphemisms like spontaneous, but when you came down to it she'd been plain stupid and his reaction was only underlining her stupidity.

'Do you think I don't know that?' The lines bracketing

his strong mouth deepened. 'I wouldn't deliberately expose anyone I cared about to that sort of danger...' he grated. 'It was criminally irresponsible of me.' He ran a hand savagely through his hair and glared broodingly—seemingly blindly—ahead. 'As it was I took advantage of the fact you've been through a hellish time and you were screaming out for comfort...'

'I'm not a child, Josh. I knew *exactly* what I was doing,' she contradicted him firmly. 'And I wanted to do it. In fact,' she added, not much caring if she sounded brazen, 'I'd been imagining doing it since I met you, so it had nothing whatever to do with being grief-stricken.' She heard the sibilant hiss of his sharply indrawn breath. 'So if you feel the urge to don sackcloth and ashes leave my emotional traumas out of it,' she gritted stubbornly.

Suddenly it clicked: his wife had died in childbirth—small wonder he looked spooked at the idea of unplanned pregnancy. Poor Josh, it was *his* emotional traumas they were talking about here.

'Crossing the road is a calculated risk, Josh,' she reminded him gently. He looked down at her slim fingers against the dark cloth of his sleeve but he didn't reject her touch. 'I know that statistics don't mean anything when someone you love is the rare exception, but childbirth really isn't normally that dangerous these days.' Her eyelashes fluttered against her cheek as she blinked rapidly before raising stunned eyes to his face. 'Did you just say you cared about me?' she queried sharply.

He looked pretty overwhelmed by her abrupt query, or maybe it was her blatant admission that she'd been silently lusting after him since they'd met—looking the way he did you'd have thought he'd have been used to lecherous females. The dark bands of colour that stained the sharp crest of his cheekbones might even have indicated embarrassment, but at least he didn't avoid her eyes. He returned her scrutiny gravely and to her amazement made no effort to deny it or shrug her comment off as a joke.

'If I did, would that be saying too much, too soon?' There was an aggressive edge to his defensive query.

Was he kidding? Swallowing the solid lump of emotion that welled in her throat, she shook her head vigorously.

'Then I admit that I care for you—I care for you too much to gratify the urgings of your body clock. I think we should get one thing straight from the outset: if you want children from a relationship, I'm not your man,' he warned her heavily. 'I already have a child, you don't—so you could call it unfair.' His broad shoulders lifted and a thin, bitter smile formed on his lips. 'It probably is, but that's the way it is. When Bridie died I wanted to blame someone, anyone.' His nostrils flared as he took a deep breath before plunging further into explanations he had no experience of giving.

'It's taken a long time, but I've finally accepted that it wasn't something anyone could have predicted or prevented. The luck factor, or bad luck factor you refer to, just makes it worse if anything. I'm simply not prepared to take that risk with someone's life again. Take it or leave it.'

In other words take him or leave him! Feeling the way she did there wasn't ever a possibility that cool choice was going to enter in her decision. Even though, deep down, she knew that having this man's babies would bring her deep fulfilment, it was the man she wanted.

Babies. Relationships…! That was all a major leap from love-making in a hay barn! She'd automatically assumed his feelings were less intense than her own—a bit of stereotyping; it seemed she was wrong with a vengeance! Her fuddled brain couldn't keep pace with what he was telling her…what he was revealing about his expectations.

'I've seen couples who can't have children,' he continued, showing her a stony, unlover-like countenance. 'Seen how the constant preoccupation with procreation can drive a wedge between them. It's possible that knowing you could have a baby but your partner doesn't want one could be even worse.'

'Josh, are you saying you see us together…long term?'

A look of intense exasperation swept across his face. 'Hell, woman, do you think I'd be telling you this if I didn't? I just want you to know what you'd be getting into.'

A sudden naughty grin chased the last lingering shadows from her face. 'Into bed with you, I hope,' she announced boldly.

Josh responded with an equally roguish grin. The amusement slowly faded from his eyes as he took her by the shoulders. 'You're quite sure you understand that my terms are not negotiable?' he asked her sternly. 'You're not harbouring any foolish idea that you'll be able to change my mind eventually.'

'No,' she lied earnestly. 'If I knew you *couldn't* have children I'd still want to be…' A sudden notion occurred to her. 'You haven't had the…? Have you?'

He gave a very masculine wince. 'Snip? No, call me squeamish…'

'Not at all,' she responded swiftly, trying to disguise her relief with a businesslike practicality. 'There are other less drastic and perfectly successful forms of preventing fatherhood.' Not to mention motherhood!

Surely when the healing process was complete he'd see that his attitude was an overreaction—understandable, but nevertheless overreaction. Right now all that mattered to her was that Josh cared for her and they could be together. Her heart was bursting with optimism. Tomorrow could take care of itself; she was going to take care of Josh.

'And I came well supplied with one of those, but I'm open to any alternative suggestions.'

'Yes, well,' she croaked, trying and failing spectacularly to match his relaxed attitude to all things intimate.

Thumbs either side of her jaw, he bent his head and let his nose gently nudge the side of hers. She felt dizzy as his warm breath whispered over her skin and her body reacted of its own accord to being close to him.

'I need you, Flora. I need you to kiss me.' The ragged tempo of his breathing deepened. 'I need to feel your hands on my body, I need to feel your body on my body, I need like hell to be inside you…' The intense melting sensation between her legs made her shift restlessly as Josh groaned deeply and lifted his head. She could see that the strain in his voice was reflected in the taut lines of his strong, vibrantly handsome face.

'Is that needy enough for you?' he enquired, his sardonic gaze sweeping over her.

'Oh, yes,' she breathed gustily. *'Definitely.'* She allowed her sultry gaze to move slowly over the intriguing contours of his face before reaching up and laying her fingers on the back of his firm, strong neck. 'I really want to kiss you too,' she confessed huskily.

'I'm all for following your instincts, angel. That was a very mysterious smile?'

'No mystery,' she assured him dreamily. 'I was just thinking I don't feel very angelic just now.' Her body was almost audibly thrumming with the slow throb of sexual arousal; it bathed her…drenched her. She wanted Josh to make love to her more than she wanted anything—including babies, she firmly told the cold voice of logic that lurked discreetly in the back of her mind.

Sinking her fingers deeper into the lush dark growth on the back of his head, she set about doing something about the kissing part. He co-operated fully with her design, fully enough to leave her an inarticulate, clinging mass of screaming nerve-endings and equally noisy hormones by the time the lengthy embrace ended.

'Oh, my!' she half sobbed. 'You kiss beautifully.' She closed her eyes; looking at him made her feel dizzy.

'You do everything beautifully.' He watched with a ferociously rapt expression the delicate fluttering of her closed blue-veined eyelids.

She felt warmly compliant as he picked her up. His splendid physique was not just for show—he was amazingly strong. He was amazing in many ways, she mused, tightening her grip around his neck.

'I think we'll do this properly in a bed this time. Up here?' He inclined his head towards the narrow staircase.

'I thought you did it properly last time.'

'True,' he conceded modestly. 'But I'm still removing hay from places hay was never meant to be, very uncomfortable. Not that it isn't a price I'm willing to pay…'

She nodded in eager agreement. 'I hate to point out a flaw in your plan,' she said as he approached the narrow staircase, 'but, as much as I like this mode of transport…' and she did very much '…I don't think this is strictly practical.'

'It's too narrow, isn't it?'

''Fraid so.'

Josh lowered her reluctantly to the ground. 'A man does his best to be spontaneous.' His eyes gleamed as he smoothed the wrinkles in her dress thoroughly with the flat of his hand. 'Actually,' he confided, 'not actually spontaneous in the strictest sense—I've been working all day on this scene where I kick open the bedroom door and throw you masterfully on the bed.' He dwelt with visible pleasure on the cherished image.

'It sounds good to me. But don't say die, all is not lost,' she told him solemnly, entering into the spirit of things. 'How about it if I get up the stairs under my own steam and take it from there pretending you carried me up?' Eyes sparkling, she looked expectantly up at him.

'That's what I like to hear—lateral thinking,' he approved.

'Right, then!' she enthused, not feeling in the mood to delay things. Hitching up the long skirt of her dress in one hand, she attacked the stairs two at a time, fairly flying up them. When he reached the top she was standing there with her arms open.

'What are you waiting for?' she asked pertly.

Josh's deep, delighted laugh rang out. 'To wake up?' he wondered wryly.

'Nightmare?'

'Dream, angel, the best dream ever,' he told her truthfully, and he'd do anything, including lie, to keep that dream alive.

CHAPTER SIX

CAN he still taste me? Flora wondered dreamily, running the tip of her tongue sensuously around the outline of her full lips. When she breathed deeply all she could smell was the scent rising from her own warm, sticky skin; it was an erotic, mind-blowing combination of sex and Josh.

When her eyes flickered open they were still a deep, aroused navy blue. Each and every individual muscle in her body was totally relaxed in sharp contrast to the knife-edge tension of moments before. Silently she sighed with voluptuous pleasure at the memories still fresh in her mind. His love-making had brought her to a pitch of indescribable anticipation that had scarcely been bearable.

Her anxiety had reached fever pitch when she'd thought that she might not be permitted the pleasure of driving him a little crazy too. Huskily she'd told him what she wanted to do and happily he hadn't been too shocked by wanton requests she would have blushed to recall had she not been transformed into a totally shameless hussy. It was strange that Josh was the only man with whom she could imagine shedding every inhibition.

Her satiated stomach muscles quivered when she visualised his face as her greedy fingers had closed over the hard, silky length of him. It had been his turn to plead when her caresses had grown more intimate.

'I wish I could stay the night,' Josh murmured beside her. He reached over to rub the end of her twitching nose affectionately with the tip of one finger.

Lying replete in the crook of his arm, Flora stretched

voluptuously and flipped over onto her stomach and propped herself up on her elbows to look at him. Josh's attention was immediately drawn to the gentle sway of her small breasts as they adapted to her new position.

'Do you have to go yet?' she coaxed, her full lower lip quivering as she tried to suppress a strange and unusual urge to pout prettily.

The thing was she just wasn't herself. Just looking at his superb lithe body made her feel and act like a sexually deprived fool with an IQ in single figures, and the crazy part was she didn't care. Crossing her legs at the ankle, she wriggled her toes in the air. The movement made her freshly aware of some unusual aches—not unpleasant ones—in her body, which still glowed from the rough intimacy of their love-making.

'If Liam wakes I like to be there.'

'Of course you do,' she responded contritely, immediately remorseful for her clinging-vine imitation. 'I understand Liam comes first.' It would be nice to know I was a contender for one of the medal positions though, she mused wistfully.

She rolled onto her back and, bringing her knees to her chest, pulled herself briskly into a sitting position. Josh didn't strike her as the sort of man who enjoyed clingy women—probably ran a mile when he saw one coming. She squared her shoulders and gave her version—and pretty good it was, if she said so herself—of the definitive non-clingy smile.

'What?' he asked, his brow forming a censorious frown. 'No humble apology for keeping me up past my bedtime…no pun intended?'

Startled, she encountered the mocking indulgent glow in his eyes—he knew what she was doing and he was laughing at her. Nobody had ever accused her of being transparent before—could he read her mind? He certainly managed to anticipate her needs with spectacular success. With a wryly self-conscious grin, she retracted the toe she'd already placed on the floor.

'Crude pun, *you*! *Never!*' she gasped, her voice oozing sweet malice.

She yelped as Josh's hand shot out to grasp her foot mid-air; his reflexes really were remarkably well tuned. For a moment he looked thoughtfully at the graceful arch of her foot before drawing it decisively to his mouth. All the time his eyes were on her face, watching the delicate fluctuations of colour, seeing the startled little gasp form when his lips touched her flesh.

'You're gorgeous, quite literally from head to toe.' His eyes touched her tousled blonde mop of silky hair.

The rasp of his vibrant voice was like a caress; a responsive quiver shuddered through her. Almost frightened by the intensity of her desire for him, Flora obeyed his gentle but firm encouragement and wriggled her bottom along the mattress until she was able to sit on his lap and wrap both her long legs around his waist.

'I thought I was coming on too str…'

He held up a finger to his lips to still her explanation. 'I know what you thought, but don't bother killing yourself being casual and undemanding, angel. I don't feel particularly casual myself…'

'*Really!*'

'Also,' he announced with unapologetic arrogance, 'I'm a fairly demanding bloke. Actually, I've rarely felt less casual,' he announced starkly.

'That's…'

Josh grew rapidly impatient with her gobsmacked silence. 'The best joke you've heard in ages? Food for thought…? Scary…*what*…?' She was staggered to see that Josh's habitual cool had deserted him totally.

'You know, you're nearly as conceited as I thought,' she told him, rubbing a loving finger softly along the deep frown-line between his eyes. 'I'm crazy about you, you silly man.' He must have been walking around with his eyes closed if he hadn't noticed that! 'I didn't think I was being *that* subtle.'

As fast as things were going, she thought, on sober reflection, that it might be too soon, despite Josh's surprisingly upfront admission that his feelings ran a lot deeper than shallow, to throw explosive words like *love* into the conversational melting pot just yet.

The tantalisingly dominant, but too brief touch of his firm, warm lips against hers left her craving more despite their recent love-making. 'You know something.' He cupped her face between his big clever hands. 'You're *absolutely* nothing like I thought you would be. In fact, I couldn't have been further off the mark.' He shook his head as if he couldn't comprehend his own short-sightedness.

Flora raised herself up on her knees and, grabbing hold of the old-fashioned brass bed frame, deliberately pressed her breasts against his chest, which expanded dramatically as he gasped for breath. The fierce, earthy gleam in his eyes made her whimper low in her throat.

'I can see how you might have thought I have criminal tendencies,' she reflected, thinking back on their inauspicious meeting, 'but I don't go around letting down tyres every day,' she promised him, licking her finger and crossing the approximate area of her heart with a wobbly finger. 'Honestly.'

Something flickered in his eyes that made her stop. 'But you didn't mean that, did you?' Of course he'd seen her before and why not? So had half the population of the country. Her face and name had been plastered on TV screens and every tabloid front page in the country.

'You already knew about my father and the court case,' she said blankly. Wondering why it had taken her so long to realise this, she settled back down onto her heels.

'Yes, Flora, I knew.'

'I don't think much of your choice of reading material,' she joked feebly, before a hurt furrow reappeared on her brow. 'I don't understand… Why didn't you say?' She puzzled briefly before her face cleared and her hunched shoulders relaxed. 'Sorry.' She touched the side of his face gently with her hand. 'I sort of forgot some people actually have a modicum of sensitivity. Sad, isn't it?' she mused. 'I got so used to everyone acting as though me and my life were public property that when someone shows some kindness I get confused.'

'I wasn't being kind, Flora.' He spoke so harshly her hand fell away. 'I made as many snap judgements as the next man in the street about you—maybe more,' he grated. 'So have a care when you place me on a pedestal I'm woefully unsuited to.'

The warning in his voice made her shiver. 'I prefer you in my bed.' Her sally didn't draw an answering smile.

'The only difference between them and me is that I got to know the real Flora.'

'Don't beat yourself up over this, Josh,' she urged. 'We've all believed cruel lies, or skilfully edited half-truths we read in newspapers, myself included.'

Self-contempt flared in his eyes as he scrutinised her beautiful, troubled face. 'God help you, angel, but I'm probably falling in love with the real Flora.'

The colour seeped dramatically from her face. 'You are?' she croaked. He didn't look as if he was joking; then again he didn't look as though love was making him deliriously happy either!

'Nothing's one hundred per cent certain in life, but I wouldn't go laying any bets against the sort of odds we're talking here.' His expression hadn't altered; he continued to watch her with the same wary expression in his silver-shot eyes.

'I don't think it would matter what the odds were,' she reflected slowly, 'which in itself is strange because I've always been the last person anyone would have called a risk-taker...play it safe Flora, that's me. I'd still want to take a shot at making this thing work, Josh, even if we had everything and everyone conspiring against us,' she declared stubbornly.

It's taken me a long time to lose my heart to anyone, but now I'm going the whole way and then some! Part of her was appalled by her frank, no-holds-barred demonstration of faith; another part of her found the experience oddly liberating.

The conflict Josh's mobile features had been clearly displaying was supplanted by a white-hot flare of male gratification as he listened to her impassioned words.

'You sound very fierce.'

'I feel very weak,' she told him honestly. What woman wouldn't when straddled across the lap of a man with a body like Josh's? Her eyes glided warmly admiring over his athletically sculpted frame; perfect harmony was the only description that came close to summing up the muscle ratio of his impressive proportions. Deeply debilitating desire flowed through her veins.

'A weak, wanton woman...I like it.'

'That's what I want to do,' she whispered huskily.

'What do you want to do, Flora?'

Her eyelids felt heavy as the heat which pervaded her body spread. 'Whatever you like,' she explained languidly.

The sibilant hiss of his sharp inhalation cut the silence like a knife. 'My God, Flora…' His voice sounded as shaky as the hand he curved around the back of her head. She gave a slow, sultry smile as he pulled her face to his. 'Have you got the faintest idea what you're doing to me?'

'From where I'm sitting,' she announced innocently, 'it's hard to miss what I'm doing to you.'

A strangled laugh rumbled in his chest, only his eyes weren't laughing—they were filled with intense, raw need. The earthy sexuality of that look made the teasing expression fade abruptly from her own face. Nervously she ran her tongue over her suddenly dry lips.

His hands spanning her waist with casual ease, he drew her up onto her knees and then, eyes still holding hers, brought her smoothly and decisively downwards again. The corded sinews stood out in his neck as his eyes closed and his head jerked back. His mind blanked and his arousal grew even more intense as he adjusted to being sheathed within the hot, moist tightness of her receptive, eager body.

'You want me…?'

A low, needy moan emerged from her throat. She couldn't speak—hell, she'd forgotten how to breathe! She could feel, though—every atom of her being was concentrated with mindless hunger on the incredible sensation of being intimately melded with him.

Each slow, controlled thrust of his body turned her insides molten and pulled her inner muscles and nerve-endings tantalisingly closer to the release they screamed for. Her fingers dug into the resistant muscles of his shoulders as her forehead came to rest against his. His face was a dark, unfocused blur, and his breath, hot and fast, mingled and merged with her own shallow gasps just as they were merging…becoming one.

He shouted her name at the moment of climax and Flora, still with her arms linked around his neck, felt her body go suddenly flaccid with the shock of release. She loosed her grip and Josh lowered her slick, hot body gently to the bed.

Propped up on one arm, he watched the shallow rise and fall of her small breasts. He ran a finger through the delicate valley the twin soft mounds formed. Flora's eyelashes lifted from the curve of her cheek. She had never in her blissful ignorance imagined that loving someone could make a person want to weep. It was the most overwhelmingly intense feeling she'd ever experienced in her life.

'I know you've got to go.'

'Soon,' he admitted softly. 'But not yet. I want to look at you a while, and maybe hold you.'

The tender expression on his face brought the tears even closer to the surface. 'I thought men didn't go in for that sort of thing,' she teased in a wobbly voice.

'Depends on the man…and the woman he's with. On second thoughts,' he added, retrieving the tumbled sheet from the bottom of the bed and drawing it up over her still-quivering thighs, 'perhaps it would be sensible to hold back on the holding bit…considering the time restraint…' he added in response to her look of enquiry.

'I'm glad you find me irresistible but I think, under the circumstances,' she remarked drily, 'it would be quite safe. Unless, that is, you're superhuman.'

'That,' he told her, his eyes gleaming naughtily, 'is a challenge I'd love to rise to on another occasion when I'm not obliged to love you…'

'Twice,' she couldn't resist adding with dreamy-eyed complacence.

'Being the modest type, I wasn't going to labour that point.' He loftily ignored her hoot of derisive laughter. 'However, if we're talking stamina…'

'I'm sure your staying power is tremendously impressive…for a man of your age.' She ducked under the sheet with a sly chuckle.

Flora was hopelessly outmatched in the resultant wrestling match but this didn't hamper her enjoyment of the rough and tumble playfulness. Love-making and laughter had never seemed compatible bedfellows to her before, she reflected, finally pleading breathlessly for mercy.

'It's unscrupulous of you to take advantage of the fact I'm ticklish,' she protested, pushing several wayward strands of hair from her hot face and grinning reproachfully across at him.

Her glance flickered downwards to where her limbs were still snarled in a deeply satisfactory tangle with his long, long legs. Her skin looked very pale against his darker hair-sprinkled flesh; a strong, athletically built young woman, she was amazed how delicate she appeared up against him. The stark contrasts between them excited her even in her present satiated state.

'I'm a very unscrupulous man, Flora.'

He had stopped smiling and her own smile became uncertain; there had been an odd, indefinable but distinctly sobering note in his voice.

'I'd better be going.' He rolled away from her onto his back and in a single fluid motion rose from the rumpled bed.

Flora nodded, unable *not* to watch him as he padded with unselfconscious grace across the room, pausing to retrieve several garments as he did so. He really was magnificent! She couldn't figure out what had broken his mood, but something definitely had.

'Not up for milking in the morning, I hope.'

Josh fastened the last button on his shirt across his chest. 'Not until the evening tomorrow, and that'll probably be the last time. Huw's plaster is due off. Actually I promised Liam I'd take him to the beach in the morning for a picnic, a sand-in-your-sandwich sort of affair.' His long lashes lifted as he looked at her. 'Wondered if you'd like to come?'

'Sand is my favourite sandwich filling,' she replied, hoping she was managing to match the insouciant tone he'd set. Hopefully he wasn't as indifferent as he sounded.

He nodded and didn't look displeased by her reply. Flora felt content with this. It would be plain daft to start getting neurotic every time she didn't understand his mood. Josh was a very complex man, which was good as well as occasionally frustrating. Being lovers required no great effort on her part—what after all could be simpler than pleasing Josh and being pleased by Josh? The intimacy of being genuine friends seemed a much harder aim to achieve, and she wanted—*really* wanted to be his friend, not just his lover. She wanted the sort of friendship that would endure. Right now, though, she was concentrating on the important things—things such as he'd said he was falling in love with her. That was what mattered.

'I'll pick you up around eleven.'

The hard kiss he dropped on her unsuspecting lips was not at all indifferent, which proved conclusively to her how justified her optimism had been.

Flora only risked immersion ankle-deep in the sea and even that gave a nasty jolt to her nervous system—it was like ice. She worked up a healthy glow though, chasing an incredibly active three-year-old around the large beach.

which was empty but for the odd person or two walking dogs or jogging.

'Enjoying yourself?' Josh caught her by the arm and swung her around. His eyes skimmed warmly over her lightly flushed features. 'Or are you lusting after Caribbean sunshine?'

The only lusting she was doing was after him. 'Caribbean sunshine has its place, but just now I wouldn't exchange five-star service and rum punches for being right here with you and Liam.' Her cheeks grew self-consciously pink as his scrutiny intensified. Her shoulders lifted. 'Call me strange…'

'I'd prefer to call you—oh, God, no!' He broke off and groaned at the crucial moment. It seemed she was never destined to hear what he would have called her—he was looking past her towards a diminutive figure heading very decisively in the direction of the water's edge. 'You can't take your eyes off him for a second!' he yelled, hitting the sand at a run.

Flora couldn't keep up with his long-legged pace and by the time she'd reached the strip of hard wet sand, rippled where the tide had recently retreated, Josh and son had emerged from the water.

'He just flung himself in head first,' Josh informed her, torn between laughter and horror as he struggled to contain his son who seemed determined to repeat his experience. 'He hasn't got an ounce of fear in his body,' he observed in a distracted, but proud parent manner.

With Flora laughter won out; she chuckled out loud as the two came nearer. Josh's capable hands were full of struggling toddler as he impatiently puffed an errant hank of dark hair from his eyes.

'I'm glad you find it funny,' he observed with a disgruntled snort.

'Well, you do look funny,' she informed him honestly. 'And there was no harm done.'

'Thanks.' He glanced down at his moleskin trousers which were wet as far as mid-thigh. 'As for no harm done, I doubt very much if these will ever be the same again.'

'And I'm sure you'll really lose sleep over that.' Josh didn't strike her as the sort of man who listed sartorial elegance very high amongst his priorities, but then he, lucky chap, looked better in the most commonplace comfy casuals than most guys did in the most up-to-date designer gear. 'I strongly suspect that you have slobby tendencies.'

'It's starting already, is it?' He raised his eyes heavenwards in appeal. 'I ask you, is it a sin for man to put comfort before fashion?'

'What?' She took off her fleece jacket and tucked it firmly around the drenched youngster who was already looking a bit blue around the edges. The fresh wind made her shiver as it penetrated the thin shirt she wore underneath.

'You want to make me over, make me presentable for all your smart, slick city friends,' he teased reproachfully.

'Huh, it would take more than a suit to do that.' Chin resting on her fingertips, she gave him a thoughtful onceover. 'Yes, *much* more than a suit.'

Actually she could think of several women of her acquaintance who would drool openly if they saw him at this precise second, with his dark wind-whipped hair all deliciously mussy and those trousers clinging like a second skin to the muscular outline of those thighs. On second thoughts, not some...all!

Josh gave a lopsided grin. 'Cow,' he observed affectionately as they puffed their way up the beach.

His puffs were due to the fact his burden didn't want to be rescued, whereas Flora suspected hers had more to do with her lack of fitness. She thought regretfully of the expensive gym she'd joined and never actually attended above twice. I'll turn over a new leaf, she promised herself.

'I think we'll just have to play the arty card. Genius is the dispensation for a lot of things, including not shaving...but then I'm sure you already know that.'

Josh placed his unhappy son on the soft sand. He lifted a hand to his square jaw. 'Actually I did shave; by mid-afternoon it's always back.'

'I'd noticed.' Her stomach muscles did a quick butterfly hiccough as she recalled the abrasive quality of his skin against her own when he'd kissed her.

'Perhaps I should grow a beard...?' he suggested innocently.

Her eyes widened in mock alarm. 'Perhaps you shouldn't, not if you want to carry on being seen with me,' she responded firmly. A girl had to draw the line somewhere.

'So shallow,' he sighed.

'I'm just not crazy about unrestrained facial hair. How would you feel if I stopped waxing my legs?'

'Severely lacerated?' he speculated.

'You're hilarious!' She was pretty sure he was disputing the point out of sheer bloody-minded cussedness; fortunately Liam distracted him before the argument got even more silly.

'Swim!' the child insisted loudly. His soft baby chin developed a distinctive stubborn tilt as he glared disapprovingly at his father.

'Not now, Liam.'

'Swim...swim!' Lying down on the sand, he began to drum his heels in time with his escalating demands.

Ignoring the synchronised display with the air of a man who'd seen it all before, Josh scooped up the rigid child and strode back towards the four-wheel drive that was parked on a gravel area just above the banks of long spiky grass that fringed the beach.

'Ordering groceries on the net is a godsend when your kid is going through the tantrum stage. Mind you, I'm assuming it's a stage. Occasionally I have this vision of a strapping fifteen-year-old lying down on the floor and screaming until he's blue in the face when I tell him to do his homework.'

'Heavens, no,' she soothed, 'teenagers have *much* more effective ways of punishing cruel parents.'

'I can hardly wait! What a little ray of comfort you are, Flora,' he breathed drily.

He placed Liam in the back seat before sliding in himself.

'Could you get the spare change of clothes from the back?'

Between the two of them they managed to strip the wet clothes off the unco-operative, already chilled child and replace them with a dry warm set.

'Pity I didn't think to pack a spare set for myself.'

'Great pity,' she agreed, letting her limpid blue gaze rest on his distracted face. 'I wouldn't mind undressing you in the back seat.'

Josh abruptly stopped what he was doing. 'I can't say the idea doesn't interest me.' The pair of sodden dungarees in his hand dripped unnoticed onto the leather upholstery as he allowed himself to match a mental image to her words.

'Lucky for you it does,' she retorted bluntly, 'or I'd be out this door.'

'Only if I let you go,' he rasped, his eyes darkening as they came to rest on her face.

This confident announcement made her pulses quicken

Flora swallowed past the sudden constriction in her throat. She still couldn't get her head around the swiftness with which they could be transported in a heartbeat from a relatively calm, companionable atmosphere into a sexually charged maelstrom that left her panting—quite literally panting, as it happened just now! She made a conscious effort to still the agitated rise and fall of her tingling bosom.

'How do you think you'd stop me?'

'Oh, I reckon I'd think of something.'

She snorted without conviction and dragged her eyes from his smouldering scrutiny. 'Shouldn't we get Liam back? It's getting late.'

'Coward,' Josh taunted gently, but his glance followed her affectionate scrutiny in the direction of the rosy-cheeked and now sleepily placid toddler in his arms.

As Flora watched Liam's head flopped sleepily onto his father's chest. Stubbornly he jerked upright once more.

'He can hardly keep his eyes open.'

'But he'll try,' Josh predicted, strapping his son into a child restraint. 'He's as obstinate as a mule. Sometimes the only way I could get him to sleep when he was tiny was popping him into the car and driving around until he went off.' He gave a shudder.

'I can't imagine where he gets that from…' Genetics had a lot to answer for. The thought pushed home hard the nagging knowledge that she'd never have the opportunity to see what their combined genes might produce. She tried to ignore the bleak little cloud that settled around her heart. Determined not to allow anything to spoil what had been a perfect day, she vowed to concentrate on what she *did* have, not what she didn't!

'Is this brother of yours stubborn too?' Flora wondered

curiously as they both climbed into the front seat, leaving Liam to fight sleep behind them.

'Jake…? Depends on who you ask. When he and Nia fight the sparks really fly.'

'But they have a good relationship…?' she wondered with a frown. 'I mean, they're happy?'

'Are your eyes blue?' he responded drily. 'I've been thinking I've outstayed my welcome with Jake's in-laws…' The expectant silence lengthened as did Flora's tension.

It wasn't so much what he'd said but the way he'd said it that convinced her he was leading up to something. It's been nice knowing you, but…? She gave a tiny angry shake of her head. When did I get so damned insecure? she wondered. Being in love was like a white-knuckle ride and she'd never been able to see the attraction of deliberately exposing yourself to that sort of gut-grabbing fear.

'It doesn't seem that way to me,' she retorted lightly. 'They seem to treat you like a favourite son.' Continued speculation about what was coming next made her feel deeply uneasy.

She knew that inevitably they'd both have to return to their proper lives—understanding partners aside, her own sabbatical couldn't be extended indefinitely. In some ways what they had together had more in common with a holiday romance. Would they find their lifestyles were totally incompatible back in the real world? Was he already having second thoughts? She tried to let the tension seep away, but her spine remained stubbornly rigid as she waited for him to speak.

'That's on account of me being Jake's brother and since he—with a bit of help from Nia—has turned them into grandparents he can do no wrong.'

'I think it's possible they like you, for some inexplicable

reason, for being you,' she snapped, irritated by his false modesty, and worried—despite a brisk internal pep talk—about where this was all leading.

'Like you do?'

'No,' she denied, shaking her head vehemently. 'Not at all like I do!'

Josh thought about that as he pulled the car to one side to enable a wide farm truck to pass. He shot a swift searching sideways glance towards her clear-cut profile as he pulled out of a passing place on the narrow single track road he was negotiating.

'Meaning you don't like me…?'

As if he didn't know…! Cheeks flushed, she threw him an exasperated, hot-cheeked glare. 'I think we've established I like you far too much for my own good—when, that is, I don't want to strangle you!'

Josh's smug expression suggested he was well satisfied by her murderous intent. 'I've decided to put my cottage—the one Liam and I live in—on the market,' he announced abruptly.

'Oh!' This was the last thing she'd been expecting.

'When Bridie and I bought it we hadn't the faintest idea how much space kids need.' Practicality had actually played no part during the heart-searching that had gone into this symbolic gesture.

Flora hadn't missed the symbolism. 'The place must hold a lot of memories…'

He didn't bother denying her quiet observation. 'Good and bad. I've known it was time to move on for some time now but it never seemed to be the right moment.'

Flora wondered if wishful thinking was guiding her hand as she excitedly filled in the blanks left by his amazing announcement—sometimes her optimism got out of hand. 'But it is now?' she prompted carefully.

'I'll never forget Bridie, but I know now that I'm not rejecting her and what we had by getting on with my life. I think the time has come to look towards the future. Hell, I can't believe I just said anything so amazingly trite!'

'If it's any comfort, I can't believe I'm crying over something so amazingly trite.' She sniffed gruffly. Failing to discover a tissue on her person, she rubbed the back of her hand across her damp face.

'What I'm trying to say is, I'd like you to be part of that future.'

'With the proviso I don't break the rules and start getting broody.' She shot a sneaky glance in Josh's direction. He was looking pretty remote all of a sudden—*and I'm surprised*...! Why the hell did I have to go wreck the moment?

'I'm sorry, Flora, but that's the way I feel.'

It wasn't as if she wanted a baby this precise second, it just made no sense to her to rule out the possibility so totally. His intransigence made her want to scream, stamp her feet and do all manner of immature emotional things, but she didn't.

'Just checking.'

'I've been doing some checking myself on houses. Perhaps at some point in the future when you're comfortable with the idea...'

'Josh, are you asking me to move in with you?'

'No...at least, not immediately. You have to appreciate that I come as a package deal...'

Flora twisted around in her seat and smiled softly at the sleeping figure of the other half of the package. 'That hadn't escaped my notice.'

'I think that's something you should think about very carefully.'

'What is it with you?' she demanded hotly. 'You say

something nice and in the next breath you try and snatch it back. I'm falling in love with you, Flora, but if you want babies look for another man. Move in with me, Flora, but you lack the maturity to accept my child!' Her impassioned voice stilled, but only long enough for her to catch her breath. 'It's as if you're looking for some reason why this won't work,' she accused, finding there was a definite pattern to his behaviour.

'Maybe,' he suggested heavily, 'I don't think I'm good enough for you.'

'Pooh!' she mocked. 'Humble really doesn't suit you—you're arrogant down to your little cotton socks. You're well aware of your own worth on the open market.'

'It does a man's ego no end of good to be discussed like a piece of meat.'

'Don't go all politically correct and prissy on me, Josh, you know exactly what I mean. Talk about mixed signals!' she grumbled. 'Small wonder I'm confused. Let's get this straight—do you actually love me and do you want me to live with you?'

'Wow! I bet you have the opposing counsel trembling when they have to come up against you in court!'

'Don't try and sweet-talk me, Josh.'

'Fine!' he flung in a goaded voice. 'Yes, on both counts. Suddenly you don't seem to have so much to say for yourself.'

'Yes, on both counts,' she breathed shakily. 'Will that do?'

'It'll do just fine.'

CHAPTER SEVEN

'I DON'T know exactly where you'll find him, Flora, but I think he said he was heading towards the lake. If you take the footpath through the woods it takes you right up to the west side of the lake, but you'll need a coat.'

Megan Jones touched Flora's arm and felt the coolness of her firm young skin through the thin cotton shirt she wore. 'Have you walked over here like this?' she exclaimed disapprovingly. 'You'll catch your death,' she admonished. 'Come along through to the fire,' she urged the young woman who just stared back at her blankly, but did as she was bid.

'There, take a seat by the fire.' She wondered worriedly where the animated creature Josh had described to her had gone. 'I offered to keep an eye on Liam for an hour or two,' she explained as Flora sat down in the chintzy over-stuffed armchair. Megan's motherly eyes crinkled with pleasure as she smiled towards the small figure seated at the low table, his expression intense as he drew a childish scrawl with his jumbo-sized crayon in a dog-eared colouring book.

The child looked up and smiled his crooked little smile of spontaneous pleasure when he saw Flora. The uncanny similarity to his father smote her to the heart.

'He's a good boy, aren't you, *cariad*?' Megan clucked warmly. She looked to Flora for confirmation of this and her smile faded. The girl didn't turn her head quickly enough to hide the sparkle of tears. 'Is something wrong, my dear?'

Flora bit her lip. 'Please don't be nice to me,' she begged shakily, 'or I'll start blubbing.'

'Do you want to talk about it?'

Flora shook her head. 'Did you know Liam's mother?' she asked suddenly. The toddler had come over to solemnly give her a page he'd carefully ripped from his colouring pad. 'Thank you, darling,' she responded gruffly, kissing the top of his dark curly head.

'No, I didn't know her. Nia didn't meet Jake until several months after she'd died...tragic...' She gave a sigh. 'But life goes on,' she pointed out briskly. 'I don't think you have any need to worry about ghosts, my dear. I've never seen Josh look so happy, not that he's ever been one to go about with a gloomy face.'

Not worry about ghosts! Considering the anonymous much-read letter crammed at that moment into her pocket, the irony of that comment brought an hysterical bubble of laughter to her aching throat.

'I think I'd better go,' she rasped huskily.

With concern Megan searched the young woman's pale face before reluctantly nodding. 'If you say so.' She sighed. 'But if you're following Josh up to the lake you'll need something warm.'

Follow...it made her sound like some meek, mild little helpmate. Does everyone who's seen us together assume I'll follow Josh wherever he goes? Flora wondered angrily as she slid her arms into the overlong sleeves of a fleece-lined cagoule. It was time to disillusion the world in general and Josh in particular!

Josh lay down his sketch-pad as he saw Flora's slim figure approaching. The welcoming smile faded from his lips as she got closer and he was able to appreciate that he'd never actually seen her angry before—not *properly* angry. He was seeing it now, though—oh, boy, was he seeing it! Warily he watched as her briskly swinging arms punched the air energetically as her long, shapely legs swept her closer.

If she'd been walking across hot coals he seriously doubted she'd have registered it. He automatically rose to his feet and brushed the dust from the dry stone wall off his trousers. Wouldn't Mum be pleased if she knew her early lectures about old-fashioned courtesy had made a lasting impact on her sons? That icy fist that had grabbed his guts suggested to him it was going to take more than nice manners to get him out of this one.

Flora came to a halt just in front of him. She was burdened by the awful things in the letter, but seeing him still did the same things to her it always had done. It couldn't all be a lie...could it?

'Well, is it true?' The trembling hand she thrust aggressively under his nose held the crumbled sheets of a letter she'd received that morning. A few scraps of paper remained in her tightly clenched fingers when he took the letter from her. 'Was your wife my dad's patient?' she asked woodenly. 'Did you follow me from London?'

Josh's eyes flickered across her face briefly before his eyes returned to the typed sheets of paper in his hands.

It was the all important response she'd been watching for. That look said it all. At that moment the tiny flicker of hope inside her died. She'd known it made no sense for anyone to make up lies like the allegations in the anonymous letter. Despite this, part of her still hadn't believed it wasn't true—not until now. All the way over to confront him she'd kept telling herself over and over again that she'd have *known* if he was pretending.

'I see.' Actually she didn't see how anyone could be so calculatingly cruel. 'You just forgot to mention it.'

Eyes filled with pain, she watched Josh skim over the

contents; his dark, lean features were drawn tight across his impossibly perfect bones. Angry, yes, he was angry, but not because he was reading meddlesome malice, he was angry because it was true and she'd found out before he wanted her to—when, she wondered bleakly, had he planned the finale?

'I didn't want to hurt you, Flora.' He lifted his dark head, his expression was sombre and his eyes shone with passionate sincerity.

The sincerity really got to her, she'd had enough of his so-called sincerity to last a lifetime—probably longer!

'I thought that was exactly what you wanted to do!' she sneered scornfully. 'Oh, I appreciate my feelings were almost incidental to your plan, it was Dad you wanted to get at through me. How inconsiderate of him to die and rob you of your ultimate revenge!' She bit back a sob and flinched back, her expression registering loathing, as he reached out for her. Had he opened the champagne to celebrate whilst she'd been weeping at her father's funeral? 'I suppose you're selling your story to the tabloids in order to spare me pain.'

Gritting his teeth, Josh lowered his rejected hand awkwardly. 'I'm not selling anything!' Actually he'd sell his soul to banish the hurt in her eyes. 'You can't actually believe I'd do that.'

'Don't you think it's a bit late to play the integrity card?' she asked him bitterly.

'Do you really think I'm the sort of man who'd deliberately court that sort of notoriety?'

'So maybe that part isn't true!' she conceded carelessly. 'If only a *fraction* of the stuff in that letter is half true it's enough to condemn you.'

'Why stop with condemnation?' The revulsion in her eyes cut him like a knife. 'Why not have a bash at sentencing too…?' Her eyes suggested life wouldn't be long enough to satisfy her sense of outrage.

'Not very long ago there were a lot of things I didn't believe you'd do, but now I know different.' She saw Josh's facial muscles tighten as he heard the crisp, cold conviction in her voice. She felt spitefully pleased. The very least he could feel under the circumstances was uncomfortable—it was the sort of pleasure that made her feel sick to the stomach.

'Actually I'd have staked my life on it.' That of course was what hurt most: she'd never trusted anyone as much as she'd grown to trust this man and all the time all he'd wanted was revenge; he'd wanted to hurt her. Objectively she watched as the colour fled his face leaving his vital flesh tinged with an unhealthy grey tone. 'Now…' her hunched shoulders lifted and she gave a bitter smile '…I think maybe there isn't much you *wouldn't* do.'

'Ask yourself why anyone would write that stuff,' he pleaded urgently.

There may not be a signature but he had no doubt as to who was responsible. To think he'd imagined he had that rat of a journalist tied up every which way—this was what you got for being a complacent idiot. This was what you got for imagining she would never find out—he'd been afraid of losing her if he told her the truth and look what was happening now. His jaw tightened with determination—he *couldn't* lose her!

'I'm not an idiot.'

She gave a bitter laugh and Josh winced. If keeping quiet had been intended to spare her pain he'd seriously miscalculated.

'Under the circumstances I think you'd better cancel that claim,' she continued stiffly. 'However, even I can see the motives behind this letter were probably one hundred per cent malicious.'

'There's no *probably* about it,' he gritted.

'But that's irrelevant. It doesn't alter the facts, fact number one being you followed me with the deliberate intention of making me fall in love with you. A simple little plan, but then they're often the best, I'm told.' Her scornful blue glare raked him, daring him to deny it. Even he didn't have the bare-faced gall to do that. Though she was sure that, being the rat person he was, he'd try and wriggle out of it somehow.

'Originally I intended to get to your father through you, yes, it's true.'

'How noble of you to come clean,' she trilled caustically. 'You know the person who came up with that old chestnut, better late than never? He was an idiot.' She couldn't imagine feeling better ever again!

A rush of dark colour seeped under his pallor as he forced himself to endure the scorn in her beautiful eyes. 'That was before...before I fell in love with you, Flora.' It sounded lame even to his own ears.

She squeezed her eyes tight shut and shook her head vigorously from side to side. 'Don't you *dare* say that,' she hissed. It made her feel physically sick when she thought of him cold-bloodedly conniving—ironically it hadn't taken much conniving! He probably hadn't been able to believe his luck; she'd been a pushover! 'I seriously doubt you know what the word means,' she informed him with icy distaste.

'Yes, I do, Flora.' If she hadn't known he was lying through his straight white teeth she might have been swayed by the sheer force of conviction in his impassioned voice. 'Because I've been immensely privileged to feel this way twice in my life.' One corner of his firm mouth quivered. 'Something I didn't think could happen. I tried to hate you, despise you, told myself that you were a cold, icy woman who didn't have a heart to break. Told myself that if the system wouldn't punish your father...'

'My father was punishing himself enough to please even you!'

The colour flooded back into his face as she flung the bitter recrimination at him. 'I tried to tell myself I was justified in using you. I even believed it for a while. But the more I saw of you, the more I knew how impossible it was to hate you.'

Even cocooned in her own private hell the depth of his sincerity shook Flora. 'If you want lessons in hate,' she told him grimly, 'look no further...'

'When something bad happens in your life—something you have no control over it's...' He swallowed and drew a sharp, ragged breath. 'You feel impotent and you want to blame someone. The court case with your father meant I finally had someone to blame...'

'My father may have made a mess of his own life, but he never harmed any of his patients. Every single investigation vindicated him on that count!'

'I know that, Flora, I just couldn't let myself believe it. I *needed* to blame someone. I wanted justice for Bridie. It was crazy...irrational, but, ask anyone, I've never been noted for my logic...'

'I can understand you needed a scapegoat, even appreciate the logic behind your sick revenge. But what I don't understand is why you carried on with it after Dad died?' A dry sob caught in her throat. 'Why did you carry on pretending? Why didn't you just go away and leave me be?' Her voice deepened and shook with outraged anguish. Why did you make me love you? she wanted to scream.

Josh shook his head and ground his teeth in frustration.

It was hellish hard wanting with every ounce of his being to hold her and knowing full well she'd reject any move he made to comfort her.

'I couldn't stop loving you if I tried, Flora, and I did try, I tried bloody hard!' he admitted loudly.

'And you're proud of it,' she suggested in a choked, disgusted voice.

'Proud! I'm ashamed. If you want to know, the thought of sitting down to share a cosy family meal with your father brought me out in a cold sweat...being rational is one thing, that is quite another. I had no idea how I'd react, but he was your father and I was prepared to give it a shot.'

'I don't believe you. If your feelings for me had been even halfway genuine you'd have told me the truth.'

'Do you think I didn't try...?' he asked her hoarsely. He raked his hair with an unsteady hand. 'I started to I don't know how many times. The longer I left it, the harder it got, and then your father died and it somehow didn't seem so urgent any more. Any obstacles between us were gone.'

'He may have been an obstacle to you, Josh...' her voice shook and the tears that had welled in her eyes began to seep out '...but he was my dad.'

'I didn't see how the truth was going to do anyone any good, and I was right, wasn't I?' He bared his teeth in a savage snarl. 'If the truth be known, I couldn't bear the idea of you looking at me like...' he lifted his head, his eyes were burning '...looking at me like this,' he finished bleakly. 'As if you hate me.'

'I do hate you!' she flashed back.

'No, you don't!' he responded with equal vehemence. 'You love me, you need me as much as I need you, and if you turn your back on what we have a day will never go by that you don't regret it. There'll be a gap in your life where I should be! You won't be able to stand it, I know, I tried to turn my back on you and how I felt…do you remember?'

Flora unwillingly recalled the time when he'd seemed to inexplicably reject her; she'd thought that was painful…only she hadn't known at the time how bad pain could get!

She was deeply shaken by the stark images his impassioned words conjured up, but she forced herself to respond with scornful indifference. 'Very clever of you to keep me dangling. Your problem is, Josh, that you're in danger of confusing real life with art. The critics may have put you on a godlike plain, but in real life you're just a man. There are thousands…millions just like you out there.' She could feel the wild tattoo of her heartbeat as it thudded against her ribcage.

'I'm the only one for you, though,' he persisted with stubborn arrogance.

What if he was right? Her mocking laughter had more to do with protective instincts than a response to any humour she'd discovered in the grim situation.

'Even when I didn't know what a manipulative, cold-blooded snake you were the situation was far from perfect. A man with a ready-made family is rarely a girl's first choice,' she told him casually. 'You're not the only one who had qualms to overcome.' She thought about little Liam and his lovely smile and she almost broke down and retracted the hurtful words. Pride held her dumb.

He looked white-faced and almost haggard as their eyes clashed and locked. It was only stubbornness that stopped her breaking that contact. She'd selected those words to cause him maximum pain; wasn't it good she'd done just that? A warm tide of triumph didn't wash over her; instead the sense of joyless desolation intensified.

A nerve in his lean cheek jumped as he slowly shook his head, rejecting what she'd said.

'Besides, I want a man who can give me children of my own, and you can't or won't do that, will you, Josh?' she reminded him spitefully.

He visibly flinched as her accusation hit home. 'No, I wouldn't do that,' he confirmed quietly. His face was as hard and still as rock.

'Flora!' he called as she turned to go.

She didn't want to turn back but something in his voice overrode her will and made her limbs respond independently of her brain. On autopilot she turned around.

'I don't believe you.'

She lifted her shoulders. 'Which part, Josh? No, on second thoughts don't tell me, I'm really not that interested in anything you have to say.'

'Whew!' Sam Taverner was only half joking when he wiped invisible sweat off his brow as he walked into Flora's office. 'Mission accomplished,' he said, plonking himself down on the edge of her desk. 'How come,' he wondered out loud, 'your desk is always so neat and mine looks like a bomb site—after the bomb's gone off?'

Flora gave a smile; it was a weak distracted affair. 'It's not complicated, you're a slob. A brilliant slob,' she conceded. Fingers tightly laced, she rubbed them against the sober material of her skirt. 'What did you say?'

'I said that you were in Hong Kong and you wouldn't be back for weeks. I thought it best to be vague...'

'Hong Kong! Why Hong Kong?' she wondered.

He shrugged. 'First thing that came into my mind,' he confessed. 'My brother-in-law is always shooting off to

Hong Kong, lucky dog, it's got a nice ring to it. Besides, if lover boy decides to hotfoot it after you it'll keep him out of your hair a lot longer than if I'd said, say... Cheltenham.'

As usual Sam's actions did have a weird sort of logic. 'Yes, well.' Flora couldn't hide her impatience with this rambling explanation. 'The point is, did he believe you?' she asked tensely.

'Well, not at first, but my days in amateur dramatics came into their own. I gave the performance of my life, if you must know,' he told her modestly.

A wave of curious anticlimax hit Flora. 'And he went away?'

'You can thank me later,' her partner responded drily.

Flora gathered her addled wits and blushed. 'Sorry, Sam, it's really good of you.'

'If you ask me, Flora, my little love, you should get an injunction out on this guy.' For once her partner dropped his amiable fool persona completely. 'I mean, he could be dangerous.'

'No, he's not.'

Her partner's gingery eyebrows shot up at the note of complete conviction in her voice. 'I don't see how you can be so sure.'

'I'm sure, that's all,' she snapped. 'Josh is harmless.' Now there was a novel notion. She'd be safer if a tiger were on her trail. 'And he's not stalking me, he's just...'

'Turning up uninvited at your flat and place of work.' Sam gave a disparaging snort. 'I always thought you were a pretty good judge of character, but this! *Harmless* is not the first adjective that springs to mind to describe your boyfriend.' It made his blood run cold just to think of what would have happened if the Hong Kong story hadn't worked. It was at times like that he wished he'd persevered with the judo lessons.

'He isn't my boyfriend.'

'Why should you feel obliged to move out of your own flat? Not that we're not delighted to have you stay with us,' he reassured her robustly.

'Because I'm not into confrontation, that's why.' Also because, although she still hadn't forgiven him and never would, now her brain wasn't fogged by the fury of betrayal she had recognised several pivotal moments when he might just have been about to tell her the truth as he claimed.

The point was he hadn't and *almost* didn't make what he had done any the less unforgivable, but how long would she remember that if he started telling her he loved her—he needed her? Or, more likely, how much she loved and needed him, she mused, recalling the arrogance of his parting shots.

'You hate confrontation…since when?' Her partner didn't bother hiding his scepticism.

'Since I last confronted Josh.'

Having met the guy, Sam found he could identify with her little shudder. 'Then you haven't actually seen him since you had your…bust-up…?'

Flora smiled. She had no intention of elaborating on what had happened, and she knew that Sam, who would be acting under strict instructions from his wife Lyn to extract all the juicy details, was agog to hear more. She'd have some news for them soon that would be shocking enough to satisfy even the scandal-hungry Lyn. She still felt pretty shocked herself. What else do I feel…?

'No and I don't want to.'

This determination not to reply to a single telephone message he'd left, or answer the doorbell when he leaned on it and stayed there, had nothing whatever to do with the fact she missed him like hell, she told herself. Who am I kidding? Push come to shove, she didn't trust herself to remember how badly he'd betrayed her if she saw him again.

For her own peace of mind Flora forced herself to identify individually each evil thing he'd done one more time. She made the worrying discovery that his sins, which had seemed very obvious, had started to get indistinct and jumbled in her head. Even if she believed he loved her that didn't cancel out what he'd intended to do, she told herself severely. She couldn't afford to start going soft…!

'Well, promise me you'll think about the injunction. I mean, if he was after me I wouldn't sleep a wink.'

My skills with the old make-up palette must be a lot better than I thought if Sam imagines I'm sleeping at all.

'Rest easy, Sam, I don't think you're his type.'

'You obviously are.'

Giving a very un-Flora blush, his partner averted her eyes and started fiddling with a sheaf of papers.

'What shall I tell Lyn? Are you going to come to the theatre tonight?'

Flora sighed; helpful friends were a pain sometimes. A person couldn't even be miserable in peace. 'You know I don't like blind dates, Sam.'

'This is a blind *double* date.'

'And that makes a difference?'

'All the difference in the world. If you can't stand this guy and things get sticky, Lyn and I will be there to make the whole thing less painfully embarrassing.'

'With sales patter like that how can a girl refuse?'

'Excellent!'

'That wasn't a yes,' she protested weakly, but Sam wasn't listening to her. She watched with amused resentment as her partner, displaying a bad case of selective deafness, made a hurried exit whistling loudly and tune-lessly to himself.

'Well, what do you think of him?' Lyn whispered during the interval. Her voice was muffled as she reapplied her lipstick.

'I preferred his last play.'

'I didn't mean the play, as you well know! I've got some blusher if you want some,' she added, regarding Flora's pale cheeks with a critical frown. 'Your lippie has worn off,' she added helpfully.

'No, thanks.' Flora waved aside the offer. 'And I'm not wearing any lipstick.'

Lyn looked scandalised by this casual confession, but maintained a tactful silence on the subject. 'What do you think of Tim?'

'He's very nice.' There was nothing to object to in the man; likewise there was nothing to get worked up about, nothing to set him apart from the common throng, not like… She pulled her thoughts up short of the precipice.

Lyn gave a smug little smile. 'I knew you'd like him,' she crowed triumphantly. 'I mean, he's *so* perfect I did worry that there might be something a bit…I mean, un-married men his age with no actual deformities are pretty rare.'

'You mean they're usually gay.'

Lyn sighed and nodded. 'Such a waste,' she bemoaned. 'But Tim's not, I made enquiries.'

Flora couldn't help laughing. 'You really are impossi-ble.'

'I'm not the impossible one. Look at you…*beautiful*!' she announced indignantly. 'You should be up to your armpits in men. I know you scare them off deliberately.

For God's sake be *nice* to Tim, and don't act too clever,' she added as an urgent afterthought.

'You know something, Lyn, you're probably on the hit list of every card-carrying feminist in town.'

Flora, under Lyn's approving eye, did smile; she didn't always know what she was smiling at as her attention showed a marked tendency to drift around the crowded foyer.

Her glass of wine was halfway to her lips when she saw him. The glimpse was only brief, before the back of a large man's head almost immediately blocked her view, but it was enough to send her nervous system into instant shock.

'Excuse me.'

She was oblivious to the startled looks of her companions who automatically craned their necks to see what she was looking at as she firmly shoved the large man out of her way. Yes, it was him, there was no mistaking the angle of that jaw. God, but he looked gorgeous in a formal dark tie.

'Look at that hair!' Lyn breathed with an envious sigh as the voluptuous redhead draped herself all over Josh.

'Look at that body!' Nice Tim breathed with a covetous sigh.

Flora *was* looking; she was looking at the way Josh pressed the redhead's hand to his lips when she ran her fingers caressingly over his cheek. She could see the way they were visually eating each other up—it was almost indecent in a public place.

She didn't actually hear Sam's anguished plea of 'Don't do this, Flora,' as she wove her way sinuously through the seething mass of packed bodies.

They didn't even notice her! She stood there with only the width of the table separating her from the couple who seemed far too engrossed in each other to notice if the ceiling fell in. Josh's dark head moved towards the red-head's ear. He said something that brought a becoming flush to her lips and a low, husky chuckle to her white throat.

It was the sexy laugh that really tipped the balance and sent Flora right over the edge. Without being sure of what she expected to happen, she cleared her throat very noisily. They both looked at her, but Flora had eyes only for Josh.

She couldn't believe it when his eyes swept over her with an expression of polite—even vaguely irritated—indifference. He didn't even have the decency to look embarrassed!

This had been the same man who had been pursuing her with passionate avowals of enduring love! Now he was acting as though he didn't know her. A small choking sound of outrage emerged from her dry throat. The irony was she had been halfway to believing him!

'It might not matter to you,' she said in a shaking voice to the redhead, 'but this man you're with is a shallow, faithless, lying rat.'

Josh began to get to his feet, an expression of cautious alarm on his drop-dead gorgeous features. 'I think there's been…'

'A mistake?' she drawled, her eyes snapping. 'Tell me about it.' So saying, she flung the contents of her glass straight in his face.

She had a brief glimpse of his white-faced shock as she placed the empty glass in his hand before she turned on her heel and, head held high, stalked out of the now silent foyer.

'Tissue…?'

Jake Prentice took the proffered tissue from his wife and sat slowly down. 'I've never seen her before in my life…I swear!' he told her earnestly.

'Well, you would say that, wouldn't you, my darling?'

'Listen, Nia…you're having me on, aren't you?' he said, heaving a sigh of relief. 'You do believe that she was a mad woman.'

His wife gave a serene smile. 'Lucky for you, stud, I do believe you, considering she's a *pregnant* mad woman.'

'Pregnant!' The way Jake recalled it the blonde had had a very trim midriff, but he didn't question his wife's assessment. He'd learnt that Nia seemed to know this sort of thing. She had either received an extra large dose of female intuition or she had a bit of witch in her—he suspected the latter.

His eyes opened wide. 'Josh…?'

'Sometimes, Jake, you're very slow,' she mused with a patronising little sniff.

'Sometimes, Nia, you like it when I'm very slow.' Oblivious to the fact they were the cynosure of all eyes and numerous low-voiced conversations since the blonde had departed, Jake kissed his wife very thoroughly.

CHAPTER EIGHT

JOSH perched on the edge of one of the many packing cases stacked in the room and watched with a resigned expression as his twin produced an outsized bar of chocolate from his pocket for Liam. Predictably his son went into transports of chocoholic delight.

'Ever heard of a balanced diet?' he enquired as Liam threw a fit—the noisy variety—because his mean dad had exerted a bit of parental control and confiscated the biggest portion of the foil-wrapped bar.

'That stuff's a parent's province, I'm his uncle... Have you noticed how little Liam here is one of the few people who can always tell us apart?'

'That's because he can spot a soft touch a mile off, and I'll remind you about that uncle thing when the twins have got teeth to rot,' Josh warned darkly. 'How are the twins?' he added, enquiring after his six-month-old nieces.

'Blooming, and brilliant. Why, little Angharad...'

Josh knew from experience that the soppy smile on his brother's face usually preceded a long rambling discussion concerning the perfection of his small daughters. In common with a lot of new fathers, Jake was under the impression that everybody else was as fascinated as him with every minute detail concerning his offspring. Josh was a doting uncle but there were limits to his devotion...

'It's good of Nia to offer to have Liam today,' he cut in quickly.

'Least we could do, considering moving house is supposed to be right up there with the most stressful things in

149

life…which would account for the fact you look like hell,' his brother mused slyly. 'It *would* account for that, wouldn't it, Josh?'

It might, after all, have been less tiresome to let Jake ramble on about the babies. Josh resisted the urge to tell his brother to mind his own damned business—he knew from experience it wouldn't do any good—and contented himself with grunting unhelpfully.

'Where's Nia?'

'In the car, she didn't want to ruin a male bonding moment. And, before I forget, I've got something for you.'

The casual mention of male bonding brought a suspicious frown to Josh's brow as he looked down at the piece of paper his twin had pressed into his hand. 'What's this?'

'As you see, a bill.'

Josh turned the innocuous scrap of paper over. 'Your dry-cleaning bill?' Bizarre even by his twin's standards.

Jake nodded in confirmation. 'Wine, the shirt was a write-off…' he elaborated sadly.

'I'm sure you're going to get to the punchline eventually. The thing is…' Josh glanced pointedly at his watch '…I don't have all day.'

'Save the sarcasm. I would have sent it to the lady, but I don't know her address—I expect you do…'

'Will you stop being so enigmatic?'

'The lady in question was tall, blonde, attractive—*very* attractive actually,' Jake conceded thoughtfully. 'Ring any bells?' He saw his brother stiffen. 'But if Nia asks, I didn't notice the attractive part.'

'Where…? When…?' Taking a deep breath, Josh regained control—at least partially. 'What did she do?' he asked tensely. Wine over a dinner jacket implied clumsiness or a defensive act of sorts—Flora didn't have a clumsy bone in her body. 'What did you do to her?'

Jake held up his hands. 'Hold up, boy, you're looking at the victim of the piece. Does *she* have a name? We didn't really reach the polite exchange stage.'

'Flora.'

Jake did his wide nod thing, the one that always irritated Josh. 'Nia thought it must be…'

'How did Nia…?' Josh exploded. 'Ah, Megan,' he grunted in a disgruntled tone. Was the concept of a private life totally alien to his family?

'Your Flora verbally abused me and then chucked her wine over me…it was red, actually,' Jake elaborated with a fastidious shudder. 'All this, I might add, was done in front of my wife, not to mention a captive audience of what felt like thousands.'

For a split second the grimness of Josh's expression was lightened by a light of unholy glee as he imagined how much his twin would have hated this public humiliation, although admittedly Jake had lightened up considerably since his marriage. His amusement speedily faded when it hit home that the attack and the humiliation had been meant for him!

My Flora, she is *my* Flora—the inescapable certainty of this ran bone-deep in him. It was just convincing her of the fact that presented the problem! His jaw tightened with determination. Wasn't it just ironic that he'd been scouring the city for her, virtually camping on her doorstep, and it was Jake who got to see her?

He glared resentfully at his twin. 'She thought you were me?'

'The thought doesn't make me happy either, but it seems a fair assumption. It's certainly not an effect I usually have on women, but then my social life has never been half as interesting as yours, brother dear.'

'You mean you've always been a dull, virtuous stick-in-the-mud.'

Jake displayed no sign of offence as he shrugged off the insult. 'It may have escaped your notice, Josh, but you've been equally dull and virtuous for several years now. I hate to be the one to break it to you, but most people have forgotten you even had a misspent youth! Don't you think it's time you stopped trading on your youthful hell-raising image? If you ask me...' he continued thoughtfully.

'Which I wasn't...'

'She was jealous.'

Josh suddenly looked a lot more interested in what his twin was saying. 'You think so...' he began, trying not to sound too eager and failing miserably.

'Nia was being quite affectionate at the time,' Jake informed him cheerfully.

'*Must* you be so smug?' Josh complained out of habit rather than conviction. 'We all know you're the perfect husband and father, you tell us often enough.' If Jake was right—which he had an irritating habit of being—then that opened up all sorts of interesting possibilities...

'I'll have you know that Nia holds you up as the ultimate example of the perfect dad ad nauseam...' his twin responded indignantly.

'I'd say she was a woman of taste, but she married you...'

'If you want...'

'The benefit of your worldly wisdom,' Josh cut in sarcastically. 'I don't. I don't know what makes you think you have the right to interfere with my personal life?' he growled, displaying a complete lack of gratitude for the brotherly concern.

'What a woefully short, amazingly selective memory you have,' Jake drawled. 'I seem to recall someone lying through his teeth to get me together with Nia, not to mention locking me in a room with her! I didn't notice you displaying any reluctance then or ever to interfere in *my* personal life!'

Josh conceded the point with a reluctant grin. 'Like you wanted to escape! Anyhow, you've always been a complete loser with women; without my help you'd still be a crusty old bachelor.'

'*Old!*' Jake protested. 'What does that make you?'

'Some people are born old.'

'Well, at least no woman has ever thrown wine in my face…at least not knowing it was me.'

Josh's expression sobered as he announced abruptly, 'She's Graham's daughter, you know.'

He did his best not to recoil from the glimmer of sympathy in Jake's eyes as his twin slowly nodded. It didn't really come as a shock to see Jake displaying no signs of incredulity; he'd suspected from the outset that his brother knew more about the situation than he was letting on.

'I did catch some of her previous public appearances, but the drastic change of style threw me a bit—icy composure to spitting fury…?' Jake let out a silent whistle.

'Was she alone?' Josh found he couldn't dismiss the disturbing thought that Flora might have been with another man from his mind.

'Well, her regal exit was a strictly solo affair, not that that means much. It's not actually very likely she went to the theatre alone.'

'Thanks for nothing.'

'Well, I didn't actually see anyone, but then if I'd been with her I'd have been hiding too,' Jake admitted frankly.

'I'm going to marry her.'

'Don't tell me, tell her.'

'What do you think I've been trying to do?' Josh yelled.

'It doesn't make any difference who her father was,' he added aggressively.

'Obviously not.' It would have taken a more reckless man than himself to contradict Josh in his present volatile mood. 'I take it you are seeing things a bit clearer in the Graham area these days?'

'I am, but Flora doesn't believe it, with some justification,' Josh admitted. 'A hell of a lot of justification, actually.'

'So you were still on a revenge trip when you took off without a word to anyone and ended up with my in-laws?' His twin gave a grudging nod of assent. 'And your motives for getting involved with the lady weren't originally entirely pure,' Jake surmised.

'What exactly did she say to you?' Josh barked, looking ready and willing to squeeze the information out of his sibling if he didn't voluntarily cough it up.

'Nothing that wasn't cryptic and damned right insulting—you two obviously have a lot in common—I'm just making an educated guess. Come along and see Aunty Nia, Liam,' he coaxed, kneeling down and holding out his arms for the toddler to climb into. Liam ignored his uncle with a sweet but stubborn smile and continued to smear chocolate over the remaining clean parts of his face.

'Talk about *déjà vu*,' Jake mumbled. That grin was identical in every way to the one his twin had frequently used to get his own way through their formative years together. If there was any justice in the world Josh would be in for a taste of his own medicine over the coming years.

'Actually I've made a real dog's dinner of this, Jake.'

His expression sober, his twin got to his feet. 'I had gathered that much, I'm just amazed that I'm hearing you admit it, Josh. What are you going to do?'

'Damned if I know, she's made it crystal clear she can't stand the sight of me.'

Jake regarded with a frown the uncharacteristic dejected slump of his brother's shoulders. He was beginning to feel quite concerned about his twin's state of mind. He needed shaking up a bit.

'I always knew you were a closet romantic, Josh, but I never knew you were a wimp!'

Josh, his expression one of seething frustration, grabbed his twin by the shoulders and glowered dangerously into eyes remarkably similar to his own. The hot fire died away as quickly as it had erupted. A grim expression on his face, he released the creased fabric of his brother's top.

'God, that's me, sensitive new age man,' Josh bit back angrily.

'You've made your point,' Jake conceded wryly with a weak grin as his brother flexed his not inconsiderable shoulder muscles. 'You're no wimp, just an idiot. Actually, there's something you might like to take into consideration when you're deciding what you're going to do next.'

'Which is?' Josh asked, kissing his son's brow and handing him over to his uncle with a firm, 'Be good for Aunty Nia, champ.'

'*Aunty* Nia says your Flora's pregnant.'

Jake watched sympathetically as his big, tough brother clutched towards the wall for support. 'She can't be,' he croaked after a short, painful pause.

'You'd be in more of a position to know about that than me, but personally I wouldn't bet against Nia's intuition.'

'*Well?*' Nia prompted impatiently when her husband returned carrying their nephew.

'Well what?'

'Were you kind and gentle?'

'Kind and gentle would have *really* put his back up.'

'And I suppose nasty and sarcastic didn't!'

'What was I supposed to do…cuddle him?'

Nia rolled her eyes. 'Now wouldn't *that* be shocking?' she observed waspishly. Men! To hear the pair of them talk you'd never know they'd each walk through fire for the other.

Well, there was no point her hiding out in Sam and Lyn's spare room any longer—Josh had obviously given up trying to contact her. It was just as well she already knew Josh's so-called love was a hollow sham otherwise the fact that his devotion had strict geographical limits—and Hong Kong was outside them—might have come as a blow.

It wasn't as if she'd expected him to hop on the first available flight, but he might have waited for a semi-decent interval before hopping into bed with the first available female! She gave a tiny shudder of revulsion as an image of the sexy redhead materialised in her head.

Flora continued to tell herself how relieved she was that Josh had no staying power, at least in the fidelity department. Elsewhere…well, the sooner she stopped thinking about Josh Prentice's staying power *elsewhere*, the sooner she could get her life back on track!

A soft holdall looped around her neck, two more at her feet, she struggled with a recalcitrant lock.

'Damn and blast it to hell!' she cursed wearily just before the key finally clicked. With a sigh she threw her bags carelessly over the threshold and followed them.

The sound of the door being clicked shut made her swing around in alarm. Josh was standing there looking tall, dark and dangerous.

He'd hurt and betrayed her in every way possible, he'd forgotten about her when the going had got tough and ye every instinct in her told her to walk—no, to *run*—straight into his arms.

'Get out!' she yelled hoarsely, picking up the nearest thing, which happened to be a soft cushion—it bounced harmlessly off his dark head.

'In my own good time,' he soothed, rubbing the side of his head. 'That hurt.'

'I wish!' she hissed venomously. 'And you won't get out in your good time, you'll get out in mine—in other words now, if not sooner! Does the green-eyed vamp know you're here?' she asked shrilly, then, just to establish she didn't care one way or the other, she added hastily, 'I *almost* feel sorry for her.'

'The only green eyes I see,' Josh murmured with provocative pleasure, 'are right here!' He looked pointedly at her flushed face and flashing cornflower-blue eyes.

'Cut out the wisecracks—and, actually,' she added huffily with a dignified sniff, 'you couldn't be more wrong!' Even she didn't believe it, and one glance at his face told her he didn't either!

'If you don't care, would you mind explaining to me about the wine-in-the-face stunt?'

'I don't think you're in any position to gripe about my behaviour, but if you must know it was just a spontaneous expression of my deep contempt for you.'

Considering the fact she hadn't had the faintest idea what she was going to say when she opened her mouth, Flora felt moderately pleased with this glib face-saving explanation.

'I'm so sorry if I ruined your evening,' she added with spiteful insincerity.

'Actually I didn't come here to discuss the extortionate cleaning bill I've been presented with.'

'Really! I didn't think we had any other unfinished business.' If he had the bare-faced cheek to present her with a bill she'd make him eat it!

'I think you know we have.' His grey eyes moved slowly over her face with almost clinical precision as though he was searching for something specific. *'Is it true?'* he asked abruptly.

Flora froze. Her mind raced frantically—he couldn't know, she told herself soothingly. How could he when she hardly knew herself? The secret was uppermost in her mind, which accounted for the fact her powers of deduction were a bit distorted just now. If I don't volunteer anything, he can't know anything. She dabbed her tongue to her upper lip to blot up the tiny beads of moisture there.

'Is what true?' Her eyes widened to their fullest, most guileless extent.

Josh's own eyes narrowed as his glance moved from her innocent expression to the heaving outline of her chest. 'You want to play it like that…?' She watched nervously as his heavy lids drooped further over his worryingly alert gaze. 'Fine,' he approved casually.

'I don't know what you're talking about.' Please God he didn't either!

'I want to talk about us.'

She relaxed slightly, but not much—*us* couldn't be classed as a safe subject either.

She carefully wiped her face of all emotion and stared at him stonily. It would be the final humiliation if he guessed how often she had dreamt of there being an *us*…if he guessed that how, even after all he'd done to her, if she'd seen him at a pre-redhead moment she might have been tempted to try against all odds to work towards there being an *us*.

'There is no *us*, and never has been.' That should do the trick! She had put her heart and soul into sounding as though she meant it—only a completely insensitive idiot could have failed to get the message in her icy put-down.

It frustrated her beyond belief to discover his silent, vaguely amused response was loaded with teeth-clenching scepticism. How could she have forgotten that Josh *was* a completely insensitive idiot?

Ignoring her little snort of annoyance, Josh contemplated thoughtfully the set angle of her firm chin, before strolling further into the room and looking around with interest.

'Nice place you have here.' He ran the square tip of one tapering finger down the spines of a row of books in her crammed bookcase.

Her own spine reacted as though it had received the caress. Just looking at his shapely hands made her feel shivery and feverish. Anxious to dismiss these distracting sensations, she said the first thing that came into her head—unfortunately her thoughts emerged uncensored.

'Can your new girlfriend actually read, or does her bosom get in the way?' They couldn't have been real, Flora decided spitefully, thinking nasty, unsisterly thoughts about the curvaceous redhead.

His cough had started off sounding something suspiciously like a laugh. And no wonder he looked smug and self-satisfied, she thought bitterly as her tortured blue gaze slid self-consciously away from the sparkle in his amused eyes. So much for icy indifference, I might just as well have put out an advert in a national newspaper in case anyone hadn't realised I'm a jealous cat!

'Being a man…'

'I'd hardly noticed,' she said wistfully, tearing her lingering lustful gaze from his long, muscular legs.

'I would never dare make a connection between a lady's cup size and her IQ,' he explained virtuously. The saintly air was rather spoilt by a lecherous grin that suddenly split his rather hard features. 'I'm more a leg man myself,' he admitted, dropping casually into an old leather armchair.

Flora wished she'd opted for trousers—not that there was anything remotely revealing about her severely tailored skirt unless you had a thing for ankles or calves. She remembered that Josh had had a thing about just about every part of her no matter how mundane. Desire made her skin prickle as sexual heat rushed through her.

'It's my brother, Jake, who's the—'

Shamed at her weak response to him, Flora knew that she'd be a gibbering basket case if he turned his attention anywhere more intimate than her legs! Besides, she didn't want to invite any unkind comparisons with his bosomy date!

Shrilly she cut him off. 'Don't make yourself comfortable, you're not staying!' she snarled. 'If you don't stop ogling my legs,' she informed him, conveniently ignoring the fact she'd been doing the same thing herself only moments before, 'I'll...I'll...' he quirked an enquiring dark brow in her direction '...I'll call the police!' That injunction was looking more attractive by the second.

'Really! That would make interesting listening,' he reflected. 'Could you send around an armed response unit? My boyfriend is looking at my legs...'

She gnawed at her quivering lower lip as she listened to him mock her toothless threat. 'You're not my boyfriend.' Boyfriend was a much too tepid term to describe Josh; there was nothing remotely boyish about him. She hated the pushed-into-a-corner, whiny note she heard in her tremulous voice. How was he supposed to believe she meant what she said if she sounded so wishy-washy?

Josh appeared to give serious thought to her statement.

'Yes, I prefer lover too, it has a much more grown-up and…intimate ring to it.'

His deep sexy purr made all the fine downy hairs on the back of her neck prickle. She no longer worried if she was in control of the situation; she *knew* she wasn't!

'Talking about Jake…' he continued, crossing one long leg over the other. Flora noticed he was wearing odd socks. She found herself wondering if he'd had a tough night with Liam…or perhaps there was a much less innocent and possibly more likely explanation for his red-rimmed eyes and unshaven chin… She felt suddenly mad as hell—with him, with herself, with stupid, bloody-minded cruel fate that had made her fall in love with him!

Flora folded her arms firmly across her bosom. 'I wasn't, you were, but I have to tell you I'm not that interested in your family.' She produced an artistic yawn.

'Oh, Jake's quite interested in you; so is his wife, Nia.'

Flora, still coping with the most atrocious pangs of jealousy, kept her expression blank as he extracted a photo from his breast pocket and held it out to her. She automatically placed her hands behind her back and mulishly shook her head. Doing exactly the opposite of what he wanted felt extremely important to her.

'I don't want to look at your family snaps.'

'Look at it!'

'Don't you take that tone with me!' For the first time Flora saw that beneath the air of laconic, laid-back amusement Josh was actually extremely tense.

'I think you'll find it quite illuminating.'

He obviously wasn't budging until she'd done as he bid so she decided she might as well humour him. Ungraciously she snatched the glossy photo from his hand, hoping the way she carefully avoided any contact with his fingers wasn't too obvious.

She felt the blood seep from her face as she stared incredulously at the image of a radiant woman in a stunning wedding gown flanked by two amazingly handsome men wearing morning dress. Josh was one of the men, but for the life of her she couldn't tell which one!

'You're a twin!' she croaked accusingly as the colour returned to her face with a vengeance. 'You didn't tell me... *Oh, God!*' she groaned as she recalled the shocked expression on her victim's face as he'd dashed red wine from his eyes.

He'd acted as if he hadn't recognised her because he hadn't! She'd never felt so squirmingly embarrassed in her life. 'Why on earth didn't you tell me?' Fists clenched, she rounded on Josh furiously. 'If you had I wouldn't have made a total fool of myself...'

Josh took her spitting fury in his stride. 'Jake thought it was my fault too.'

'He must think I'm...a mad woman. I must be to care who you choose to canoodle in public with!' She didn't notice the white-hot flare of satisfaction in his eyes as she miserably visualised the sort of rampant speculation her little stunt must have created. With an anguished groan she buried her face in her hands. 'God, she was his wife...the one...'

'With the D cup.' He nodded solemnly as she squirmed some more. 'Yes, that's Nia.'

'She's beautiful.' Amazing how much easier it was to admit that now she knew the lady in question was married to Josh's brother, that she wasn't a rival...what am I talking about, rival?

A sudden rush of relief flooded through her. 'That means you haven't...?'

'Looked, touched or had improper thoughts even about another woman.' He shook his head solemnly from side to side. 'Innocent on all counts. Does that make you feel better?'

Flora flushed rosily. 'I could care less.' She knew her denials were futile, she just couldn't hide her feelings from him, but she felt obliged to make an effort. 'Did she—your brother's wife, think...?' Flora began in sudden trepidation. All she needed to make this day complete was to discover she was responsible for splitting up what had looked like a blissfully happy couple.

'Don't fret, all is peaceful on the marital harmony front. Nia has an exaggeratedly high opinion of my brother's integrity.'

'You mean he *would* cheat on her?' she demanded, her glare one of shocked disapproval.

'I mean I've been insulting Jake since I first mastered the knack of stringing a few words together, the habit's become ingrained. Jake would die before he'd hurt Nia, the man's besotted.'

'Well, he looked it,' Flora recalled wistfully as she recalled with horrible clarity what his besotted behaviour had done to her when she'd thought that he were Josh. 'I still can't believe there are two of you,' she murmured in a stunned voice.

'There aren't!' Josh bit back swiftly.

'Have I hit a nerve?' She didn't need any convincing; there couldn't be anybody else quite like Josh.

Josh didn't deny it. 'It's a common misconception.' His tone of voice suggested it was an irritation too. 'But we're just two people who happen to look very much alike... though I must admit I'm pretty insulted that you couldn't tell the difference. Nia could right off...but then Nia's a bit of a mystic on the side—must be the Celtic blood,' he mused. 'Talking of which, she said something about you...'

'Nothing flattering, I'm sure,' Flora reflected, blushing to recall what sort of first impression she must have made. 'But it can't be any worse than the things I've been saying about her,' she admitted guiltily.

'Jealousy will do that.'

Flora gritted her teeth. 'I can't decide if you're just plain stubborn or you really believe you're irresistible!'

'You're in denial, at least about this,' Josh qualified cryptically.

His relentless confidence made her want to scream, especially as she knew it was justified. 'Don't you ever give up?'

'Never,' he confirmed. 'Are you in denial about the other too?'

Flora's expression was distracted and confused but not suspicious. 'What other?' she enquired innocently.

'The being pregnant other.'

'Oh, God!' she gasped. She took a stumbling couple of shaky steps towards the nearest chair but the buzzing in her ears and the black dancing dots before her eyes got so bad she just folded up, cross-legged, onto the floor before Josh, who had dived in her direction as soon as the colour had dramatically fled her face, could reach her. 'How... how?'

'It's true, then.' Josh didn't know whether to join her in a collapsed state on the floor or bang his head against the wall. If he'd been using said precious head this mess wouldn't be happening! He'd done several things over the years he wasn't proud of but he'd never despised himself more than at this moment!

Flora pulled herself into a kneeling position and rested her bottom on her heels. She'd never seen anyone look so wretched and distraught as Josh did; he'd aged visibly in the last thirty seconds.

Somehow she'd never pictured the father of her first child reacting like this to the news he was about to be a father. Some romantic dreams it seemed persisted even in the face of adult cynicism, but then she always had been a hopeless romantic at heart.

'How did you know? I hardly…' Even Josh's persuasive powers were not enough to open confidential medical files.

'What can I say?' he asked hoarsely. 'My brother married a witchy woman. You may laugh…' Flora didn't feel like laughing at all '…I did myself the first time, but she definitely has a spooky ability for this sort of thing. Maybe she is just extra smart at reading body language, who knows…?' He sounded as though he didn't much care about the method he'd learnt the truth, but the truth itself was bothering him more than slightly.

Flora ran her fingers through her feathery crop and pulled herself to her feet; her expression was sober. 'I don't care what you say,' she warned him, her small chin lifted to an obstinately determined angle.

'So tell me something I *don't* know!' Josh grated harshly. 'You're not going to faint or anything, are you?' he added with gruff suspicion.

'No.' Decision glowed in her blue eyes as she bit her lip. 'I know how you feel, Josh, about having any more children—' she swallowed the constriction in her throat '…but I won't have an abortion,' she announced grimly. 'No, don't say anything!' she pleaded, placing her hands firmly over her ears. 'I can't and I won't!' she insisted loudly. 'This is my baby and you don't need to have anything to do with it.'

The mention of abortion had made what little remaining colour he had seep steadily away. His eyes burnt with anger in his otherwise immobile features as he met her defiant glare head on.

'I won't even dignify the notion I could wish any child of mine harm, let alone actively seek it with…' Flora could hardly bear it when his deep, emotion-packed voice broke.

'I thought…' she began. Seeing her outstretched hand reaching out towards him, she snatched it self-consciously back.

'I know what you thought.' The reproach in his eyes made her cheeks burn afresh with shame. 'I'm interested in how you figure that I won't need to have anything to do with my own child?'

She looked at him with undisguised scepticism. 'Are you trying to tell me that you *want* to be involved?'

That dream was quite stubbornly persistent, but there came a point, she told herself, when optimism was ever so slightly silly and as she listened to his response she knew that this was the time. The prospect of fatherhood would do what all else, against the odds, seemed unable to: it was going to make it impossible for them to be together. There weren't any workable compromises.

'*Want* isn't the right word precisely,' he began cautiously.

Flora tried hard not to flinch. 'I didn't think it was, somehow.'

'It's about responsibility. I've told you before that I turned my back on Liam briefly once, and I've never forgiven myself. I'm not about to make the same mistake twice.' The memory seemed to release a torrent of self-condemnation in him. 'If it hadn't been for Jake…'

'Not that again!' she yelled suddenly, drawing his startled gaze. 'I'm sure your brother is great, but he was only doing what brothers are meant to do in that situation. You'd do the same for him, wouldn't you?' she challenged.

'Sure,' Josh conceded. 'But you don't know it all. I drank…'

'Drank!' Rolling her eyes in exaggerated horror, she pressed her hands to her cheeks. 'Big deal! We all get hurt, we all mess up and most of us crawl back. Only I forgot Josh Prentice doesn't lose control, he doesn't mess up and he never crawls. For God's sake, man,' she told him in exasperation, 'you're a fantastic father to Liam!' She fixed him with a blisteringly sincere stare.

'Are you defending me?' he asked in a voice of wonderment.

'Only against your worse critic—you!' she announced, gruffly defiant. She tried not to think distracting thoughts about how much she'd liked it when Josh had lost control in some situations. The fact she lusted after him…loved him to bits…just made doing what she knew she had to harder—*much* harder! 'What I'm saying is no reflection on what sort of father I think you'd make.'

'It's hard to forgive yourself for…'

'Being human!' she responded with heavy sarcasm. 'The point is, I don't know how hard it will be having this baby, but I do know it would be a hell of a lot harder with you watching every move I make waiting for something bad to happen. I'm sorry if this sounds brutal, but I want to *enjoy* this pregnancy. It's something very special.'

She saw his strong throat muscles work before he finally responded. 'Are you trying to tell me that having me around would make you…?'

'Me jumpy, nervous, unhappy? Probably all three.' But not nearly as unhappy as it would make you, she thought sadly. 'I know that was your original intention.'

He flinched; his hurt eyes silently reproached her. 'I told you, Flora, that that was before I fell in love with you.'

'If you really love me, Josh, leave me alone. Let me

have the baby. I want him, you don't.' He could have denied it, but she knew he wouldn't.

The conflict on his face was only a weak shadow of his internal struggle.

'Do you really think I could abandon you and our baby?' He looked at her as though she had lost all sense of reality.

'I know you don't want him,' she wailed miserably.

'I want you, Flora. Marry me.'

CHAPTER NINE

FLORA gave a faint, wispy gasp. Her knees quivered wildly. 'You can't be serious!'

'I've never been more serious in my entire life,' he revealed grittily.

Despairingly she tore her gaze from the compelling conviction in his eyes. She shook her head slowly in denial.

'Are you mad?' she croaked, showing what she considered an amazing amount of restraint under the circumstances. 'I know you don't like feeling helpless, Josh.'

'True, but it's a theme I'm getting tiresomely familiar with of late,' he chimed in grimly.

This solution was a bit extreme even for him. 'But doing something…doing *anything*, especially *this* anything to make yourself feel as if you're in control is not a good idea.'

In control! Was she joking? 'I haven't been in control since the first moment I met you!' he declared, his resentment very obviously smouldering. He threw her a harassed, driven look. 'My life wasn't so crash-hot terrific before,' he growled. 'But at least it had some sort of comforting predictability.'

'Then you ought to be careful about who you decide to stalk in future,' she felt pushed by his perverse logic to point out.

'Hell!' He stopped, an arrested expression stealing across his dark face. 'Predictable! Like it was a good thing… *Did I really just say that?*' he appealed to her, a comically horrified expression spreading across his handsome, haggard face.

'I take it that was a rhetorical question. Or has your short-term memory gone the same way as your sanity?'

'I sound so *old*,' he announced in a shaken voice that, if she hadn't been so deeply shaken, might have made her smile. 'If I go on like this I'll be as boring as Jake before long,' he observed acidly.

'I didn't see too much wrong with Jake.' How could she when he looked so like the man she loved?

Josh shot her a sharp, not altogether pleased look. You don't say,' he responded in a disgruntled tone. 'Actually we're chalk and cheese, nothing alike, the original odd couple.'

'He sounds better by the minute,' she mumbled provocatively.

'You love me really,' he shot back carelessly, though had she seen his eyes she might have revised the careless part.

She watched, stifling her frustration and growing panic as he recommenced his monotonous pacing of the room. It was, she admitted, probably the only time she'd think monotonous in the same breath as Josh and, if she was being scrupulously honest, she liked it that way.

'I do…?' she echoed faintly. It occurred to her she ought to be objecting to this sort of cocky confidence.

He stopped his panther-like pacing and looked directly at her. Now she forced herself to analyse his expression she saw that he didn't look particularly confident, just fierce, driven and deeply distracted.

'It's blindingly obvious,' he announced. 'I love you, you love me.' Jaw clenched, chest heaving, hands balled into white-knuckled fists, he paused to let her deny it.

The significance of her silence was deafening. The pu

pils of his eyes visibly expanded and a bone-deep thrill shot through her as their eyes clashed and melded. '*We have to get married.*'

'Why? Do you think I'm likely to be ostracised by polite society? Grow up, Josh,' she sneered shakily.

He ignored her sub-standard attempt at sarcasm. 'You need me.'

How horribly true. Her chin went up. 'To be a martyr…thanks, but no, thanks! You've made your views on fatherhood crystal clear.'

'That was before this *fait accompli*, that changes everything.' His grim voice was laced with the crushing strain he was feeling.

Everything except the way you feel, she wanted to shout. 'This baby isn't a *fait accompli*!' she yelled. 'As hard as you obviously find it to believe, I *want* this baby.' Her intensity drew his narrowed gaze to her face. 'Until you do too you can keep away from me…us. If I do drop dead,' she flung recklessly, 'you'll have a role to play, but I have no intentio—' She didn't get any further.

He moved with astonishing fluidity for a big man. He grabbed her by the shoulders and hauled her roughly towards him until her tender breasts were pressed close to his heaving chest. His eyes blazed down at her. The rage that consumed him was a tangible thing, like static it danced in the air around them.

'Never, *never* make a crack like that again.' The soft staccato words emerged from compressed, bloodless lips. 'Do you hear me?'

Overcome with remorse, she nodded. 'I didn't mean…'

Josh released his biting grip on her. His fingers curled around the soft nape of her neck before sliding upwards across her scalp. 'I was her husband, Flora, I should have been able to save her.' The memory of that failure still haunted him, she could see it in the stark pain in his eyes, hear it in the harsh unevenness of his tone. 'I tried to blame fate, your father when the opportunity arose, but deep down I knew, I always have, that the responsibility was mine…'

'But that's…' He hushed her automatic horrified protest with a finger pressed to her lips. His words continued to carry the same implacable conviction.

'It was me who wanted to start a family straight away. Bridie just went along with what I said to please me, she always did, which was very convenient for a man who likes to get his own way.' His voice was laden with bitter self-derision. 'Her family blamed me, they never wanted her to marry me in the first place, and they were right,' he asserted grimly. 'But I won't let anything happen to you,' he vowed fiercely, threading his fingers through the bright strands of her hair.

'It already has…I fell in love with you, Josh.' She heard the hissing intake of breath, felt his chest swell and saw the flame that smouldered for a fraction of a second before igniting to an incandescent blaze in his eyes. She closed her eyes dizzily as his lips swooped downwards.

'But that doesn't matter!' she protested just as she felt the first touch of his mouth against hers. He froze. Flora felt his big strong body quiver with strain as he held back his lips still almost touching her own. She trembled feverishly; her desire for him was so strong she could taste it on her tongue.

'It doesn't matter that you love me!' he echoed in a disbelieving whisper. The warmth of his fragrant breath teased the ultra-sensitive flesh around her ear. 'That I love you…what sort of insanity is that, Flora? It's *all* that matters.'

'That's too simplistic,' she persisted tearfully, and, oh, so tempting…!

Breathing unsteadily, he brought his forehead to rest against hers. 'I know we had a bad start. Hell,' he ejaculated unsteadily, 'that's the granddaddy of all understatements! But I'll make that up to you, I promise… Can't you forget the past…?'

'I can,' she told him with sudden complete conviction. 'But you can't, Josh. Don't you see *that's* the problem?'

His thumbs moved compulsively over the smooth, firm angle of her jaw. 'Even if I accepted that, which,' he told her stubbornly, 'I don't, what's your solution—something mature like refusing to see me again? You could always have your friends tell me you'd gone to Australia this time, why mess around with half measures? Hong Kong! Did your pal really think I'd swallow that one?' he enquired scornfully. 'I warn you, Flora, it wouldn't really matter where you went to—you see, I'd follow you to the ends of the earth!'

'You would…?' Emotion clogged her throat.

'Do you doubt it?'

Looking into his eyes, she didn't. She almost heard the sound as the last threads of resistance within her snapped.

'I don't think I could not see you,' she confessed brokenly. 'I love you so much it hurts.'

Josh's head fell back and he gave a long, juddering sigh of relief. When he eventually looked down into her eyes his own glowed with heart-stopping tenderness. 'I've waited a long time to hear you say that.'

'But that doesn't mean I'm going to do anything drastic.'

Like give myself permission to be happy? She suddenly saw clearly the stupidity of her fearful stance. She had nothing to lose and everything to gain.

This is it, girl, you've found your man. So this isn't the way you imagined it would be; life's no fairy tale, it's complicated. What are you going to do about it? Sit and whine, or get off your bottom and go for it? Life with Josh had the potential to surpass any dream she'd ever had.

There was no point pretending this wasn't going to be a tough nine months for Josh. Her pregnancy was not something they could ignore, it was bound to be a massive problem for him, and his ambivalence was painfully understandable. But she could help him to be positive about it, she *knew* she could. Don't just stand there bleating like a dummy, Flora, make it work!

'And marrying me would be drastic?'

'Does it get much more drastic?' she asked wryly.

It was a relief to finally come to terms with the conflict that had raged within her. She still felt apprehensive, but now she was fired up and determined. It was time to start doing something positive—something like marrying the man she loved and showing him that the past couldn't hurt them! It would be worth the wait.

Josh was unaware of what she was thinking; his expression had grown darkly sombre. 'How about having a baby? That's the definition of desperately drastic in my book.'

'It's the definition of fulfilling in mine, Josh.' Her face shone with a new serenity.

'Have you seen a doctor yet?'

'Yes.'

'Who is he? I'll check him out...'

'In case he turns out to be an addict?'

Josh winced and his eyes darkened. 'I didn't mean...'

'To interrogate me? I know what you mean to do,' she added quietly. 'You mean you'd like to wrap me up i cotton wool and treat me like an invalid. I knew you'd overreact if I told you… Well, I won't have it, Josh.'

'The way I recall it you thought I'd insist you had an abortion,' he reminded her grimly.

Flora flushed defensively. 'Do you blame me?'

Josh narrowed his eyes and didn't reply immediately. 'Actually I was going to point out that twins run in our family, it's something we ought to mention to your obstetrician.'

Flora's mouth and eyes opened wide simultaneously. *Twins!* She hadn't considered that. *'We…?'* she managed, regaining a little of her composure. 'When you say run, Josh, just how many twi—'

Josh cut her off abruptly. 'I'm not going to be a silent partner, Flora,' he warned her.

She trembled but didn't protest as one of his big hands curled over her flat belly. It was the first time she hadn't felt lost and lonely in a long time.

'You have to promise me if at any stage during this…' he swallowed as though saying the word was hard for him '…*pregnancy* you are at risk in any way you'll put your own well-being first.' His voice firmed as he met her startled gaze sternly. 'Do you understand what I'm saying, Flora?'

She did. If it came to a choice between her and the baby he wanted her to choose herself. How could she promise that, when even though the life within her was hardly formed the same couldn't be said for her new and powerful maternal feelings?

She wanted to hug him and tell him everything was going to be all right, but she knew he wouldn't believe her. 'I understand what you're saying, Josh, and I have to tell you I don't much care for your tone.' She tried with limited success to lighten the atmosphere.

'The word *tough* springs to mind. And just for the record,' he added a shade belligerently, 'I don't much like you not telling me you're carrying my child. Were you going to…?'

'I don't know,' she admitted in a distracted voice. 'Can't you just be optimistic…?' she suggested wistfully. 'Do you always have to be…?'

'Practical! One of us needs to be!' he thundered.

Flora's mind was racing. 'If I marry you will that constitute practical?' It was practical when compared to the alternative. The alternative, a life minus Josh, didn't bear contemplating.

'You mean it?' he grated. Gloatingly triumphant, his glowing eyes moved hungrily over her face. 'You better had!' he warned her grimly.

She lifted her hand and pressed her fingers to his lips. 'Stop,' she pleaded, 'before you demonstrate what a classically macho overbearing husband you'll make. I know I'm probably crazy, but the simple truth is you were right—I'm not sure I can live without you,' she announced with a sob. To hell with pride! 'It seems wicked to say it, but I'm not sure I'd want to live without you.'

When she managed to blink away the tears from her eyes she saw that Josh seemed to appreciate the enormity of her husky confession. In fact he looked so stunned she wasn't sure if she'd scared him off with the intensity of her feelings.

Her doubts only lasted a few seconds before he groaned harshly and lunged towards her, his arms lifting her off the ground as his lips offered hungry, incontrovertible proof of his pleasure.

When he finally drew back Flora found herself standing in the circle of Josh's strong arms with her head on his shoulder, conscious of the soothing background throb of his steady heartbeat. She inhaled deeply, her senses greedily drinking in the unique male fragrance that was just his alone.

'I hope you realise that a kiss like that is equivalent to an engagement ring?'

'A real rock,' she agreed dreamily. 'I knew this would happen if I ever opened my door for you.' She gave a contented sigh and rubbed her cheek against the thin fabric of his shirt, breathing in the smell of the warm musky scent of him. A sharp thrill of sexual desire shot through her. 'You've no idea how hard it was not to when you were hammering on it for what seemed like hours. I thought you'd never go away.'

'That didn't seem like hours, it was hours, and if I'd known for sure you were here I would have put up a stronger resistance when that pair of butch security guys expelled me from the building!'

'I didn't contact them,' she promised, lifting her head. 'It was the neighbours. This is a very respectable building.'

'I feel I know all the neighbours personally—the whole damned building came to watch the floorshow when the heavy mob arrived. Actually the general consensus from those who know me seems to be I'm a pretty respectable type myself these days.'

'Do I detect a tiny note of regret there?' she teased lightly.

'I regret a lot things, Flora,' he admitted with none of the levity her own voice had contained. 'But, believe me, meeting you is not one of them. Believe me too when I say I'll make you the very best husband I know how.' He just hoped to hell that was going to be good enough! Tenderly his fingers trailed down her smooth cheek.

The throb of sincerity in his voice brought an emotional

lump to her throat. She turned her head to kiss the palm of the hand that caressed her face.

'I believe you, Josh.'

'We've got a lot to plan, there's no point hanging around. We don't need anything fancy...' He looked ready to dash off and collar a willing priest right there and then. If she was going to do the wedding thing, she thought, it might be quite nice to do it properly—after all she had no intention of doing it more than once. Right now she had more urgent things on her mind so she didn't think it necessary to break this to him straight off.

'I think you should get your priorities right from the start.' Rather boldly she flicked open the top button of his shirt and made a gentle circular exploratory movement over his hair-roughened skin with one curious finger. She lifted her eyelashes to take a sultry little peek at his reaction. It was promising—*very* promising!

'You put forward a very convincing argument,' he admitted throatily.

Flora took him by the hand and led him towards her bedroom door. She knew for sure that, no matter how much they had going against them, as long as he continued to look at her like that they had more going for them!

Flora loved watching Josh work. He attacked a canvas with bold, sure strokes, yet there was nothing insensitive about his rich, vibrant style. He liked to paint her and there were several portraits stacked around the walls that lovingly showed the many stages of her expanding girth.

The light in this studio Josh had created in their new home still excited him and Flora approved of things that made Josh happy. She made Josh happy, but she was also aware that she and the child growing big within her were responsible for the growing tension she sensed in him.

It still felt strange being Mrs Prentice, but not unpleasant strange—no, a long *long* way from unpleasant! The reality of being with Josh surpassed her wildest dreams. He'd indulged her when she'd told him she wanted their wedding to be a special day to share with their family and friends, though he'd had a hard time keeping his impatience in check as the preparations were being made.

Flora didn't actually have a lot of family, but the enormous Prentice clan more than compensated. Liam had made a delightful page, and though Flora had thought at first that she'd never be able to look at Jake and his wife without blushing the couple had soon put her at her ease. Nowadays the brothers complained that the two women were constantly conspiring together behind their backs.

Josh tried hard to hide his anxiety from her, but she occasionally—more often lately—caught a fleeting fearful expression in his grey eyes that you could almost taste. It made her ache with bitter-sweet empathy. She knew that until she had safely delivered their child Josh wouldn't be able to throw off the ghosts from the past that haunted him—that haunted their union.

Quietly so as not to disturb him she got up from the canvas studio chair. The combination of the flimsy chair and her bulk made quiet hard to achieve. Josh turned around and she responded before he'd asked.

'I'm fine. I could just do with a stretch.'

She didn't mention the nagging pain in her back because Josh had a habit of overreacting to every trivial ailment, and as often as not she responded crankily in return to his concern, and before you could blink they were arguing. Hormones might be responsible, but Flora found she had lost her appetite for conflict; happily for them both that was the only appetite she'd lost.

'Anyone home?' Alec, Josh's agent, came in through

the garden door bringing a sharp blast of cool air with him. 'I have to come and thank this brilliant husband of yours.'

'I wish you wouldn't feed his ego,' Flora pleaded drolly.

Alec regarded her uncertainly. He could never quite work out when Josh's new wife was joking. 'I sold those shares!' he announced exultantly to Josh who was regarding his canvas with a critical eye.

'What shares would those be?'

'What shares?' Alec shook his head disbelievingly. 'The man says what shares!' he repeated to Flora.

'I heard you the first time, Alec.'

'I've made a small fortune!' his agent enthused. 'I could retire, not that I'm going to,' he added hastily.

'I'm relieved,' Josh responded drily. 'And happy for you.'

'Why,' Flora wondered out loud, 'would you take Josh's advice about shares?'

Alec looked from Flora to Josh. 'She's joking…right? She does know…?'

'Know what? Do you dabble…?' She broke off as Alec broke down laughing like a drain. 'Why do I get the feeling I'm missing something here?' she appealed with growing impatience to her husband.

'When Jake and I were eighteen we inherited some money from our grandmother about the same time we were given a project in school which involved investing—on paper—a given amount of money on the stock exchange to see if we could make a profit.' He shrugged and laid down his brush. 'I did make a profit, only I did it for real with gran's inheritance.'

'That was reckless,' she murmured. But not entirely unexpected, she thought wryly, having come to know her husband's reckless streak. Though he was more the mother hen upon occasion with her than the bold reckless pirate he reminded her of.

'That's what my mother said, amongst other things, when she found out. The outcome of that first foray was that I discovered early on that I had a knack for making a bit of money,' he explained diffidently.

How much? she wondered as she watched Josh frown repressively at his agent, who seemed to find his last off-hand statement incredibly amusing.

'Being a card-carrying member of the financial establishment must have hurt your credibility as the rebel artist with attitude.'

Josh grinned at this side swipe. 'On the plus side it meant I didn't have to dance to the tune of money-grubbing philistines like Alec here—nothing personal, mate.'

'Today, my friend, you can do no wrong,' Alec assured him sunnily.

'You're rich, aren't you…?' Suddenly she understood the fact he hadn't shared her concern about the extortionate price label attached to their lovely new home. He could obviously afford to be blasé. 'I mean *really* rich.'

'It's all relative, but I suppose I am,' he conceded, wiping an oily smear from his hand with a cloth.

Flora's eyebrows arched. 'And it didn't occur to you to mention this before we got married?'

'I was having a hard enough time getting you to the altar as it was,' he reminded her candidly. 'I didn't want to risk you having moral qualms about being hitched to a dirty capitalist. Besides, it doesn't really matter, does it?'

Alec, a very literal soul who had missed all the subtle interplay, began to bear the worried look of a man who was witnessing serious marital discord. 'He gives loads of stuff away, Flora,' he piped up anxiously. 'That new ward at the children's hospice… The research…'

'Shut up, Alec!' Josh snapped.

'Yes, shut up, Alec,' Flora mimicked, her warm glance still resting on her husband's flushed face. 'Can't you see you're embarrassing Joshua?'

Alec gave a relieved sigh. 'She doesn't mind, then.'

'No,' Flora agreed softly, 'she doesn't mind. Besides, like the man said, it doesn't really matter.' Her glowing blue eyes were transmitting an unambiguous message of love as she gazed over at the tall man she'd married. 'We've got our priorities straight,' she explained.

'I love you!' Josh, much to his agent's acute discomfort, breathed fervently.

Flora smiled contentedly as a warm glow enveloped her. 'If you two gentlemen will excuse me…I thought I might have a nap before Liam gets back from Oliver's. What time are the Smiths bringing him back?'

'Don't worry about that, you just rest. I'll deal with Liam.'

Flora stifled a yawn. 'Maybe I'll let you. You know, there are compensations for having a husband who works from home.'

'Even if I am always under your feet?'

She appeared to consider the question. 'On balance,' she conceded grudgingly. 'I think I quite like having you around.'

Josh looked in and found Flora still asleep after he'd bathed Liam later that evening. He decided to put the little boy to bed without disturbing her. Several stories later— he'd resorted to simple and effective bribery when the toddler had taken some convincing he couldn't go and climb into bed with Flora—Josh closed the door quietly on the sleeping cherub.

Anxious not to disturb his wife, he cautiously opened their bedroom door.

'What are you doing?' He looked with a confused frown when he discovered her kneeling on the bedroom floor with her upper body resting on the rumpled bed.

Flora paused in her panting to cast him a withering look; her face was blotchily red and sweaty. 'What does it look like?'

'Oh, God!' Josh went completely still. 'You're not... you can't be!'

'Want to bet...?'

Josh's white, bloodless lips moved, but nothing emerged. The aghast silence lengthened as no coherent words formed in his frozen brain.

The almost feral sound that emerged from Flora's lips jolted him from his catatonic trance.

'Ambulance...' he gasped. 'I'll ring, or shall I drive...?' He thrust his shaking hands into his trouser pockets and hoped that wouldn't be necessary. 'And the Smiths will come over for Liam. Don't go anywhere!'

Flora found a cold spot on the bed cover and pressed her cheek into it as a merciful gap occurred in what seemed to be one long, unremitting contraction. What had happened to slow and gradual...?

'I'm not going anywhere and neither are you...*please*, Josh! I've already called the ambulance, but I'm pretty certain that they won't get here in time.' Being a relative novice at this sort of thing, she might be wrong—only she wasn't taking any chances. If Josh wanted to get out he'd have to step over her to do so.

Josh shook his head. 'That can't be right,' he babbled,

raking a shaky, distracted hand through his dark hair. 'First labours are long, everyone says so…'

'Try telling that to this baby! Oh!' She gasped, turning a pain-distorted face towards him. 'It's started again… *Josh!*' she pleaded, stretching a fluttering hand towards him. 'I don't know what to do.'

At the sight of her pain-racked little face he grabbed his own gut-freezing fears unceremoniously by the scruff and put them firmly to the back of his mind. Flora needed him, and, inadequate though he felt to the task, he was going to help her through this any way he could.

'It's all right, sweetheart,' he crooned, getting down on his knees beside her. He brushed the damp hair from her eyes. 'I'm here.'

The small hand that slid inside his tightened as she turned to rest her head against his chest. 'I woke up,' she said, 'and it was just happening. I rang the ambulance, I didn't want to worry you too soon…'

Josh's expression tightened. 'You can forget about tiptoeing around my feelings, angel, I'm fine. Just think about what you're doing.'

Right at that moment her body was telling her exactly what she had to do and she couldn't have ignored the instructions if she'd wanted to. 'You know how I said I didn't know what to do…?'

Josh nodded.

'I do now! I've got to pushhh…!' She groaned.

Somehow Josh managed to get her back onto the bed. The sweat was pouring down his face, but not from the effort of lifting her.

Although he'd always known what the end result was meant to be, he'd been too caught up in his recurring nightmare, the one when he lost Flora, to be prepared for the emotional and physical impact of the warm slippery body of their new daughter when she landed in his hands.

Tears mingled with the other moisture on his face as he placed the stridently complaining baby on her mother's chest.

'She's absolutely perfect!' he breathed incredulously.

Then all his attention and concern returned anxiously to the new mother who was quietly sobbing. He placed his hands palm flat on either side of her face and moved them very gently, slowly downwards until they came to rest on her slender shoulders as if to convince himself she was still there.

'You're all right!' he breathed wonderingly.

'Better than that,' she replied, tearing her eyes from the small dark-haired bundle in her arms. '*Much* better. You look better too,' she added. The moment was made more perfect because she knew that the last barrier to their happiness had been lifted...she watched him realise it too. Two perfect moments in one day!

'I feel...' He flexed his shoulders and rolled his neck. At a loss to describe the feeling of a planet-sized burden being lifted. 'I want to laugh like an idiot.'

'Go ahead!' she advised jubilantly. 'You did it!' she told him, triumph shining in her teary eyes. 'I *knew* you could.'

'From where I was standing it looked to me like *you* did it.'

'We did it, I knew we could,' she purred complacently. It was amazingly easy to dismiss a fraught few minutes back there when she'd thought she couldn't! Poor Josh, she'd told him so in no uncertain terms.

'We can do anything together! Though next time,' Josh modified, 'I'd prefer not to do this much *everything*...'

'Next time!' she mocked, grinning at the expression of

amazement that spread over his face when he realised what he'd said.

'I didn't mean that's up to…'

'I know what you meant, idiot…what's that?'

'The ambulance crew, I expect.'

'Then you'd better go let them in before they break down the door, or wake Liam.' Hers eyes widened. 'What will he say when he wakes up in the morning and finds he's got a little sister?'

'He won't wake up to find a little sister because his little sister and his mother will be safely tucked up in a hospital bed.' His 'this isn't negotiable' glare stilled the protest on her lips. 'Do this for me, Flora. I want you to have a proper check-over.'

She nodded. It wasn't much of a concession to make when you thought about the enormous one he'd made. 'About her name,' she called out as he went to leave the room. 'I thought Emily for my mother. Emily Bridget has a nice ring, I think… Do you…?' She gave him a tentative half-smile.

Tears glittered in Josh's eyes. 'The day I followed you turned out to be the luckiest day of my life!' he announced authoritatively, his deep voice throbbing with conviction.

'Mine too, baby,' she crooned softly to their daughter. 'You don't know it yet, but you've got the best daddy in the entire world.' And I have the best man, she thought as she sat back to enjoy a brief, blissful moment of quality time with her new daughter.

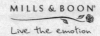

MILLS & BOON®   0306/03b

Live the emotion

_Medical
romance™

HER BOSS AND PROTECTOR *by Joanna Neil*

Dr Jade Holbrook's first day in A&E doesn't go
as planned. She discovers her landlord, Callum
Beresford, is also her new boss! Jade knows she
hasn't made a good impression on the handsome
consultant, and is aware that he is watching her
every move…

*A&E DRAMA: Pulses are racing in these
fast-paced dramatic stories*

THE SURGEON'S CONVENIENT FIANCÉE
by Rebecca Lang

Theatre Nurse Deirdre Warwick is determined that
the two children left in her care will have the best
life possible. When Dr Shay Melburne enters her
life suddenly, Deirdre finds herself falling hopelessly
in love with him – and then he offers her a marriage
of convenience…but can he offer her his love?

THE SURGEON'S MARRIAGE RESCUE
by Leah Martyn

Adam Westerman is a successful Sydney surgeon and
has returned to the Outback to find the beautiful
ex-wife he's never managed to forget. Charge
nurse Liv Westerman fears Adam has only come for
custody of their child. She finds herself hoping that
he has come back for both of them…!

On sale 7th April 2006

*Available at WHSmith, Tesco, ASDA, Borders, Eason,
Sainsbury's and most bookshops*

www.millsandboon.co.uk